HAIDEE BELSHAW was born in Northern Ireland and was educated by Quakers in Lisburn and at St Columba's College Dublin. Subsequently he graduated in Mental and Moral Science at Trinity College Dublin and is a Fellow of the Royal Anthropological Institute London. He was also a founding co-director of Eurotek (Ireland) Ltd.

He has bred Aberdeen Angus cattle, hatched and farmed the native oyster in Ireland and Scotland and raised ornamental poultry; on the African birds, he wrote the only comprehensive book in existence, *Guinea Fowl of the World.*

He is married with six children, and has lived for many years in the Wicklow hills from where he and his wife worked and travelled extensively. Their chief interests lie in the natural world, human pre-history, psychology and mythology.

Cosmic Leap is the second instalment of *Saba's Choices*. Part one *Mother Lake* was published earlier this year.

I0675196

SABA'S CHOICES

COSMIC LEAP

HAIDEE BELSHAW

Namste
Dum Spiro Vivo

SilverWood

Published in 2014 by SilverWood Books

SilverWood Books Ltd
30 Queen Charlotte Street, Bristol, BS1 4HJ
www.silverwoodbooks.co.uk

ISBN 978-1-78132-267-3 (paperback)
ISBN 978-1-78132-268-0 (ebook)

British Library Cataloguing in Publication Data
A CIP catalogue record for this book is available from
the British Library

Set in Sabon by SilverWood Books
Printed on responsibly sourced paper

For my wife Deirdre – without her unfailing encouragement and constructive criticism this book would never have been written

CONTENTS

ACKNOWLEDGEMENTS

I would like to express my sincere thanks to my copy editor Averill Buchanan, my guide Helen Hart and publishing assistant Emily Heming at SilverWood Books, and my illustrator Emily Daly for their patience in perusing, checking and correcting the text, and assisting with artwork. I'm also indebted to my children Marcus, Michael, Lara, Sarah, Karen, Alan and their partners for their unstinting support and for providing varied technical services.

EELFOLK VILLAGES

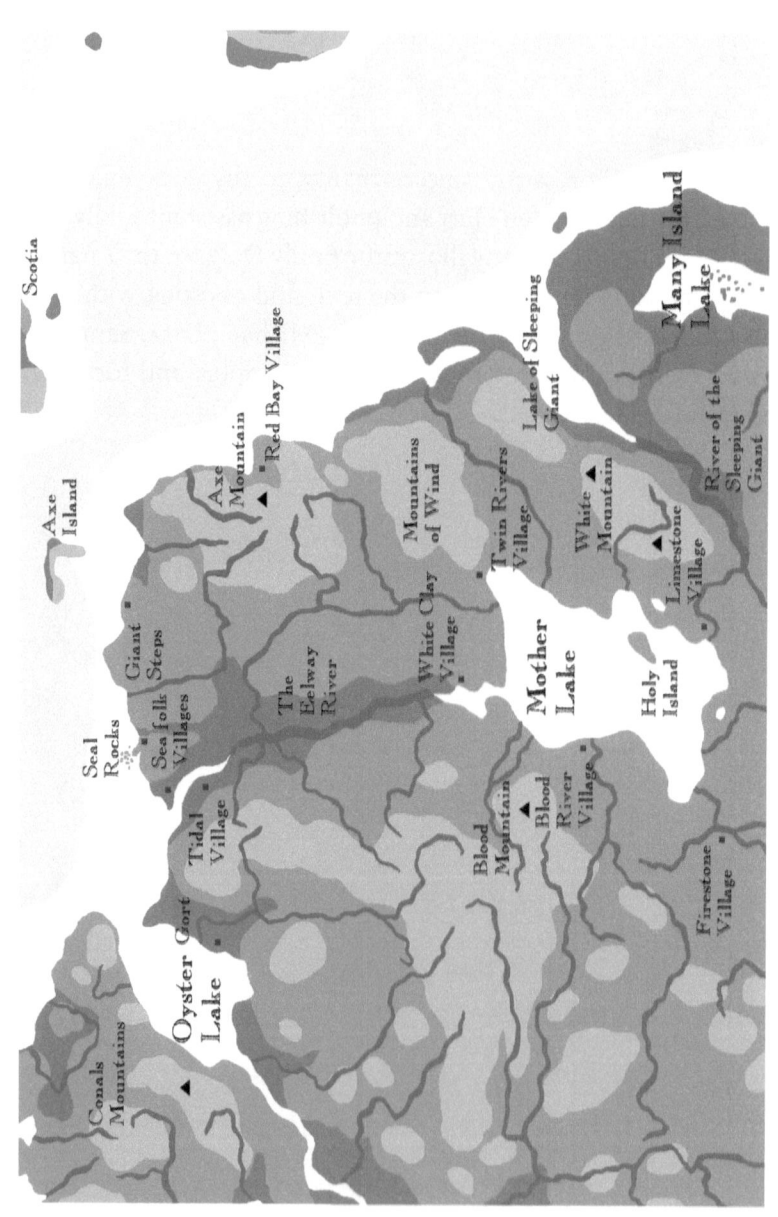

SABA'S NEW ROUTE

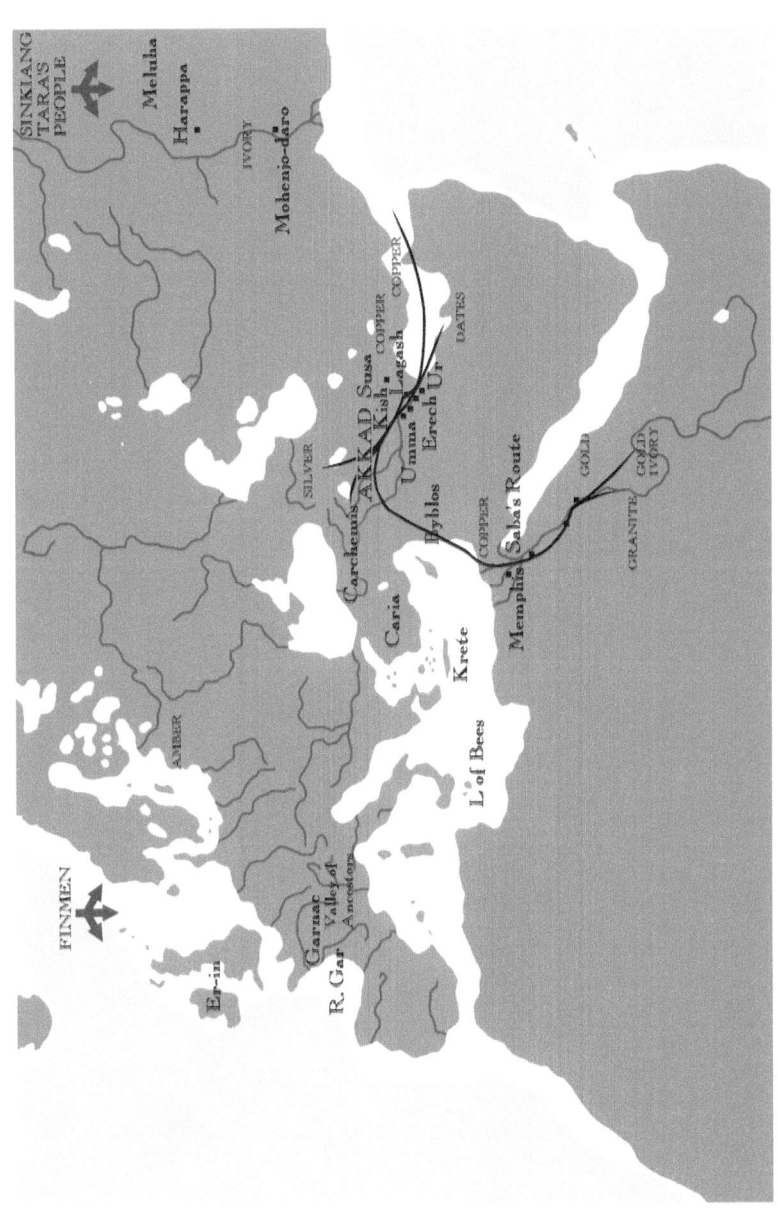

THIRTY-THREE

THE WHALE ROADS

The voyage along the coast of Albion was uneventful. They sailed straight into the sunrise until the Cymru cliffs were in view, then turned southwards, keeping them on the eastern horizon. The plan was to make landfall in Larmorica as speedily as possible so they could place Aengus within the influence of the Garnac healing chamber and begin the procedure that they hoped would cure his afflictions.

Among the ship's company, only the twins, Kalliste, Amlodi and Bethel knew that the cloaked woman who set out with them was Saba – the Wise One of the Eelfolk, the recently anointed Great Kaheen of the whole island of Er-rin – and not her kinswoman and lookalike Sedana, who was substituting for her in the Kaheen's lodge on Boand's Plain with Bride and her Seiors' collusion. The Er-rin travellers were elated that because of the size and versatility of the Kretan vessel it wasn't necessary to beach, eat and sleep on shore each evening, as curragh travellers invariably did unless blown off course by a gale. A couple of curragh builders had enlisted with the Kretans in the hope of learning how to construct such a novel concept in sea travel. Hermes kept just sufficient men on watch to steer, lower sail if necessary and cast overboard the stone anchor inset with fire-hardened oak spikes. The veteran Larmorican crew claimed to be the widest ranging fishermen on the Grey Ocean, although this was disputed by their Euskaldun kinsfolk. They knew every stretch of the waters and alerted Hermes to any passages with submerged rocks. One evening a storm blew up and they ran all night before the wind with full crew on oars to keep the ship facing into the waves.

They had brought such quantities of sundust and smelted metal aboard that there was no need to call and trade for tin at the southern point of Albion. Saba had not wanted to be recognised by Olwen at the wells of Suil, as there were always some Clanspeople there who would eventually carry the news back to Er-rin.

Before leaving Er-rin, Amlodi had been sworn to secrecy on the matter by Bride, and Kalliste would do whatever Aine wished. Bethel was regarded as a shaman to whom any confidence was a matter of honour. Besides, Bethel felt he could never betray the incredible Eelwomen, who utterly beguiled and confused him with their entrancing looks and mysterious gifts. They didn't evince the usual reversals of attraction and repulsion for an outsider with brown skin that he so frequently encountered in the northern lands and grey sea margins. They merely accepted his appearance with a friendly curiosity. He supposed this was because when they read his thoughts, and maybe also some of his memories, Bethel ceased to be a stranger or pose a threat to their imagined security.

Since his ordeal with Maeve and her allies in the caves beyond Shinan, Aengus had withdrawn into himself and communicated little, even to Aine and Saba who ministered to him constantly. Bethel, too, kept a sharp eye on his condition when not sharing steering duties with his old friend Hermes. Amlodi was saddened for his former singing pupil; Aengus's voice had held more promise than anyone he'd ever met, and he spent his time, when not crewing, hovering like a bodyguard around Aengus on the little raised deck and talking endlessly. Amlodi was not only popular for his singing voice, he was also frequently in demand for his stock of sagas and funny stories. Some of these he learned from his mother's companion whose name he was given. This wanderer had arrived many yuls ago with traders from the amber sea and made his home on Boand's Plain. Amlodi was fascinated by Kalliste and her gymnastics; she returned this interest in him as a man and a minstrel, and sometimes pleasured him, calling him her blond giant.

Saba was quieter than Bethel ever remembered her being. She often sat on deck, her green eyes staring into the distance as if she was in a daydream, or stood leaning over the prow rail, auburn hair swirling in the wind, listening intently to sounds from the sea apparently beyond her fellow travellers' hearing.

The ship was constantly attended by schools of dolphins who leaped around them, grazing the water, their backs arched in tight formation. Their speed was ten times faster than the humans could ever hope to emulate. Saba caught Bethel admiring them and, as usual, read his thoughts. 'I too would love to be able to swim like our friends.' She smiled and her eyes gleamed with excitement, the first Bethel had seen in a long time. Some of the crewmen wanted to dip lines with coloured feather lures for mackerel. They were not at all pleased by the continual presence of the dolphins and threw a few ballast stones at them. Bethel saw Saba's flicker of annoyance but the dolphins were impervious to such a feeble threat.

'Drop your lines here off the starboard bow,' Saba told the crewmen.

Two men obeyed her and to their amazement, time and again the fish hurled themselves onto the lures and were left in peace by the watchful dolphins as the lines were repeatedly dipped and drawn out of the water. The men stared respectfully at this woman they believed kin to their Kaheen. She too must possess magical powers.

Three or four dolphins were now taking turns to ride the bow wave just a foot or two in front of the prow, skilfully avoided the projecting snout glistening on the waterline. They vanished at the sound of a high thin squeal from Saba that startled everyone on the boat.

'Why did you do that?' Amlodi asked. He had been admiring the dolphins with her.

'Look!' She pointed over to the port side where two very large shapes were bobbing in the gentle swell. They were black with a dazzling white throat, belly and patches on the sides of their heads facing the ship.

'Those epolar are dangerous,' Amlodi warned her, doubting if she knew them as he did.

'Not to us, they respect the Eelfolk,' said Saba. 'We know them as orcas – giant dolphins. See? They are standing up to inspect what we're doing. Aren't they smart?'

Amlodi was still doubtful. 'The Euskaldun call them grampus, but does calling them by a different name change their nature?'

'I think it does,' said Saba. 'People label things as they perceive them. The name reflects that, and how others will respond as well. Perhaps the thing – in this case, the orca – responds in turn to our attitude. If I label it as harmless or friendly, then will become so to all humans and they will be encouraged to get to know more about it and respect it.'

'That's an impressive argument, that the nature of things and creatures can be affected like other people, by our attitudes.'

'Orcas prefer fish but some of them will take a dolphin or seal quite happily. I don't want any more death on this voyage than necessary.'

'So you warned the dolphins,' said Amlodi.

'Yes. There's plenty of fish for the orcas. They won't be angry with me.'

Meanwhile the orcas dived and after a few moments breached skywards out of the water close to the ship. The onlookers could estimate their length at four to five men. They hurled themselves sideways, hitting the water with tremendous smacks and causing a splash that drenched everyone. Saba laughed. 'See, they're playing with us.'

'You mean you can talk to all these creatures?'

'Only a little and not as we talk, but I hope soon to understand more.'

'Could I also learn?' Amlodi asked eagerly. 'You know that Aengus and I could mimic the deepest bellows of the red stags so well that they used to come to fight, thinking us rivals.'

'Perhaps you might succeed, because of your tuned ear. Their sounds go way above and below the ranges that most people can hear. My senses were developed by the bats in the Raven's cave where I spent my yuls of learning. Aengus and I used to exchange such high-pitched whistles that ordinary folk heard nothing. Only Aine and Sedana detected us because they also trained there. And I can feel the deeper tones of the great whales through my body rather than my ears. Besides, one of my totem animals is the narwhale – One-horn – who sometimes talks to me in dreams.'

'What on earth is that?' Amlodi asked.

'He lives equally in the sea and in spirit world,' explained Saba, grinning. 'A white whale with a long horn coming out of his head.'

'Is it because you are Kaheen that he speaks to you?'

'No! It's because of my Finmen ancestors. He and the Great Bear are their totems and through them, mine also.'

Bethel pricked up his ears at this piece of news and interrupted their dialogue to enquire who the Finman was.

'It's a long story. I'll tell you sometime.' Saba squeezed Bethel's arm to indicate she wasn't trying to exclude him from the discussion. 'Those two guardians have such powerful magic, I love and fear them in equal measure.'

'Does One-horn come to you often in dream?' Bethel asked.

'Yes, Bethel, and especially on this voyage. Because I saved the life of one of his whale people, he tries to protect me and he's taught me how to listen to the songs of all the whales. They seem so mournful and yet so beautiful.'

Amlodi broke in, unable to contain himself.

'Don't forget your promise to teach me. I've never wanted anything so much!'

'When we leave Albion for the open sea, there will be opportunity enough to see and hear them. We'll go in the water.'

'I've never dared to swim in the open sea, but for such a chance, I'll do anything.'

'As we humans swim on the top it doesn't matter how deep the water is. We shall learn together – and don't forget, our friends will be there to help.'

'Your friends maybe.' Amlodi grimaced.

'But I've heard the Eelfolk say they're safe on the water as long as they're with you,' Bethel interjected.

'Yes, they spread that rumour.' Saba sighed. 'But do you always believe all the stories you hear?'

'Well, I've never yet had cause to disbelieve any stories about you,' said Bethel backtracking.

'Our wise ones have a saying: trust, then verify,' she said.

'They're probably right. But for a goddess in human flesh I must make an exception,' Bethel responded.

'Your facility with the Clan tongue has improved too fast. The choice of words is more flowery than accurate,' observed Amlodi wryly.

'We can excuse a lot to so proven a friend and ally,' Saba said, defending Bethel, and the warmth of her gaze flooded over him like a torrent.

On the third day, the ship passed the isles that some call holy and the Larmoricans call the cat because of the likeness they once had to a sky figure before the sea swallowed up many of the villages and changed the contours of the land. The ship put in for fresh water. The Larmoricans knew some of the islanders and exchanged greetings and gifts for the water and fresh food. The isles were known for their lobsters and ormers, and the crewmen cheerfully stowed away several sacks of each.

The islanders also warned them to look out for pods of the larger whales. There were more than usual and their deep-sea fishing had been ruined by them during the past moon. When they tried to drive them away with spears, their curraghs were overturned and some crew had been lost. As the ship drew away from the port, little black pirate birds with long shafted tails harassed the sea swallows for their catches of whitebait. Eventually the swallows opened their scarlet bills and the fish dropped seawards, to be snatched before they touched the waves. One large pirate bird was doing the same to a herring gull and the crew muttered something about it being a poor omen for the rest of the voyage.

Before long they saw five of the great baleen whales swimming close to the ship, as if it were a new whale-like creature. One of the Larmoricans seemed to take it as a dare in what he considered virtually his home waters. He was accustomed to chasing and, if lucky, killing one of the creatures. Before anyone could stop him he climbed down the footholds on the prow, secured the line of his spear around it and launched the spear into the tail of one of the beasts as it passed. The barb sank in and the tail lashed upwards as the whale dived. The slack of the line whipped up, catching around his outstretched forearm, and tightening with the speed of a striking snake. The man's arm ripped from his shoulder socket as the ship's bow pitched forward, lifting the stern from the water; then the line snapped. His other arm, rigid with terror, still gripped one of the footholds tightly but as the blood welled from his wound he fainted and toppled into a watery trough.

One of the crew shouted to save the man in the water and Bethel considered diving in to grab him, but Saba's face was white. 'The fool deserves to die!' she said, choking with anger. 'What can you do for him? Nothing will staunch that flow.' She stamped her foot, switching her tirade to cover all foolhardy fishers. 'Why are they so stupid and greedy? There's plenty of fish for everyone and the worst of all is that these giant creatures are friendly. They recognise our intelligence. They could teach us so much about the sea and its underwater creatures. Some day people may want to live there too.' She shut up and went to sit by Aengus who appeared disturbed by her outburst.

Hermes decided it was more merciful to let the Larmorican sink, and that happened quite quickly. As the whale and his pod receded into the distance, Bethel imagined a thrash or two of its tail would dislodge the spear, but that it would be a long time before it approached another ship. He wondered how good the whale's memory was; would it now hold a grudge against all humans or could it understand that though they seemed tiny, their minds and behaviour was different? If whales thought of humans as humans thought of ants or bees, they wouldn't bother to be friendly or even curious, assuming what Saba said was true.

That night found them on a calm open sea with the pregnant moon lighting their way. Hermes kept the sail up in a light wind and checked the course by the Great Bear when it appeared in the twilight. Saba and Amlodi climbed down the footholds on the prow and straddled the projecting snout at water level. There, Saba distinguished the deep-toned sounds of the fin whales so that Amlodi could follow their sequences. They were not really sad at all, she pointed out, no more than the curlew or the nightingale letting their kinsfolk know all was well wherever they were. In the dark sea around the ship there was a sound of sucking and welling as other whales surfaced and spouted, then swam lazily past.

In the morning, Saba got Hermes to tie a couple of ropes from the stern and drop them in the water. Then she and Amlodi got into the water, holding on to the ropes, and trailed along behind the ship, keeping one ear immersed as long as possible. The songs were amplified underwater, as were the squeals and clicks of the dolphins sporting around them. It was so obviously enjoyable that Aine, Kalliste and Bethel took turns to join them. The water was cold but the sun was warm and dispelled any goosepimples as the sunbeams enveloped their flesh. Kalliste and Bethel decided that when they got back to Krete it would be fun to trail behind a boat skimming on planks of wood.

Aine had her arm over a dolphin's back. 'Don't they feel odd – so vibrant inside that skin yet it's as tough and shiny as old pine gum. Not a bit like any fish I ever touched.'

'That's because they aren't fish,' explained Saba. 'They breathe air as we do through that blowhole behind their head, and they don't swim tail sideways like fish but like us, moving tail or legs up and down.'

'They're too trusting for their own good,' Bethel grunted. 'Most tribes hunt and eat them.'

'But they are much smarter than our wolf dogs,' protested Aine.

'Some people eat wolf dogs too, and even humans for that matter. I've seen the bones all too often when whole cities were dying of famine.'

'What are cities, Bethel?'

'Places where large numbers of people all live together as in a village.'

'How many?'

'More than you could imagine, Aine. Some have a few thousand. Really big cities may have many times more than Fion's whole army.'

'How is it we have never heard of any? Are they all beyond the Middle Sea?'

'Melusine told me there were once several cities on the shores of the Grey Ocean in the west, after the ice giants retreated from the northern lands like Er-rin and Scotia, in the time when the starry beast we call the crab ruled the spring sunrise.'

'That would be two star yuls ago,' Aengus interjected suddenly, in his slurred speech.

'Congratulations, it's well your brain is still working,' Bethel commented. 'Anyway, Aine, at that time there were many cities built on sea coasts as far as the land of Meluha, even further to the east than my homelands of Akkad and Sumer. But when the giants went north and the ice melted, the sea rose higher and overwhelmed them, and a star yul later it happened again when the winters got warmer. After that, new cities were built well inland on riverbanks safely away from floods.'

'How can so many people survive together without getting in each other's way – or find enough to eat, or talk to the High Ones?'

'By being organised into disciplined sections and social groups, each one serves another with their particular skills, and all of them – including the farmers and hunters living outside the walls and growing or collecting food – are protected by a standing army, like Maeve's permanent bodyguard only far larger.'

'What's discipline?'

'Following orders and sets of rules – like the crew of this ship obey Hermes, who in turn is responsible for the safety of all, including the ship. It's not easy and everyone has to give up a lot of freedom to belong to a strong and wealthy city.'

'Why would they want to belong to such a limiting way of life?'

'How could bees survive without belonging to a hive?'

Aine glanced at the others listening to their discussion.

'I'm not sure I would like to be a hive bee. Don't some of the bumble bees live in tiny groups?' Saba chipped in.

Bethel sighed. 'It's much too complicated a process to describe easily. When we get to Krete I'll be able to demonstrate how citizens live and explain more of the details.'

'Who says we're all going as far as Krete? If Aengus gets cured in Larmorica won't you have to return to Er-rin and be the Kaheen again?' asked Aine.

'Who knows what the Spinner has decreed for any of us,' said Saba enigmatically.

After a rest on the quarterdeck at sun high, and with some mackerel fillets in their bellies, Saba and Amlodi went down the ropes again. Amlodi had managed to memorise passages of the low-pitched songs and reproduced them for Saba's comparison while the fin whales were still singing. The others were lazily resting on deck, but were suddenly startled by an anguished yell from Amlodi. Everyone looked out in amazement to see Saba riding on the back of an orca. She was clutching the tall dorsal fin and called out to them – somewhat nervously Bethel thought – that it was all right and not to worry, they would see her again soon. They stood thinking it was a game as before, when the dolphins would give them short rides; the orca would soon turn back. But instead it continued to swim off at a much faster speed than the ship. They soon diminished to a distant speck and then vanished from sight.

Amlodi climbed back on board, shaking with shock. 'We were trailing quietly when that monster rose from the depths below us and pushed Saba until she let go of the rope. Then he nuzzled her away from the boat and slid beneath her until she sat athwart his back and could grasp the fin – down there it looks as big as a sail on a curragh. It was terrifying. On other voyages I've seen those creatures rip a dolphin to pieces, even attack a grey whale, tear its tongue out and leave it to die. Yet she says they're her friends.'

'The dolphins or the orcas?' Kalliste asked.

'Both I suppose. But what can we do now?'

He stared at the others as though waiting for an oracle to bring him comfort.

'Nothing to be done,' said Aine slowly. 'Saba has powerful spirit helpers.' She tried to sound more certain than she was, to give Aengus some comfort. He was trying not to break down. Something seemed to have given way in his mind and he now relied on his mother for confidence like he had when he was a small boy.

Meanwhile Aine's face brightened, and she looked tense and alert.

Bethel was about to ask her what it was but she signalled him to be quiet, then sat down and subsided into a trance as though she had eaten the food of the little people. She remained like that for the rest of the day and all night. The others left her alone, trusting she would tell them about her experience when recovered. Hermes and the crew were dumbfounded by the whole episode, but seafarers learn to take almost anything in their stride and they knew the woman they thought of as Sedana was a kinswoman of the Kaheen. Besides, only a witch could have done the things she did with the wild sea creatures; witches could take care of themselves. Bethel agreed with Hermes that they must continue the voyage; their primary goal was to get their injured friend to Garnac as soon as possible.

The next morning, they sighted the northern coast of Larmorica and repeated the pattern of travelling down the eastern side, as they had done near Albion. Aine whispered to Aengus and Bethel that she had been in touch with Saba who was communing with Narwhal and would have weird news for them when they managed to meet again. Bethel wondered privately if that would ever happen.

THIRTY-FOUR

THE DREAMING LAND

Only after Saba disappeared with the epolar did Bethel realise how deeply attached he was to her. Without her he felt a light was extinguished. It was as though the moon had set but would not reappear from underearth and he would be deprived of her comforting beams forever. Aine tried to comfort Bethel but her close resemblance to Saba was merely a constant reminder of her mother's absence. The effort expended during her psychic communion with her mother and Narwhal had so drained her that after this exchange she could not re-engage to discover where Saba might have gone. Bethel wished he shared Aine's certainty that they would all meet again.

Hermes proceeded south and then west until the tip of the Larmorican coast was confirmed. Then they sailed parallel with it for much the same distance as they had when they passed the coast of Albion earlier. They sought and reached a narrow peninsula pointing to an island. Passing between these two stretches of land a wide bay could be seen, and across that, standing like a finger to the sky, was the tallest stone pillar in the western lands. It dominated the bay and served as their guide. As they neared it, a jumble of creeks and inlets became visible. Close to the pillar was a passage through which the sea swelled like a river in flood. Their Larmorican pilot navigated this to reach the small inland sea filled with islands which the Garnac men called the Morbihan.

The Grey Ocean tides that rose and fell so many paces in this area created a rhythm of waters swirling and eddying around the islands and land spits. Only the quiet lagoons reflected the dune pine trees on their calm surfaces. Many curraghs were beached in the protection of these lagoons. On an island plateau near the passage mouth lay the temple to the Eyed Goddess which, Bethel explained to Aine and Aengus, was the most sacred in all Larmorica. Its mound was as tall and wide as any among the Temples of Light in Er-rin. A curragh was putting out from the narrow beach in their direction and rowing hard to breast the headstrong currents. They hove to and waited for the passengers who hailed the ship. They could hardly believe their eyes as they picked out Saba seated in front of two stately attired women; all three wore scarlet and green cloaks. Saba led the way up the climbing pegs to the foredeck looking none the worse for her wave-cresting ride.

The Kretans introduced the twins to Fleur, the Seior mistress, and a younger woman of Saba's age named Aelise, who was Melusine's daughter. Bethel hadn't met her when last in Garnac and she gave him a searching stare as they saluted. Bethel, intent on questioning Saba, was forced to restrain his curiosity. Fleur welcomed the Eelfolk warmly; she had already made preparations for all of them, and for Aengus in particular.

Saba had apparently arrived in the early morning and Fleur, imaged in advance by Melusine, met her on the beach where the epolar deposited her. Food and warmth at the Seior lodge rapidly dispelled the effects of the exposure she had endured. Bethel suspected Fleur had been as amazed as the rest of them when she saw her alighting from the giant beast's back, but a Seior mistress is never surprised. To Aelise, in training with the Seior mistress, the appearance of a sea spirit on a whale's back was a feat so outrageous for a mere human – even a Kaheen – that she regarded Saba with a superstitious awe accorded only to the semi-divine offspring of the High Ones in the ancient myths.

The ship moved forward over vast reaches of oyster beds in the shallower water towards a river mouth harbour. Looking back at the sacred island in evening light, under the deep shadows of the sun, it seemed to be a place of enchantment protected by the entities who served the loved and dreaded Suil, known as the Eyed Goddess in Garnac.

They tied up at a berth that had been occupied when Hermes and his crew left by a vessel from the Two Lands, an incredibly powerful kingdom located south of the Tideless Sea. Some of their citizens had settled in Krete as traders and craftsmen.

'Do they prefer Krete to their homeland then?' asked Saba.

Bethel hesitated. 'Yes, many of them actually do. They find a greater freedom here without the restrictions imposed by their masters. It's a long explanation and will keep for another time.'

'I'll hold you to that and exchange it for part of my experiences with the Narwhal, which you are desperate to hear about.'

Bethel laughed. 'You have me there. They will both have to await our convenience.'

As well as the usual smith's village, the Ker – or elders of Garnac – had provided another guest village upriver for the use of outland visitors and traders. Here they were free to follow their own practices and customs without intruding upon the locals. These, in turn, could invite anyone with interests in common back to their lodges. A sheltered bay on the southern bank offered sufficient depth of water where heavy-timbered ships could lie safely in spite of the huge daily tidal exchanges. As it was low tide they all climbed out on a sand bank where the water was knee-high. Amlodi, Hermes and the crew made themselves at home in longhouses whose dimensions were suited to the widely disparate groups of outlanders, whether arriving by ship, or overland with ponies and cargo laden slipes from the amber sea or the mother river. A curragh transported the remainder of the party over the river to the wide peninsula dedicated to underearth daimons. Here stood the stone pillar, tall as twelve men, which they had marked out at sea. Fleur and Aelise pointed out the different rock shrines and chambered mounds as they made their way to the healing chamber selected for Aengus. Nearby was a Ker village called Mairequer where patients were housed and cared for between periods of treatment. Aengus and Bethel, his personal healer, were allocated space there while the women, accorded honorary sistership, lodged at the main Seior enclosure of Garnac.

In Mairequer, they met S-bastien, the austere Master of the Seers, and Sugaar, curator shaman of all the shrines, with whom Bethel would be co-operating in the care of Aengus. It soon became evident that Sugaar felt he had a special relationship with Aelise and was most disturbed when he noted her interest in Bethel.

Saba and the Seior healers discussed Aengus's case with Sugaar, which Bethel felt was in deference to his position as he doubted the shaman would have any new ideas to propose. Sugaar agreed that the optimum prospect of securing a perfect joining of the mutilated members would be to remove the old scars, bind the freshly opened edges with appropriate salves and allow the healing power of the trembling rocks to work their magic. Sugaar and Bethel were both skilled in surgery, but Saba insisted Bethel should perform the task next morning. Sugaar was about to protest that he, as intermediary with the daimons, would not allow the most prestigious healing facilities in the world to be taken over by two virtual outlanders, but he was quickly overruled by both Fleur and S-bastien who, as religious and civil leaders of all the Larmoricans, would brook no argument. Bethel could foresee the quality of their relationship descending even lower than the current comparative disregard.

Sugaar suggested that a night in the soothing atmosphere of the chamber would compose Aengus for morning surgery. Then the Crystal, the daimon of the chamber, might forge an affinity with him to advance his healing; perhaps she would give him a dream to comfort him. To his surprise, Aelise warmly supported his comments and a bed of skins and fresh juniper branches was prepared in the big circular chamber. At the back there was an almond-shaped stone of the Crystal almost the height of the roof slab, which was seven paces long and about a man and a half above the floor. After the others had left, Bethel remained with Aengus to enlighten him about the procedures.

'Few patients who come here are initiates and most wouldn't comprehend our knowledge. Axular taught you many of the ways of measuring and estimating. Here we can not only estimate and record the coming of spring by the position of the constellations at sunrise, we can guess when the Sky Giant will try to swallow the moon or sun and scare him away or make him vomit them back.'

'What else is recorded here?' Aengus mumbled.

'Look at the carvings on the stone. Each of those snakes with curved necks stands for a solar day – see the sun in the centre? Now there are four pairs of groups divided down the centre and facing left and right. The part-completed snakes stand for half and quarter days. The two notches separating the topmost pair of four and five days show they are also used as a total of nine. The totals of the six lower groups measure the number of days of each of the four phases of the moon over nine moons, two hundred and sixty-five days altogether. The small sign inscribed at the base of the stone helps us work out when the moon exerts its strongest pull on the tides and when that coincides with the day of a full moon. Do you follow me?'

'Yes, I think so,' he muttered, nodding.

'Because that's when the strongest tremor happens, and Sugaar and his people must drum their loudest to match the biggest magic.' Bethel left him with enough burning torches so that he and the Crystal could see each other if she appeared.

Aelise was waiting for Bethel and invited him to walk with her down one of the long avenues of stones stretching across the country-side. She was not as tall as the Eelgirls and was more stockily built, like most of the Clanspeople, but she was pretty and made the most of her looks. Her dark hair was trimmed to shoulder length and loosely tied back. Her face and torso were painted with fine, blue undulating lines, spiralling from navel and nipples and curving up around her neck and ears. Like Saba, she wore a necklace of alternate jet and amber beads, but lacked the famous amber bracelets on her upper arms that Saba had inherited from the Allmother.

Aelise told Bethel that she had noticed him the first time the Kretans arrived in Garnac, but training disciplines with Melusine prevented her from getting to know him properly. He knew from experience that many white girls were keen to pleasure a dark-skinned outlander until they discovered that the colour in itself made no difference. Saba was the only one who had indicated this with complete frankness, but had added that what really intrigued her were Bethel's shamanic skills.

In her mother's absence, Aelise wielded a lot of influence in Garnac. So as well as finding her attractive, Bethel felt it would be socially unwise to ignore her obvious interest in him. She explained that Sugaar was indeed one of her playmates, but too jealous for her liking. He would have to spend most of the night performing rituals for success in the healing of Aengus so he would neither miss them nor make a nuisance of himself, and she felt that once they were recognised lovers it would be too late for Sugaar to take action. Their walk and talk became increasingly amorous and the moon fell low in the sky before Bethel arranged another assignation and left her at the Seiors' village.

Next morning Bethel performed the surgery on Aengus with Saba, Aine and Sugaar in attendance. He removed the scars on both Aengus's organs with the sharpest of Hermes's obsidian blades, while they recited spells to reverse the evil ones placed on him by Maeve and the traitorous Eelwoman. Fresh salves were applied to pintle and tongue – they would first protect the raw flesh from his saliva and urine, then accept them so that the healing properties of each could also do their work. The scar tissue was wrapped in a linen cloth by Sugaar for use in rituals that he performed during each healing session.

If Aengus bravely withstood his torture from Maeve, he compensated this time around with yells and moans, demonstrating his renewed dependency on his mother. Eventually, Saba gave him a draught of mind-dulling herbal juice to ease the pain and let him sleep.

Sugaar stalked away without a word, taking the tissue with him.

Saba and Bethel left Aine to sit a while with Aengus and check if his dreams were being sent by the Crystal.

'I'm glad you worked on him and not Sugaar,' Saba said to Bethel. 'There's something about him I don't trust, apart from his jealousy about Aelise.'

'You noticed that too.'

'I couldn't miss it,' she said, smiling. 'And since she's fallen so hard for you the least you can do is keep her happy, in return for the Seior's promptness in seeing to Aengus. Others have to wait much longer. Besides, I have a premonition you will need her on your side for help in the future. Perhaps we all will – it's not clear.'

'I'll do it willingly. You must know I've already started, but you also know very well the one I really want to be with.'

'There's a fitting time for everything,' Saba scolded him. 'I guessed you began last night and I think Sugaar may have too.'

'Can he stop us?'

'Well, he won't complain to the Seers or the Seiors – neither would forgive him for exposing someone of her status in taking pleasure with an outsider – but he may try to revenge himself on you. Mind your back.'

'What happened with your Narwhal?'

'Much of our communing was beyond explanation in words, but he did warn me that my struggle with a woman who went in the sea would continue in other lives. He predicted great peril but communicated that he would help me as long as I could get myself to seawater. As I seem to spend my life getting in and out of dangerous situations, that's no novelty.'

'Did he send the epolar for you?'

'Yes! Such an opportunity to meet him outside dreams is unique. There is a true sympathy between us.'

'I've never heard of such a thing, even in ancient sagas. You're a unique person.'

'If I am it doesn't make life any easier! You want to ask me about the ancient temple on Suil's Island.'

'By the Mother, you're reading my thoughts again!'

'At least I'm honest about it.'

'Do you think there's a chance for me to see it and worship the goddess stones inside?'

'Only the Seer master is permitted to visit the temple once each yul. The penalty for others is death, exacted by Suil herself. If you think you are powerful enough to risk that, you might manage to persuade Aelise to help you.'

'Perhaps she'll lead me there,' he quipped. 'What better service could I offer the Eyed One?'

'You know that the chambers are mainly used by the Larmoricans and their kinsfolk to incubate important dreams. Many of them are premonitory, so watch you aren't discovered even as you enter!'

'Oh, everybody looks for a big dream to receive something special. Melusine told me about that when I was here before.'

'Well, we've been invited to attend some of the dream councils. Come along if you value your honoured position.'

'I'm as eager to know how they employ dreaming to control their lives as Amlodi could ever be about his whale sounds. Aelise and I shall exchange a few confidences.'

Bethel and Aelise were once again walking the ancient stone alignments where people communed with their ancestors and invoked their aid during the festivals. 'Not only sky spirits but those beneath the earth follow the lines of power upwards. Can't you sense them, Bethel?'

Aelise halted at a grove of willow and cut Y-shaped twigs for them both. 'Hold each arm of the twig and walk across the line of stones,' she instructed.

As Bethel did so the tail of the stick twitched upwards as if it wanted to leap from his hands.

'Now walk alongside the stones,' she said.

As long as Bethel walked close to the stones the twig pointed upright. Aelise looked relieved.

'You couldn't be a true shaman without sensing that force,' she said. She took his arm again and rubbed her head on his shoulder. 'Tell me about your dreams. Do you usually wake feeling frisky?'

'If you mean not tired, that's correct. But if I woke with you by my side, I'd always feel "frisky", as you put it.'

She chuckled, 'I think we're going to see "eye to eye" as the goddess exhorts us.'

Bethel seized his opportunity. 'In that case will you help me to worship in her temple?'

'You must know it's forbidden.'

'I'll take that risk, and offer her my life if she wills.'

She sighed. 'It will depend on the quality of your adoration. Our dreams may register her approval.'

Next morning, Fleur allowed Saba and Bethel to observe a children's dream-telling session in Melusine's lodge.

'Before we go in, I want to explain why dreams are so important. When we learn how to use them constructively, we become wise long before the normal age of elders. We act with greater confidence and assurance than our inland neighbours because we are in closer touch with the three worlds. Our neighbours are scared of us because we live on the Shaking Land. That's funny, for we're not magicians of course – we merely serve the daimons below – but it's also useful to encourage their fear. We don't enjoy fighting and it keeps them from pressuring us or wanting to live in our territory. There is little crime among our people – the dreaming would soon search it out – and our elders chastise the odd person who breaks a taboo, or pardon them if they can supply a good enough reason for doing it.'

'How early do you listen to children's dreams?' Bethel asked Fleur.

'As soon as they begin speaking. They are dreaming before they are born and they grow and learn through dreaming. In the morning each family group discusses their dreams and the children are taught to develop their dream situations just as in waking life. If a child reports a falling situation, which is common, we tell them that's wonderful, and ask them where they fell to and what they found, or suggest that next time they fall, they should travel on until they find the spirit that caused them to fall.'

In Melusine's lodge a little girl of ten or twelve yuls was describing how, when she was walking back from the beach with her paddle, she was chased by a strange man on horseback. He cornered her, stuck his spear into her and killed her. She was very upset. Aelise took her hand while her mother bathed her eyes with diluted nightshade juice.

'But you're not dead now, are you?' said Aelise. 'So he couldn't have really killed you. You only thought you had died. You must go back into this dream tonight, grasp the man's spear when he comes at you – you will be given the strength if you ask for it – and demand he tells you why he wants to do this. If he says he was angry or frightened and wanted to hurt you, tell him that that was silly, you could have charmed him. Now he must give you a gift, like a song or a new skill, and in future he must come if you call on him to help you in other dream adventures. Understand?'

'Yes, Aelise.'

'No matter what frightening thing threatens you, never give way. Force it to talk to you and it won't harm you. If you win it over, its spirit must help you in future dreams or when you're awake and in danger.'

'That was a good example, Saba,' said Fleur. 'We find that before they become adults, fear and anxiety have vanished from their dreams. Instead they bring inspiration and pleasure to ordinary life. Come and see the children at the fire festival in a few days time. You'll see how confident they are. If anyone – child or adult – brings back a gift of a new dance or song, they demonstrate it there, and if it adds to our knowledge or skills, the elders incorporate it into our lore and reward them for their contribution.'

When Bethel returned to collect Aengus from the chamber for his second session, he was still sore but in a better mood.

'Don't try to talk yet. Just keep the pads in your mouth for another five days. Then you will be eating delicious soups and stews.'

Aengus nodded and sucked a long drink of water through his rush stem.

'I've got something else to show you – look!' said Bethel.

Suspended from the ceiling slab by a thread was a stone weight carved in the shape of a whale with a very long tail fluke extending at right angles to its body. The tip of the fluke dipped into the end of a concave tray filled with powder so that when the weight began swinging, which it would when the tremors began, a trace would appear on the surface of the powder.

'The length of the trace records the strength of the tremors and we can transfer these to calendar strips of wood as a permanent memory.

At the end of each yul they are compared with tides and moon phases to show how the cycle is created by the daimons.'

Aengus nodded vigorously to show he understood, and raised a thumb and little finger in admiration.

'The whale image symbolises the weight of giant ocean tides crashing through the channel into the Morbihan and making all the land shake.' Bethel put his arm around Aengus's shoulder. 'You're being a good patient. It will be worth the discomfort, and when your tongue is whole again, you will talk and sing without a lisp.'

Aengus glanced downwards meaningfully.

'Yes, that too will be back to its old self,' Bethel said reassuringly.

The blowing of the long horns signalled the start of the festival. It included physical contests as well as dancing and singing competitions. Aelise appeared wearing a golden breastplate and wrist guards. She held a big Clan longbow; the guards would protect her from the back snap of the bowstring, which was severe for a woman. Her arrows were shot long and accurately into a target sapling and she challenged the girls to have a go. Kalliste shook her head a little contemptuously.

'My people never use long bows,' Saba explained. 'Besides, I don't want to damage myself.' She looked down at her generous breasts. 'Archery is better suited for men.'

'I thought you were a famous warrior, Kaheen,' said Aelise.

'My companion taught me to use the long knife and axe. Do you have any spear throwers in Garnac?'

'We don't use them. They are neither fast nor accurate, but there are a few trophies which were gift exchanges. They are hanging in the Seers' longhouse.'

'Can I see them tonight?'

The bed of embers for the fire walk had been burning since dawn and glowed hotly in shades of red and white; any child over seven could accompany their elders. Aelise took the hand of the little girl who had told her dream, while her mother took her brother and sister and joined the rows of waiting celebrants. Saba looked enquiringly at Aine and Bethel.

'I think we should show solidarity with our hosts.'

Kalliste began protesting about the risk.

'You're one to complain about risk, you and your bulls,' said Saba.

'I've no problems with things like that,' Kalliste retorted.

'I've never done it before,' Bethel told Saba.

'With your training in the deserts you should be able to adjust your mind without the ritual prayer and fasting,' she chided gently. 'Those children do it without thinking. It's a game they play with their elders. But just in case part of your mind becomes doubtful I'm going to bond with you. We must show a brave front before Aelise and the others.'

'You know I don't care about her as such, but you are right – I mustn't let the Eelfolk and the outsiders down.'

Saba put her hands on the crown of Bethel's head and neck. There was a momentary pain in his ears and then a great peace, as though he'd just swallowed a sacred drug. In a few moments he was no longer in full control and knew that Saba was guiding his thoughts. He felt like a spirit inhabiting two people: she was in his mind and, more frightening still, he was in hers, experiencing some of her memories.

Saba and Aine took Bethel's hands and kicked off their slippers, following the marchers striding unflinchingly across the embers. Bethel felt a searing blast of air rising around them but knew with a sense of growing exhilaration that he was not being burned. Then they were across on the other side and he was crushing their hands in triumph and relief. Bethel glanced around but no one else was acting as though they had done anything unusual.

Bethel's bonding with Saba ceased the moment they stepped from the flames. He stared into her eyes and wondered if she had learned as much about him as he had about her – probably a lot more, as she was controlling them both. He was shocked by this exceptional encounter, and realised it would be some time before he could assimilate the few raw memories gleaned from this amazing woman.

'Don't worry, Bethel, you are stronger than you believe,' said Saba. She turned, obviously not wishing to discuss anything further about it, and walked away with Aine.

Aelise caught up with Bethel a little later. 'I was going to take you on the fire walk when I saw you being escorted by those witches.' She was patently jealous, but when he explained it was his first experience, her look changed to puzzlement. 'But you didn't make any preparations for it. You must be a very powerful shaman.' She became more serious still. 'Perhaps that's just as well. I'm afraid you've made a bitter enemy and it's partly my fault.'

Bethel guessed to whom she was referring.

'When Sugaar realised you and I had been together I told him to get lost, and he went wild with fury and swore to kill you unless I refuse to see you again. I've never seen him so angry. I also suspect he is doing something out of spite to disrupt Aengus's healing process, perhaps changing the incantations.'

Bethel, in turn, grew angry. 'If I find he's done anything like that, then he's a traitor to his calling and his curatorship. In my country that's punishable by a nasty death. If he thinks his threats will affect our friendship he's mistaken.'

'That's how I feel too,' Aelise said eagerly.

Bethel resolved to watch Sugaar closely.

THIRTY-FIVE

BITTERSWEET HAUNTING

Saba had dreamt of Fion many times since the slaughter on the clifftop. Sometimes she fantasised that he wasn't really dead, merely gone on a long absence, similar to the fifteen yuls they had been apart before. Perhaps one day she would meet him on the spirit plane and love him as she did at the Temples of Light. Did spirits make love between themselves? She wondered. On her first night at the Seior lodges she dreamt of lovemaking. The man in her sleep was unknown and only partially visible. She felt him running his hands over her face and neck, armpits and breasts, his lips touching hers, until her nipples became hard. Finally his fingers traced her hips and stroked the moist hair between her legs. She moved eagerly within his embrace, seized with desire, but nothing he did satisfied her, and as his teasing slowly became a torment she awoke angrily to find herself in a sweat, but alone. Her nostrils twitched as she recognised a familiar scent, but with an almost imperceptible odour added to it.

She leapt from her couch and, snatching a blanket, strode to the entrance of her cubicle to look around outside. All was still. A couple of dogs were curled fast asleep; no one had passed in or out to disturb them.

The following two nights she awoke because someone was tapping her on the shoulder, and a shaft of moonlight filtering through the wind hole over the couch showed a man's figure standing there. He slowly turned around and there was no mistaking Fion's face. She spoke his name but as she sat up, the figure disintegrated into a dense cloud of dust specks that the moonbeam caught wafting about in the faint breeze.

The next night she went to sleep with his image and scent firmly fixed in her mind and soon began dreaming that he once again stood beside her and touched her on the shoulder. She awoke and stretched out her arm to him, softly calling his name. This time her hand touched the flesh of his stomach – solid flesh – and she recoiled in wonder.

He wore no familiar clothes or ornaments, standing upright in the fullness of his manhood, and looked just as she had known him the evening he had rescued her from the clutches of Cairla a generation earlier. Was she dreaming that Fion was a reality or was she truly awake and finding that somehow he had returned from the spirit world? She pinched her own skin and felt the pain. He knelt down and put his arms around her, telling her how dreadfully he had missed her and how he had tried to materialise through her dreams so many times in vain. He felt so cold to her touch that she invited him underneath her sheepskins.

'Do you recall how you once asked me again and again to make you warmer?' he whispered in her ear. 'Now it is I who need your warmth.'

'We'll see what we can do about that,' she said. Soon she was left in no doubt of his physical reality.

'The gods have granted me leave to come back to you because the fire of our love would not be quenched by my earthly oblivion or translated to the spirit world,' he explained. 'My nascent body energy is still feeble but will be nourished by yours every time we make love. As the sunlight would still harm me I must restrict my substance to visiting you when the softer silver rays melt the darkness. So let us walk and talk and make love under her friendly silences.'

His demands were great and Saba finally fell asleep from exhaustion. When she woke the sun was halfway up the sky and he was gone. However, she was beyond any doubt that he had indeed been with her, and the marks of the love bites on her body convinced Aine when she decided to confide in her, if only to reassure herself of her own sanity.

Aine was excited and also troubled by this turn of events. It must be a miracle if it were true; yet could Saba have somehow dreamt it up? She had conceived and energised the tulpa bear whose reality was sufficient to cause Maeve's death. Saba had previously explained the technique and how it was still too advanced for her, but Aine knew her expanding consciousness would one day enable her to project too. Saba's bear was a projection from herself, but from what substance could she project an image of Fion to herself other than in dream? There was an uneasiness in the back of Aine's mind, echoed by a lump in the pit of her stomach.

She slept with her mother for several nights and nothing further occurred. Eventually they both came to believe that Saba had undergone a hypnotic nightmare and somehow caused the marks to appear on her skin, since shamans could produce bleeding wounds when in trance.

The only other person wise enough to consult on such an intimate topic would be Bethel and Saba didn't want to embarrass him, not so much because his desire and admiration for her was strong, but rather because he was pleasuring Aelise to help achieve their prime objective in Larmorica, that for which they must subordinate any other goals or wishes. Aine returned to her own sleeping couch and Saba said no more about the matter when they went to visit Aengus by day.

Amlodi came to take a temporary leave of his friends. He had inveigled an invitation to go with some Euskaldun he met in the village on a fishing trip back to their homelands far down the coast. He explained they would be far out at sea for many nights each way following shoals of saithe, a favourite fish with all the Clanspeople. Sailing as they did in long seagoing curraghs, he would have superb opportunities to pursue his study of whale songs because many of the greatest beasts swam alongside the boats as though they were curious and would even allow some humans to stroke them. He was composing an epic ballad for voice, drum and flute, incorporating his version of their tonal chords and rhythms. It would be a first in all the Clanlands and he freely acknowledged it would never have been possible without Saba's instigation and help.

The Eelfolk were struck by another of his unusual talents. Amlodi saw with his inner eye a different shade of colour for every note he sang. His friend Larmor, and later Aine, painted pictorial accompaniments to his ballads on bark and rock surfaces using the colours in the surreal way he saw them. The wider spectrum of whale sounds excited him as it would a musician first introduced to the world of birdsong. He later persuaded Aine to complement his whale epic by painting coloured images of the beasts and their songs on rolled linen cloths that he could carry on his travels and open out as a backdrop wherever he sang and played his ballads to a new audience.

Fion began to appear to Saba for periods each night, gently wooing her all over again as he reminded her vividly of enjoyable or intimate moments they had spent together. They relived the memories of paddling down the Mother Lake to watch the mating dances of her birds, spying on the white hares in moonlight from the secrecy of their forest pool and listening to the chilling cries of peregrines circling the Cualan hills while Fion tracked a deer during their moon of music, as Saba described that idyll of ease and pleasure in their lives following the harsh battles on Boand's Plain.

'I never really went away, you know, after I was flung over the cliff top. But it was impossible to make you aware of me until a powerful being in the skyworld showed me how.'

'Who was that being?'

'I dare not say or I would lose my ability to materialise. You must trust me that this being is working for the welfare of us both.'

In the days that followed, Saba often seemed distracted or dispirited. This was particularly remarked by Bethel, who kept as close an eye on her as on Aengus. He asked Aine if she noted any changes.

'Yes, but when I ask her she says all is well and changes the subject.'

'You seem to know more about this than you're telling me,' Bethel said.

'I'm not sure she would wish me to talk to you about it but I am extremely worried.'

'I don't want to intrude on a private matter, but if it's as serious as I divine from your manner, you are duty bound to tell me. We both love her and you know I have some little power to help her. It's sad she doesn't feel she can confide in me.'

'As to that, she was upset because she encouraged you to pleasure Aelise in order to further our projects, even though she knew of your feelings for her.'

'Tush, that's done all the time and I assure you, this project's giving me plenty of fun in two directions.'

'Well, two things are worrying me and they may be connected. Firstly, when Saba was communing with the Narwhal she confided in me that he told her she would soon be thrown into danger.'

'That's a condition she's well used to, from all I've seen and heard.'

'Yes, and she couldn't believe anything would happen to her here among Melusine's friends. But secondly, since she's been here she's begun dreaming of Fion and his ghost actually appeared to her. I stayed with her for some nights and nothing further happened, but she's acting the way she did before, except that she won't talk about it. In fact, she's denying anything is going on. I was uncertain but now you have corroborated my worries, what can be done?'

'Try keeping her company at night again.'

'She'll have none of it!'

'Then the apparition will have returned. We must both be on guard for any change or new development, no matter how slight. Then we'll decide what action to take.'

'I thought she was so well protected by her guardians!'

'There are as many subterfuges and deceits in the spirit worlds as on earth. How else could so many sky wars develop?'

'So guardians can only protect us to some extent?'

'Of course, otherwise we'd have no personal freedom to make choices and allow the multiple destinies woven by your Lady Spider to operate and be selected.'

When told of Kalliste's past exploits in bull dancing, some of the Larmorican youths challenged her to give a demonstration. Unable to refuse a dare, she asked Aine to help her organise a trial. But they were shaken when they saw the size of the Larmorican bulls – twice as big as any in Er-rin or the Cyclades! The Larmoricans laughed at them.

'These aren't your island toy cattle brought in by boat. They've always roamed freely here like the boar in the wild forests. We manage to partially tame some of them, the cows at least.' The bulls' shoulders were at human height and their curved horns were longer and wider on their broad heads. They were only handled by several men with spears at the ready. The girls asked Saba's advice; how could they dance with such monsters?

She shook her head. 'You at least, Aine, have the faith learned in the Raven's cave. And you, Kalliste, saw the child ember walkers who have faith that in special circumstances ordinary effects don't happen. When they are absorbed in the intricate gestures of the ritual, every part of their body is focused. These points of concentration are all that matter in the fire dance. You, Kalliste, are equally skilled and versed in concentration. If the bull were as big again, you could dance with him because you will be aware of nothing else. And don't forget your friends – we won't allow you to fail.'

Kalliste tossed her head at Aine. 'You are only my catcher and bull distractor. I must face him and decide the moment to leap. What if he reacts differently? The slightest error means death.'

'Take heart. Remember how my mother rode the giant orca who

is only an enormous dolphin. These bulls are just bigger versions of the ones we know. They all think the same way.'

The trial bull dance was to take place at the next new moon games. On the day before, the Garnac herdsmen caught and corralled one of the feistiest bulls, leaving him plenty of ash leaves and water. Onlookers from all parts of Larmorica gathered curiously at the corral. Was this a new mascot to embody the divine Sky Bull when they dressed up with their horned masks and bull genitals at the sacred dances. Surely they were realistic enough?'The strangers bring a gift from a new dream,' they were told.

'One of them will dance with the bull himself.'

A great crowd assembled to witness the new ritual. A hundred men with shields and spears formed a large circle to ensure the bull didn't gallop away. Kalliste and Aine appeared from the Seior lodge wearing white feathered robes decorated with the flat, yellow bracted Carline thistle, emblem of all the coastal Clans. Its petals and splayed leaves, like the united rays of sun and moon, symbolised their unity.

When the bull was released and pranced forward, they dramatically discarded the robes, displaying their well-oiled athletic bodies painted in yellow with black designs. To Kalliste's annoyance the taurine teasers and musicians began drumming and whirled bullroarers to incite the bull and build up the atmosphere; she had no wish to enrage it before she was ready. The heavy drum beats did just that and it charged her directly. But this bull was huge; his horns, even when lowered, were level with her breasts, so that when she ran towards it, relying on its surprise to grab them, she modified her somersault to allow for its upward toss. All went well; she landed on its hind quarters and executed another backwards somersault over its tail to the ground where Aine steadied her. The crowd went as wild as the spectators on Boand's Plain. 'Again, again,' they yelled. But the bull was enraged at the indignities heaped upon it by these puny wasps with their stinging spears.

Kalliste realised she was in serious danger. Saba was standing within the circle close by and spoke a few words to her. Bethel appeared and took Saba's arm as he could see how tired and nervous she looked.

'We'll work on him together!' Bethel whispered.

Saba pressed his hand gratefully and they concentrated their wills on the bull's eyes. From madly scraping the earth and bellowing with fury, it calmed and faced Kalliste, standing stock-still with head up.

Seizing the opportunity, Kalliste skipped forward, leapt up to grasp its horns and vaulted to its shoulders where she executed a forward somersault, landing astride and beckoning Aine, who vaulted up from the side, to join her. Both dancers banged on his flanks with their heels. The bewildered bull moved around the ring with a lumbering gait while the girls stood up on his rump. Aine helped Kalliste to climb up on her shoulders and wave at the crowds. After a circuit or two, Kalliste dived to a handstand on the bull's shoulders and landed on her feet with a sideways flip, while Aine somersaulted to the ground on the opposite side. The two finished their display with a run and double somersault that ended at opposite sides of the circle, where they bowed to the bull and the crowd in turn, with arms raised triumphantly in the horned invocation. The spectators were reduced to silence when they walked up to the bull, stroked his head and led him meekly back to the corral.

Bethel grinned wickedly at Saba. 'I'd love to be here if someone tries that trick at the next games.'

'So would I! You always seem to be on hand when help is needed,' she said, with a slightly wistful twinkle in her eyes.

'I foresee you needing lots of help to climb the peaks in your destiny. I'll always be on hand if you let me.' He spread out his arms, palms upwards. 'As part of my shamanic training I spent many yuls in mountains far to the east of Akkad and practised arcane disciplines with hermits to whom the goddess directed me. I learned to pass back through the Gates of Horn to the dream senders, opening a way through time, and to extract whispers from what, to other adepts, was deep silence.'

'I'm sure to have need of you,' said Saba. 'But not just yet.'

Hermes was urging his people to depart soon. He wanted to recommence the voyage homewards before the seasonal storms of the Grey Ocean arrived in the bay of the Eusquerra. But Kalliste refused to leave Aine who, like Bethel, had no intention of deserting Aengus and Saba. So he agreed to delay a further moon at the behest of Bethel, whose concern for Saba was increasing daily.

Bethel was also convinced that Aengus, though physically repairing well, would require greater psychic help than was available in Garnac. He would not easily regain his amatory function or singing skills. Maeve and her shaman were too subtle to kill him. They knew well the extent of damage inflicted on the young man by singling out these two organs, thus destroying the lifelines between his intangible self and material nature: his speech, his poesy and his ability to extend his temporal existence through his organ of generation, which in turn opened the way for the ancestors to quicken a new scion of his lineage within the chosen mother.

In the days that followed, Saba still kept her own counsel about the exchanges with her nightly visitor. Her feelings about Fion – for she ceased to doubt that it was he in whatever form – were changing from scepticism to sympathy. At times when they made love he was rougher and cruder than before, but his words were gentler and more persuasive.

'How do I know you really are you and not a masquerading spirit?' she asked him. 'Do you recall what emblem I stuck on my shield with my own blood?'

He whispered the answer, for she could not read his thoughts. 'I'm happy that we are bonding so wonderfully,' he said. 'You nourish my spirit every night and I know that I'm sapping your energy, leaving you drained and feeling like the victim of a forest daimon. But it need not be like that.'

'How so?' Saba asked.

'If we were together all the time, I would no longer exhaust you.'

'And how can that happen when we exist on different planes?'

'I need you desperately on my plane,' he begged. 'You see, every male spirit must meld with a female spirit in our world to become a whole being and it should be someone with whom there was a carnal bond in the life just ended. Almost all the women I knew are still alive except Boand, and she has already melded. Maeve has demanded from the mistress of death that I must become her other half.'

'But that's wrong! When did you have any connection with that evil slut?'

Fion told her about his enforced contract with Maeve after his rescue from Mastell's island and how she had forced him to seal it. He added that a spirit ancestor of Saba's was trying to help him avoid the demand, but Maeve, in turn, had appealed to the Fire God, one of the Sky Lords whom she had always worshipped. Unless Saba helped him he was lost. Was her love equal to that? He touched her face, wet with tears.

'You are the only person I ever loved – far beyond Grainne who you met in Cualan. I know you will not fail me now. You never have.'

Saba felt herself torn in two and retreated to pray to the goddess for wisdom and advice. To Aine and Bethel's consternation, during the following days she seemed to be sinking into a torpor not unlike that portrayed initially by Aengus, although he at least had his periods of lucidity. Saba reflected how her love and affection for Fion had blossomed to its greatest extent during their moon of music. She had felt like a free soul, bound no longer to any obligations. They had celebrated each day with renewed energy, catching their joys like flutterbys on the wing.

'Fion's sacrifice at the clifftop ensured my survival and victory,' she reasoned. 'My power might not have been sufficient to defeat Maeve and her shaman. Maeve will now annihilate the positive life force in his spirit for countless ages when she takes him as her other half. I truly owe him my life here and because of our love bond, the least I can do in return is help him in the spirit realm. I know there is much left undone in my skein on middle earth, but I will pick up the threads on my next incarnation and fulfil this wyrd. I learned from Raven how to forge the memories to endure in a new body. Bethel is a fine and extraordinary being. I may miss forever the glories we might have accomplished together, but no choice remains for me. At least he and Aine will never leave Aengus until he finds wholeness again. My decision is made. I shall take the potion of immortality. My spirit will join with Fion's, and Maeve will find us impregnable.'

Without further delay she prepared and drained the cup in front of the hearth fire in Maire's lodge. When the mixture was past regurgitating, she lay down to compose herself, but instead received a blinding revelation: the leering face of her old enemy appeared first in the fire, then gradually materialised close to her own. There was that pervasive smell of Fion, with the something extra. Saba recognised her mistake too late.

'Now you are all mine and powerless to save yourself,' Maeve gloated. 'Fion has been my creature since that stupidity on the clifftop. That was his last voluntary action. You thought you were finished with me when your cursed bears mangled my body. Well, now it's I who will torment your spirit and control it as I do with Fion. It is me, in Fion's guise, who has visited and coupled with you every night in dream or reality since you came to my homeland. Ha! You didn't know my roots suck strength from this earth. You can guess how I enjoyed the process through him, making you shudder and pant and take him to the heart of your being. How I longed to interrupt your orgasms and let you know it was me, but then we wouldn't have broken down your will sufficiently to persuade you to drink the poison which even now you can feel numbing your limbs. I don't think we could call it a love match, do you? But I know and possess you body and soul, thanks to your stupid loyalty to that oaf.'

Saba grunted a horrified retort: 'Then I also possess you.'

She crawled over to the fire and pushed her feet into it. The excruciating pain helped her to separate her mind and to establish contact with Aine, transmitting her catastrophic predicament in a flash to her before she lost control and sank into darkness, substituting in her mind's eye the image of the Allmother's face.

THIRTY-SIX

HOW FAR IS FAR ENOUGH?

Aine, Bethel and one of the Seiors arrived to find Saba with her feet scorching in the hearth. They carried her to a couch, where they checked her breath and pulse and confirmed that she was in a deep coma. Aine explained that the potion of immortality had no antidote. After enquiring what herbs it contained, Bethel rushed off to his pack and returned with a liquid which they forced into Saba's mouth, drop by drop.

'It will stimulate and fortify her body to combat the lethal herbs, for I'm sure she's fighting hard,' Bethel muttered.

Aine prayed to Allmother, Narwhal and Suil and begged their assistance. She recalled her ancient Mother's advice to think of her in times of deadly peril; this was surely one such time. Later in the night, while Aelise and Bethel changed the burn dressings on Saba's feet and Aine dozed in Saba's cell, the Allmother appeared to her. Her face was grave.

'Your mother's condition is critical but all who love her on this plane are interceding for her with the goddess.'

'Can you help her, Old Mother?'

'Bethel and the Seior must support her fighting will. I have spoken with her ancestral guides. Narwhal or I shall come to you when you have agreed on a definite plan of action. We on this plane cannot do that for you.'

Aine filled Saba's scrying skull and set it where she could glance at the water's surface. The Seior employed numerous spells and incantations to revive Saba from her coma or exorcise whatever spirit possessed her. Inside a circle of light formed by flickering lamps, Maire and Aelise led the chant of an ancient rhythm, hypnotic in its effect.

Bethel felt his body convulsing as energy surged from deep within to radiate with sweat from every pore. As the drumbeats reached a peak Aine saw a face appear in the water, which changed from misty to clear. The face wore a vicious smirk, a look she had never forgotten. Aine shuddered and the others gathered round to discover what was upsetting her, but Bethel was the only one who saw anything. He had never seen Maeve up close but guessed from Aine's demeanour whose face it was. The eyes stared victoriously into the shaman's, challenging him to do his worst as though she were far beyond the reach of any mortal.

Bethel ransacked his memory for something to use as a weapon. 'Aine, I knew a black-skinned shaman who, with enormous effort, could call back spirits as solid beings and they could function as in life for brief periods because they used his energy and substance, but they so exhausted him that he spent his days and nights in a near comatose state when they were materialising.'

'Could a shaman from this country do it too?'

'I don't see why not – if they were strongly connected in the other worlds.'

'So the ghosts of Maeve and Fion must be getting their energy from a living shaman?'

Kalliste interrupted. 'Do you remember, Aine, when we were Maeve's captives and she dispatched you to guide her fleet of curraghs? After you left she spoke to me in Larmorican, as I understood it better, and she had an evil-looking woman companion whom she left to oversee Fergus when she marched north with her army. I recall her telling me that this Scathach was a witch who accompanied her from Larmorica to help her develop her magic powers.'

'Oh!' Aine exclaimed. 'And Melusine told us that when Maeve's evil shadow escaped from her in the caves, she must have fled back to the country she came from.'

'You mean she might have returned here with one of the Larmorican fishing boats?'

Aelise became excited. 'Listen, Melusine my mother is imaging me that the medium is indeed Scathach and she wants the Seior and Ker dreamers to begin searching the land for her. She has already visioned her likeness to Maire.'

'She may have eluded Melusine but she won't escape so easily from all the Seiors combined,' Bethel said. 'And now we know that Maeve has centred her power in Saba's body until it becomes lifeless and has taken the spirit over completely, perhaps the Seiors could trace the force back from Maeve to the medium.'

'If we could find Scathach soon and bring her here, maybe Suil the Mother will give us power to make a transference,' Aelise suggested.

'But then we will have thrown away any advantage of surprise. We need the daimons' help all the way with this,' Maire said. 'If we don't locate the medium quickly, Saba is lost to us and with such additional energy these evil ones will wreak havoc in Garnac in our efforts to undo the spell on Aengus, as well as help his mother. Have you noticed the earth tremors are much stronger since Saba's been in a coma?'

The vigil at Saba's side continued for several days, during which time Hermes went to see Bethel. He was desperately upset. A few of his Kretan sailors had got drunk on the Larmorican herb-laced apple wine and violated some Euskaldun women in the travellers' village. The women complained to the Garnac elders who viewed this broken taboo with great severity, but determined to reserve punishment until their menfolk returned from their fishing expedition on the Grey Ocean.

Hermes knew the Euskaldun would demand that the guilty Kretans become their slaves; no amount of gold dust or metal stored on the ship would buy them off. The Kretans were terrified, for they feared all of them would be blamed and punished and never see their homeland again. There was a movement to seize the ship if Hermes would not put to sea. This, and the fact that the vessel almost foundered when crossing the bay of Euskadi during the storm season on their way to Garnac, made it imperative that he depart.

When Bethel protested, Hermes interrupted: 'I wouldn't dream of abandoning you all. There's a trade route across country to the Tideless Sea, the route most travellers take since few ships risk the tricky sea journey. It starts further along the coast, down the great river Gar and past the Valley of the Ancestors. There's a short porterage at the far end but you won't have trade goods to carry. I'll bring the ship to the harbour on the Tideless Sea, at the other end. I'll wait there however long it takes. I promise I won't leave without you. The Larmoricans know the route well and the Seiors will send a guide with you.'

There was nothing they could do to dissuade him. Bethel reasoned Hermes was right and that he would die rather than break his oath. He wanted the shaman to take some pouches of gold dust but Bethel knew from experience they would merely cause trouble. With caravans in all countries, backpacks were searched each time travellers entered a new territory and if the gifts offered were not considered satisfactory, the carriers went in danger of losing their possessions and their lives.

One of the things Bethel found so refreshing about the Eelfolk was that they never cared about material objects, and he knew Kalliste would agree; one could always get more. They were utterly self-reliant compared to the people in the lands with whom Bethel was familiar. Saba and her daughter were so confident of their ability to survive and obtain whatever they needed, and completely confident that the Earth Mother would never forsake those who were truly at one with her.

Bethel explained to everyone the predicament Hermes was in. Hermes made his farewells and embraced Kalliste, promising he would collect her and the others. Bethel was certain he would never dare face her mother in Krete without her.

The day after Hermes left, Amlodi returned with the Euskaldun fishing fleet. Some of the Euskaldun whose partners had been violated swore vengeance on the Kretans should any of them return. A little later Aelise reported that one of the Seiors, in a searching dream, flew past a village to the north where the atmosphere struck her as bleak and strained compared to everywhere else in the land. She paused and peeked in each lodge and in one of them glimpsed a female shaman in a trance. She was certain from the description she had been given that it was indeed Scathach.

Aine prayed to the Old One and was answered instead by the Narwhal. Later she nervously discussed with Bethel the steps he envisioned must be taken. When the healer considered them he became equally apprehensive. They were to place themselves completely at the mercy of the wild creatures. Bethel hid his sense of unease from Aine knowing she possessed more 'hupomone', as Kalliste called it, than he did, perhaps as much as Saba herself. She would never count the cost for this venture. Her mother and brother were more important than her life.

When Aine and Bethel explained to Amlodi the part they needed him to play, he became so excited at the prospect of such an incredible and exotic marine adventure that concern for safety didn't enter his head; Bethel felt ashamed of his own petty worries. Maire sent a contingent of Seiors to enfold Scathach and her village in a blanket of darkness and bring the evil one, under hypnosis, to a lodge near the beach where Saba would be waiting. They had to ensure there would be no subconscious communication with the possessing entity lodged in Saba's mind.

The ritual transfer of possession began with a group of Seers drumming softly and chanting syllables of power in low-cadenced tones. Maire and her Seiors burnt herbs and heated brews even Bethel could not identify. She anointed Saba's lips and genitals with a black ointment, then smeared it on Aine, Scathach and Bethel. It was essential that an adept of the opposite gender conduct the procedure. She wafted the pungent vapours and smoke in slow sweeps across Saba's skin with a vulture's wing. Aine lay on her back alongside Saba, and Maire stared intensely into her eyes for what seemed an endless finger of time. Eventually Aine began dolphin breathing – she expelled all the air from her lungs, then filled them to the fullest capacity and held the breath as long as possible before blowing it out very fast and sucking in fresh air. This was repeated compulsively as she sank into a trance mode from which her spirit could reach out and empathise with Saba and Maeve.

Bethel stretched across them both, pressed his mouth over Saba's lips and sucked the breath from her lungs, then blew it into Aine's mouth, which was open and ready for him. This continued for so long that he almost fainted from dizziness, even though he snatched a fresh breath between each transfer. He began to feel as though he were working in a twilight zone, interrupted by small flashes of lightning. Eventually Saba began to scream like an animal in torment. When the noise subsided, Aine, in her turn began to moan softly. Then they knew they had successfully transferred Maeve into Aine's mind and body. Even if she was aware of what had happened, she may not have resisted the spells to the extent of putting Saba's life in danger, thinking that she could as easily hurt and control the mother by possessing the daughter.

The most challenging and dangerous parts of the operation were yet to come. Scathach's body was still lying on the floor beside Aine. Aelise and some of the Seiors picked them both up and transported them swiftly down to the beach. Bethel followed, praying that the Narwhal had arranged all that was needed for Amlodi, as their success depended on the speed of the next procedure.

To everyone's relief Amlodi was waiting in the water and with him were two orcas. They swam as close to the shore as they dared without beaching themselves, and when Amlodi scrambled onto the back of one of them, the Seior waded into the water and passed up Scathach's body so that he could secure it between himself and the dorsal fin.

When Bethel was seated on the back of the second, the manoeuvre was repeated with Aine and the orcas sped smoothly away as though responding to an invisible signal – or perhaps they understood the urgency. Bethel and Amlodi grasped the women with one arm and the dorsal fins with the other. As they traversed the channel and entered the Grey Ocean reaches, Bethel expected the ride to become more violent as the waves got choppier and higher and the swells deeper, but the beasts travelled through them rather than over in an exhilarating manner that was unlike any curragh or larger ship the pair had ever experienced. Bethel understood how Saba must have felt with her orca. Amlodi and Bethel couldn't communicate because of the rush through the water – they could just about breathe between avalanches of flung spray – but they were both wondering if these were the same orcas they had met on the way to Larmorica. How wonderful to be friends with these powerful creatures and to be allowed to ride on their backs if it pleased them! They seemed as docile as ponies, but whose orders were they obeying? The Narwhal or perhaps the Earth Mother herself? Bethel shivered at the thought of being a puppet for such mighty beings. They were hardly out of sight of land when Amlodi's jaw dropped and his eyes widened, fixed on the water before him.

'A zeroi!' he yelled.

Bethel glanced up and beheld a huge whale floating calmly in the waves as though waiting for them. If the orcas were four times larger than the dolphins, this whale was at least twice the orcas' size. His massive head was blunt ended and appeared a third of his body. As they floated alongside the giant his mouth opened like a hillside cavern to display dozens of stalagmite teeth standing like stones on a dancing floor. The creature had the majesty of a god, but was so gentle. The orcas were stationary and Bethel was close enough to touch his enormous tongue. The eye on their side flickered as though signalling the men to get on with it.

During the final leg of the journey, Aine had been writhing and mumbling and Bethel was beginning to worry just how he was to overcome the daimon, which by then must have known that they were trying to transfer her to Scathach. He smacked her face to rouse her from trance and she began screaming and attacking him. Amlodi, as previously prompted, thrust fragments of a fiery stinging herb into Scathach's orifices to distract her with the sudden pain. To their consternation a stream of evil-looking vapour spewed from her mouth, it grew and swelled until it towered over them like a monstrous black fart, paralysing them with its coldness and stench until they couldn't move. Aine stopped fighting, as though she had just awakened.

'How can we make the transfer from me to that thing? I can feel Maeve getting stronger each instant and my will fading.'

A jet of orange flame rose from Aine's mouth and climbed upwards to centre inside the swollen gas field. She moaned.

'I'm being ripped apart! Old Mother help me!'

Bethel lost control. 'Is there never any justice?' he shouted at the sky which had turned sulphurous yellow. 'She did what she did out of pure love. Must she lose her immortal spirit as well as her life?'

Glancing down, Bethel saw an old woman take Aine into her arms, declaiming imperiously in word-sounds familiar to him from the Mother Lake. She seemed to be challenging the tongue of fire. A series of thunder claps sounded out, then stroke after stroke of lightning forked around them, cutting through the black gas cloud. It exploded like a giant tree in the centre of a forest fire.

The old woman turned to Bethel. 'Transfer the spirit now!' she commanded.

Bethel glued his mouth to Aine's lips, inhaled fully and vomited the contents down Scathach's throat. Amlodi and Bethel immediately rolled Scathach onto the zeroi's tongue and jerked backwards; the jaws snapped shut like a tree falling and he dived slowly without a backwash. When Bethel turned round the old woman had vanished and Aine was astride the orca. He clambered on behind her, Amlodi did likewise on his. The orcas began circling as though waiting for a signal. Then the zeroi surfaced again, opened its mouth and coughed. A lump of tar-like stuff shot from its throat and splashed into the water.

'Is that what he did to her?' Amlodi muttered fearfully.

'What is that?' Bethel asked himself aloud.

'I don't know but it's not Scathach,' Aine replied haltingly. 'Pick it up and bring it with us. Someone is telling me you will need it soon.'

One of the orcas stopped by the lump and Bethel managed to lift it from the water. It was the weight of a grown wolf, grey-black with variegated streaks, glutinous with a familiar sweet earthy odour. Bethel was keen to cheer Aine.

'How are you feeling?' he asked her.

'Terrible, but now that bitch fiend is gone, I'll be all right. The Old One saved me and gave me strength. Saba's awake and improving too. Her body is fighting the poison now her possessors have left.' The orcas were well on their way to the coast at their amazing pace.

'Where do you think the zeroi will go with Scathach?' Bethel asked.

'The big squid whale? Oh, the Narwhal knows an underworld lake in the land of the ice giants where only whales visit. He'll keep her there frozen in her live body for a long time. They cannot be destroyed, you know.'

'So Fion's spirit went too?'

'I hope so since she controlled him. That awful display of elemental rage settled it all. You know Saba's guardians had to confront the great Fire Lord, not just Maeve and Scathach.'

'Eternal Mother! Since the Fire Lord lost this confrontation, he will take his anger out somewhere. I pray his vengeance will not descend on us.'

'Well, since it seems our guardians had to call on the Mother herself in their extremity, hopefully we are still under her protection.'

Bethel knew that the great gods, if angered, must be appeased and he thought of how worried and fearful Aelise had been to discover that the Seiors had been informed of their temple visit. Aelise, jealous of Bethel and Saba's intimacy at the firewalk and bull dancing, had decided to risk all in an effort to keep his affection and agreed to take him to visit the Eyed Goddess in the island temple. They spent the night there celebrating her fertility, and in the morning sunrise Aelise interpreted the marvellous spirals of life and death carved on the walls perhaps a sky age earlier by their ancestors from the south, before the northern ice glaciers melted and vanished from the land. Bethel's determination to see the carvings close up stemmed from casual information proffered by Melusine. She believed that they equated with symbols of glorious Tara, an eastern Goddess of Wisdom who had appeared to Melusine in dream. Bethel was not disappointed when he saw the equivalent symbols, and concluded there must indeed be a connection between her and Suil the Eyed One. In one engraving he saw the three wyvre serpents spiralling up out of the island in the sea, indicating the tremendous earth forces empowering the Shaking Land and their origin from the same goddess, both there and in Meluha.

Later Aelise discovered they had been seen entering and leaving by a Seior, who was shocked at the desecration and reported the matter to S-bastien and the Ker, as well as the Seiors. S-bastien convened a council of as many Seiors and Ker as he could gather at short notice to decide what actions to take. Sugaar grumbled that the strangers from the Kretan ship had been trouble since they landed and had they not been friends of Melusine, he would have formally accused them sooner of a list of charges.

Firstly, the youth sent for healing was cursed by such powerful spirits that their own daimons couldn't lift the spells laid upon him. Secondly, the brown man had defiled their maiden priestess and enchanted her. Thirdly, the Kretan sailors broke the Larmorican laws of hospitality and raped their kinsfolk. Fourthly, the brown man forced their priestess to take him into the sacrosanct Temple of Suil, and who knew what blasphemies they committed there. Lastly, evil spirits from Er-rin now possessed this sea witch known as Sedana, also her daughter and a northern shaman, and had taken them away on the backs of orcas. Was that not enough reason to destroy them all, especially the brown man? If they did not, the underearth daimons would surely wreck vengeance on the people of Garnac for permitting it.

S-bastien and Fleur announced they would retire and consider what judgement must be meted out to the guilty ones. After a brief adjournment, they returned and pronounced that all the strangers would be banished forthwith, but that Bethel must be sacrificed for his desecration of Suil's temple. Aelise, having overheard what transpired, took the opportunity to advise Aengus and Kalliste and brought them to the lodge where Saba – now fully conscious – was still recuperating. The person in imminent danger was Bethel, and the Ker, at Sugaar's insistence, were already posting lookouts along the coastline to seize him if he returned.

While they discussed what could be done, Kalliste told them of the plan concocted with Hermes. If Amlodi could persuade some of the

Euskaldun fishermen to bring them all down the coast in their curraghs to the river of the ancestors, they could proceed in a single boat to the port of Narbac on the Tideless Sea.

Saba discovered she was able to communicate again with Aine – the seemingly impossible mission was accomplished and they were already on their way back. She told Aine of the council's decision regarding Bethel and said that Kalliste and Aengus would wait on the spit of coast where the orcas had collected them and try to distract the lookouts. Kalliste and Aengus left straightaway to spy out where the guards were stationed. When they met up, Amlodi would persuade his Euskerran friends to help Bethel escape and arrange a rendezvous for them all on one of the outer islands in the bay.

'Aelise, I know of your affection for Bethel and the risks you are running for all our sakes. Melusine and I will be forever in your debt,' Saba told her.

'Well, it looks as though I must come away with all of you as I'll be deemed equally guilty for helping. Besides, you'll need a guide through the Valley of Ancestors. I know it and no one else will dare take you now. I'll go and find out what sacrifice is intended for Bethel. May the Eyed One help Kalliste or Aengus to find him in time.'

Saba dragged herself up from what might have been her bier and raided the Seiors' store room for herbs. She brewed a restorative to counteract her bodily sickness and made salves for her feet. After drinking it she was disturbed to see the floor and walls of the lodge shaking before her eyes. She must be in a worse state than she realised.

As the orcas rapidly neared the coast, the sea became disturbed; great masses of water moved in swells and deep troughs as during a mid-ocean storm. There was no sign of any people on shore, lookouts or friends, but the river was rolling in choppy waves and large rocks bobbed up and down in the water like twigs. Tall trees on the land lurched grotesquely, some cracking and smashing to the ground.

A low rumbling sound rose to a thunderous roar. The orcas unloaded their passengers and shot out of the bay at incredible speed, as though this was the last place on earth they wanted to be. A gap opened in one of the river banks and a sour reek of rotting debris streamed past their nostrils. They stared in horror as tree roots and earth poured into the widening maw. From the opposite bank they were just in time to see the great stone pillar – the tallest monument of human engineering in all Larmorica – as it rocked and then vanished from sight with a mighty crack of shattering rock.

Shrieks and yells of fear and fury erupted from a group of village men who appeared as magically as the fissure in the earth. Bethel, Aine and Amlodi were surrounded, and the menacing gestures indicated they would be severely beaten. One of them pointed at Bethel and screamed at the others to seize him and tie him up; Amlodi and Aine were temporarily ignored and each ran for their lives. There was no hope of rescuing Bethel immediately, but if they could get away, a chance might come later. To their surprise no one followed them. The men marched Bethel towards the Seior lodges. The ground was still shaking and quivering as Bethel made out the shapes of Kalliste and Aengus. They had both been hurled off their feet by the quake, and decided to stay put on the ground when they saw the guards flock to the shore.

Aine elected to take Aengus and trail Bethel and his captors. She could keep in touch with Saba and be prepared for any opportunity that might arise. Amlodi and Kalliste went to the nearby travellers' village to seek out the Euskaldun fishermen. They found them easily, for everybody had huddled together while the severe shocks lasted. Amlodi explained they needed to get away urgently – their little company, and Bethel in particular, was being blamed for the earthquake. The men looked surly.

'We will gladly take you and the sick boy, but not the Kretan and her female friends – and certainly not the brown man. The Kretans are now our enemies because they abused the laws of our kinsmen here, and since he has defiled the sanctuary of the Eyed Goddess how do we know he is not being pursued by the furies of vengeance who may destroy us all?'

Amlodi pretended to agree. 'If we accept a few crumbs maybe we'll get the cake later,' he whispered to Aengus. 'Show us where your curraghs are beached and we'll meet you there.'

'On the spit near the river mouth.'

'Oh, I know the place.' It was close to where they had landed a little earlier. 'We'll see you there at sunset.'

'That won't be long.'

Aine and Kalliste found Saba still in the long house but feeling better, especially as she now realised the shaking earth was not due to her poisoned senses. Aelise had not returned.

'I fear something has happened to her,' Saba told them. They flitted softly like shadows towards the Seer's lodges and encountered a distressed friend of Aelise. She explained that Bethel was also blamed for the earthquake and destruction of the pillar stone. He had been bound to a log and at sunset would be launched on the ocean with his skin slashed to attract any sharks that might be sent by the daimons. Aelise had tried to slip in to release him but had been caught by Sugaar and now her life, too, was in danger.

Sugaar held Aelise head downwards, her hair in one hand and a knife at her throat, he was snarling at Bethel. 'You pretend not to fear me, brown man, even if I cut her throat. Don't think you will float out to sea and get rescued by your fish friends. You'll go straight to the daimons by the entrance they so thoughtfully provided for my purpose.'

Aelise struggled desperately. 'Let me go, you filth. You wouldn't dare talk to him like that if he wasn't so tightly bound.'

'As for you, bitch, you've proved yourself a traitoress to Larmorica and unfit to succeed your mother. You will suffer the same fate.'

He stripped her and bound her to the log, facing Bethel.

'You can comfort each other in your last moments,' Sugaar sneered.

He began dragging the log towards another wide crevasse newly opened by the quake, only a few paces away.

As the women ran they could see Sugaar dragging the weighted log towards the fissure. It was easy to guess his purpose. There were no witnesses, for everyone had rushed to protect what they could during the quake. Saba had brought with her the spear thrower and weapon that Aelise had shown her after the festival, as though guessing she might need protection, but she feared they were still too far away. Sugaar reached the fissure and hauled the log up to stand on its end for a final taunt at his hated captors.

'Show the daimons how you enjoyed yourselves,' he gloated.

As he began heaving forward, Saba, still fifty paces back, aimed and flung the spear with all her strength. It sang in the air like a javelin and curved down over his back before the barb entered high, grazed his spine and found the heart. He gasped and collapsed, dragging the log with its human burden backwards on top of him.

Saba and Aine ran up to Bethel and Aelise and cut their bonds with obsidian blades. Aelise and Bethel rolled over and shook their cramped limbs back to movement again. Aelise stared at the spear through the shaman's back. 'Let's go before the others return and find Sugaar.'

'They won't find him,' declared Saba. 'Help me, Bethel.'

They slid the body over the edge of the fissure, but never heard it land.

'He's reached the underworld already,' Bethel laughed. 'Now let's fly!'

Saba's party assembled at the beach where Amlodi and Aengus waited by the curraghs with two of the Euskaldun. When they saw the other five and who they were, the Euskaldun refused point-blank to take them.

'Bethel, where's the lump of stuff the whale coughed up?' Aine asked.

'It's over there' – he pointed – 'where I dropped it during the quake.'

Bethel and Aine went together to the side of the spit where they had waded ashore. He picked up the sand-covered mass and rinsed it in the wavelets. The Euskaldun gave low whistles and spoke rapidly in their dialect to Amlodi.

'They'll take us all the way to the southern river and give us two curraghs for half that piece,' he told them excitedly.

'Why?' Bethel was curious.

'It's the magic base from which the sorcerers of the Two Lands extract the perfume of the gods. They would give the whole Kretan ship for it.'

'Now I remember the smell! Isn't it called ambergris? We use it in my country as well,' said Bethel. 'Tell them it's a deal if we can leave instantly,' Saba told Amlodi.

'What about our packs?' grumbled Kalliste.

'Look, we've got our lives. When most of the Garnac people realise their sacred pillar is smashed, the Ker, their Seers and even the Seior will blame us, along with Bethel. Even Maire won't be able to stop them killing us in case their daimons do worse damage. Come on, Aelise, you'll be blamed as well.'

'Saba is right as usual,' agreed Amlodi as they pushed off in the curraghs. Bethel was clutching the precious lump under the watchful eyes of the Euskaldun.

Crouching in the boat behind Saba, Amlodi chuckled. 'Well, you've got your medicine bag, and I've got my scrolls, flute and horn so we can at least make music with the whales.'

Saba smiled in agreement, but her eyes were fixed thoughtfully on Bethel and Aengus in front. A kaleidoscope of puzzling images flipped through her mind. Were their trials only just beginning?

THIRTY-SEVEN

ORCA'S WORLD

Garnac watchguards noticed a knot of people stumping about on the distant sand strip, arguing furiously. Moments later an agreement seemed to have been reached. A dozen or more figures placed three of the four big seagoing curraghs into the adjoining deep-water channel and pushed off hurriedly. The guards signalled the alarm back to the nearest village but they knew it was already too late. Most Garnac boats had been smashed and sunk or hurled out to sea. Another six or seven people picked up the remaining curragh and tramped away towards the visitors' lodges.

Amlodi was in the second curragh, just behind Saba. Although they had all jumped into the boats at high speed, the Euskaldun fishermen took great care to avoid being near the dread sea witch or the brown shaman who had, with the Ker priestess, broken the sacred taboos on Suil's Island and probably brought on the earthquake. So it was that Bethel and Aelise found themselves with Saba and Aengus. Aelise did not want to be parted from Bethel after their recent ordeal together; she believed she had stolen Bethel away from Saba, and felt uneasy being so close to Saba. Saba didn't seem to mind, but if her mood changed, what might she do to her? Saba, reading her mind, tried to put her at ease with smiles and a show of friendship, but the fear still lurked in Aelise's subconscious.

The open sea outside the bay was savage after the earthquake. It seemed like a different season from that which had greeted Bethel, Aine and Amlodi on their return with the orcas. The serene Earth-Sea Mother had transformed into a sullen, raging hag by the vicious onslaught of the underearth giants, and she reacted to equal their violence. Ripped out headlands, rocks and banks rendered the contours of the coast barely recognisable.

They found that all their skill and experience was needed to avoid bumping into splintered tree trunks, roots and floating carcasses while keeping the curraghs pointing out to sea. The Euskaldun beside Amlodi translated the rapid comments of his companions in the third curragh: 'All these animal bodies will attract the sea daimons and sharks to drink the blood and feed on the rotting flesh.'

During his sea expedition with the Euskaldun, Amlodi had learned how to manipulate the oars and thole pins with which each curragh was fitted, instead of the customary paddles employed by the northern peoples. The oar provided greater leverage and speed through the water. He demonstrated the technique to the others.

Amlodi had also struck up friendships among the Euskaldun and was saddened when many of them refused to put to sea with his friends. To his amazement he discovered that one of these rugged fishers, Orthonac, was a kinsman of Axular, the teaching priest at the Temples of Light back in Er-rin who had tutored Aengus and Aine in languages and sky symbols. Axular's mother was an Euskaldun from one of the high mountain villages perched above the bay of Euskadi. Orthonac was the son of her younger sister. He had twinkling black eyes and brown hair flecked with red, a strong, beaked nose and olive skin like Kalliste. He was powerfully built, like the ash-blond, blue-eyed Amlodi. Each looked as though he could pick up and carry a horse across his shoulders.

They had already formed a close friendship and Orthonac was determined to accompany Amlodi and his friends on their journey. He didn't know all the reasons for this adventure; he just hoped the shaman, whom his mates called the sea witch, would accept him. He'd been watching her since they set out and believed she possessed powers like a Laminak, an Euskaldun demi-goddess, and these could be frighteningly mischievous. At other times, he thought she resembled Ursana, the bear goddess, so fierce were her eyes.

One of the rowers in the third boat pointed to a long fin in the water beside them. 'Bad shark!' he shouted in halting Larmorican.

A patch of water reddened in the sea not far off and they could see the carcass of a cow jerking and swivelling as three or four sharks ripped and tore at it. As they rowed onwards, more and more fins showed in the angry water. Some of the tiger sharks looked as long as the curraghs, and one or two began bumping against the skin sides as a feeding frenzy developed around them. The Euskaldun beat and stabbed at them with the fish tridents strapped under their seats. A few dolphins, skipping and plunging alongside Saba's curragh, vanished. Everyone was so distracted that no one noticed an enormous tidal wave creep up towards them. There was no time to do anything except yell.

Tall as two boats end to end, the wave's frontal trough suddenly sucked the curraghs up. Then they were borne upwards through the churning crest and tossed about as lightly as twigs. Desperately, everyone swam to capture and upright their curraghs. Bethel found himself clinging to the lump of ambergris and Aengus helped him push it back into a boat, which he and Amlodi had just righted.

From the boat they were able to help Orthonac, Saba and Aine fight off an attacking shark by jamming a broken spear vertically between the creature's jaws. Kalliste and Aelise, who swam like fish, were helping an injured Euskaldun who could hardly swim at all. Bethel saw a screaming Euskaldun vanish under water with two sharks. The others held Bethel by the feet and stomach while he vainly beat off one of the sharks with his fists; but even if he could have reached the man, it was too late. There seemed to be only two boats remaining and everyone was hanging onto them. He became aware of several giant shapes swimming beneath him. What new monsters were these?

Then Bethel heard Saba's piercing whistles and realised she was 'talking' to a pod of orcas. They were actually driving off the sharks. Wondering if she had called them or if they arrived through some other agency, he began helping some of the others back into the boats. There was still no sign of the third curragh. Saba's little group was all accounted for but a second Euskaldun was missing. Almost everyone had gashes and wounds on arms and legs, but were fit enough to carry on. As a result of the tidal wave they seemed to have drifted much further out to sea, away from the chaotic nightmare of sharks and floating debris. Saba was still in the water communicating with the orcas, one was nuzzling her and she stroked it tenderly.

The remaining Euskalduns were completely demoralised, in shock from the shark attack and the wave, and now they were confronted by this spectacle of the witch and her orcas. They feared these creatures even more than sharks because they were so formidable; nothing in the sea threatened orcas. The sea witch was obviously in league with them; she hadn't been able to save the lives of their companions. The four remaining crew pointed this out in a frenzied plea to Orthonac.

They were determined to sever all connection with the witch and her followers and head straight for their homeland.

The two remaining boats were still drifting out to sea and southwards. Both curraghs had some secure oars, tholepins firmly in place, so the Euskaldun suggested they take one boat and leave the other with Saba's party and Orthonac, if he was crazy enough to go with them. They were prepared to row home – the currents and wave patterns were in their favour and they were sure the witch could whistle up a wind to fetch her boat southwards to the Gar. They demanded their share of the ambergris as arranged. Their companions had paid for it with their lives and its value would help compensate their families left behind.

Saba and Bethel looked at each other and agreed the argument was reasonable, but Aine and Kalliste thought it was callous to leave them with only two oars. 'Suppose we don't find a current, you can hardly see the coastline from here,' Aine said.

'That's true,' Saba replied, 'but in their view we're not really far out. They must go much further to catch the sea roads and may need their oars, as we have seen, for protection as well as for propulsion. Besides, I have a wonderful idea to remain within site of the coast.'

Bethel and Amlodi divided the hunk of ambergris in two with their blades and gave one half to the Euskaldun, while Orthonac told them that the others bore no ill will; they were inured to such reactions from strangers when faced with unusual events connected to Saba. Orthonac was delighted that the group had accepted him so readily on Saba's assessment. She had talked to him through Amlodi, but he didn't know of her skill in mind reading. He was prepared to serve her and obey her commands. Furthermore, he was greatly taken by the other three superb women in the little band; to be able to travel with so many beautiful and talented females to places he had only vaguely heard about made him ready to undergo any hardship. He hugged farewell to his companions as they separated and rowed away.

'It was well we tied our packs under the seats,' Amlodi said, smiling at Saba. 'You still have your medicines and I have my flute.'

'We all have blades and flints in our pouches and Orthonac has an axe on his belt,' added Aengus.

'I also have a few hooks and a bit of line in my pouch,' said Orthonac. 'Curraghs get overturned more often than we like to admit, and waves washing over us can carry off our gear and fishing tackle. There's always some fish to be caught in the kelp forests offshore.'

Aine patted Saba's arm. 'I know you're reading my mind,' Saba told her, 'but I'm not strong enough to hold the rope myself. Maybe they will accept Amlodi and Orthonac.'

'What ploy are you weird ones concocting now?' Bethel asked them.

Saba said nothing; she was concentrating on one of the orcas still swimming around them. She knew him well, not only by his mental patterns, but by the configuration of scarring on his hide behind the dorsal fin. It was the same one who had carried her to Garnac and one of the two that had brought Bethel and Aine out to deliver their enemies to the sperm whale.

'I'm sure Amlodi or Orthonac could do it,' murmured Aine. 'They're both so strong.'

'Yes,' Saba mused, 'with the lead rope tied round their waist. The orca is prepared to try, I believe he enjoys helping me – us,' she corrected herself. Saba explained to the others how she and Aine thought the orca would solve their travel problems if Amlodi and Orthonac were not afraid to work with it. To her surprise, they both agreed at once; with Saba in control they felt sure of a successful outcome.

'Just show us what you want us to do.'

'You can go first, Amlodi, as you've already ridden on the orca,' Saba suggested. 'Tie the rope round your waist, ease into the water and the orca will let you mount him as before, hang onto his dorsal fin and through you he will tow the curragh southwards to the big river. We don't know how long it will take to reach it, but if we become desperate for water or food we will arrange a landfall, or perhaps Orthonac will be able to catch some fish.'

As though she had sent out her thoughts as well as the words, one of the orcas swam alongside holding in its mouth what, to it, was a small tuna.

'Grab it, Orthonac,' called Aine. Kalliste and he heaved the fish on board with an effort. The orca's teeth had almost severed the head from the body and the tuna lay bleeding, its length stretching past four of the astonished passengers. Orthonac hacked a large slice from the shoulder with his axe and handed it to Amlodi. 'Eat that before you get in the water,' he chuckled. 'It will keep you going so long I'll be able to get a sleep before my turn!' The girls laughed. 'Well, there's our next few meals provided for,' smiled Saba. 'Don't neglect to thank the sea spirits for this bounty.'

When he was ready, Amlodi eased over the side and the orca positioned itself so that he could sit in front of the tall dorsal fin, facing backwards. He looked quite small perched on the great back. 'Ask him to start slowly,' he called to Saba. The orca obliged, the slack tightened on the rope and the curragh began to glide through the calmer water.

There were long swells with only a rare white-tipped wavelet.

'How goes it, Amlodi?' called Aine. 'Fine,' he shouted back. 'The rope is comfortable, but it's not so easy holding on to the fin.'

'Just as well it's not slippery like a fish fin,' remarked Bethel.

'Why isn't it like a fish?' asked Orthonac.

'It's more like holding a tough seal's flipper,' Bethel replied. Orthonac had been watching intently; he knew when his turn came he would be both eager and afraid. He was most anxious to shine in front of Saba and the others, but inwardly quailed at the prospect of meeting and actually riding on a whale big enough to rip him to pieces, as he had seen them do to seals and other creatures.

The others had started on their fresh fish diet. The raw, bloody meat assuaged their hunger and quenched their thirst. The Euskaldun had estimated it would take their curraghs three or four suns to reach the Gar estuary, depending on currents and winds. Amlodi and Orthonac were taking about ten shifts between them to cover from sunrise to sunrise. Bethel and Aengus tried a turn each but tired more easily. At one point the orca took a break to chase down one of the big fish predator groups with the remainder of his pod, which was tagging along with him.

Large flocks of gannets – sprightly monarchs of both sea and wind – were also chasing the median fish shoals such as mackerel. Conspicuous by size and wing span, they outclassed the gulls with the dazzling brightness of their plumage, pale blue dagger bills and broad webbed feet. The crew watched as they dived repeatedly with tensely sprung pinions, which then half closed to a rigid W-shape only a few paces above the waves before the clean-cut plunge. Their dives were almost a part of the flight pattern – all the birds dashed into the breakers and rose again, the rhythm of the entire flock maintained in a jagged pattern. Saba pointed out to Bethel a lone pair of northern divers. Similar in size, they flew low and fast over the water like kingfishers, with attenuated neck and thin black head held straight out and slightly drooped, making their backs look hunched. The pair uttered one lugubrious, almost human sounding wail, which, to Bethel's amazement, Saba mimicked perfectly; he had never heard such a curious cry in his life.

Bethel mused that her command of sound as well as language was another magical accomplishment. Had she developed this in the Raven's cave she spoke about? Saba told him that when mating the birds cried continuously; they also uttered a crazy cackle so disturbing in the darkness that the Eelfolk called them lomrs.

The curragh flew along at more than twice the pace it might have achieved with combined sail and oars; indeed, to have travelled any faster would have damaged the boat skins. All four of the men, when they were mounted on the orcas' backs, experienced a sense of wellbeing, but at the same time, of being mentally probed by sonic pulses and a low-pitched vibration that passed not only through their ears but up their spines into their heads. Aengus quite enjoyed this 'zinging' sensation and was beginning to look more hopeful. Ever since his ordeal with Maeve and Scathach, he had experienced occasional flashes of second sight. These informed him whether an event would turn out well or badly, and he felt sure the orcas were a good omen.

On the second day, they passed two river mouths and long stretches of sandy beach bordered by pine forest. These eventually changed to marshland and then they found themselves in an estuary as wide as a bay. The breadth of it reminded Saba and the twins of their Mother Lake. The orcas turned into the bay and showed no sign of slackening their pace. The passengers were delighted, for the tides and currents around them looked quite powerful.

Aine turned to Aelise. 'You said you had been this way before?'

'Yes,' Aelise replied, 'but rowing needs a lot of effort. When the ancestors' river narrows, we will leave the curragh with the villagers there, if the orca will take us that far. At this time of year the rains swell the rivers and the tidal flows are more dangerous.' The estuary they were entering was a large tidal basin, the first two thirds of it sea that graduated to fresher water at the ancestors' river mouth far up on the left.

The evening air was filled with myriad frogs and toads droning and ribbeting from their hiding places in the vast reed beds, and an enormous variety of birds: gulls, geese, ducks, grebes, herons, bitterns, kingfishers, ospreys, kestrels and other predators. Mostly the birds regarded the travellers with indifference. They had rarely been hunted, certainly not by humans. Aengus felt he could almost reach out and catch them with his bare hands. He recalled how he and Alan, in the northern coastal waters, picked up defeathered guillemots when they moulted after breeding and brought them back to roast on the beach. Orthonac had lured several ducks with his line and a sharp hook in a fillet of fish. He waited until the duck was swallowing the fish, then jerked hard, catching the hook into their gullets. He planned to roast them when the boats landed at the settlement near the tidal mark where this ancestors' river mouth narrowed.

Two of the orcas swimming near the boat submerged and sidled over towards a flock of mallard. Just breaking the surface, they spat out some regurgitated fish and vanished again. Some of the mallard spied the fish and paddled over to sample the bait. Then a little wave turned into the black-and-white form of the orcas surrounded by a glass-like bubble of water as they made their strike. Three mallard disappeared; the others flew off in alarm. The orcas reappeared, spouted and slapped the water with their flukes as if to say, we can do that anytime.

Next morning the landscape began to change. A few trees and shrubs appeared along the banks and grew in number quite rapidly as they moved along. The water became clearer, then slightly greenish. They passed islands covered with bushes and saplings; then appeared the mouth of the ancestors' river. Saba announced that one of the orca would tow them on to the tidal limit. She had begun to think of it as her orca, with all the obligations of a mother to a giant child who has been helping them all. She owed it a duty of care in return; the shallower river might be dangerous for it. She transmitted these thoughts to it with her love and gratitude, thanking it and the pod for their patience.

When they arrived near the settlement, Orthonac, whose turn it had been to tow, found Saba and Aengus beside him in the water. He watched in amazement while Saba turned to the orca as an old friend. She stroked and tickled its body and it shimmered with a frisson of delight, ducking away and returning to her like a giant playful puppy. After a time she placed her arms as far as she could around the orca's head and laid her forehead against it. She found before, as with the Narwhal, that this way she could exchange thoughts and impressions more easily. She made Aengus clasp her neck and shoulders so that she could share some of the impressions with him. Orthonac climbed back into the curragh as it was obvious that Saba and Aengus didn't need him.

Saba was consoled by the notion that now she could telepathise with this lovely and intelligent creature, it might even help her to find a remedy for Aengus. She spent a long time linked with him in psychic empathy, during which it transmitted a myriad visions to her. She saw that dolphins had told it about the shark attack, but that during Saba's mortal crisis the spirit of the Narwhal had summoned it to help her. It and its companions were pleased to have saved Saba and her friends at that time and would do so again if the need arose because they travelled all the seas of the world. It showed Saba many scenes of the orcas' history and way of life. She began to receive images that at first confused her. They involved eons of time in the past when orcas were smaller, like dolphins, and walked on land like otters. They found the seas more agreeable and remained longer and longer in the water. Their limbs adapted to permanent swimming and they developed their own form of propulsion, unlike that of the fishes, and more suited to their organ of breathing. Their bodies also grew to an optimum size to enable them to hunt most efficiently and outwit all other predators. From the beginning, their intelligence was superior to non-mammalian creatures and it gradually increased, fuelled by their insatiable curiosity.

Saba was offered views of their varied hunting techniques. Big sharks they could kill without a bite, smashing into them at high speed; a few thumps disabled them completely. Large whales, giant squid, seals and smaller mammals, penguins, tuna and shoals of smaller fish – each creature and each hunt merited a unique strategy. A combination of creative flexibility, bat-like echo location and their telepathic ability to co-operate in pairs or packs of thirty or more placed them so far ahead of any other sea creature that the oceans became a leisure ground for them.

The orca was amused and pleased to hear that the blond man was composing a musical on whale life to play to his people and told Saba that he would need to hunt for more ways to emulate the many sea voices. Hearing was more important than vision or scent to all sea life. Sound was used for recognition, courtship, hunting and locating companions – even a moon's swimming distance away. There were taps, knocks, thumps, bangs, creaks, grunts, chugs, warbles, peeps, clicks, deep throbs, whistles and endless trills. The orca predicted that understanding the songs of whales would engender human interest, but it might be a long time – two star yuls, going into a water age – before numbers of humans came to live in the sea with whales and fish.

Saba also learned that beneath the surface of the sea the water was as varied and contoured as land. The orca told her that fish swim in different layers of water depending on the densities of salinity and temperature, and rarely depart from their chosen layers. These are like paths in three dimensions, some being higher and others much lower, depending on the moon's attraction. Warmer water travels nearer the top of the oceans from hot sunny parts of the world until it reaches the cold north lands, where it cools and becomes saltier and more dense; then it sinks to the bottom and returns like a great cold river flowing low down. There are upwellings from hot springs on the sea bottom, like fountains, said the orca. These carry lots of food and are loved by multitudes of fish who flock around them, as do all the ranges of predators. These were the orcas' favourite places. So much happens in their seaworld they rarely become bored, the orca said, and they are just as curious about any land animals available to them.

They had studied Saba's kind since humans first lived by and in the water as a primitive bipedal species. They eventually concluded that these two-legged animals possessed a cleverness and adaptability to match their own. This was why they were keen to establish some form of communication. Saba was the first who could share pictures or vision memories. They had found a few people from other tribes who communicated a little with them but never as coherently as she could. Saba's people – or 'Two Legs', as they had long ago been nicknamed by the orcas – could invent ways to live and amuse themselves under the sea and the orcas would help them. But the orcas agreed that Two Legs were dangerously competitive among themselves, and with all other creatures. Such efficient and ruthless killers might in the end destroy everything, including the sea creatures.

The main reason they wanted to work with Two Legs was because of their smartness and inquisitiveness. But they also wanted to work with them to teach them the vital importance of co-operating with natural things. Other species were not enemies to be wiped out in fear or in fun. If they could persuade Two Legs how vital all plants and creatures in and out of the sea were to their own survival, they would feel satisfied.

Because their mastery of the seas allowed them leisure time for thinking and dreaming, one of the orcas' favourite pastimes was to spend a tide floating vertically among the giant kelp beds. They noticed that many kinds of fish not only hid from predators in the seaweed but that they appeared to benefit from their experience. The orcas allowed the weed to caress and tickle their hide and to colour it a rusty red; it seemed to stimulate their brains and encourage visions and dreams.

Among other things, they dreamt of Two Legs coming to dominate all parts of the earth. Flying through the air like enormous birds, entering the sea in larger and larger boats, decimating the great whales for food and materials, eventually poisoning the sea water, and destroying all life because they could not agree to share the earth among themselves or with other creatures. On learning that Saba was visiting special dreaming places on her way to the Middle Sea, the orca asked her to explore the future for all of them. They themselves could not see far enough into the distance and were deeply fearful. The pod would come to the Middle Sea, as they often hunted tuna in that region. If she envisioned them there they would come and learn the good or bad tidings she might have gleaned.

THIRTY-EIGHT

THE CAVE IN THE MIND

Aelise assured Saba and the others that the villagers, welcoming new blood, would gladly provide additional oars and the sail on a stepped mast needed to row upstream. So they dragged the curragh well up the bank above the river and secured it with stones. Then they waved farewell to the orcas and watched the three sky-hopping in a row down the middle of the river. The orcas, in turn, were taking a last look at the first Two Legs that had ever managed to communicate with them.

The village, set well back from the river, presumably to avoid flooding after rains, was also afforded shelter and privacy from prying eyes by the trees and scrub growing around it. Aine wondered if the villagers thought of themselves as forest or river people. A few long houses contained the inhabitants. There were only eighty or ninety of them and it was soon obvious they all belonged to the same family.

Aelise explained to Aine and the others that the main trading route went on up the Gar, bypassing the river of the ancestors. The only outside social contact these people had was with fishermen, and visitors from Garnac and other Ker lands that made a pilgrimage to their ancestors' caves. The folk here would treasure new men to sleep with their fertile women, especially vibrant and exotic strangers like Amlodi, Orthonac and Bethel. Offspring from men such as these would possess high value.

The people remembered Aelise and considered her and all the Ker from Garnac and the northern areas distant clansfolk. Countless generations before, their common ancestors were the families of the first shamans living in caverns along the valley. Those people were planted there by the Great Mother and her spirits, who taught them how to create the rock paintings and carvings that released spirit animals and ancestors to help them celebrate rituals.

A feast was held to celebrate the strangers' arrival. They roasted the ducks procured by Orthonac, lots of river fish and snails, and succulent little animals like tiny deer which, to the visitors, were called rabbits; their flesh was pale like waterfowl but with an earthy flavour and deemed by Saba's group to be fine eating.

When they discovered that the three adventurers would couple with three of their ripest and most alluring girls that night, the people were more than happy to prepare a mast, sail and extra oars for the curragh, and to provide Bethel and Aelise with proper winter clothing. They had been wearing makeshift loincloths since their ordeal with Sugaar and the earthquake.

Promising to return by the next moon, the visitors left at dawn and followed an ancient trail into the denser forest lining the valley.

'It's only about three suns' trek,' said Aelise. 'The trail is kept clear by the trickle of pilgrims going to worship at the sacred walls.'

Bethel liked the forest. He had had little time to appreciate it during his visit to Er-rin where there had been endless wars, chases and escapes. Apart from the brief birdsong at morning and evening and the scolding of jays and squirrels, there was a whispering activity, which he found soothing. Huge trunks rose out of the plush leafy carpet on which they walked. They often had to climb over the raised roots of giant beeches and oaks; these dwarfed the thinner alder, hazel, elm and the sturdy, dark, stone pines filling the occasional space where a giant had fallen and taken down its neighbours. Leaves made a soft swooshing sound each time they lifted their feet. There was no noticeable breeze, but a musty odour rose from the fungi, creepers and roots themselves.

Bethel remarked that they hadn't seen any animals, but Aengus pointed out that they were making far too much noise, like wild pigs rooting through the loam for tubers and rhizomes. He had lost none of his hunting skills and in the evenings he took the bow the villagers had lent the group and disappeared through the leaves. He returned before long with their evening meal, a deer, and this one kill satisfied the whole party, leaving enough to hang in a tree for breaking the morning fast.

On the third day, the trees thinned to scrub and Aelise pointed out a line of cliffs that seemed to rise vertically out of the river. There were several steep paths on one side with occasional steps cut where necessary. When they reached the head of the defile, a broad grass plateau spread backwards from the remaining cliff tops. Twenty or thirty people turned out to greet them. They were the acolytes of a powerfully built shaman named Ka-ren, who remembered Aelise and hugged her warmly. Aelise told her that she had brought Saba to experience the dreaming caves and hinted she might be able to penetrate further into the historic past of the ancestors, beyond the period of the sacred paintings and sculptures on the walls. Ka-ren explained that Melusine had already visioned her about Saba and she was in great hopes of learning all she could about their past.

Saba's group learned that Ka-ren's immediate tribe comprised about five hundred people who lived in contiguous lodges under several overhangs of the cliffs. Everyone was introduced and space found for the guests among the lodges. As the day was late, they settled down with bowls of stew and cups of beer or herbal wines to relate some of their adventures, diplomatically omitting the friction at Garnac and some of the orca exploits, which they judged would be unbelievable and perhaps engender a loss of confidence in their group.

The next day, Ka-ren's acolytes showed them some of the limestone caves with their magnificent paintings, which used the walls' natural rock projections to support three dimensional figures. Saba touched a deer whose head and shoulders seemed to be emerging from the wall. While the walls were physically impenetrable to humans, they acted like a dense barrier of fog or smoke which allowed the spirits of animals or shamans to emerge in visible form and communicate with true Seers, who could also travel back with them and see whatever mysteries were permitted.

'It's here that our two worlds can meet and exchange thoughts,' said Ka-ren proudly. 'While you are here we will hold a ceremonial gathering, and ask you to join with us on a shamanic journey. I understand you are adept in visionary travelling into past and future.'

'Only at certain times, not always under my control,' Saba replied.

Her group was intrigued by the variety of cave shapes and rock formations. Some contained huge spaces and high vaults; others had long narrow tunnels, which those allowed access had to squeeze through. Aine remarked on the imprints of hands placed below paintings, some dipped in paint and laid on, others outlined by a cloud of paint which must have been blown over them. In one cave Kalliste gave a cry of recognition and pointed to a painting of a double-bladed axe.

'These are the most sacred symbols on our islands as ritual objects and as paintings. We believe they came with our ancestors from the east. How old can that picture be?'

Ka-ren looked at Saba as an expert on the past. She wasn't certain but hazarded a guess.

'As much as a great yul?'

'How old is that?' asked Kalliste.

'The time it takes all twelve constellations of the animals to pass through the spring budding and sowing.' Seeing Kalliste did not comprehend the time span, she added: 'If we count a generation as twenty yuls, then well over one hundred and forty generations.' Everybody gasped.

'Were our ancestors living that long ago?'

'Oh, yes, and much longer than that,' Saba told her.

'So the people who painted that image must have been ancestors of us all, and it was sacred to them as well,' Kalliste mused.

'What do your people think it means?' asked Bethel.

'Sacred axe blades were given to men by the gods, along with the use of fire. Well, the axe blade, with fire, enables us to clear parts of the forest to grow food and cook it. The twin blades fitted on either side of the axe handle symbolise the wings of the butterfly; this is a promise of immortality from the gods. The butterfly breaks out of its chrysalis like a soul from a dying body and after a brief honeymoon here, flies off to heaven,' answered Ka-ren.

Nothing was planned for the following day as people always rested after the customary reception feast that Ka-ren gave them. Saba decided this would be an opportunity to teach Bethel the technique of lucid dreaming. She had found no time to keep her promises of initiating him into some of her powers. She chose one of the incubation caves and, as Aine was so proficient, brought her along accompanied by Kalliste. Aine and Kalliste had established a sympathy similar to the one between Saba and Bethel.

The participants were given cups of a brew to induce an onset of the lighter sleep most conducive to this kind of mental activity, where the sleeper becomes aware that he is dreaming and can take partial control of the action. If sleeping with a partner, the difficult trick was to synchronise both dream and dreamer to share the same dream. This might happen once a year with normal lucid dreamers, but Saba and Aine, having trained for years in the Raven's cave, had developed their skills to take control of sympathetic minds just before entering sleep and bring them along into a chosen dream.

Each of the couples had already found their chosen mate to be highly agreeable sexual partners, so they lost no time in activating and encouraging the chakras of Bethel and Kalliste to awaken and combine in higher flights of ecstatic rapture during the dreaming than had ever been possible in waking states. Then they were flying, higher and higher, at first towards the moon until they could see the ridges and craters on it, resembling the earth. 'So the star houses are probably real worlds like our world and the moon,' thought Saba to Bethel. 'All of them have their protective spirit lords like Earth Mother and Moon Lady.' They swooped down and began gliding, first up the river Gar, then over the forest until they saw the sea and wide, curved coastline bisected by a river mouth and a large village.

'That is the way we must travel,' said Saba. The scene darkened and without warning they were waking up on their mats in the cave.

Kalliste and Bethel were overwhelmed by the experience. Saba and Aine had been there many times before and were bombarded with questions as they walked back to their temporary lodges. Aelise saw them coming and was consumed with jealousy that Saba had chosen Bethel as a partner. She knew that Bethel now had eyes for no one but Saba. However, she hoped against hope that she might find some miracle to get him back for herself. That night she awoke with a plan in her mind. If it worked, her problem would definitely be resolved.

The following quarter, on the night when the moon was darkest, Ka-ren judged it auspicious to hold the Dreaming Search. With her own acolytes she invited all the shamans of the Clan and Saba's group, enough to provide support without distraction. The main sanctuary cave was chosen because the entrance was large and could enable half the colony to be distant onlookers. The ceremony began with the headmen blowing their rams' horns in unison to warn those in the shadow world of the important event taking place.

Ka-ren, dressed in her full shamanic regalia, was standing at the back of the cave with her acolytes and a group of drummers and flautists on either side. They beckoned Saba and her friends forward. Aelise was standing beside Ka-ren; she had attended these kind of ceremonies several times before. A cauldron of dark liquid was being stirred over a fire by two of the acolytes and Aelise. They wore skin loincloths and their bodies were painted in red overlapping triangles. Ka-ren clapped her hands and the music began, slow and low-pitched. The acolytes and shamans hummed an accompaniment. Saba knew the brew would be hallucinogenic and wondered which of the potent roots had been chewed for it. Each of the Clans had their own recipe and prided themselves on its power and magical attributes. Ka-ren was singing an invocation to the tribe's guardian spirits. Aelise and the acolytes brought a cup of the brew to everybody inside the sacred tenemos. To Saba, the brew was strong and tasted like rotting swamp wood.

The effects of the drug were rapid. Saba experienced a violent sensation of nausea. The semi-darkness in which they stood grew brighter, and the cave seemed to expand as the walls melted away to reveal great throngs of people and animals clapping and stamping in rhythm with the drums. Saba glanced at Ka-ren. The shaman's face was red with beads of sweat breaking from her pores, as were the faces in the crowd. By contrast, Saba's friends appeared ashen and strained. The cave darkened again and she felt herself accelerating so fast through a tunnelled landscape that everything was blurred. Finally, she slowed down and was back in the cave again.

But everything was different. There were groups of people, many wearing skins and woven garments of a type unknown to her. Several of the men and women were painting figures on the cave walls. Three men with small drums sat in a corner beating out a lively rhythm, to which was joined the sound of three men and three women playing bone flutes. No one appeared to see her; it was as though she was invisible. She could not understand the language they spoke but could mind-read sufficiently to know everyone was excited. Though wearing antiquated clothing, all the people behaved and chatted together just like they did in her own time, although she sensed the period was long, long ago.

The tunnel swirled about her twice more, and each time she shuttled through it at incredible speed, going further and further back. The second scene showed her people who looked different from her own. They wore crudely tanned and roughly sewn animal skins and their foreheads receded sharply back from their eyebrows. They still exchanged words and sounds but their deportment seemed less socialised. They kept lookouts posted outside the cave, as though fearing an attack from animals or strange people. There were numerous bones lying around; she saw a human skull with a high forehead sitting in a corner. The incongruity worried her – if that skull belonged to a human of her own type, it was not valued much, and certainly not respected. Was this species ever at war with hers and had it lost the struggle for the cave or possibly for its own survival?

In the third scene the cave was gone and she found herself on the edge of a wide bay. The shore was furrowed by numerous small rivers spreading out most likely from a mightier river higher up. The beach was gritty and behind it stretched lines of odd looking trees with tall, scaly trunks. Their tops were crowned with masses of long, flat, narrow leaves with bunches of strange fruits hanging from the branches. There was a skein of people on the shore with digging sticks and baskets collecting what looked like cockles, clams and razors.

Many more were out in the water where the waves broke over their heads; they carried nets and spears. The people were all naked with long flowing hair, and many women had skin baby pouches tied over their shoulders. These people looked exactly like her own folk. They reminded her of Alan and the twins, and of scenes at the mouth of the Mother river. She could hear them talking and calling to each other in peculiar tonal jabbering and clicking sounds.

The sun was so hot, Saba felt like throwing off her own clothes and joining the natural fishers for a romp in the waves, but she remembered that she would be invisible to them. By their looks and bearing these must be her real ancestors, but how far removed in time? Their attitudes seemed more distant and the sexes remained in two different groups that were less convivial and civil with the other. They were carrying loaded baskets to a distant fire on the beach and there were some large fish in their nets.

A great weakness blanketed her. Saba remembered that on her earlier visions she had seen Aine's figure standing beside her. Though neither had exchanged a word or thought, she felt Aine's excitement. Then why hadn't she travelled back to the shore? Had they gone too far? She now felt tired and feeble and found herself lying down. A mental darkness enveloped her mind, but she could detect two or three entities in the distance reaching out and calling to her. One of them, stronger than the others, was pulling her with a spider's thread around her neck. This stirred a memory of someone wresting possession of her from Maeve and Fion. They had brought her back from a state close to death. The thread had stretched to a fraction of its thickness and must surely break; but no, it held, and little by little she forced herself back from the treacly shadows towards a glimmer of fire in the distance. With the last tiny effort of willpower she could muster, she pictured the thread snapping her back and discerned Bethel's anxious face staring down at her and holding both her hands. The flutes and drums were playing insistently but ceased when she sat up, freezing cold. He rubbed her arms and legs vigorously and Aine held a cup of hot water to her lips. 'We willed you back with all our strength.' They both hugged her. 'This must never happen again.'

'Great Mother, thank you for giving her back to us. What happened?'

'The drug was too strong,' she murmured. Her head was clearing and she saw the worried knot of people around her. Aelise was at the back, trying to avoid her eyes, but Saba stared at her head, forcing her to turn round. As soon as their eyes locked and she divined her thoughts, all became clear. Once Aelise had decided that she could never match Saba in any way, the only remaining method of getting Bethel back was to eliminate her, and what could be more appropriate than to slip a double strength portion of the roots into Saba's cup. Now the goddess had sided with Saba, Aelise knew there was no hope for her.

Saba's fury was partially directed at herself, as well as Aelise and the young male acolyte who had assisted her. He had developed a passion for her during her last visit, when it had been reciprocated by Aelise. He was pleased to help in furthering her scheme, since the lethal dose was intended for a witch, as Aelise described her. Saba was about to condemn the acolyte to blindness, reserving a slower fate for Aelise, but her mind cooled and she realised the ultimate futility of this kind of revenge. However, she informed Ka-ren of the situation.

Ka-ren was horrified and ready to mete out the ultimate punishment. Under Saba's advice the two culprits were named and shamed to all the Clan. Ka-ren did not want Aelise to remain at the ancestors' river and would have cast her out to be at the mercy of the forest people, but Saba determined to bring her along with the group and watch her closely. This turned out to be a more scalding experience than anything else she could have devised.

When Bethel and Saba were finally alone, she flung her arms around him saying this was the second time he had saved her life. He looked at her sadly.

'I always thought it was the happiest moment of my life to have met you. Now I wish I had never set eyes on you. You have entered my blood like a fever and when we are not together I burn for you.'

Saba looked him full in the eyes, holding his face with both hands. 'Believe me, you have become the lord of my life, and my sole concern is for your and Aengus's wellbeing.'

'Aengus is my concern too. Don't forget, I am his healer since we tried to cure him at Garnac, and were it not for Sugaar we might have succeeded.'

He looked at Saba. She didn't appear even a bit older than the day he first laid eyes upon her, Aine and Sedana at Whiteclay village by the Mother Lake. Maybe Fion's belief that eating the clay conferred a long-lasting youth was true after all. Her sea-green almond eyes still twinkled and her lips were as full and kissable as ever; her figure was as agile and alluring as that of her daughter, who must be only half her age.

'Is this a good moment to ask you those questions we spoke of on Hermes's ship?' Bethel asked.

'One or two anyway. You already part shared my thoughts on the fire walk.'

'All right! What was the most exciting thing that ever happened to you?'

'My encounter with Fion the day he rescued me from Cairla. I was only eighteen yuls. That dreadful and shocking episode overthrew my world.'

'Who do you most admire or envy?'

'I admire the Old One for her knowledge and far sight, but I don't envy her because she is no longer here on earth. I envy the person that I hope to become – I shall have experienced so much more and developed my powers and talents as far as I am able.'

'Who do you love?'

'You first of all.' She took Bethel's face in her hands and kissed him with a long searching kiss involving ears, neck, lips and tongue until Bethel, who reciprocated each movement, was panting with excitement.

'Like that, you see?' said Saba. 'What gives you most pleasure?'

'Understanding new people and new animals.'

'What irritates you most?'

'People with false intentions, whether malevolent or stupid. If they anger me, I study them to find their weakest chink, at which I strike.'

'What is your greatest secret?'

'You can only keep a secret from the living, not from the ancestors or spirit powers! The fact that Sedana is taking my place as Kaheen of Er-rin. That's enough. Now it's my turn and I'll only ask one question. How would you like to be remembered?'

'You only ask me because you can read my mind already! I want to be remembered as the lover and eternal friend of a beautiful part human, part-divine female, and like her, I want to expand and develop to the utmost the powers and abilities I was born with, with her help and guidance.'

'I promise to help you all I can. You might do the same for me. There is so much to learn on this journey we undertake.'

Bethel sealed his agreement with another passionate embrace.

'After our explorations of Krete, I want you to come to Akkad with me'

'Have you particular reasons for such a journey?'

'Yes, especially if our visit to the Isle of Bees is as unsuccessful for Aengus as the operation in Garnac. There is a great Healer in Ur, Lao Tzu. He is an old and dear friend and one of the reasons I must return there is to spend time with him while he remains alive. I feel certain he could work wonders for the boy. The other reason is my concern for my half-sister, Sarah. She has long passed the correct age for a woman to marry in our country and if our father dies – he was unwell when I last saw him three yuls ago – his eldest son will marry her off as soon as he can. He thinks she is too high-spirited for a woman, and she is. We were playmates for many yuls.' Saba became interested.

'I would certainly like to meet this girl you were so fond of. Why should we not visit this woman and Lao Tzu, even if Aengus finds a bee cure. The whole country and its people sound fascinating.'

Eva, the chief shaman and leader of ancestor valley, did all she could to make amends for Saba's near tragedy. Saba recounted to her and selected storytellers everything she had experienced on her journeys into the past and they were intensely grateful for her revelations.

Ka-ren invited Saba to visit a secret cave with her, which had recently been discovered further up the valley. They set out one morning when everyone else seemed occupied. The cave was small but filled with stalactites of crystal white, and the walls glittered with milky quartz and mica particles. It possessed a strong aura of mystery. The walls were free of any carvings or paintings but they seemed equally diaphanous, as though there were many entities behind them that wanted to express themselves. Saba was completely enthralled and requested to spend some time dreaming there alone. Eva agreed and showed her a flat niche in the rock that formed a potential sleeping pallet. This was already dressed with willow branches, dried bracken and grass to make it comfortable, as Eva spent time there herself at full or dark moons to seek lunar experiences. She offered to leave Saba for as long as she wished to perform a dream incubation. Saba walked around for a while to get closely acquainted before settling herself on the pallet and closing her eyes.

She felt her sensing spirit leave her body on the ledge and rise high in the air outside the cave. She began hurtling along as she had during her time travels, first towards the moon and then past it into black space. Her flight appeared to continue for ages, even though she was travelling at such speed. At long last she decelerated and landed gently on a sandy surface. A steady, white daylight pervaded everything but there was no sign of sun or moon. All around her was desert – a few patches of soft sand but mostly a rough, unfriendly scree; in both the near and far distance were mountains, coloured in gradations of blues and browns. Her immediate vicinity looked like a dried-up riverbed which was completely barren of all life. In front of her lay a strange object. It appeared to be a desiccated root, its shape like that of a giant mangrove tree. She went up to it and walked around it – it was the only object loose from the earth within sight. It had many old projections and she sat down on one of these, perhaps to feel less alone in this bleak world. Within a moment she felt a jolt of energy leap up from the stump between her legs and shoot through her body. Nothing else happened and so she sat on the ground beside it and waited. Eventually something would occur. Even though the quality of light did not alter and no darkness fell, she estimated that at least two days passed by. Then something moved on the root. It was almost too insignificant to be noticed but she kept watching the area on the root where she thought movement had happened. Slowly, a large knot in the wood began to open. It revealed a sunken, multifaceted eye, which swivelled towards her; each of the facets seemed to be inspecting her, as though they all had different functions. Then nothing else happened for another long period. She tried speaking and singing to the root, but got no response. The eye flickered as if indicating something. On a notion she walked over and impulsively laid her hands and forehead on the ancient wood near the eye. At once pictures and ideas began forming in her mind in the same way they had when she communicated with the orcas and the Narwhal. The mind or brain, if such it was, seemed to be trying to tune in to her wavelength of comprehension. Soon the picture became clearer.

'If you help me, I will share with you my mind. Also, I will teach you how to strike the ground for water and make it flow.'

'I can divine already,' thought Saba.

'But I need a mighty river,' protested the Root, for so she thought of it. 'You must follow the bed of the river all the way to that mountain and when you reach the location I indicate, you must follow my instructions.'

'Why do you think I will do this?' asked Saba.

'Don't you want to gain knowledge and return whence you came?'

Saba pondered. Was she in a customary dream situation where she could return if she closed her eyes and slept? She was not sure. This place was more strange and yet more real than anywhere she had ever been or dreamt of. How old was the Root? It gave the impression of immense antiquity. What might it know and share with her if she did help it? It looked like a long and arduous trek but it might be worth it. She didn't doubt the Root's sincerity – it was too ancient to care about deceit and it certainly needed help. How long had it lain in the riverbed? As many generations as her folk had lived in the caves, or ten times longer.

Its eye opened as she replaced her hands on it.

'So you have decided to help me! Very wise. When you reach the mountain, climb up about halfway and you will see a large hollow with a white stone standing in the ground like a pillar. Strike the stone with this splinter of my body that I am giving you. Then take shelter under the overhang at the side of the hollow until the water arrives. The earlier you leave, the earlier you will be back with me.'

Saba wondered if everything would be as simple as that, but set out at once up the gravelly bed of what must have been at one time a mighty river. No doubt this had made a great lake of the immense pan she could see just beyond the Root. On either side of her the sand dunes rose up for one to two hundred feet, and yet the bed of the river was so wide that, rather than feeling shut in, she seemed to be following a broad corridor leading endlessly forward.

The only landmarks she came across were outcrops of smooth stone, which looked lonely in this inert world, bereft of any kind of vegetation, insect, bird or animal. Even a scorpion would have been welcome to break the monotony, she thought. So the wearisome trudge went on. Had there been sunsets and sunrises, many days and nights would have passed. However, the temperature and light were unchanging. She never felt hungry, which was just as well, for there was nothing to eat or drink. But she got tired regularly and lay with her back against a dune to rest. She felt that her body needed spells of darkness as her mind needed sleep and dreaming, so surely she must be awake. How awful to live in a world like this even if she could, like the Root, survive without food. When she finally arrived at the mountain, she was travel-stained, rock-bruised and mentally weary, but set about the climb. Eventually she saw the hollow and the quartz pillar and, running forward, struck it with her splinter, which was as long as a walking staff.

Saba waited a long time. Then she was rocked by a deafening explosion far above her and saw a section lifting off the mountain top and fragmenting into tiny bits, which filled the air. She recalled the Root's words: 'Shelter under the overhang!' It was small but adequate and the stones rattled around her. Next she heard a whooshing roar and saw a wall of water three men high rushing down on her. There was nowhere to escape to and as the water enveloped her, she swam for the surface as if she was in a towering wave at sea.

At the bottom of the mountain the water settled into a steady flow along the old riverbed and Saba found she could float and let the current carry her along. At last she could see the Root ahead. The water swirled round it and picked it up to float away like herself. She swam the last few strokes to it and clambered on top. The river was now emptying out across the giant pan basin, and the water was calming as it did on the surface of a lake. She leaned forward, laying her forehead on the wood.

'Congratulations,' it visioned her. It was swelling and expanding even as they communicated. 'Now it's my turn. But I can only siphon information to you in small bites. You will have to return and visit me often to receive and discuss all the detail of the knowledge which will be your part of our bargain.'

'I would like that, but is it possible?'

'It can be arranged. Keep your head against my wood for a while so that we can program each other's minds to transfer and absorb knowledge speedily.'

Saba knew she had found the Root by dream, but they didn't seem to be in dream on this planet or world. Everything was too real.

'Are we near the earth I came from, or a star house, or much farther away?' she asked.

'Much farther away,' it answered drily, 'but that needs a long explanation. Next time, I think. You wondered if I was very old, as you walked up the riverbed. The answer is yes, far older than you ever dreamt of. I am not only older than your world, from its beginnings, but older than many others, which I outlasted, transferring from one to another as each expired. You came here in dream, real or not, and now your mind has the coordinates of where I am, so next time you can return at the speed of thought. Your deep self heard my cry for help across the cosmos and I will thank you always for answering it. When you want to visit me again, just picture me as you go to sleep.'

She glanced around. They were now floating on a vast shallow lake which would obviously rise up the sides of the dunes surrounding the great pan, like a small sea.

'Stretch yourself along my trunk and close your eyes,' the Root instructed.

She did so and to her amazement found herself waking up in the cave of the stalactites.

THIRTY-NINE

THE ISLE OF BEES

The sea gods and winds were kind, and the Kretan ship cruised smoothly from the moment Hermes collected Saba's group at Nar.

After exchanging fond farewells with Ka-ren and her people, Saba and her crew had rowed and sailed up the river Gar for half their journey. Then, when the river bent southwards, they left it and the curragh and began trudging east through the forest along the traders' track. This was uneventful, except for when they lost the trail crossing an expanse of rocky ground. They were returned to the track by some forest dwellers in exchange for a stag Aengus dispatched for them. They arrived in Nar nearly two moons after leaving the caves and only needed to wait a quarter moon for Hermes's ship to arrive. He and the crew had contended with severe storms that blew them off course for days at a time. In case of other wintry gales and pirates from the two big islands, Hermes proceeded by steering a course east and then south, keeping about fifty miles off the coast. Soon they entered the sphere of the underearth giants and their volcanic mountains perched on small islands, which the crew had to pass quite closely on their right before entering the Sicel straits and encountering the giant volcano of Etna. Two of the other volcanoes and Stromboli were alive as they passed. The first wasn't burning but its stench drifted for miles. Steam fumaroles made the sea boil and sulphurous geysers sported on land. Stromboli was flaming, and as its eruptions cause tidal waves, the Kretan pilot, who knew the coast, kept the ship as far away as possible. However, they could still see lava flowing into the sea and sending up clouds of steam.

They passed through the Sicel straits and immediately saw the wide red glow in the sky. One crater was erupting violently and sending up bombs of lava from its summit, far up and out over land and sea, in a monstrous firework display. This was completely unexpected and some of the panicking crew suggested a sacrifice be made to appease the great giantess. They started to draw lots to decide who it should be but Aelise raced across the deck and tried to launch herself over the side. Amlodi and Saba, who happened to be right there, grabbed her legs and pulled her back again.

'We don't need a sacrifice. One of my friends has died already,' announced Saba. A young orca from the pod keeping the ship company had inadvertently risen to blow in a dangerous part of the sea and been struck by a volcanic bomb the size of a mighty oak tree. The others had blown earlier and, seeing the conditions, dived fast and deep to avoid the danger. Saba wondered if they now regretted travelling to meet her from the Grey Ocean.

Aelise lay at the side of the deck where Saba and Amlodi dropped her. The small group had treated her as a pariah since they left and she felt her sacrifice was a way to expiate her attempted crime against Saba.

Saba, who had seen in an earlier dream that they would reach the Isle of Bees safely, held up her arms and announced to the crew that she had made a pact with the giantess Etna and they would all pass the lava gauntlet safely. She urged them to chant a prayer to the Mother and row hard, which they all did, still having faith and fear in their sea witch.

Hermes, who was keeping close watch, pointed out to Saba and Kalliste a small dugout canoe almost crossing their bow wave. Saba told Hermes to stop their boat instantly while she climbed down the pegs to examine the occupants, who were clearly hurt. She found a man, a woman and two children all suffering from severe burns. They gently lifted the woman and children up into the vessel but the man couldn't move. Saba crouched over him in the dugout; Bethel brought down her medicine bag, but all she had was a burn salve. The man had been lying over the boy to protect him, and both back and front were terribly burnt. As Saba rubbed her salve on his chest, the charred flesh came away exposing his ribs; the burns went even deeper. He was beyond speech, but his eyes were pools of pain. She foresaw he might continue in that state of agony for quite a time before dying. Bethel, who was still beside her, helped her to lift him into the water and release his body which floated quietly away. No words between them were needed. The mother and children were not so badly burnt. They lay under the shade of the awning where Saba made them as comfortable as possible with her salve. Kalliste knew a little of their language and explained that the ship was going to the Isle of Bees where the priestesses were famous for healing the sick. The patients stammered their gratitude.

A storm buffeted them after they left the area of Etna but subsided just as darkness dissolved in the soft dawn light. Straight ahead they saw a flat-topped rock jutting out of the sea. 'The Mother was with us this night,' announced Hermes. 'That's called Filfla, the altar rock. It was once joined to the mainland before the sea rose. We have been blown half round the island.' He ordered the helmsman to steer to starboard, keeping back from the cliffs. They all took long drinks from the remaining goatskin bag, and thought at first that the sea had got into the water during the storm. Then they realised the saline taste was from the caked salt on their lips and faces.

On the mainland, grey-white cliffs dropped to water level where their colour changed to a pale honey and the rocks became sharp, angular weapons. On the headland stood a mighty stone temple, the largest building Saba and her children had ever seen. It dominated the whole landscape and the onlookers stood in awe. Many of the stone slabs on top seemed crooked and lying at odd angles, and the building had a silent and empty look. But the grandeur of the edifice still conferred a sense of numinous serenity.

Kalliste explained that some years ago there had been a terrible earthquake. The others shuddered; the experience of the Garnac quake was too recent. The earthquake had shattered more than half of the island's temples. Then there was a drought, and since many of the water cisterns had been destroyed and there were no rivers on the island, water was in huge demand. Finally a pestilence struck. It was claimed some of the sick pilgrims brought it from the great deserts to the south of the Tideless Sea. About three quarters of the population died. For once, the bees and their precious honeycomb could do nothing.

At the invitation of Bee Mother, peoples from islands to the south called Pantel, who were part Berber, came to assist the stricken population. It was several generations before life returned to a vestige of its former quality, and the great temples that had fallen into neglect lacked the craftsmen and women to restore them, or sufficient priestesses and worshippers to maintain them.

The bees, which had been decimated by the drought causing a dearth of flowers and nectar, were restored and restocked from the southern deserts. The newcomers took over the fishing, harvested the crops and performed other tasks where necessary. The remaining folk tended the bees, maintained the temples and welcomed the sick and pilgrims who came again to worship the Mother.

The recent storm had disturbed many shoals of fish in the water and Hermes thought it would be politic and courteous to make a catch as a present to the islanders. Everyone agreed and the nets were let down. Orthonac and a few of the Kretans got out poles and lines for the larger fish that would undoubtedly pursue the shoals. They baited hooks with sardines from the first net catch and soon saw dolphins and tuna in hunting mode. They caught a few big tuna, which required a lot of crew to lift them over the side. Hermes almost choked in disbelief when Kalliste told him about the orca supplying their curragh with a small tuna to save them journey time in fishing. She told the others, 'You will see two of the most sacred temples close to the great harbour when we make port.'

They entered the harbour, which was like an inland lake with promontories, headlands and creeks. A party of priestesses and helpers met the ship at the dock and immediately took charge of the injured mother and children. Kalliste, who had visited the island several times and knew the Bee Mother and many of her priestesses, was taken to visit them, but the others were obliged to wait by the ship.

'You are not sick or known guests. If the Bee Mother invites you, we must introduce you first to the bee guards so they do not sting you to death,' one of the helpers told them.

'That's how they maintain their privacy,' joked Kalliste as she left the ship.

Some time later a bee priestess came and selected Saba, Aengus, Aine, Bethel and Amlodi to follow her. The others were told that food would be provided and she thanked them profusely for the catch of fish, part of which Bethel, Aengus and Amlodi carried with them, leaving the tuna for the crew and islanders to divide.

The Bee Mother's temple was a short distance from the harbour and contained the chambers and halls of the most sacred mysteries, several levels all carved into solid limestone. Guests and patients were lodged in and around the second and third temples not far away. All the temples on the island kept and cared for hives of bees, but the Bee Mother and her most experienced priestesses studied and worked with the swarms held specially sacred and with whom they communicated best. These all resided at her main temple.

They were introduced to the Bee Mother, seated formally on the throne where she received the pilgrims. She was a short, fat woman with a regal but not pompous demeanour and kind eyes. Only Kalliste understood and spoke their language, but the Bee Mother, a few of her priestesses – or Melissae – and Bethel spoke Kretan.

'My Kretan friend has been telling me all about you,' the Bee Mother said, smiling. 'And about Aengus's cruel assault. His afflictions are outside our usual practice, but we will do what we can for him starting tomorrow. The burnt ones are already being treated in our Tarxien healing temple.' She pointed out a mass of buildings a brief walk away. Bethel thought that beside them, the Mother's temple looked quite small above ground. He was staggered when he toured the massive area cut into the rock underneath.

The Bee Mother, whose name and title was Melitodes, assigned one of her Melissae to be their guide and protecting custodian with the island bees. She led them to the Tarxien temple to organise sleeping quarters and a meal. Next morning Melitodes would prescribe treatment for Aengus and, as a rare privilege, conduct them around some of the sacred parts of the temple. She also wished to hold a long discussion with Saba; she felt they could advise each other on several matters. Kalliste had told her of Saba's remarkable seeing abilities and even powers to intercede with the gods. Perhaps Saba could assist Melitodes to reverse the evil spell laid upon the island.

The Tarxien temples formed the largest complex in the Isle of Bees. There were three distinct buildings, the smallest of which lay to the east, used as lodgings for the sick. Part of the main area, including the spacious forecourt and curved façade, was walled off as a formal area for large public ceremonies. A number of smaller buildings also provided temporary accommodation for the hundreds of people who still lived there, mainly tending the sick pilgrims. The central building was twice as large as the eastern and western pair. It was constructed in three main and three smaller apses, which led into each another through sacred lintel porches. Floors were paved with ashlar slabs. Each apse contained a large seated statue of the Earth Mother. There were areas for ancestor worship and interaction with rituals unknown to Saba and her friends, animal sacrifice, storage for water, oil and grain and, of course, large spaces for the ubiquitous bees who also acted as guards, oracle creatures and providers of the treasured honey.

Honeycomb was the main medicine and core treatment for the range of illnesses and diseases displayed by the pilgrims coming to the island; it treated interior inflammations and was applied to external wounds and burns. Wax, royal jelly, curative sting venom – all were produced by the bees. It was obvious to Saba and Bethel that without bees the priestesses and other islanders would never survive. They upheld a reputation of both hope and fear to outsiders. They attracted wealthy pilgrims seeking a cure for their maladies and frightened away would-be conquerors and pirates. The bodies of intruders stung to death and floating far out at sea were visible to outsiders' boats and demonstrated that the threats were real. Crime on or off the island didn't exist; human peacekeepers or warriors were not needed. All the inhabitants could be involved in productive pursuits. What a happy outcome.

Next day in the harbour temple, the Bee Mother organised a team of Melissae to take charge of Aengus. Kalliste and Aine went with them as Aengus was feeling strange and not entirely himself. There were times during the past few moons when he seemed to be another person – a nervous person – and Aine was the only close companion he would tolerate. Phoebe, the leader of the Melissae, was intrigued by this aspect of his personality. Apparently she had met such behaviour before and explained that Melitodes believed it was a special gift from the Earth Mother. They went to Kordin, another neighbouring temple of healing, where Phoebe conducted an initial diagnosis through Kalliste, discussing Aengus's history, background, outstanding events and memories. Then she gave him time off while she consulted about his condition.

Aengus, Aine and Kalliste, with their guide in tow, set out to explore the lovely coast of Melita, as the natives named the island. It was renowned for its abundance and variety of flowers which, as it was still winter, were only in bud. They provided the bees with vast varieties of honey, some of them highly medicinal.

'I hear there is even one called poison honey which induces a stupor to begin with, then severe illness for several days and sometimes death. The few bees which attend this poison plant are reared on it and conditioned to collect from no other. Is that true?' Kalliste translated Saba's comments to the priestess who verified the facts.

Saba and Bethel began their talk with Melitodes, who launched directly into her worries.

'You will have heard that this part of the world has been put under a curse by a powerful underearth giant. For yuls the skies have released less rain and dew so crops and livestock, bees and people have been suffering from increasing water shortages. As the plants and flowers are not as luscious as they used be, the bees produce less honey and our livestock yields less fat and milk. Our creatures don't breed so prolifically and may die of diseases related to the long droughts. The mainland and people beyond the Pantel Islands were also suffering but even more so: their earth turned into desert sand and the farmers were forced to emigrate. Some retreated into the mountains and some were invited to come here and replace our own lost farmers and fishermen. It's only a short day's boat trip to Pantel and another to the Berber coast. We all get along well and even our languages have similarities. Now our population is growing again, but because of the continuing famines we are barely managing to feed our people. The Mother only knows what will happen if the sky water supply goes on shortening. We rely on it as we only have small springs on the island. You know that we worship and preserve the rituals of Gaia the Earth Mother, and Persephone, her daughter, who spends part of each yul underearth and then, supported by her faithful spouse, reappears in the spring to bring fertility back to the land. But lately, each yul the fertility is less. One of the underearth giants is withholding the gift from her, and her consort, the dark lord, cannot undo the curse. We need a powerful magician who will go down and foil the giants' curse and assist Persephone to bring back fecundity to the world.'

Saba was shocked and sat in silence for a while before speaking. 'That is a task for a goddess, no ordinary mortal.'

'From what I hear, you are no ordinary mortal. I can see your charisma. As you sit there, I know you are reading my thoughts before I speak them to Bethel, and sometimes power gleams and shoots from your eyes to a degree that frightens me.'

'I will give you my answer within the quarter moon,' Saba said. 'But whether or not I attempt this task I feel I should warn you that the outcome you desire is unlikely to be successful. Our lady the Spider weaves the woof and warp of history – even the curse will be included.'

'But you have managed to defeat – or at least bend – her destiny before. We beseech you to intercede for us!' begged Melitodes.

'Kalliste has been telling perhaps more than the truth. Anecdotes become magnified as they pass from mouth to ear. What you ask is far beyond my ability.'

'All we ask is that you at least try. No one can do more and I feel you are our last hope.' Melitodes looked at the two of them. 'Come. I will show you some of our mysteries and the miracles of our mentors and protectors.'

She led them down sets of steps and passages below the ground. They opened into a series of large chambers, each of which was entered through sacred trilithons; the ceiling and walls of each room were painted in a different design with red and green as the dominant colours. One room was washed in red paint and seemed intended for animal sacrifice.

'Yes, the stone knife is for pigs, goats, sheep and birds; we sacrifice no humans, not even invaders, and we have no criminals. We sacrifice to the Mother and the Lady Persephone. All maladies can be treated by an exchange of confessions or substances developed by bee healers among the Melissae.'

The next room was painted with a tree of life, and vines, tendrils, leaves and fruits.

'What are the red fruits?' Saba enquired.

'They are the sacred pomegranates carried and eaten by Persephone, you shall taste some soon.'

A superbly carved room with the ever-present limestone pillars and trilithon doorways led into a cult room where esteemed clients could consult an oracle. Questions and answers were exchanged with the seated goddess who nodded or shook her head in reply with a variety of booming sounds. The next room was decorated with a hexagonal frieze coloured like a honeycomb. Then came the great pit occupied sometimes by the giant rock python, Meilikhios, whose body was inhabited during the rites by the dark lord who led Persephone back and forth from their kingdom of dead souls each autumn and spring. The bell-shaped pit closed in from above so there was no escape without rope or ladder.

'Sometimes invaders are sent to visit Meilikhios. If he judges them unworthy to remain he escorts them royally to underearth.'

The last chamber was the most ornate in the entire labyrinth. The trilithon entrance was set in a concave façade and curving slabs were built across the façades in a corbelled semi-circular dome. The pillared niches held statues of mother and daughter; an inner space, dark and discreet, led from it.

'That is an underworld entrance inviting those who wish to, to come and go.'

Many seed grain pits lay alongside a water cistern. 'This is living water. It's been specially treated for our medicines and to mix with the seed grain and pig morsels from the decay pit so that we produce excellent crops.'

'How does the water become alive?' asked Bethel.

The priestess pointed. 'You see that egg-shaped wooden barrel? We fill it with water from a holy spring, we add a few handfuls of powered bone or horn, then handfuls of rock dust ground fine with a wooden pestle. Later, it is stirred with a flat-bladed wooden ladle, with thin leaves of copper and silver hammered on either side of it. The stirring is important: first, slowly from the left towards the centre, so that a swirl is created; then, repeat from the right. The urn is closed tightly by a wooden lid with a hole in the centre, covered with a cloth and left for three quarters of a moon. The water from this promotes growing and healing.'

'You have this miracle at the Mother Lake: the white clay Fion and Maeve were fighting for,' Bethel said to Saba. Then he turned to Melitodes. 'I thought no metal was allowed on the island?'

'That's true – no weapon or tool,' said Melitodes quickly, 'but ornaments and jewellery in copper, silver and gold are constantly brought as donations or appreciative gifts after successful healing. We have a hidden chamber of these things.' She put a hand quickly to her mouth, then smiled. 'I should not mention such things, but you have become privileged friends. I feel you, Saba, are not interested and you, Bethel, are not greedy. A long time ago, the person who was Melitodes then was shown in a dream how to construct the ladle to create living water.'

Saba looked at her curiously.

'Did the Melitodes of that time say who told her in the dream?'

'I don't think she told us or it would be in our history record, I will ask the recorder to search her memory. Why is it important to you?'

'Oh! People sometimes tell me things in dreams. I just wondered.' Saba was thinking of the Root. That was secret too, she reflected.

*

Aengus was examined for several days by Phoebe and her troop of Melissae. They decided on an appropriate treatment for him and took him to a small lamp-lit room at the rear of the main temple complex. Four of the Melissae stripped and washed him, handing him a cup of steaming xahxieh, prepared from the poppy. Arranged in the clothing of seductive dancing girls with their faces, hands and feet painted in vivid red and green, they each took a pot of honey and smeared him from head to foot. Standing him on a platform, they began an undulating dance around him, chanting a lilting song with soft harmonics. Then a fifth girl appeared, naked and painted in sinister black and yellow stripes. She was so alluring and pretty that Aengus deemed her to be an apparition of a goddess. She held in front of his eyes a clear glittering stone swinging gently backwards and forwards from a thread. In turn, the Melissae darted in from their dance and slowly licked honey from his body. The girl in front licked his eyes and lips, thrusting her honey-coated tongue in his mouth. The licking became faster and more exciting until he felt an enormous and uncustomary erection.

They laid him down and the black and yellow girl mounted him. He was tremendously excited, but try as he might, no orgasm was forthcoming. Aengus refused point-blank to let them apply a stinging bee in a wicker basket to his glans or throat and subsided in exhaustion. The Melissae brought him back to Melitodes, confessing their diagnosis and treatment to be only partly successful.

Saba and Bethel walked around a few of the island temples, stopping at Mnaidra to visit the mother, boy and girl they had pulled from the boat at Etna. The mother had endured severe facial burns and decided to remain in Melita and apply to become a priestess. The children were healing well and begged Saba, whom they idolised, to let them go with her when the ship left. Stephanie and Se-Bastien were twelve and fourteen. As far as they were concerned, Saba had saved their lives, and what's more, she was magical, a goddess; they would do anything for her even if it cost their own lives. Saba consulted Bethel.

'They will be better off in Krete, if it's only half of what Kalliste claims for it. They are both old enough to be useful and flexible enough to learn new languages and customs.'

Saba had negotiated that the ship's crew should be allowed on the island with a bee guide for every eight of them, and they often met up with Saba's group. Hermes had bags of gold dust from Er-rin on the ship, a few handfuls of which would cover the cost of food and healing.

Hermes, Orthonac, Aelise and the twenty crew members were fascinated by the bees and by the peculiar customs of the islanders. The small cattle were taboo and kept only for their milk and manure. Each parish sacrificed its own pigs and sheep and this meat satisfied their needs. Everyone ate fish five days a quarter moon. Generally, the islanders were a little nervous of the bees. They were controlled by the Melissae and ignored the other inhabitants, unless they upset them by accidently breaking a hive. Offenders were quickly stung to death, as were stray fishermen who landed uninvited on the island.

There was a strong empathy between the bees and the Melissae. They reacted to each others' upsets, and the bees were often consulted about problems. It was Melitodes who could best interpret their feelings. Some of the Melissae worked with the carvers, herbal healers, weavers and water managers. However, Melitodes spent most time in familiarisation with the warrior bees and queens. They bred in strains from distant lands to develop immunities and improve stinging efficiency. Some of the special hives had crystal lids or side panels fitted so they could observe the worker bee dances and other more subtle communications within the community.

Aengus, Amlodi and Aine were not so taken by the Isle of Bees and its people. They felt the whole atmosphere somewhat sinister; even so, Amlodi composed a musical composition on the bees themselves. They spent a lot of time on their own and with the ship's crew from whom they gleaned a grasp of the Kretan tongue.

As the spring festival was near, Saba decided she would humour the Bee Mother by agreeing to act the part of Persephone and spend three nights in the so-called chamber of darkness, although she knew there was no chance of success. Next night was full moon, a propitious moment for her to perform the ritual myth with the Lord of the Underworld. Bethel had done his utmost to dissuade her, although he shared her view that it was only a theatrical performance. He was worried by how seriously Melitodes was taking the matter. Beyond doubt, she was a powerful shaman and she and all the bee priestesses believed fervently in the reality of the undertaking.

Saba wore a blood-red robe given to her by the Melissae and was reminded, as she entered the chamber of darkness, to be sure and address the python as Meilikhios. As the stone slid into place behind her, leaving her in an inky blackness, she could hear the rasping of the great snake's rough skin on the floor. She was reminded of the occasion when she was enclosed with Maeve's wild bear in the western caves of Er-rin. She did not know that the snake was hungry, not having eaten for three moons. She concentrated all her mental powers in an effort to contact and, if possible, control its presence and its actions. It reared up its head to her height. First one and then the other of her waving hands touched its neck and fastened firmly but gently on it. This was the most bizarre and upsetting act of mind transference she had ever attempted. Even her session with the Root had not seemed so fraught with danger. She remembered it and her guardians, Old One and Narwhal, and prayed for extra power to match the ravenous creature.

She did not succeed in reaching its thoughts as she had with other opponents. Her eyes were now getting used to the blackness and her other senses peaked. No doubt it could sense her far more effectively. She could feel its hunger and knew it must be diverted for the three nights. She also felt its cold implacable nature. Its body was thicker than her hands could encircle. Bethel had told her pythons grew to twenty feet or more and this seemed to be one of these. She continued to project her mental force and love for all creatures towards it and thought she felt some of the tension leave its neck. It slowly swayed forward and placed its head against hers. She was gaining greater access to its feelings, alien though they were. Its hunger cravings faded and it became curious about this biped who was having such an effect on it.

It wound a coil of its body around her shoulders and drew her gently towards the rear of the chamber. She felt a breath of fresh air on her legs and bending her knees noticed a low tunnel leading off the chamber. Softly disengaging herself from its coil she crawled down the passage and went around a corner where a beam of sunlight shone along the wall. The python was following her and they emerged into a sunlit pit. The python obviously spent much of its time basking there. She was amazed at its size – more than three tall men in length. It could swallow a goat, or a small human, without difficulty. She knew that all snakes could dislocate their jaws and expand their body to engulf larger animals. Even the Kaheen's pretty grass snakes in Er-rin did that.

The great snake coiled itself on a flat slab, waving its head and neck in a lazy motion. It was inviting her to bask in the sun with it. If she relaxed with it, might it change its mind and crush her? Her rational mind was cautious but instinct told her it was safe. She sat down and stared him in the eyes, projecting again her love and warmth. It stretched out and laid its head on her lap, closing its eyes. By the third day, they had reached some sort of understanding. Saba spent most of her time with it in the sunshine, which it loved. In that somnolent state its hunger pangs diminished and she felt safe enough to sleep beside it.

That day she began dreaming and was transported back to the lake on the alien star. She found the Root had put out tendrils and planted itself near the shoreline. A young tree had begun to grow. It was as friendly as ever and pleased to see her. She explained her involvement with the festival of renewal from underearth, the snake Lord of the Underworld and his queen.

'These are myths and parables designed to show inner truths to those with wisdom and understanding. Nothing is ever lost. When a creature dies, its body will, of course, rot and disintegrate until it becomes minute particles. These particles will disperse and link up with others to become a new plant or animal. You might be a dandelion and get eaten by a sheep, which in turn is eaten by a human. Part of its essence transfers to that human. Thus it achieves new life; everything is part of everything else.'

'What about my thoughts and ideas, or music I compose?' Saba was thinking of Amlodi and his glorious songs.

'These too live on as part of the collective minds of nature and individual memes. Ideas may be reused to create something else. It's the same with thought patterns and musical sounds.'

'So not only the seed grain survives and renews, all the eaten or discarded grains do as well,' mused Saba.

A dark but powerful shape entered her mind. 'I am Persephone, daughter of Zeus and Gaia, queen of the underworld and consort of Pluto. I am strongly in the mind of the Bee Mother. We inspire each other to do great things. In your mind I am but a thought pattern, but I still have a kind of existence. In the future I am passed on as a myth through generations. Since you have conceived of me, I now tell you your notions are correct – we cannot influence constantly changing nature. The drought and famine Melitodes is experiencing will get worse and her civilization must change and move, or be extinguished. Perhaps you can help her to understand this.'

Saba awoke and heard the stone in the dark cavern being pulled back. Her three days and nights were over. The first thing she did was to order food for the python.

'He will eat something large. Did you think it might have been me?' she asked Melitodes.

'I am happy to see you alive and in good spirits. Had you been less than is claimed, Meilikhios would have kept you in the underworld. Did you communicate with Persephone?'

'Yes, but the future for your culture here is not good. In the far distant future I see the island prosper and be famous for other things. She cannot assist your wishes or influence the natural flow of events. Conditions like famine and drought will slowly worsen. I advise you to seek a new land where you may continue your excellent work. I will be happy to transport two teams of Melissae and their bees with us when we leave. They can resettle in Krete or some of the other islands. Kalliste and her people will look after them. I beg you to let them go and ensure the future of all you love.'

'I will think about it. Your advice seems to come from the goddess. Tomorrow we will celebrate your efforts for us, combined with a farewell feast at Tarxien. Your ship's crew and everyone else are welcome.'

The Kretans went fishing with islanders, who knew the favoured spots, and returned with an array of sea creatures. The big tuna and swordfish from far out, dentici, sprats to crisp in oil, mérou, mullet and even a fekruna to be barbecued in its shell as a delicacy. Pigs and goats were sacrificed, roasted and broiled, herbs and roots gathered. Representatives of leading crafts and all the parishes were invited. The bees were informed and demonstrated their approval of the feast and acquiescence to the proposed travel arrangements to set up new colonies. The feast took place in the forecourts in front of the Tarxien temple and the evening was really spring-like, as though Persephone sent her blessing. After the fish and the meats, they drank myritis, a mixture of honey, wine and myrtleberries. Saba and her companions delighted in the dried sweet and sour pomegranates. The Kretan crew fraternised well with the islanders and Aelise announced that she was determined to remain and learn from Melitodes to become one of the bee carers.

Preparations for departure began the next day. Melitodes organised hives of bees in the care of her two top bee experts, who each took four assistant Melissae with materials for smoking the hives in case of upset. Stephanie and Se-Bastien were now clear of their burns, thanks to the honey, and revered the little creatures. The ship was very full and everyone was squeezed into a tight space.

Saba placated a worried Hermes by promising that Pluto and Persephone would give them fair weather and a smooth crossing so he chose the southern route home, along the Berber coast, which had the most constant winds.

FORTY

ELECTED TO PARADISE

Four nights into the voyage and again the gods had been kind. With strong westerly winds behind them, Hermes steered a course due south, then east along the African coast. For the first time in his career he didn't find it necessary to make landfall for storm shelter or water. Rowing could take six to eight nights but the strong wind shortened their journey by half.

The island of Krete was visible to the north-east, which meant they were approaching the south coast where Kalliste's family lived. They owned the chief palace called Phaistos and the nearby seaport Aygia Triadha. Hermes set his course, keeping a small island on his left and a long peninsular spit of land to the right. Two large ranges of snow-capped mountains lay inland, one to the left and the taller one straight in front.

'See the high mountain? That's Mount Ida, with the Dikte Cave to its right, where our ancestors began. It's the most holy sanctuary on the island,' Kalliste explained. Their approach to the harbour of Aygia Triadha was so swift and smooth that they drew up at the crowded jetty almost before anyone noticed or recognised the ship with Kalliste and Hermes at the prow. With yells of delight, runners started out to the factory house and even to Phaistos itself where Kalliste's mother, sister to Hermes, lived and ruled, showing that she was held in warm esteem by her people. A reward might also be expected for news of the favourite daughter. A group of people poured out of the factory house and down to the jetty.

'Look! There's Hephaistos, Ariadne's consort and man of magic,' said Hermes.

A tall, black-haired, strikingly handsome man with a limp was making his way towards them ahead of the others. He flung open his arms towards Kalliste, who responded more coolly.

'How is my glorious niece? You look fitter and healthier than when you left! You'll never guess how I've missed you.'

He grinned delightedly at her sardonic expression.

'I could say the same,' she retorted.

Hephaistos turned to Hermes and Bethel. 'Welcome back to you both, but in what country did you find such magnificent women?' He indicated Saba and Aine. 'Those sisters are worth an emperor's ransom. Tell all at once. 'Bethel, who knew him of old, brought Saba forward. 'Meet my queen, and the most powerful shaman the world has ever seen, so mind what you say – or even think.'

'So then, this is her sister?' Hephaistos asked.

'Our names are Saba and Aine,' said Bethel's 'queen' imperiously, deciding it was time to shed her disguise. 'This is my son Aengus, and my friends Amlodi and Orthonac.'

'I look forward to long discussions with all of you. Such friends and such a long adventure must engender many wonders to intrigue our ears.' He gestured at the ship's crew, 'I also see many new faces over there. However, before we start, I hear the hoof beats of my paramour – she will be with us very shortly.'

In the distance they could just discern two mounted ponies galloping towards them at full speed. The scene held all the fascination of a horse race and they watched entranced as the drama of Queen Ariadne's entrance unfolded. Her pony was a full hundred paces ahead of her companion's, and covered with a lather of foam and sweat. She raced until almost on top of the group, then reared the pony in the air, swept off its back with a flourish and ran at Kalliste. This time there was no doubting the warmth of affection between them.

Ariadne was still a raven-haired beauty, though close to middle age, and remained lithe and active, as her vault from the pony testified. She was shorter than Kalliste, who was level with Aine. She had wide eyes and mouth, a long straight nose and her small hands were strong enough for a capable horsewoman.

'I was so worried when Hermes did not return last summer, but thanks be to the Mother you're here now.'

'It will take a moon to tell you all our adventures,' breathed Kalliste, arms still around her neck.

'Well, we'll take that moon.'

Ariadne hugged Hermes and Bethel, and on learning the status of Saba and Aine, greeted both with formal cheek kisses and invited them to stay with her as long as they wished – or even live in Krete, since they were such friends of her daughter.

Saba, whose command of Kretan was still limited, explained through Kalliste about the bees and their keepers and the whole situation on the Isle of Bees. More than just welcoming, Ariadne seemed overjoyed and announced that they would have pride of place in her palace, which overlooked the widest grasslands on the island. They were trying to increase the island's honey production so the new strains of bee and their keepers' expertise would be invaluable.

'You could not have brought a more treasured gift,' she told Saba.

As a trading nation, one of Krete's main exports was honey to the land of Khem. She already pictured sending another ship to the Isle of Bees for a cargo of hives while the Bee Mother remained favourable to Saba's advice. She would swap or trade items like coloured textiles, wine or decorated pottery, whatever would please them. She had heard of their aversion to metals.

The other rider, a pretty blond girl, was holding both ponies. Ariadne turned to her.

'This is Chrestena! She is my inseparable companion. Go and rub down and water the ponies, then bring them back harnessed to carts.' She turned back to Saba. 'They will convey the hives back to Phaistos so the bees suffer the minimum disruption in the shortest time. Now, let us all repair to our factory here for a refreshing meal and to make each other's acquaintance. I want to meet those new faces from the ship and see what qualities their owners possess, so everyone must come.' They set out in several groups. Numbers of friends of the old crew, including Hermes's family, had by now turned up to welcome them and exchange news. Minerva and Datemi begged to be excused; they would not leave their charges until the hives were settled and the bees content. Ariadne and Saba promised to send them over food and cordial.

Aine took Kalliste's arm. 'Is Hephaistos your father? He seems a racy character.'

'He's certainly not my father. He's tricky. Watch out for him. However, he and my mother are well-matched partners and he's very talented. Wait until you see the jewellery he makes.'

'Your mother seems shrewd and very smart. What was that word she used about Chrestena who took the ponies?'

'Ah! That means someone who can be both companion and carer and whom one cannot do without. Mother bought her from an Akkadian trading ship. She was from the Black Sea. My mother's people sailed here from those countries about fifty generations ago, after the flood when the waterways opened up and ships could pass through. Now they are the landowners and merchants because they are the most able.'

'You mean, the rulers and overlords?'

'Not exactly. Our society works as a meritocracy, so anyone who is clever or talented can rise to the top of their calling, be it healer, merchant or artist, though it's a bit harder for slaves.'

'When we have more time you must explain about slaves – why you buy them and so on.'

'That will take a day's discussion on how our society works!' exclaimed Kalliste.

The factory stood in a square at the end of a long narrow street leading up from the quays. The ordinary houses were one and two storeys tall, but the factory was three storeys and looked enormous to Aine. She glanced at Aengus and Amlodi to see if they were impressed. Saba had probably seen them in her visions, she thought.

'That's the biggest house I've ever seen,' she said to Kalliste.

Bethel interrupted. 'Wait till you get to Phaistos and Knossos, and then to some of the palaces in the Akkadian Empire where we must go if Aengus is to meet the healer I told you about.'

The front entrance led through some antechambers into a great hall. All the floors were tiled and the pillars and walls were of dressed stone. The walls were painted with brightly coloured frescos featuring lifelike scenes of seascapes, both under and above water.

Brilliantly tinted fish traced their way through red and green seaweeds. Squatting on the bottom were octopus, clams and conger eels beneath rocks. Above the water level were twenty- and thirty-oared ships in full sail, with men on deck blowing triton shells and passing what looked like whales and other strange creatures. Gannets and cormorants swooped above the waves while storks and ibises paddled at the water's edge.

Above the doorways on one side of the hall were large images of the labreus, or double axe, which they had seen in one of the ancestors' caves.

'Those signs show that the rooms are dedicated to our ancestors. They have a suite on each floor. We worship and commune with them daily, bringing them food and wine,' Ariadne explained. A long trestle table was set out in the hall with dishes of dried fruits and nuts, baskets with slabs of fresh bread and jugs of wine and water. A large steaming cauldron of deliciously scented fish stew was carried out and everyone picked up a bowl to receive a helping from it.

A throng of another twenty or thirty men and women streamed in from various art rooms and workshops in the building.

'They are artists and craftsmen who work in the factory with Hephaistos,' Ariadne told Saba and Aine through Kalliste.

'Do you think he would let me work and learn from them?' Aine demanded eagerly.

'Yes, I think you're tough enough to take their banter – especially that from Hephaistos,' said Ariadne, regarding her quizzically.

'She loves all forms of artwork,' Saba explained, adding that Aine was collaborating with Amlodi on a combined painting with flute and drum recital based on the theme of marine life and sea creatures.

'Like the fresco above us! When it's ready we'll hold a gala music evening to come and listen, and I'm certain that our lute and lyre players and timpanists would love to take part with you.'

'Did you know I play the lute?' Kalliste smiled quickly. 'That's something else Aine and I have in common. We can swap instruments and teach each other.'

'Aengus, Bethel and Orthonac are also good flautists,' said Saba. 'Amlodi is a champion singer, as was Aengus until his misfortune.' She told Ariadne about Aengus's unhappy saga and their quest for a healer.

Bethel praised the fish stew. 'I've spotted nine types of fish and shells.'

'It's one of our favourite dishes,' said Hephaistos, passing nearby.

'Yes, and he's stolen my top cook to come here and make it,' grumbled Ariadne. When Hephaistos heard of Aine's love of art, he was delighted and immediately offered to work with her himself. She accepted gratefully, acknowledging Kalliste's conspiratorial wink from behind him. Ariadne had been moving around talking to everyone. She banged her bowl with her wine cup.

'We are going to hold a welcome home party for my daughter. In ten days time it will be Phaistos's festival of Ekdysia and we shall hold both celebrations together because our friends from all over the island always come to join us.'

Bethel, who had lived on Krete for several years, explained to Saba and Aine, 'The festival commemorates a girl called Leukippos who was very boy-like, and when she grew up she was changed from a girl to a boy by a powerful shaman. He/she went on to perform great exploits. Some day when we are storytelling, I'll get one of the bards to recite the tale.'

'How far away is Phaistos?' asked Saba.

'Oh not far, about three thousand paces,' Bethel replied.

They came in sight quite quickly, just as he predicted. Ariadne insisted they all leave for her palace at once.

'Look! It's perched on the top of that ridge looking over the Messara plain, the largest flat expanse on the island. It's well stocked for hunting.'

The Phaistos palace, built around a central courtyard, was a much bigger construction than the factory. There was a colonnaded entrance leading through several antechambers to a reception hall. Out of this rose an impressive staircase and landing that opened in turn onto a great reception or ballroom. All the walls were painted with sumptuous frescos on pastel or terracotta backgrounds, the tiled floors and plaster ceilings had geometrical designs. At the end of another corridor, Saba could see more stairs leading to the third floor. She guessed there were more than a hundred rooms of many shapes and sizes. The west wing had the labreus or double axe symbol of immortality painted or carved over the doorways. These, like the ones in the factory, must be dedicated to the ancestors. Also, just like the factory, the floors and walls were of hardy, dressed limestone and each floor was supported underneath by massive pillars. Being situated on a hillside allowed the architects to execute different levels of terraces radiating from curved courts to outer sets of rooms.

Saba and her group were assigned rooms on the north side overlooking the plain. The grassland was dotted as far as the eye could see with anemones and narcissi blooms, and with groves of flowering almond trees nearer the palace.

Servants brought each of them two sets of clothing. Their own clothes were sadly dilapidated after extensive travelling; several of them still had only the scanty forest clothes obtained after their sea adventures.

The clothes included sandals, loincloths, kilts, shirts and tunics in wool and linen for the men, and for the women delicate sandals, blouses, short and long skirts, cloaks, robes and close-fitting tops in multicolours, which revealed their breasts and created amusement. Kalliste explained they would wear some of these for the festival, and said that she and Ariadne would show them how to apply the customary makeup for eyes, lips and hair.

Hermes reminded Bethel that he had left his 'whale stuff', as he described it, on the ship; he was afraid for its safety. Bethel had previously become friends with Merer of Edfu, one of the chief Egyptian perfumers and an influential man in world trade. The Egyptians lived in their own separate village near Aygia Triadha, as did groups of foreigners in most countries where they conducted a consistent business and wished to preserve their own culture.

Bethel had outlined to Saba some facts and stories about the Egyptian civilization – how it was one of the oldest and most famous in the world, and how the geometrical funeral mountains to their Pharaoh kings were the largest ever known. He had visited the Two Lands twice on Kretan ships and seen them for himself. They didn't keep ancestors' bodies in parts of their palaces as the Kretans did but they admired the Kretan embalmers as masters of their profession. This was the main reason for the exchange of apprentices from Egypt to learn the art, for art it was. In exchange, the men from Khem brought all kinds of new technology into Krete. Merer helped Hephaistos to construct a reciprocating lathe in his factory. This helped to carve, smooth and polish wood or stone. Simply operated by a foot treadle and cord wound around a pole, it spun back and forth like a horizontal fire drill.

Saba and Bethel were sitting in Merer's house drinking Egyptian beer and nibbling sweet cakes while Bethel discussed his lump of ambergris, still the size of half a wolf. Merer privately agreed with Bethel that Saba was a magnificent woman and presented her with a phial of amber essence, which he felt would suit her perfectly. When she smelt and approved this novel offering, she kissed him on both cheeks and invited him to visit her in the palace.

After haggling for some time, in exchange for the ambergris Merer offered Bethel a choice of twelve sea voyages back from Ugarit or a whole yul's lodging in a suitable house in any Egyptian quarter of any major city in Akkad or Egypt and an allowance for food and slaves during that period. Bethel accepted the offer provided that Merer included a piece of amber, of exactly the same hue as Saba's bracelets, which he had noticed in his shop. He eventually agreed and told Bethel he would send him an inscribed clay cylinder recording their deal. The chief members of the communities in the cities where Bethel might be would honour this contract on seeing the cylinder.

Bethel didn't show Saba the amber and slipped it in his pocket as they walked away. She was impressed at the bargain he had negotiated and, knowing the origin of the ambergris, said she presumed their guardians were looking after them.

The festival was to begin the next day. At the ball in the evening, everyone had to wear not only fancy dress with masks, but dress as the opposite sex to celebrate the meaning of Leukippos. The ladies' breasts would naturally be hidden under tunics and cloaks.

Friends of Ariadne and Hephaistos began arriving from the three other kingdoms on the island. They all wanted to meet the fabled newcomers, the two shaman women in particular. The elderly Queen Europa and her consort Paulus, the Minos of Knossos, were the first to greet them. The shamans' command of Kretan was now more than competent for social occasions and they assented to sit in on the sessions after the festival when Kalliste and Hermes were scheduled to regale all the interested friends of the host and hostess with the most exciting tales of their adventures. Kalliste insisted Saba and Aine were needed to explain many things that puzzled her about their unusual powers. The glamour, regal presence and faint underlying sense of danger that emanated from Saba and Aine as personalities meant they were sought after in any company.

Trestle tables were laid out in the large courtyard for food and drinks, and anyone among the citizens and freemen who cared to come was made welcome. Music for dancing was provided in the courtyard, and upstairs in the more sedate ballroom two sets of six-piece bands played. The bands comprised lyres, lutes, drums, bone and wooden flutes, and stone or clay lithophones. Amlodi, Aengus and Orthonac all offered to play as stand-ins while others were resting.

To get the party upstairs off to a good start, Ariadne had her slaves serve everyone with what she called a stirrup drink. This tasted like diluted absinthe and was prepared from the popular mastika plant growing wild on the island. Later in the evening it was mixed with valerian-scented carob wine. The fancy dress disguises were so effective that only Saba was able to divine the sex and identity of the wearers.

The tables were laden with platters of beef, mutton, pork, geese and ducks, pigeons, hares, dried berries baked in bread pastry rolls, quantities of nuts and kernels, celery, carrots and asparagus, roots and bulbs. There were jugs of red and white wine, rowan beer and loaves of freshly baked bread everywhere. Wooden platters and cups were set out for those who hadn't brought their own.

Saba and Aine loved the ladies' costumes and were surprised by the wide variety of hairstyles. They were in gales of laughter at the buffoon costumes of the men disguised as women. Those who couldn't shine as sexy women, turned themselves into grotesque caricatures of the top ladies. The two Eelwomen were not excluded: several people wore red wigs, an easy clue to their identity, as red hair was unknown on Krete. Amlodi who was a huge success sang a falsetto ballad so superbly that the crowd demanded he sing outside too. Bethel and Orthonac employed body paint to emphasise their breasts and nipples. There was line dancing, eightsome reels, weaving conga lines, circular hortas performed at high speed and a fine demonstration of the famous Crane dance by a troupe so proficient they behaved as if it was a set piece performed in the calendar of festivals. The celebrations lasted until dawn when flocks and couples in the courtyard straggled away towards the village and the folks in the ballroom sloped off to their rooms.

Aine overheard one woman say to another, 'That bash was fabulous compared to Diotema's last moon.'

'Yes, the poor thing ran out of wine in the Zagros ballroom and had to resort to Egyptian beer.'

After the celebrations, few appeared before midday and by then slaves had cleared the previous evening's debris. Most folk looked a bit wan and jaded, so Ariadne judged it a good time for her friends to be amused by Kalliste's and Hermes's accounts of their adventures, elucidated by asides from the natives themselves. The proceedings were interspersed by 'ohs' and 'ahs' and gasps of disbelief. Saba's exploits with Maeve and her bears followed the battles of Mother Lake and Newgrange. At Saba's request, Aengus's ordeal wasn't mentioned and to satisfy Kalliste's sense of drama, the events at Garnac and adventures with the orcas were held over for a second sitting.

Europa and Ariadne clasped Saba's arms afterwards.

'Did you really strike two men blind?' Europa asked.

'Well, only in extremity and I'm not proud of it, Europa. The people of my family were born to heal, not maim. I hate battles and wars.'

'I'd like to know how to materialise an imaginary bear that will destroy people!' Ariadne exclaimed.

Saba explained that all such feats were only developed after many years training in a dark cave, from which one only ever saw the stars. Saba and Aine's mind reading abilities were also suppressed. This enabled them to stay a step ahead and avoid undesirable conversations before they started.

A day or two later, Kalliste found time to discuss Kretan society with Saba, Aine, Amlodi and Orthonac.

'I know your first query is about slaves.'

'Yes, and about citizens, freemen, servants and your merchant trading venturers.'

'This is the fabric of our society. At the top are a few priestly families like those of Europa, Ariadne and Diotema of Zagros – ten or twelve at most. Then there are the wealthy merchants, hundreds of them – they hold most of the wealth in the island. The citizens are the backbone of our society. They are composed of all who have distinguished themselves in their fields, also healers, artists and the like. Men and women have the right to vote and decide all major issues. Freemen are farmers, fishers, some artists, all craftsmen and so on. The best of these will become citizens by election, as you yourselves did by popular vote just after the Ekdysia. You will be invested with your insignia tomorrow. I'm breaking a confidence to tell you this but I know and trust you'll keep the surprise a secret. Servants are freemen with their children, those who have lost their possessions or property and depend on the richer classes to pay them for their labour. Kretans do not fight in wars like the folks on the mainlands all around us. They don't capture slaves. However, we sometimes buy them if they have qualities we need or if we take pity on them. Remember, if these people were not made slaves, they would have been killed at the end of a battle. They were selected as prime specimens from a captive race to do well and survive. Usually they are well treated by their owners so as to maintain their good health, and allegiance is vital for trustworthiness and harmony in the household. As they are completely looked after, they don't have the worries of servants in settling costs and expenses.'

'But you own them like animals, I'm told, and can kill them for disobedience,' said Saba. 'That's no way to treat another human creature.'

'The slave is taken in as a member of the family and if they show love and loyalty that is reciprocated. They are frequently set free after ten yuls for loyal service. If a slave killed someone or performed a bad action, the owner must get the city council's permission to mete out severe punishment or have it carried out on their behalf.'

Kalliste's argument was forceful and the Eelfolk felt they would reserve judgement until they learned more. They still believed humans could own animals, but not other people. Bethel told them that in the Akkadian Empire and in Egypt slavery was the norm and the conditions much stricter. The Kretans were considered easy-going hedonists and didn't extract sufficient work from their servants and slaves.

Next quarter moon, a fox hunt took place from Phaistos. Kalliste and her friends were each fitted out with a pony and set off into the early morning. Hephaistos's hounds sniffed out a big dog fox. It streaked off through the scrub, which was dotted over the grass plain and interspersed with groves of oaks and nut trees. The fox led them a fine long chase and at last bolted down a hole in a bank. The sweat-lathered ponies first cooled down, then took a drink from a nearby river. Diggers were trying to smoke the fox out.

Aengus grinned at Orthonac, who had not ridden much before and was trying to ease his aching muscles. 'Come for a walk instead.'

They wandered over to where the bank petered out beside the river. As Aengus expected, he found a smaller hole close by the water. 'He's gone for a cooling swim.' Meanwhile the hounds found the second hole and tracked the fox to the water's edge, where the scent died and the fox was long gone. The pack began casting around for a new trail. Aengus and Orthonac walked their ponies for a few thousand paces upstream where Aengus pointed to a little promontory. Orthonac followed the line of Aengus's finger and spotted the big fox sitting on top with his tongue lolling out and watching his pursuers.

'Let's say nothing – it earned its freedom. Anyway, they can't even eat it!'

Most mornings, Aine worked alongside Hephaistos in the factory. He found her such an apt and precocious pupil that he forgot to make the passes he usual tried on pretty women. He thought her painting excellent and was helping her improve her carving and polishing. She was also learning to cut stones, execute filigree work in silver and gold, and build up bracelets and rings. Bethel visited them once or twice and the second time he ordered a commission, handing them his piece of amber. He requested a pendant cut in the shape of a labreus or double axe. He didn't need to warn them to keep it a secret. They had all seen Saba wearing her impressive amber bracelets – heirlooms from the Old One – which acted as magical talismans and toned so well with her auburn hair.

It was close to the spring equinox, which Saba always regarded as her birthday, never having learned her real one. She had counted back, with the Old One and Mara's help, the events contained in her life and knew she would be thirty-five this yul, with Aine and Aengus nineteen yuls.

Merer of Edfu, who had called on Saba shortly after their visit to his shop, had been telling her about many of the customs and inventions of the land of Khem. He found her highly intelligent and they soon became firm friends. After hearing some of her exploits, as stories of these had flown around the island, he used the Kretan word 'arête' to describe her, meaning not only supremely beautiful but valiant and heroic. He explained that the Egyptian astrologers, in their time calculations, divided the day and night into twenty-four fixed time segments numbered from sunset to sunset; each segment was designated one hour. The hours of darkness and sunlight naturally varied with the seasons; the sunlight hours increased as the equinox approached. She agreed that these were useful divisions of short time.

Amlodi had been practising for some time with the Kretan musicians to complete and polish his whale symphony. He loved the chosen venue, which was situated in the biggest natural labyrinth on the island in some hills beside a village named Gortyn, or as Saba laughingly called it, a half hour's pony ride from Phaistos. When the day of the gala arrived, all the members of Saba's group, except Bethel, were playing in the 'orchestra'.

Aine's painting, redone on a fifteen-foot-long roll of linen, like a great fresco transferred to textile and fastened onto two poles, was unfurled as a backdrop. It depicted a vibrant panorama of marine life and was much admired. It possessed a teeming energy that seemed to tap into the larger than life power of the music. Orcas formed the major attraction in it.

Orthonac had his high-pitched flute, the txistu, made from a vulture's thigh bone, which contrasted with the deep yet haunting sounds of Amlodi's walrus bone instrument, which sounded like a shakuhachi. There were reed and wooden flutes and panpipes. Kalliste handled a lyre and a lute which she had cajoled Aine to practise while on board the ship from Nar. Aengus borrowed one. All the instruments that had been played at Phaistos were there, and more unusual ones like pans of water, leather whips, rock gongs and rams' horns. Amlodi chose the harmonies of throat singing to exploit the acoustics of the Gortyn caves, where the sound carried over great distances and the cavern acted like a drum, responsive to every snatch of noise.

Saba and Bethel went to the concert with Ariadne, Hephaistos, Hermes and his partner Eurydice. 'Do you play an instrument?' Bethel asked Saba.

'In this instance I put a higher price on the intoxication of listening than on the joy of being skilful.'

The labyrinth was entered through a small hole in the hillside. Inside, passages and galleries ran off in various directions. They were given tapers and lamps. Without these Bethel would have been hopelessly lost, but Saba's years of training in the Raven's cave stood her in good stead. Many of the passages opened into huge caverns as large as the main one, lit with torches and lamps, where forty or so musicians and singers and most of the audience were assembled on seating mats. Saba thought an entire city of people could hide and live down here. Europa and some other queens hastened in and took their places. After a brief pause the symphony began.

The audience was transported to a great ocean where they discerned the waves and seabirds; lower menacing tones signalled sharks and monsters. Some deep voices sank below human hearing and the mimicked dolphin clicks could only be heard by those attuned to the squeaks of bats. Seafarers in the audience recognised the sounds of the great whales, blowing when they came up for air and slapping the water when they breached. They were enthralled by the long-distant humpback songs as Amlodi used to hear them underwater. The sound of the oars in Kretan ships blended with deep squeals of orcas hunting down seals. The audience was mesmerized and at the end went wild with enthusiasm.

Ariadne made a congratulatory speech to Amlodi, saying that his symphony aroused more feeling than any music played for many yuls.

She thanked all the players and singers and hoped they would play again soon. She welcomed the newcomers to the island and announced that because of their exploits and assistance to her countrymen, they had elected Saba, Aine, Aengus, Amlodi and Orthonac as citizens of Krete, an honour rarely accorded to strangers. Bethel was already a citizen and all the other visitors from the ship were welcomed as freemen, to remain on the island if they wished.

Europa reminded them that the bi-annual Minoan funeral games and festival of the ancestors would be held between equinox and solstice next moon at Knossos and hoped her new friends would all attend and compete in the sports. Kalliste had already scheduled herself and Aine for the bull running. The Minos had to choose a hero for the sacrifice of the Minotaur. Orthonac thought of putting his name forward and told Bethel of his intentions. 'With only five quarters to go you will have to practise every day. You must tell the Minos here and now, and arrange to stay in Knossos where the bulls are,' Bethel advised. He did so and was accepted gladly. Only a few brave young men were prepared to risk life and limb to kill the bull in single combat.

The labyrinth seemed so impressive that Saba wanted to return and explore more of the caverns. She and Bethel set out one morning on two ponies, bringing a supply of torches and lamps in case Saba wanted to dream there.

Bethel had been back to Hephaistos's workshop, for the amber pendant was ready. Hephaistos and Aine had made a superb object the size of a flattish gull's egg with a tiny hole at the back and fine gold and silver wire threaded through it with a strong silver clasp to secure it around Saba's neck. The twin axes and central body were cut and polished with a splendid simplicity. When the rough outer surface was removed revealing the translucent electron, as the Kretans called it, they could see a small butterfly trapped in the left axe blade and deemed it to be a momentous omen for her spirit life in the future.

Bethel presented it to Saba outside the labyrinth where it sparkled in the sunshine. She studied it for some time before allowing him to place it around her neck with a mutually passionate kiss. She was lost in amazement at the provenance of the jewel and still more astonished when Bethel told her that Aine made it under Hephaistos's supervision. 'It's already my talisman, worn for you three,' she told him.

Saba entered one of the caverns with interesting vibrations. They found a comfortably even floor to lie on.

The dreaming came to Saba swiftly – first earthquakes and a volcano, then tidal waves that devastated towns and palaces a thousand yuls in the future. A new race took over the island, replacing the queens with kings. They established a mind set spearheaded by an androgynous goddess, giving her name Athena to a centre on the mainland. From there, fresh ideas emanated through the Kretan world, around the Tideless Sea and beyond. She would provide inspiration to successive minds, sufficient to survive until the spring constellation of Aquarius. The avatars of that age would not be solitary males and females but amalgams of both, seeing the end of gender conflict and bringing greater light and consciousness into matter.

Saba had a vision of Athena: a powerful figure arrayed in Amazon warrior skins, with a little owl mascot on her shoulder and arms outstretched, proclaiming that to the sons and daughters of fire, she would give more fire. Her fire was a divinely energetic and transforming flame, provoking inventive acts of creativity. Other calamities occurred, with thousand-yul gaps. Each time the labyrinth served as a welcome refuge for those living in local castles and villages.

On their return to Phaistos, Saba recounted her dream but found neither Ariadne nor Europa unduly worried when they heard the timescale of the predicated disasters.

'A thousand yuls is a long time. I suppose most societies suffer dislocation within such a period. Not even our great-great-great-grandchildren will be around to see it.'

Orthonac went to Knossos with the Minos and learned how to fool and dodge the young bulls with coloured capes. His mentors, who thought this first trial would end in calamity, began to believe he might survive because of his keenness, strength and seeming aptitude with cattle and bulls.

Europa invited Saba and Bethel to visit her a quarter moon before the games with the intention of sifting through Saba's mind and discovering what this shaman could predict closer to their own times.

'After the games we should think of departing for Akkad,' said Bethel. 'Merer tells me that a mutual friend, who recently arrived from Ur, heard that the ancient healer I have in mind for Aengus was returning to Meluha.'

'How soon?' Saba asked. 'Within a yul, I imagine.'

'How long was your friend travelling?'

'Two moons perhaps, depending on when transport was available.'

'Then we must travel sooner and work faster on our Akkadian studies.'

The palace at Knossos was the most important on the island, several storeys taller and more capacious than Phaistos. The walls were covered with frescos infinitely more elaborate than any in that palace. There were street scenes that pictured four and five-storey buildings. They featured wide window spaces and dozens of people engaged in domestic, festive and religious activities. Many frescos showed repeated patterns of roses, lilies, antelopes and bizarre humanoids called monkeys. Entire rooms were covered with panoramic views of both pastoral and cult pageants, which made her feel as if she was standing to one side but actually living with the players, paying homage to the goddess of the mountains or pouring libations to the ancestors.

Europa lodged Saba in a set of connecting rooms that would contain all her friends when they arrived. During the several days they spent together, Europa asked Saba about herself and her ancestors. She was keen to know more of the Old One and of Saba's communications with her. How was she involved in interceding with the gods to rescue Saba's spirit when it lay in peril? How had Maeve's spirit been captured into another's body and taken away by the sperm whale to a supernatural prison beneath the frozen earth?

'This justifies our beliefs about our ancestors, that we are right to pay them homage with food and perfume and so keep them alive in our minds as long as we can remember them. They continue in our stories and legends, in our poetry and myths. They in turn will care for us, protect us from the ill wishes and mischief of malevolent ghosts and spirits. They talk to us in dreams and teach us to distinguish the wise dreams from those with bad advice sent by such ghosts.'

Saba nodded. 'You're right. And don't forget those priestesses and priests who absorb the food and perfume of the dead, who take upon themselves any bad fortune that may cause confusion in the exchange of prayers accepted or gone astray.'

The Minos was pleased that a stranger of new blood was prepared to mingle it with Kretan blood in the bull worship. When he heard that

Orthonac was able to perform as well as the other aspirants, he chose him as the current hero to represent the sun against the bull as hero for the Queen of the Night.

'The symbol of his curved horns can be seen repeated in the uterus and womb of every woman as a warning that the darkness is in us all. The bull spirit in woman bleeds every full moon. The shadow must be defeated by each male hero or absorbed by the female heroine to achieve greater spiritual growth.' Paulus remarked.

Orthonac looked at Europa for confirmation of Paulus'words. She nodded emphatically.

'I can show you the bulllike horns of the uterus image in the belly of any female opened by a vulture on a tower of silence; our mothers brought this religion of the bull god and his symbol inside our bodies, representing the regenerative potency of the birth and death shapes of the moon where it was worshipped for thousands of yuls in the Black Sea lands, anciently known in our stories as the sweetwater sea, before the salt sea broke into it.' Orthonac kissed her hand. 'I will not disgrace your faith,' he promised.

The festival games began with races, high and long jumps, hurling boulders, spears and flat wooden solar discs, wrestling, boxing, a sea-swim won by Bethel, and a tree-climbing competition won by Aengus. Everyone took part in some sport as a participation mystique to honour the Goddess of the Wild Things.

Next day came the bull running, when the young bulls were let loose among the crowds of people anxious to win fame by vaulting over their backs as often as possible. Kalliste secured the most vaults.

On the final day the bull fight and sacrifice took place. At the bottom of a terraced hill, hundreds of men formed a great square with long shields and spears, presided over by the Minos wearing his lifelike bull's head mask. Orthonac, with a couple of spare spears, wore a brightly coloured shirt and kilt with yellow and red stripes to indicate the sun. Two spearsmen stood behind him to drive off the bull if he was about to be killed. The bull was large and black with traditional horns curving skywards. Boys had been taunting it since early morning and by midday it was in a savage mood.

Orthonac had a gold and black cape big enough to hide behind, and by sweeping it and dodging from side to side could fool the bull as to the position of his body so that when the bull charged the horns slid past him. He also had what was called a muleta, a brigh red coloured piece of cloth folded double over a tapered wooden stick with a sharp point at the narrow end. This was used to defend the man, tire the bull and regulate the position of his head and feet with adroit passes back and forth in front of his eyes, hopefully to bemuse the bull when preparing to plunge in his spear. A spearman held each in turn for him. When the bull was driven into the square it made straight for Orthonac and the game of death began. Sometimes the bull charged the square, as though to escape, only to be faced by a wall of shields and many pricks of spear points. Within a half hour his shoulders and back were running with blood. The sight of this spurred the crowds on the hillside to greater excitement and they began shouting 'Kill! Kill!' The bull alternated between fits of fury and moments of exhaustion. Orthonac knew he must take advantage of the latter to place his spear accurately. Although he was much taller than the Kretans, the bull was big too and he would have to partially leap up from the front, gripping his spear halfway, to employ sufficient force to drive it down between the shoulder blades into the heart. He was also becoming tired and knew he must act while he still had the strength to strike home. The crowd was now in a frenzy of excitement. His own heart pounding as the bull halted, Orthonac dropped his muleta, leapt over the head and plunged the spear with all his might between the shoulders. The blow was strong and well placed but the bull's head jerked up and back involuntarily. The horn pierced Orthonac's thigh and they both fell sideways, Orthonac's leg still impaled on its horn. The two spearmen dashed over and lifted him up, disengaging the horn before the bull could roll further in his death agony.

Saba and Aine raced between the ranks of spearmen to Orthonac's body. Saba stripped off the costumed sash he wore at the waist and began winding it around his thigh, near the groin to staunch the flow of blood.

Orthonac's stroke had killed the bull and the crowds were shrieking approval. Many of them didn't even see he'd been wounded. The sacrifice was made, that's what mattered. The sun was victorious, even though he was being carried away. The Minos made a proclamation, praising the sun hero stranger who gave his blood to the Minotaur. He sent him the bull's cojones to be ensouped and help in his recovery.

Saba's swift action prevented him losing too much blood. She checked that his leg bone was only fractured, not displaced, and bound it up with healing salves of comfrey and oregano. The spearmen carried him to a room in the palace, and Saba left him with Aine who helped him to sip a reviving herbal tea. She went to wash for she was covered in blood from Orthonac and the bull. She hoped she had managed to stop infection entering the wound, but only time would tell. In any case, he would be out of vigorous action for the next two moons. Ariadne and Europa came to Saba's suite where Bethel and a crowd of friends had gathered to praise her. 'You have just demonstrated more of your talents,' Europa said, 'healing and speed of mind.'

'A healer cannot do otherwise.' Saba replied, shrugging.

'Now that you are all here, why don't you take the opportunity of seeing some of our small islands? They lie to the north-east. Thera has palaces and works of art as fine as any on Krete, although the island is tiny. Now the storms are dying down, the sponge diving season is open. That's fun too.'

Stephanie, who was now thirteen, offered to stay and nurse Orthonac. The honey had proved effective, her severe burns had healed well and she was delighted that her face was clear. Her brother remained with Hermes as a trainee sailor. An invitation came to take one of the Knossian ships for a moon. There were many in Knossos who wanted to get to know these extraordinary newcomers. Kalliste was insistent that the ship should sail directly to the Astipalia sponge islands lying to the north-east between Thera and the mainland. Then the passengers would stand a better chance of capturing some of the new season's sponges in fancy sizes and colours. Within the first moon most of the season's prizes would be lifted. The local divers, with their yuls of practice, would obviously be able to go deeper for the little animals than the amateur fun-seekers.

Ships from other islands like Naxos and Rhodes, and from Caria on the mainland, were there already. Sponges were in demand around the known world. They had a hundred uses inside and outside the household – in the bath, as dish and cleaning cloths, as swabs and pads in surgery, for painting and art work, as a portable lightweight alternative to a drinking cup for the traveller, as a contraceptive pessary soaked in olive oil, as supports for blisters and fillings for reclining cushions. The honeycomb species were the most versatile.

The ship bypassed Thera and sped on to the islands. Close to shore, sponges could be taken by dragging from a boat, but this often tore them. It was much better to dive and select the choice ones. Saba's group could dive for one hundred and twenty or thirty pulse beats, but the islanders and mainlanders could descend two hundred feet and remain twice as long. They laughed at the fun-seekers.

'Don't worry,' said Bethel, 'if you practise hard for a day, you'll be able to hold your breath twice as long and if you gather round, I've a secret to show you.' He borrowed a couple of grouper fish from a nearby boat and gutted them, preserving the swim bladders. He showed the little group how to blow up the bladders with little puffs of air from the mouth, not a deep blow from the lungs, which would not be good air, as much of the oxygen would have been used up. The diver then brought the contraption to the sea bottom, weighted with a stone, and gulped the air when his own supply was fully exhausted. In a couple of days they could outdo the native divers, who were jealous to find out the secret of the sweet air bag; and when they did find out they all blew it up the wrong way, with deep breaths.

One of the young divers from the mainland was outstanding in the water. Saba's group, who were all as experienced at swimming as walking, watched her with amazement under the rising sun. This young diver behaved as though she was part human, part-fish. She could swim at two or three times their speed or that of any of the other divers, her arms skimming the waves and flashing in the air or by her sides. She mostly swam with the up and down wriggle of a dolphin and seemed to shuttle just as fast underwater.

Aengus and Amlodi dived in beside her to study her incredible technique. She slanted a flashing smile at them, dipped her head underwater and disappeared. They waited expectantly but the water all around was a calm glittering sheet in the early sunshine. Then Aengus called out in surprise and pointed. They could see her head bobbing in the sea many hundred paces away. This time she flashed back along the surface. She was pleased to climb on the ship when invited and share some food. She wore no loin cloth and her dusky body was superbly proportioned and shining with oil, so the salt water beads on the lines of her joints glittered like jewels in the sun. Jet black hair covered her head in tight curls. Her name was Medea and she had come over from Caria with a companion who was back on shore with a bag of sponges. She spoke a halting Kretan with an accent that even Bethel, with his knowledge of languages, had not heard before. They became friendly and Medea took to sleeping on the deck. Amlodi was completely smitten with her. Medea reinforced the feelings of oneness with nature that he had developed with Saba and the orcas. He enjoyed with her, to the limit of endurance, the ravishing feeling that his life was blended with the flow of the tide and the course of the stars. He was always alive to the charm of beauty and Medea revealed to his flesh a sensuous enchantment with the yielding and yet mastering transports of a woman in love. She taught Amlodi and Aengus to shuttle under water. She swam hardly moving her arms, lazily wriggling her whole body; once in a while she would open and close her legs with a snap that made her almost leap out of the water.

To save Medea and her friend Zita from making the daily trip back to the mainland in their tiny canoe with their heavy catch of slimy trophies, the friends suggested that they hang the sponges in nets around the ship to dry and rewash. When re-dried, they could carry ten times the cargo. The girls could now sail on the ship to beds and ledges much further away for as long as necessary to exploit rich pickings. The others were surprised how their diving skills improved by descending with Medea and Zita. They were also shown how to select the valuable sponges by their softer texture, shape and colour. No longer appearing like dark blobs clinging to rocks, their purplish hues and sweet fragrances could be distinguished when raised from the foam to glisten in the sunlight. Saba felt sad that the sponges died so swiftly overnight while the hot air sucked out their moist vitality. Then all their lovely colours drained away when they were washed and re-dried, leaving wrinkled yellow clumps of tissue.

The first time a family of sharks went furrowing the sea with their triangular fins close to the ship's hull, Medea rose from a dive just in front of them. Amlodi dug his nails into the palms of his hands, petrified by what might happen. But Medea cut capers within arm's length of the monsters who, instead of going for her, hurriedly slipped away. She laughed, climbing up the pegs on the prow.

'They don't like the scent of my skin. Each morning I sponge my body with oil infused with ground rock dust and they turn tail when they think I'm chasing them.' She emitted a startled whoop and vanished in the water like a stone. She returned in a few moments with her fingers carefully inserted in the gills of a jet black torpedo fish which the others didn't recognise.

'These are hard to find. The sea god has sent it for you,' she said triumphantly to Aengus. 'I will help you.' She had heard with great sympathy of his phallic disability. 'In my country it is a cure for many ailments.' She held it towards Aengus: 'Let its head just touch you on the groin.' He was enthralled and nodded his willingness. His groin felt as if it was exploding, and he yelled and swooned. Medea dropped the fish in surprise and Amlodi caught Aengus. Together they lifted him back on the ship. He was numb in his hips and legs but seemed fine by next morning when he was eager to test out his cure with Medea, only to be disappointed once again.

Everybody was diving in the earlier part of the day before the sun got too hot. The following morning a dark, glistening hump rose out of the swelling water, then a dorsal fin, much taller than the sharks. Saba cried out and swam towards it. The thirty-foot body under the dorsal fin positioned itself beneath her and suddenly she was on its back, racing away at a phenomenal speed into the distance.

Bethel and the others guessed it was her orca friend but those on the ship and in the water who had never seen such a sight were horrified. When three more giant fins appeared, the swimmers raced to get out of the sea.

'Those are killer orcas!' shouted one of the sailors. Most of them had witnessed these animals ripping seals and sea birds to pieces. Even Medea the mermaid, as she was nicknamed, was shocked. 'It's all right,' called Aine, 'Saba is friendly with these creatures. They won't hurt us. You can stay in the sea.' The three others of the pod were moving around the ship and spyhopping with half their bodies bobbing above the waves. Bethel, Aine, Aengus and Amlodi jumped into the water and swam towards the orcas to demonstrate there was no danger. The orcas played around them but didn't show the intimacy that Saba's one displayed to her. Medea, seeing the great beasts meant no harm, joined them in the water when Amlodi beckoned, and was delighted to swim as close to the orcas as the others. Everyone else remained on the ships and boats in which they took refuge.

'Don't worry,' Aine told Medea. 'Saba will come back when they have had a talk in peace.'

'How does she talk to them?'

'That's a long story. They share thoughts.'

When an hour went by, most people either gave Saba up for dead or resigned themselves to a long wait. Suddenly they were both there in the water. Saba was laughing and patting the orca's back. All four creatures gambolled around for a while and Saba reintroduced her friends. The orca remembered Amlodi, who spent such a time riding on his back when towing the curragh. They soon renewed friendship with the other three members of the pod, and with Kalliste and Medea, who considered themselves to be privileged humans. Saba explained that no one else on earth cherished such a friendship.

When Saba's orca heard they were going to Africa for a yul – Bethel had assured them it would take that amount of time – the orca intimated to Saba that it and its pod would spend at least as long swimming around the world, as they customarily did, visiting northern and southern oceans. On their ride together, Saba told it all her relevant dreams regarding his race. She explained that in the world upheavals under the sign of Aquarius they would not become extinct because of their versatility, as many other animals would. She reminded it that they could communicate in dream through the spirit of Narwhal. It said that it and the pod would remain until the ship left. None of Saba's people were in a hurry to leave the islands, they all felt that Krete was a delightful place to live. A strange word came into Saba's mind by dream that night. It was 'hoonanea', meaning passing the time in ease, peace and comfort. She wondered if it came from the orca or from her old acquaintance the Root.

FORTY-ONE

SARAH AND ABRAM

After a storm blew them past Cyprus, Hermes's ship landed in Ugarit. They had travelled with Hermes because Ariadne insisted that he take them when Kalliste refused to let Aine leave without her; she was determined they would never be parted.

All the coastal towns and ports in that part of the world were now under the control of the Akkadian Empire, since the Emperor Naram Sin had extended its authority from the southern ocean to the Tideless Sea. Hermes warned Bethel that any persons 'of interest' who landed within the Emperor's jurisdiction were to be impounded and brought to Akkad, his capital city on the middle Euphrates, so he could judge how useful or amusing they might be to him. Bethel had little doubt that the Eelfolk, and Saba in particular, who could not easily hide her charisma, would attract his attention. Therefore, Hermes planned to bring the crew off the ship when it landed, leaving Saba's party to come ashore after dusk when they were less likely to be noticed.

Bethel had found an Akkadian clay tablet awaiting him in Phaistos from a kinsman of Sarah, with whom he shared the same father, asking his urgent help on her behalf since their father was now dead. Women in the empire, and all the patriarchal societies around it, were not free agents. They were considered too mischievous and, with very few exceptions, were under the supervision of fathers or other male members of the family until they married, when a husband or a temple took charge of them. Bethel and Sarah had been very close as children. He was very concerned about her and his intention was to proceed as fast as possible to Harran or Carchemish, where his family owned properties, and locate her. Their father had been renowned as a benevolent prince, but large numbers of his relatives and followers were not so considerate and he guessed that Sarah, who was always more of an imp than her sisters, would be accounted a nuisance and quickly disposed of. Her mother belonged to a sect of the ancient Sabian religion and his father had married her to maintain good relations with that tribe, which was spread across Harran, part of his principality. Their father, in turn, was a vassal of the Emperor. Bethel's plan was to sort out Sarah's problems, and since Carchemish lay on the northern Euphrates, they could rent or buy a barge and take it all the way downriver to Ur, near the southern ocean, where his friend, the famous healer from Meluha, resided at Enheduanna's court. He was provisioned by Ariadne with pouches of silver and gold to purchase all their needs.

His father once introduced him to the vicereine and high priestess of Ur, Sargon's granddaughter, and he knew his family name would secure their admittance to that renowned city. Accordingly, Bethel went ashore, engaged rooms at an inn and was fortunate to find five camels, which were as rare as horses. He ordered them to be made ready to travel at first light. They would follow the trading route north through the desert, and branch off to avoid the local towns and villages where inquisitive officials might hope to gain favour with the Emperor by seizing them. The three Eelfolk, and even Kalliste, were so much paler than Bethel; they would be too conspicuous. So Bethel purchased enveloping desert robes for all of them. These would be advantageous in shielding the identity of the owner as well as protecting them from the hot sun, blowing sand and chilly nights. He added camel fodder, dried dates, water bags and five knives of the toughest quality bronze. Everyone carried knives in Akkad and anyone who didn't was at risk.

In a city the size of Ugarit, walking after dark was dangerous. All sightseers and officials had long since gone home. After dusk Bethel led his little party, dressed in their desert clothing, off the ship to go and get a substantial meal. Who knew where they would have the next. Bethel asked the innkeeper about ferries to cross the Orontes river, which lay in their path, and learned that there was only one vessel big enough to take the camels they needed for the pack route further north. There was a contingent of guards on duty day and night, with a toll booth and lodges on each side of the river. It was the main intersection for goods passing to Akkad by sea from the Nile Delta and the Kretan islands. There was even a bridge under construction, said the innkeeper proudly. Their alternative was to aim for a higher part of the river nearer Ugarit and attempt to swim over.

As they were all excellent swimmers, it was the camels that concerned them. They were assured this particular breed swam well but were as stubborn as all their cousins. Bethel arranged a collecting point with one of Merer's associates for messages, if assistance or transport was needed. Hermes's sailors would contact them from time to time.

As soon as they left the outskirts of the city, they were confronted by the desert. The trio of Eelfolk had never seen or experienced such an immense tract of sand before. The impact of its bleakness awed them; the horizon was like that of an ocean – endless expanses of sand as dangerous as the sea. The tall dunes threatened to blow or spill over and bury like a wave; but at least one could swim up through a wave, not so with a dune. The only creatures they met were long brown snakes and scorpions. They marvelled at how the camels feet splayed out to prevent them sinking in the sand.

By afternoon they had rounded the range of hills inland of Ugarit and before long reached the river. Even upstream, it was a formidable stretch of water. However, the current was presently sluggish. The camels would not be swept away; they merely needed encouragement. Two people steadied each of their heads and tried to mind the packs. The camels were reluctant to enter the water and needed Bethel to follow and twist their tails. Saba and Kalliste took the head of the first, Aengus and Aine the second; then they returned for the other three.

The group re-dressed in their robes, refilled the water bags, tightened the loads and set off on the three-day trek to Carchemish. At night they curled up beside the animals for warmth and pulled their hoods over their faces to protect themselves against the insects. 'That's the last time I sleep with a camel. They stink!' Kalliste complained.

Carchemish was a small, ancient city with many gates in the protective walls and Bethel relied on passing through one of the more insignificant ones used by horticulturalists to bring their produce to the city market in the early mornings. They slipped through the gate well before dawn, just behind some farmers carrying milk and cheese and were happy to purchase fresh produce for a breakfast. The dates had been wonderfully sustaining but they were glad to get some variety.

This was the first Akkadian city the Eelfolk saw properly, for they had arrived into Ugarit at night and left again before first light. Massive guardian walls, six paces thick, were the first surprise. Inside were paved streets with channels down the middle carrying garbage and water. There was a sleepy watchman inside the gate and a stream of farmers carrying goods and chattering to each other. They had worked hard on their language studies in Krete and made themselves understood with the innkeeper in Ugarit. But the farmers' dialect and thick accents baffled them completely.

Bethel laughed. 'Not everybody speaks like them, but you will find the Carchemish speech different. However, the people you meet will also speak Akkadian.'

As in Krete, the streets were narrow except around the public buildings, which were also two to three storeys high.

'Remember this is an outpost. When we go downriver, we'll pass much larger palaces and cities. In Akkad itself, there are fifty times the number of people you saw in Krete.'

Bethel lodged them in another inn and led Saba off to visit his mother's family estate. They found two of Sarah's sisters with her elderly mother; they all lived on the same property. The Sabians were one of the old sects who still worshipped the great goddess, but surreptitiously. It was frowned on by the Akkadian state, which declared that the gods of sun, moon and storm were all male and supreme. Most of the goddesses were demoted to consorts, except in one or two cities like Ur, Lagash and Erridu.

Sarah's sisters hugged him and told him that his father's eldest son, by another mother, had inherited the principality. Bethel explained about his friends at the inn. Sarah's mother pointed out there were many empty rooms; they would be upset if the friends didn't stay with them. They were impressed by Saba and also amazed by her name, which was sacred and reserved for a goddess in their faith. Bethel and she had long dropped 'Sedana' – they were now too far beyond Er-rin and Garnac for anyone to carry news back. She acknowledged her title as Queen of Er-rin.

Bethel was told how the new prince, his elder brother, had married Sarah off soon after their father's funeral. Her mother's family was uneasy about the wedding. Her husband, Ruben, boasted a bad reputation, ill-treating his wives, slaves and animals. Bethel and Sarah were both thirty-five but most girls living in the neighbouring countries were married by twenty yuls. Sarah had never wanted this – she loved her freedom.

Her indulgent father had permitted this and overlooked her pranks and tricks, though other family members thought her father's indulgence of her independence was outrageous. They approved of Ruben, despite his morals – he was wealthy with an appropriate estate across the city.

News of Bethel's and Saba's arrival spread quickly and Sarah paid them a visit with four slaves in attendance – Ruben was showing his importance. She grabbed Bethel around the neck and whirled him in a wild dance. To her surprise, she rapidly took to Saba, recognising another free spirit. Sarah insisted on bringing Kalliste, Aine and Saba to buy more clothing next day; their desert robes were travel-worn and Sarah wanted brighter colours for them all. After shopping, they went, as strangers must, to worship in the temple to Shamash the sun god with Bethel, his kinsman Lari, and Aengus. Sarah's family was shocked by the identical likeness between Aine and Saba and couldn't believe such grown-ups as Aine and Aengus were her daughter and son.

Saba could tell Sarah was very unhappy with her new husband, who seemed a brute. She had wanted to marry a distant kinsman, Abram, but no one favoured him because he defected from the Sabian cult and seemed to be turning away from the official state gods to become a desert mystic. He owned an oasis near Larsa, was a pastoralist and disapproved of slaves.

'Why is the Sabian cult so different from the empire religion?' Saba asked Bethel.

'Sabians worship the spirits who control the star houses in the sky, especially Deneb in the swan constellation because she keeps company with the northern stars, the eternal ones who hold the world in their circle. Deneb, with her great wings, comes down to Earth and collects the spirits of our ancestors, then transports them up into the sky to the bear where the seven rishis protect them. So that's when we see her setting behind the burial mound aligned on the back hill marker. Then she rises again next evening and brings them with her.

'They also worship the Strider, and Sirius his son, at the summer festival in Egypt, at the site of the Lion Sphinx where Thoth and Dumuzi are buried beside the three geometrical mountains. Then Sirius summons the great Nile river to flood and yield its fertile mud for another harvest. The tribal name Sabian comes from the Egyptian word for star – SBA – that's why there was consternation when I introduced you as Saba – it's a title of the divinity.'

'Then you don't acknowledge the Sabian faith, but your mother and relations do?'

'Yes, Sarah and I used to discuss religion while growing up in our father's palace. We are free thinkers, but we pay lip service to other faiths to keep their followers happy. You know each city has its own guardian deity. People who argue and fight about a faith are zealots and bigots, but others pretend or fabricate excuses and start religious wars to conquer more land, slaves and wealth. All are destructive to our world and to themselves.'

'Perhaps a time will come when we can persuade Abram.'

'I must pay respects with my elder brother to my father's vault under the palace. We don't get on well with my brother so I won't bring you in case there's trouble. Sarah wants you to come with her to see how gloomy her house is and tell her what you think of Ruben. She hates him already and I'm worried she will run away. He is an important state official here representing the empire, and the consequences for Sarah if she leaves could be very serious.'

'I can't get used to this society of fear and domination over women. They are treated like children all their lives. I would never tolerate it.'

'Our Sabian race, who came here long ago from the Araxes plain to the north-west between the sweetwater seas, is one of the few tribes left where women have a high degree of freedom and autonomy, but not if they marry outside the faith as Sarah has done, forced by the new prince.'

'Your elder brother!'

'Well, half-brother,' Bethel conceded sadly.

'Can't she be bought out of this marriage? Or could you find some way to put pressure on the prince or Ruben? Do you know the Emperor? Could he sort it out?'

'I dare say he could but I don't know him and I certainly won't get an introduction from my half-brother or Ruben. They both know how close Sarah and I used to be, even though I've been away for so many years.'

'Where were you for so long?'

'Pursuing my training in Harappa, the principal city of learning in Meluha, for six yuls, then in Egypt and Punt for three yuls, Krete for two yuls and two more on the northern voyage to Er-rin.'

'So when you left here you were twenty-two and she twenty-one?

I'm surprised you weren't in love when you were so close.'

'We shared the palace with about six hundred others. Besides, we used to fight a lot.'

'So you probably were in love, or she with you, that's how attraction works, love and hate are opposite sides of the same stone.'

'But she was my sister, not someone to mate and have children with. I wouldn't think of it.'

'I was told in Krete that the pharaohs married their sisters.'

'They are supposed to be divine. Perhaps Hathor or Ra works a magic to keep their children healthy.'

It was arranged the next day that Bethel would pay his respects at his father's tomb while Saba paid an overnight visit to Sarah's new home. They set out on a pair of mules, with Sarah's slaves running behind.

When they arrived at Sarah and Ruben's mansion, it looked dark and gloomy. Saba tingled at the threatening atmosphere. In the reception hall, the keeper of the household told them this was an unfortunate moment: Ruben was disciplining one of his other wives because she spilt a bowl of hot soup over him. As though to confirm the excuse, a terrifying scream, cut off in mid-sound, was heard from the east wing.

Sarah paled. 'I know this woman. She was kind to me when I came here as a bride. I must intercede for her.' She hurried across the central court to the east wing. Saba followed. What kind of man was this, she wondered.

A scene like a torture chamber met their gaze. They saw a woman, mouth tightly gagged, hanging from a beam by her wrists about two feet off the floor. Ruben was a corpulent swarthy man in middle age. Not wearing his official beard, his neck looked fat and wrinkled. He wore a vicious expression, and the look in his eyes when he turned on them and ordered them to leave emphasised how much he was enjoying himself. His lips and chin were covered in blood. A massive slave stood impassively behind him. Ruben was systematically cutting strips of skin from the woman's body, neck to groin, back and front. A pool of her blood was collecting on the floor beneath her.

'Stop at once! You're killing her!' yelled Sarah.

'Hah! There are plenty more where she came from. She's an example for you. Make sure you never offend me. Who the hell is this?' Ruben snarled at Saba, who stared at him in a very strange manner. What a diseased mind! She could tell that, before his fun was interrupted, he had intended to disembowel the wretched creature. Into her own mind flashed a picture of Brude doing the same thing to one of the Seiors during the battle of Boand; she had been too late to save her then.

As Ruben swung his arm for a deep thrust into the woman's belly, Saba, who was taller, leaned over his shoulder and slit his jugular vein and trachea in one deft movement with the obsidian blade she carried hidden. The blood gushed over the slave who stepped forward to defend him. Saba's movement was so fast and unexpected that all the slave could do was support the sagging corpse. Sarah was dumbstruck and frozen. Saba quickly cut the ropes holding up the woman's wrists, laid her on the ground and ungagged her. She reached in the medicine pouch, which never left her belt, and forced some herbs into the woman's mouth to dull the pain of her flayed flesh. Sarah rushed to get sheets to wrap her wounds. Neither of them paid any attention to Ruben's body in the wailing slave's arms. Sarah yelled for the slaves to fetch salves to smear on the woman's wounds.

Saba knew the woman would live if she survived the infection that usually followed wounding. Another slave rushed off yelling to the gate soldiers for help – his master had been murdered. A dozen rushed in and stared at the scene in stupefaction. There was little time to collect their thoughts. Sarah took Saba's arm.

'How could you do it so fast! The evil brute! I can never thank you enough. But what shall we do, far from our own people? The governor himself will exact punishment. What have I got us into? I'm so sorry.'

'I had to stop him. There was no other way.'

The soldiers surrounded them and debated what to do. The leader barred them in an inside room and sent for the governor. Such a crime was too serious for anyone else to decide on the nature of a fitting punishment.

Sarah still had her slaves, who adored her. She ordered two of them to sneak out of the house before the news spread and a hostile crowd gathered. This was Ruben's domain and his followers would seek revenge.

'Take the mules and go quickly to my family's estate,' she said. Bethel would be back the next day and he was their only hope of rescue. The other two slaves brought them food from the kitchens.

Saba didn't seem as upset or worried as Sarah thought she ought to be. Perhaps she could not understand their danger, that as Ruben's assassins they would suffer torture and a horrible death. But Saba knew they both had a long future ahead of them and was not concerned; these events might open doors. Perhaps she could even turn the situation to their advantage. At least Sarah was now free. But Sarah was unimpressed. 'What's the point of being free and dead?' she complained.

'We're not dead yet!' Saba said, smiling. Her aplomb and positivity were infectious and Sarah calmed a little. This woman truly possessed great power, thought Sarah. Perhaps Bethel really had got lucky when he met her on that strange island – Sarah knew some of the story from him. Since she had met Abram three years earlier, she was no longer jealous over Bethel.

Abram came over as soon as he returned to his Sabian property. The news was all over town. Two women had been caught for killing the governor's marshal, and the governor was away, attending his Emperor in Akkad. A chief scribe now deputising for them both was petrified that if they escaped or were lynched by Ruben's people he would be held responsible. He knew the Emperor roasted men in oil for failure. He rode over to assure himself that the prisoners were secure and was struck by Saba's manner; she addressed him through Sarah. 'You realise I'm no ordinary citizen but a visiting queen from a distant land. Your Emperor himself will want to meet me before sentence is pronounced. You'll be in greater trouble if you do not send us to him.'

This was his way out. The relieved scribe appointed a royal barge to be prepared at once to transport the prisoners downriver to Akkad. He posted a full complement of soldiers to accompany them. He was taking no chances. After dark the two women and their slaves were escorted secretly from the house in a wheeled wagon and onto the barge, which set off at dawn. Once again they were closed in the central cabin and heavily veiled.

Bethel and Aengus came to Ruben's property next morning seeking news. One of the household slaves told them about Saba's interview with the scribe and explained that the two women were now on the royal barge. Bethel and Aengus noticed a tall man as powerfully built as Amlodi trying to eavesdrop on the slave's story. Aware that they had noticed him, he came over and explained that he was a friend of Sarah. He was visiting the city from his lands near Larsa and wondered how she was. Bethel remembered Sarah's recital of their friendship and decided to confide in him.

'You must be Abram. Sarah told me about you. Why didn't you offer her marriage before that bastard Ruben?'

'Your brother doesn't like me and organised the thing in my absence.'

Bethel remembered Saba's comments about petitioning the Emperor and her suggestion that they get a royal introduction. He respected Saba's sangfroid and ingenuity, realising she probably engineered the barge and escort as a way of getting to see Emperor Naram Sin. He told Abram, who looked distressed, that his party was going to buy a barge that day and follow the royal one down river. Maybe they would find a way to help the women. Abram begged to be allowed to join them. He blamed himself for Sarah's sorry episode and was willing to give his life to assist.

So it was that the party set off that evening, only half a day behind the royal barge. They expected in vain the prisoner's barge to put in at Mari for the night and Abram, who knew the King of Mari, developed notions of collecting some men, overpowering the soldiers and stealing the girls away in the darkness. At Akkad the royal barge was tied up in the inner harbour. The walls in the gateway beyond were over ten paces thick; they enclosed a square courtyard whose sides were fifty feet high. The gate was defended by turrets on each side, so that when the gate was closed, a small garrison on the walls could defy an imposing army. In the distance, rising above the two-storey houses and patios, they could see an enormous square temple, each wall over a hundred paces long with three flights of wide steps, hundreds of them. At the top was a tall square tower with a flat roof for sky ceremonies. Saba enquired what it was and was curtly told it was Nannar, the moon god's ziggurat. Saba and Sarah were marched up a wide street to the palace. It seemed that a banquet was in progress and they were confined in a small room to await the Emperor's pleasure. Saba sat down cross-legged and composed herself for contemplation. Sarah paced up and down.

'I wonder if my slave found Bethel or your friends. He said he intended to take a barge downriver. Do you think he will follow us?'

Saba didn't say she was already mentally communicating everything to Aine and knew precisely what they were doing. 'I believe that's very likely. One thing is sure, he and the others won't abandon us.'

Naram Sin was entertaining his provincial governors and some vassal kings and princes with the usual troupe of musicians and dancing girls. His sukkal, or aid, sat behind him to remind him of his guest's names and titles, which bored him. He only became interested when he heard news of a minor victory or insurrection. There were at least five or six every moon in his vast empire. Nothing was happening tonight and he was very bored. Administrators were dull people anyway but they were too afraid to say anything novel or witty. He only needed to raise a finger at someone and his guards would remove them instantaneously. Later, he might punish or reward and dispatch the lucky ones with a curse or a quip.

His sukkal whispered in his ear that two women were waiting below to be examined and sentenced by the governor of Carchemish. One of them looked highly exotic with red hair and eastern features. His Highness might wish to view her before the governor was alerted. They knew his penchant for outlandish foreign women. Why not, the Emperor thought, it would enliven his evening. Although middle-aged, he was a soldier and had kept fit all his life. He left the table and waved his guards to remain on duty. They entered the prisoners' room where Sarah was still pacing. To him, she was merely another raven-haired beauty of which there were dozens among his wives. The red-haired one, though, was a different matter altogether. She was seated, looking composed as though she didn't have a care in the world. She rose up in front of him like a tree unbending.

'I salute Your Highness,' she said in softly modulated Akkadian with a very strange accent. He started back. 'Who told you what I am?' He glanced at his sukkal who shook his head.

'I can read the thoughts of others. Permit me to introduce ourselves. I am the Queen of Er-rin and this is a kinswoman of my partner.'

'Where is Er-rin and how have you got into this situation?'

She explained lucidly and briefly.

'How did you know this Ruben was about to kill his wife after flaying her?'

'I read his thoughts also, Your Highness. Two good reasons for one knife thrust – I also rid my friend of an evil husband.'

'So what am I thinking now?'

'That I am a very unusual woman. You're wondering what it would be like to possess me.' He sneered. 'You might easily have guessed that.'

'Then test me again with something more difficult.'

He thought of a woman he had ravished on horseback during a military campaign in the Taurus mountains. Saba described every detail, including the fact that he had thrown her to his men afterwards, something he had forgotten. Naram Sin was deeply impressed.

'Suppose I keep you here and have this other woman executed for the assassination?'

'She is my friend and must be safe. Otherwise I will not read people's minds for you and anticipate your other needs.'

'By Shamash, you are a true witch. I'll pardon her also if you join me at once as you are.'

She nodded and followed him from the room. He left orders to feed Sarah and clothe her in garments suitable for the palace. The governor of Carchemish was informed that Naram Sin had dealt with the culprits on his behalf.

After Saba had spent a few moons with Naram Sin, the subjects of his palace and empire were performing their tasks like clockwork dolls – they were terrified of the red-haired witch whom he was treating as the new Empress of Akkad. He brought her with him everywhere – to meet his generals, diplomatic emissaries from tribute nations and city states, his own governors, the chief priests of the temples, the communities of Naditu, the merchants, chief scribes and tax collectors.

Saba read their thoughts to Naram Sin, taking care to reward generosity, competition and co-operation and resolving to punish the bullies when she passed on their thoughts to the Emperor. She never forgot the memory of her childhood tormentors at the Mother Lake. The result was that Naram Sin's popularity rose to unknown heights because of the good and clever judgements he made. Consequently, the power and prestige of the empire was enhanced – from the hostile Gutian nation across the eastern mountains which they raided for slaves, to the currently friendly Egyptians beyond the western desert, and north and south from sea to sea. His bitter rivals in several of the city river states ground their teeth when such news was reported by their ambassadors and spies.

Saba easily made friends with Naram Sin's tiger, which had been given to him when a cub by the King of Mohenjo-daro to grace his zoo and water gardens. It was stripping an ox shank with an air of quiet menace which changed instantly when she walked down to its enclosure. The tiger came to her and rubbed its head on the poles in front of her, inviting her to scratch its ears and cheeks, licking her fingers and purring and growling gently.

'Look at her magic. He's never done that with a stranger before,' marvelled the keepers.

Saba installed her friends in the palace. Aine, Kalliste and Sarah were her attendants, while Bethel, Aengus and Abram acted as emissaries and advisors. Every wish was attended to and they enjoyed their high status and indulgences for a while. So many institutions and social groups here were novel and sophisticated beyond their experience. But such tempered and tested adventurers were not prepared to relax in luxury for too long. Abram brought Aengus and Bethel to see his flocks and herds on his riverside estate outside Mari. They also went hunting and served as extra ears for Saba. Aine and Kalliste spent their time extending their expertise with the city jewellers and gold smiths. They thought the highly ingenious craftsfolk clever, but not as artistic as Hephaistos.

Saba, while still enjoying her new-found power and statecraft, wearied rapidly of Naram Sin and set about finding him exotic new playmates. She discovered his favourites were among the African races. Empire ships visited the horn of Africa for ivory, unusual birds, animals and girls. The Egyptian captains brought similar objects of delight from beyond the Nile, and girls – stately girls from western Africa, tall slim maids from the central lakes, pygmies from the jungles – beauty and allure was the criterion. For advice he still had Saba.

Abram enjoyed going to the temple to argue about religion and faith with the priests and scribes. They referred to him jokingly as the thinker son of Tera. His ancestors in the Sabian community revered Elil, the Sky god, as supreme lord of light and power. He was a transcendent first-cause god who ruled his people sternly like naughty children. Abram believed that the proper place of worship was on the tops of mountains or in the desert, but allowed that the ziggurat, the artificial tower mountain erected by each temple, was the holiest place to be near God in the city.

For the Sabians, the time of the great summer festival of Sirius and Dumuzi was approaching and Sarah demanded that Abram accompany her to Egypt, the land of Khem, with the annual tribal migration to worship and celebrate. She requested that Aine and Kalliste go with them.

Next morning there were loud wails throughout the palace. The body of Shar Kalli Shari, Naram Sin's eldest son, was found in his bedroom with his throat cut from left to right, just as Ruben's body had been found after Saba executed him. It appeared the killer was eager to place the blame on her. There were plenty of resentful residents in the palace to ensure this mischievous rumour spread like sand in a storm. Naram Sin brushed aside such an allegation peremptorily, refusing to accept that Saba could be capable of such a thing. She was not a blood-drinking daimon of the desert. On the other hand, she had killed Ruben, and did have a son of her own, Aengus, who might attempt to supplant his dynasty. His second son was only fifteen.

Saba herself was perplexed by the murder. She could not divine who the culprits might be. They were certainly not in the palace or among any of Naram Sin's followers she had ever met. She was esteemed in the city and the countryside. People loved her wise judgements and decorous behaviour with Naram Sin, who took her with him across the empire. The more she considered this situation, the uglier it appeared. Until the assassin was found, Saba and her children were in danger. They must either be imprisoned, where they would probably be poisoned, or disappear at once. Naram Sin announced she and her family must leave immediately until he ordered their return. They could go further downriver to his great aunt who was vicereine and high priestess of Ur.

Aine, Kalliste, Sarah and Abram were all staying at Abram's oasis. Only Bethel and Aengus remained in the palace. Saba could see the danger Aengus was in as a result of the succession rumour. They left that morning, incognito, wearing hooded robes on the barge. Many folk had seen Aine leave with Sarah and Abram a few days earlier and were confused about who had gone where.

On the barge, Saba retired to the inner cabin and composed herself to telepathise with Aine. She conveyed the situation at the palace and urged Aine and Kalliste to proceed with Sarah and Abram as pilgrims to the Lion Sphinx for the festival. She described to Aine the impersonation of Deneb she herself had planned to stage and suggested that Aine could take her place for the occasion, as she once did with Fion. She was still afraid that avengers of Naram Sin's son might follow them before Aengus even met Bethel's friend the healer.

During her sleep that night, Saba concentrated deeply on the Root, her old advisor, and was rewarded. The Root had put out shoots and branches. It was a prime mangrove tree growing beside the new lake. Saba congratulated it.

'I suppose next time I see you there will be an entire forest around you.'

'That would be easy. It's the pursuit of wisdom beyond dream we must engage in! Well, what are your current concerns?' When Saba told the Root what had happened, it was clear he wasn't interested in the murder and announced that it must work out, for her future was not over.

'How do you know it's not my destiny in another life?'

'That's true. Petty human lives are so brief.' He sighed. 'I see you are now involved with people who will cause a great headache for your world, in the age of the fishes and even into Aquarius. Three world religions spawned by Abram's transcendent god. Few fight as furiously as siblings of the same family of idealists.' His single eye narrowed.

'There is a succession of wars, deaths and suffering woven by Lady Spider. I suppose she has a greater design where mankind and nature, thinkers and feelers will learn to care for each other. The threat of survival for all planetary life forms must be faced before life from here can expand throughout the universe. Your descendants will stand on your moon and the moons of other planets that circle this sun and watch the Earth rising and setting. If the game is played correctly, life from this planet will expand forever. 'You are going to meet and befriend a precocious woman whose name will remain in history longer than the approaching wars, past the new era when women will regain their position of egality or gylany. Tell her my prophecy and that her giparu will hold sway in the top city of the Twinrivers again before long.'

The mangrove quivered before continuing. 'We may meet again before your final destiny unfolds. I send a gift with you – a device powered by the sun and made in your own future world. Switch it on in the rest room. It enriches the air you breathe – especially good for infirm patients like your partner's friend from the farthest east. It will prolong his remaining life span until his loved ones return.'

She found on her pallet a tiny silver box with a knob and grill on either side. She pressed the knob and felt on her face a little rush of cool dry wind coming through the grill. It made her feel refreshed and very wakeful.

The party arrived at Ur next day. Saba sent a clay tablet inscribed by Naram Sin into Enheduanna's giparu, or palace. An attendant soon appeared and led them to her rooms. They saw a tall, well-proportioned woman in her sixties with a delicate profile and gentle intelligent eyes, which met and interpenetrated Saba's. She registered the look of approval and greeted Bethel and Aengus.

'I feel your warm hearts, so would welcome you, even without Naram Sin's recommendation.' Her eyes twinkled as though she guessed the truth. 'At least remain in this community of peaceful women long enough to involve yourselves in our activities as artists, unless you wish to become Naditu.' She recalled Bethel's father; the priestesses had prayed for his spirit. Bethel enquired about his healer friend.

'His body was too frail to return to Meluha. He is living with us but needs constant nursing.'

'Can I see him?' Bethel asked.

'Of course! He enjoys stimulation. Did you know him well in Harappa?'

'Five yuls. He had a housekeeper and several foster children.'

'Yes, he still has a granddaughter, Tara, to whom he teaches his wisdom and lore.'

'I'm hoping he will be able to help our son Aengus.'

'I'm sure he and Tara will do all they can.'

Enheduanna turned again to Saba. 'My spirit guardians tell me you too are a dream woman and commune with spirits of great power. I would love to get to know you and discuss our viewpoints.'

Bethel went off to see his old friend while Saba talked to Enheduanna about Aengus.

'You have brought him to a house where sympathy and joy go hand in hand,' she said. 'We believe life is not worth living without universal love. Lao Tzu will cure Aengus if it is humanly possible.'

FORTY-TWO

TARA

Bethel returned eventually with a pleased look and told them that Lao Tzu and his granddaughter, who was already a yogin and healer, would both be happy to work with Aengus. 'Lao Tzu dreamt some time ago of my bringing Aengus here. In this dream, Aengus was named "the boy with the golden voice".'

They all went to pay respects to the old sage. His hair flowed long and white, and his visage wore a thousand wrinkles and a merry glint. He was lying on a couch with a rug in spite of the heat, and he greeted them by waving his fabulously gnarled hands. Saba, on impulse, presented him with the silver box and showed him how to use it when short of breath. He felt invigorated within moments.

A girl was seated with her back to Aengus. She turned around as he entered. She was of a svelte build, with firm, strong hands. Straight black hair framed the most strikingly beautiful face he had ever seen. He didn't think of it at once, but her face resembled Saba's and Aine's, except that her nose was smaller and her sky-blue eyes were even more almond-shaped. She had the same wide cheekbones, full lips and heart-shaped chin as his mother and sister.

She was gazing at Aengus with strong interest but frowned when he spoke. 'The rest of you tallies with grandfather's description, but that's not the voice I expected.'

'My voice isn't the one I'd hoped for either,' he muttered.

'Give him time. This is why he came halfway round the world, like ourselves,' said Lao Tzu. 'We will start lessons tomorrow.'

'Lessons in what?' Aengus queried.

'The way of all things and the secret of life itself,' he replied.

*

The four venturing to Egypt reached the Sphinx, or Hu as he was commonly known, at dusk when most pilgrims were squatting around their supper fires. Saba mentally advised Aine to be on site and prepared before dawn, to climb on the huge statue's back while it was still dark, and await the rays of the rising sun.

'Your Kairos is now at hand and you must take your chosen place in the world,' said Saba and told her of the star constellations which would occur so that she could predict them to the Sabians flocking to the sacred site. Kalliste helped her fasten the pair of white goose-feathered wings they had made for the occasion and climb on the back of the Sphinx. At dawn, when the sunbeams brushed across the great stone head, she stood up, naked, and sang the Sabian hymn to the sun.

This fabulous looking red head with hair spread, wings outstretched and sunlight shining through her like a flaming halo brought the entire audience of thousands down on their knees. It seemed as if the spirit of the Swan momentarily possessed Aine's splendidly formed physique, balanced on the shoulders of a sixty-foot-tall lion's body with its noble human face. Even Kalliste, standing ready to catch her, was persuaded that Aine became the apotheosis of Deneb. She didn't know that Aine and Saba had actually exchanged personas in the past. From that time onwards, the Sabians were convinced that Deneb had entered into Aine and she was now part-divine. Her every need was cared for. The Sabians, who were renowned goldsmiths, made a crown for Aine in the shape of a coiled cobra fixing its eyes on the beholder as a symbol of Inanna, the great goddess of both Sabians and Sumerians, and known to the Akkadians as Ishtar. It complemented the amber bracelet Saba had given her to enhance their resemblance.

Saba and Bethel were finding out what a remarkable woman Enheduanna was. She had been appointed by the Emperor Sargon when a young girl to be high priestess at the moon temple in the most venerated city of the empire. At fifteen yuls, she was the only suitable member of his own bloodline to rule there, having been a precocious child, able to read and write in Sumerian and Akkadian, highly numerate and already a famous poetess. She arrived in Ur with the chief Naditu from Sippar as companion and quickly learned to be as proficient a Naditu herself.

The Naditu were highly talented women who first lived in a female community in Sippar; later these communities spread to all the other cities. They could inherit and own land, slaves and property. They could be merchant traders, healers, lawyers and artists, almost always from wealthy families who gave them an excellent education and could afford to endow them generously when they became members of the community compound. Supposed to be celibate, they owed no allegiance to husbands or children, avoiding the hazards of childbirth and male domination. There were several hundred houses of Naditu and their servants lying within a walled and gated compound. The high priestess lived there too, in her own separate giparu that was superbly landscaped with trees, water and flowers and that emanated peace and beauty. Here she gathered around her the cleverest and most creative poetesses, storytellers and scribes in all Akkad for the greater glory of Inanna, or Ishtar as Naram Sin and his people called her. Naram Sin claimed her as his patron deity and cause of his victories. He glorified her through Enheduanna, knowing she treasured these myths and poems above all others in her dramatic and epic verses. He lavished huge gifts and many properties on her and her giparu to ensure the constant outpouring of her hymns and dramas to ennoble himself and the empire.

Daily prayers were offered on the ziggurats of the moon and sun temples, but in her giparu, Enheduanna maintained an exclusive shrine to Inanna, as supreme goddess of love and war, at which Naram Sin worshipped during his stopover tours around his vassal city states.

Enheduanna related to Saba and Bethel the story of Sargon's semi-divinity as asserted by Naram Sin. Sargon's mother, who lived in the king's palace at Kish, became pregnant by a wandering visitor, claimed by Naram Sin to be a godman. As a result, each of Sargon's descendants was part-divine, like Gilgamesh. Sargon's mother, terrified of the king's wrath, disguised her pregnancy and when the baby boy was born, put him in a rush basket and abandoned him, floating, in the king's watergarden by the Euphrates. He was found by the queen and brought up as an adopted child. He became ensi to King Ur Zababa, who was killed when Kish was attacked by Lugalzagesi of Uruk. In revenge, Sargon murdered that king and destroyed Uruk. Thus began his victorious road to empire.

Aengus was happy to spend each day with Tara. Lao Tzu explained that though he called her granddaughter, the title was honorary. Yuls earlier, Lao Tzu had been a monk seeking enlightenment and travelling west from the fabled Huang He river in the distant east for two yuls. He came across Tara's family in the country north-east of Kham. The whole tribe was dying from an epidemic. He did what he could to ease their suffering with his meagre herbs and potions, for he travelled light, even for a hermit. They begged him to take with him their little daughter of seven yuls who was not sick. She was named after the high Goddess of Kham, the White Tara, who would surely protect them both. They all knew the hazards of the terrible journey: south through the highlands of Kham, then over the passes of the holy mountains where the ice never melted and the only food was lichen and fungi, and finally floating down the endless river to Meluha and the hot lands. They stayed in the largest city, known as Harappa, where he hoped to continue his studies with the holy ones in their ashrams. It was there he met Bethel, a fresh young student of the mysteries. They liked each other and worked together. Tara grew up speaking her own and the Harappan tongue. She learned yoga and argument, healing with herbs and with sound; but Lao Tzu himself could heal by faith. He wanted to travel further before he died and Tara would not leave him, so they sailed on a trade ship when the winds were favourable for Dilmun and then upriver to Ur. This city was recommended to them, even in Harappa, for its high culture.

Aengus was making strides in his yoga lessons because of the attractiveness of his teacher as well as his desire to be cured. They began with the concept of breath as life force and air. She taught him to breathe with the required postures to develop his lung muscles. He recalled his diving practice with Medea and made Tara laugh when he told her about the shocking torpedo fish. When she took hold of his hands to show him the meditating positions, he marvelled at her fingers, so thin and delicate. Yet the girl could generate prodigious strength in all parts of her wiry body. Was it the yoga discipline combined with her natural vitality?

'You know a lot about music and voice, so we can skip over tones and scales, but for this moon we need to teach you how to produce overtones using vowels and mantras. Every day I will scan your body and aura, then allow tones to project through me into you. These will touch your brain, your nerve circuits and ki energy system. In particular, it will help your sacral and throat chakras. The frequencies and my visualisations will vary each day on the parts of your body needing healing. You must realise that the intentions are at least as important as the toning effects I sound into your nervous system while the movement is being visualised. This creates new connections and enables a body movement to be relearned.'

Their lessons were very intensive: twelve hours a day with breaks for relaxation when they played games and told each other their histories. Sometimes she allowed him to kiss her ears and neck, but that was all.

'When your voice is cured we can cure your other affliction too! Yoga trains a man to withhold or release his semen at will. There must be a mystical transformation where the male and female learn to become divine figures, like Lord Shiva and the goddess Tara. We find the full realisation of our nature through our love and empathy for each other. Love and worship of the human body leads to supreme bliss, which is reached on both the spiritual and carnal planes by our psychic interchange when immersed in each other.'

Tara took a waxed tile and drew for him a sarvatobhadra mandala, symbolising the explosive energy of the radiant and auspicious goddess Viraj, identified with Earth and sound. She urged him to repeat often the mantra OM HRIM in his throat, and then she danced seductively around him while chanting:

My singer, from that earthen drum
What sweet music you bring.
Who can bring such music as you my singer?
Take, take me in your arms
Sling me about your neck and play on me
Play on my body till
We give the drum's sweet note.

'Your mother told me you had a golden voice that would outshine the man you left on Krete,' said Tara.

'That was Amlodi. He could dispel darkness with light using his voice,' Aengus explained.

'You and I will do the same – and greater things. I want to use the healing sounds learned from my grandfather to extend his work, and with such a voice as yours, you could help me achieve things never done before.'

Tara didn't have Saba's ability to read human and animal minds, but she did telepathise with Lao Tzu and her friends, and soon developed it with Aengus when she learned Aine could read his thoughts.

Two moons later Aine and her friends arrived back in Ur from their visit to the Nile festival. Aine had also predicted, at the summer solstice, the immanent conjunction of Hermes and Deneb with the flood in the sky often depicted as the Milky Way streaming from the Sky goddess's breasts. The Sabians proclaimed Aine an avatar of Deneb and part-divine. The Sabians inhabited a colony in an independent city and trading port named Byblos, which lay on the coast between Ugarit and Egypt just outside the reach of the Akkadian Empire. They wanted Aine to come and live there with them as their high priestess. Kalliste was happy. It was but a short boat ride north to Krete.

Aine discovered Bethel's friend Merer kept his central trading base and shipping in this free port, from where he traded with Nar, Phaistos, Akkad, Egypt and the Black Sea nations. As promised, Merer would put a house at the disposal of Bethel and his new family. They would be close to Aine and Kalliste, and could visit their friends in Krete and other places when they wished, as Merer's ships shuttled between them regularly.

'All the Sabians I've met are so agreeable, especially your relations. I'll be happy to stay and serve them if that's what they want. Especially if my mother's quest is at last over,' she said to Bethel.

Tara came to Saba and Enheduanna one morning.

'I have good news,' she said. 'Aengus has regained his old voice.'

Saba was overjoyed. She hugged Tara tightly and kissed her. Then she asked if Tara would link minds with her; they shared so many mental qualities. Slightly shaken, Tara hesitated, then nodded assent.

'I have wondered about you too,' she murmured.

'We must hold a celebration for this cure and to greet your lookalike daughter and her friends.' Enheduanna gave orders for a banquet. A hundred of the Naditu were invited as were all Enheduanna's close friends, Saba's group and some well-known artists, musicians and prominent citizens of Ur. While everyone was finding their seats Aengus and Bethel carried Lao Tzu in on his couch. He wasn't going to miss his granddaughter's triumph. Aengus and his new friends were grouped with Enheduanna, who sat on the capacious antique cedar and gold throne that had belonged to the notorious Queen Pu-Abi, whose courtiers were all interred with her.

White wine from Carchemish was served with ice from the gippu storage pits. Tara and Aengus were hailed as the guests of honour: Ur-Nanshe, Akkad's most famous singer and dancer, was greeted with coos of applause. Saba guessed she was there to judge Aengus's prowess as well as to entertain the guests with her own program.

They served sturgeons' eggs, hot mounds of spiced rice and African pearly fowl that had first been seared in a tinuru, then finished in a domed oven for moistness and succulence – it was an Egyptian novelty. Next a roasted boar was carried in.

'What fun,' Aengus exclaimed, 'I haven't tasted forest pig since our feasts in Er-rin.'

'It's a luxury in our country,' Enheduanna explained. 'The boar roots up the crops in the fields and dies in the desert. There are no forests here for it. Unless you know how to cook it properly, it makes people ill, so the priests have banned it for the common people.'

'Our Folk eat it all the time. We also eat shellfish a lot, yet I'm told it's forbidden here because it rots so quickly and can poison the eater like a destroying angel fungus.' Many delicious dishes followed. Then it was suggested that Ur-Nanshe perform for them. She danced to flute and drum and sang a sad ballad of how Dumuzi was banished to the underworld. Then she announced that Tara and her pupil, who had lost his voice under torture and recently recovered it, would perform. Tara was wearing a green robe and splendid apple-green jade necklace given to her by her family on leaving home. She began by singing mantras, and then got Aengus to accompany her with vowel tones, followed by the harmonics of overtones, until each of them was singing five or six tones simultaneously. The timbre and pitch were amazing, and the audience was transfixed.

For two yuls, Aengus had been deprived of his singing voice; it felt as if his throat had been imprisoned in a metal collar. Singing eases the spirit's sadness and Aengus suffered constantly when he thought of his manliness, as ineffectual as his tongue. Then Aengus began one of his old ballads, an ancient one of the Mother Lake, filled with battles, defeats and conquests. It was a voice that carried one off and away with whatever emotions were being expressed. Spanning three octaves, it could be low and dulcet or project to a prodigious distance so that his listener's skin bristled. From high notes of triumph it descended to a growl lower than anyone thought possible, then rose and three or four differing tones sounded together. Not only the immediate audience was mesmerized, but people around the whole community and beyond were smitten by the liquid sounds.

Listening to Aengus's voice, Saba held Bethel tightly and remembered Enheduanna's fable of the mystery of the nightingale who sang away her life while pressing a thorn into her heart. It had allowed its blood to fall and encrimson for ever the petals of the pallid rose it so loved because the rose had relinquished its colour to increase its exquisite perfume.

Ur-Nanshe ran up and kissed Aengus's hands, telling him she had never dreamt a man could sing so enchantingly. She begged that their company set up a musical drama with supporting cast for Aengus and Tara too, for her singing possessed a low magical vibrancy. Aine and Saba were so proud of Aengus that they threw their arms around him and cried for joy. Aine looked at him archly. 'Has Tara cured you altogether?' Glancing over she saw Tara blush crimson and say, 'I believe so.'

The whole group, who all knew the history by this time, laughed delightedly and congratulated the young couple.

Sarah had no intention of returning to Carchemish and refused to meet with Bethel's step-brother. She could never forgive him for forcing her to marry, nor did she care to face Ruben's followers, who blamed her as much as Saba for his death.

While they were on the pilgrimage to the Sphinx, Sarah and Abram suffered bitter words about their divergence in faiths. The hurt was greater because although each still loved the other, neither would back down on their beliefs and dogmas, Abram being the more violent idealist. Saba advised Sarah that the best option was to hold a peace conference, compromise some of their attitudes and differ amicably on the rest. Abram was attending his flocks and herds on the oasis when Sarah sent him a message with Bethel.

'Be there at starlight, under the palm tree which faces the Bear. We will end, I beneath you, all the bad blood between us.' After this tryst she privately decided she would marry Abram and become a pastoralist. They decided to make a covenant with each other to reconcile their differences in faith and mores. Sarah asked Saba and Bethel to form part of their little council. It was agreed they would recognise and accept each other's concepts of the gods and their powers over man. Abram held to his stern but caring patriarch who watched from the heavens, but was entirely transcendent, all powerful and all good.

Sarah and Bethel's god lived in the heart of everything: humans, stones and stars. He grew and developed as life itself did, with the human mind spearheading nature's operations. God was as good or as fallible as man himself, developing and striving to be greater as consciousness increased. God, self, man and the tiniest specks of life that underlay nature were all equally immortal, because in their different modes, they were never extinguished. The cells died, rotted, regenerated and grew again, contributing to a universal mind shared by all. Saba was deeply impressed; from what she learned and understood of the Root's teachings, these two together must encompass the truth about the universe.

Ur-Nanshe and Enheduanna were writing and producing a musical drama that would embody one of Enheduanna's epic poems to the glory of Inanna. Enheduanna entitled her epic, 'The Treasures of Darkness'. As Inanna was an androgynous goddess of infinite variety, embodying the qualities of male and female, war, peace, love, death, rain and regeneration, they thought the acting role would be more effective if split between Aengus and Tara, each with half their faces painted as daimonic or seductive.

The drama described Inanna's courtship and marriage to Dumuzi in the first act, and they thought it would be fitting to devote these two acting roles to Abram and Sarah, with the singing voices projecting from behind the backdrop. Thus they could hold a spectacular wedding ceremony with their speaking voices incorporated in the dramatic performance.

The pageant, which was held at the moon god's temple, the largest building in the city, was a wild success. Sarah and Abram mimed the gods at the sacred wedding, and simultaneously participated as real bride and groom, eating fruit from the Huluppu tree of life in full Akkadian pomp. Ur-Nanshe played Ereshkigal and lived up to her reputation. The golden voice, beautifully supported by Tara, outshone everyone to the glory of Inanna who, as morning, evening and star of the sea, received her due.

A sumptuous feast followed. Wine, beer and myriad other drinks flowed down the throats of half the population of the city. The two proudest people in the building walked back through the cultivated woods, a little light-headed, towards the giparu. Saba, mother of the golden voice, and Enheduanna, the author and director of the concert drama, discussed everyone's roles and declared that such dramas should be a regular feature in Ur.

Suddenly, without a whisper of warning, blankets were thrown over Saba's and Enheduanna's heads; their arms and legs were clamped and tied, their bodies rolled up in large rugs and they were thrown over the backs of mules. They estimated the ensuing ride took them well outside the city walls, and ended in a building that smelt like a barn. They were lifted off the mules, unrolled from the rugs and thrown on straw. Then there was silence as their captors departed. By next day they were thirsty. Someone came into the barn, made a small hole in the two bags over their heads and dribbled water into their mouths through a cloth funnel. A voice spoke.

'You are being held for a ransom from the Emperor. We cannot remove the bags for our safety and for yours.' Who were these men? They spoke with a very foreign accent, thought the women. Later they heard running footsteps and a new voice.

'We didn't get the witch. She's been seen around the giparu. We'd better find out who we've captured.' This newcomer was apparently in control. He untied the bags and removed one. First he saw Enheduanna and recognised her.

'Well, we grabbed this one correctly,' he said. 'But who is in the other. We can lift the bag now. If it's not the red head she can't bewitch us.' When he saw Saba he started back, thunderstruck. 'It's the witch! Her magic has undone us! She can be in two places at once.'

It was indeed too late – Saba managed to lock eyes with him. The other guard didn't realise what was happening. But the hypnosis was already working.

'You can leave us alone, I want to question them,' said the newcomer.

The first guard left with obvious relief. Saba was now in full charge of the newcomer.

'What is your name and where do you come from?' she asked him.

'My name is Yurba and I am a Gutian chief. We are here to exact retribution in wealth and lives for those taken from our tribes in the Zagros mountains.'

Saba's eyes narrowed. 'I see it clearly. You are the one who killed Shar Kalli Shari, Naram Sin's son.'

'It was easy. There are thousands of Gutian slaves in the empire. They go everywhere and are not noticed. We can take their places and neither the Akkadians nor the Sumerians know the difference.'

'Why do you hate Naram Sin and the empire so much?' Saba asked.

'Because they never cease to attack us. They want to conquer our lands, but it's not so easy. We hide in the mountains and they can't reach us. They destroy our villages. The people who live in the villages that surrender are taken to Akkad as slaves. My family's village would not give up easily, but instead of praising our warriors for fighting bravely as we do among ourselves, they burned everyone alive. They did the same in the other villages that resisted. This war has lasted many generations and my brothers and I mean to end it. We are building a great army in the high mountains where the men are well hidden. When we are ready we shall attack Akkad, and all the Gutian slaves in the empire will rise and destroy their cities and villages as they did ours.'

Saba sat in reverie, visioning the truth of his story. She foresaw that the Gutians and their allies would indeed destroy the Akkadian Empire in the future; they would be aided by an exceptional drought and famine lasting several years. She foresaw that Akkad and most of the northern city states would be laid waste. Mari to the north, her own favourite Ur, the holy city of Kish, ancient Uruk and the other adjacent southern states might perhaps be saved but her vision for them was dark except for a vision of Namu, the youngest deacon of the Sin moon temple in Ur, whom she saw as the future king, rebuilding temples and ziggurats, city walls and palaces.

If the Gutian wars across the Zagros mountains and beyond had been cruel and unjust, Lady Spider was going to sort it out. However, Yurba was guilty of killing Naram Sin's son and for that he should pay. Naram Sin had been lenient with her; she would not repay him with treachery. This was a personal matter. Yurba must settle his debt.

'Now that we have seen your faces will you kill us if you can?' Saba asked.

'We must, to keep our identity hidden.'

She skimmed a few crystals from the chip of poison honey in her pouch and placed the powder in cups of brew for the guards.

'Give these to your men and tell them you are bringing us back to the giparu because a huge ransom has been arranged with Naram Sin and will be given to you on our safe arrival. You must find us two mules to ride back.'

'Yes, lady.'

When they arrived back, they found the city was being combed for them. There was wild rejoicing among Saba's group, the Naditu and the citizens of Ur. Enheduanna was loved by everyone. Kidnapping for ransom was becoming all too common in the cities. Saba charged Yurba to get on a barge going north, present himself to Naram Sin and recount his story. She asked Enheduanna to inscribe a clay tablet to go with him and give their opinion of what should be done, as her own writing ability was still poor.

'Besides I want to retain my good memory. I have noticed that most of your best scribes have weak memories.'

'How can you hypnotise someone for so long?' asked Enheduanna.

'I have given him mnemonics to repeat each sunrise to reinforce my commands.'

When they knew everyone was safe, Sarah and Abram returned to live on the oasis. Tara and Aengus were going to sail by ship from Ur, catch the monsoon winds to Meluha and savour the gylanic society of Harappa. They would take farewell messages to Lao Tzu's friends there, and explain that his illness prevented any hope of return and that he intended to shed his chrysalis within the city and civilization of Ur. They could visit his tomb by the temple where he had been made so welcome. Saba and Bethel promised to remain with him as guests of Enheduanna until Tara and Aengus returned.

'By that time, Enheduanna, we shall have written down many epics of all the countries we passed through, some of which we learned from your lands,' Saba remarked. 'You promised to relate, first, your story of Ziusudra, the great flood and the ark in which he rescued the creatures. They found land again near the sweetwater seas. For this the gods made him part-divine.'

Saba shared her vision with Tara and Enheduanna, as expounded by the Root, about the new Sky age, which would follow the Zodiac stars of the Bull, the Ram and the Fishes, when all peoples stopped fighting and came together to rescue their world.

The three resolved to collect and copy the myths. Tara would look for them in Meluha. Enheduanna suggested Saba compose and create new works about Er-rin. Saba now foresaw the value of stone carving and the baked clay tablets for writing. These would outlast other materials and be found and read again in the age of the water carrier, even if everything else was destroyed and obliterated, both from human memory and from leather and linen scrolls.

While researching in the cuneiform archives of the city of Ur, Saba was moved to pick up certain tiles from a dusty box. She found the script difficult to decipher and consulted Enheduanna. The tiles related an ancient legend. Many hundred yuls earlier, before the Akkadian or Egyptian empires began, two sages named Sesostris and Thoth from Ur attempted to visit Egypt by way of the southern sea and find out if some travellers' stories were true. The trading ship was sailing west to the horn of Africa, and they were told that the kingdom of Egypt could be reached by sailing as far north up the African coast as possible and going overland for two suns to a great river. They found a little port called Tumilat and a boat-building yard with a couple of Egyptian barges tied up at the quay. One of the sailors with them, who could interpret what the locals said, told them the barges had originally been dragged through the marshy land from the river named the Lord Nile, and were used to trade down the African coastline but could not navigate out in the open sea. Their ship had been damaged on the journey and the locals agreed to help some of the sailors repair it while the sages travelled overland with their interpreter. Yuls later the interpreter returned via the Tideless Sea and the Twinrivers, and related that the sages were revered and living in Egypt because they helped Egyptian priests develop a written language.

During the next moon, Saba and Enheduanna received messages from Naram Sin by emissary on a royal barge that bore inscribed tablets for both. He expressed his delight that Saba had found and sent the criminal Yurba to him. He had publically denounced the man on his own confession for the murder of Shar Kalli Shari and had arranged his summary execution by being boiled in oil. He could not understand by what magic Saba had persuaded Yurba to travel alone without guards and give himself up at the palace. Naram Sin's second set of tablets announced his gratitude to Saba and her entire family, and decreed that no further blame or rumour would link them to the murder. This news was to be promulgated up and down both great rivers.

The last tile was a personal entreaty to Saba to return to Akkad and assist him as she had done before. Conditions in the empire had deteriorated since she left. Droughts and subsequent famine in the north afflicting the fertile lands between and beyond the rivers were forcing large numbers of people to relocate. They blamed the Emperor for not interceding with the gods.

In remembered time, there had always been a surplus of grain, livestock and game. Saba pondered long on what action she should take about this entreaty. That he had not ordered her back was a promising start for their relationship if she did choose to join him again. She didn't want to return to Akkad. She found her new literary compositions enthralling. On the other hand, calamitous events were threatening. She understood the enormity of the approaching war but her prescience didn't extend to knowing whether the Gutian attacks would happen in two moons or two yuls. Having foreseen the general result, how useful might her efforts be to help her friends, or any parts of the empire, such as Kish and the southern city states?

To attack an empire with hope of success would require an army of significant size. Naram Sin kept a standing army of thirty thousand men and could raise perhaps three to six times that number. He had allies in the kingdoms north of Carchemish, but they would be nearer Akkad. Who would help Ur and Kish? Their garrisons were light, for no danger had threatened them in generations. She remembered the ancient legend she had found in the archives. Why was her hand guided to those tiles? She discussed it all with Bethel that night.

The main conclusion they reached was that the garrisons of the southern cities must be reconstituted so as to seem impregnable. Naram Sin would not accept any reason for that, even if Saba could persuade him of a Gutian threat. Enheduanna could help by offering prizes for proficiency in the martial arts to all young people, male and female, and excellence in education to encourage intelligent leadership.

'We should send messages to Merer and Hermes to meet with us in Byblos,' Bethel commented.

'That's a great idea,' said Saba. 'I think I know a way to entice Merer to link with Hermes and Ariadne in bringing ships down the Nile and into the southern sea. We can stay with Aine and Kalliste they can help persuade the others.' Saba also sent tablets back to Naram Sin saying she would act as his advisor on the condition that she spend alternate moons, or equivalent time periods, away from him to pursue her own objectives. Enheduanna was taken into their confidence and thought they were concocting a shrewd scheme. It secured her own future in Ur; she promised to co-operate in every way.

Bethel and Saba invited Tara and Aengus to go with them to Byblos to visit Aine and Kalliste and meet some of their old friends. They decided to travel by the mule caravan route from Mari across the desert, thus avoiding any embarrassment in bypassing Akkad on the river route without seeing Naram Sin.

FORTY-THREE

REUNION AT BYBLOS

Enheduanna promised the four adventurers that she would talk to Lao Tzu every day and procure whatever he needed. He was breathing better than he had done for a long time, thanks to Saba's magical air machine, and was convinced he could now survive for yuls to come.

The journey by barge upriver to Mari was uneventful. Enheduanna sent with them tiles of greeting and introduction to Enmetena, King of Mari. Saba knew they would have to buy transport and supplies to equip their caravan for crossing the desert and the two oases, Tadmer and Nashala. On arrival at the palace, which occupied a large part of a vast city, they requested an audience with Enmetena and learned that he was out hunting on the edge of the western desert.

Saba's presentiment that they would meet the royal party on the way made her decide to set up their caravan at once. She bought eight mules and ten pack donkeys for their baggage and gifts, and for the four servants who had accompanied them from Ur. She was determined to travel light, although it was customary for people of their rank and prestige to bring a much larger entourage, mainly for protection, as the western desert was famous for brigands. Water bags were selected for the animals, best quality barley meal for all of them, and dates and pomegranates; they would buy any other travelling requisites from the south. Saba took Enheduanna's tiles with her, leaving gifts for the king at the palace.

No one entering the great palace, spread over five acres, would have believed that fifty yuls earlier it had been destroyed by Emperor Sargon on his foray northwards to the Tideless Sea. He had also destroyed Ebla, one time pearl of the north, and its renowned tablet archive containing hundreds of thousands of records of trading accounts, history and religion from the earliest period of that city and the empire's civilization. The angry citizens of Ebla helped the new king of Mari to restore this archive and during the intervening years they managed to reinstate and enlarge it far beyond its former prestige.

Side towers protected the mud brick perimeter walls. Inside were a series of open courtyards surrounded by sets of rooms, many two storeys high. The internal room walls were plastered and painted with ceremonial and mythological scenes. There were public rooms for meetings and entertainment; two very large squares for caravanserai and bazaars where foreign and local merchants might bring their goods. The entire building was locked and guarded at night, as it held both the royal and the chief tax collector's treasury. Mari imposed a tax on all goods passing up or down river and on the transdesert routes of caravans from Arabia, Byblos and the northern cities.

Saba and Bethel assembled themselves with Tara and Aengus on the leading mules. Aiesa, the cook, followed and three male servants, who were all experienced fighters and handymen, brought up the rear behind the pack donkeys.

On the morning of their second day, they came across tents with a large number of people in attendance. It was easy to guess this was the entourage of the royal party, but they were surprised to discover them engaged in the sport of hawking. The King was entertaining some friends with a match. Saba halted and settled down her caravan to await the King, who was bringing his guests back for a light meal. She told the trio beside her to expect another surprise, and as the King's party arrived, his honoured guests turned out to be Sarah and Abram. King Enmetena was the first friendly and personable ruler they had met, apart from Enheduanna, since leaving Krete (or Kaptara as it was known to the Akkadians).

His Majesty was hugely impressed by the Kaheen of Er-rin, as everyone always was, and when he discovered she was unacquainted with the noble sport of hawking, he forgot his friends awaiting him and their repast and introduced her to his collection of falcons. They were perched on large boxes with broad top frames to provide support for their talons. There were six saker falcons, four peregrines and a golden eagle. Saba called Aengus to her side and explained to King Enmetena that she and her son were the only ones of her party unused to falcons, the sport being unknown in Er-rin. The birds took to Saba as soon as she spoke and whistled with them, and through her they showed a toleration of Aengus. Enmetena was so astonished that he unhooded all of them, even the eagle. Had they been dogs their tails might have wagged.

'Should we introduce our birds as well?' Sarah smiled impishly at Bethel.

'No!' retorted Abram. 'We'll show her a few tricks after the siesta meal, I'm hungry.'

Several large open-ended tents had been set up to provide shelter from the burning sun for the tables of food and all the people. Behind them, Saba noted the big broad-wheeled carts for which Mari was famous. The drinks were mainly alappanum, a barley beer flavoured with pomegranates, and himrum, another fermented beer with aniseed. Both were shared from large bowls using tubes like straws. The food was simple but sumptuous: bite-sized canapés on garlic-flavoured unleavened bread with mutton, hare, gazelle and locusts, roasted or poached; broad leaves spread with fruits, shoots, bulbs and seeds dipped in sweet or bitter juices; mersum cakes with pistachio nuts.

The king shared his drinking bowl with Saba, Abram and Sarah as the principal guests. They discussed the progress of their match. Ten casts were flown by each party during the morning, with the weights of the quarry deciding the winner. So far the weights were adjudged equal. They agreed that two more casts each should decide the match, to be restarted after the siesta.

When Sarah and Abram learned the reasons for the caravan heading to Byblos, they decided that they very much wanted to join Saba and the others. Sarah wanted to get to know Aine a lot better, especially since she had been appointed to such an honoured position as titular leader of the Sabians in Byblos, the religion of Sarah's family. She and Abram had heard so much about the calibre of the friends who shared the family's adventures in such exotic lands that they could not resist what might be the only chance of ever meeting them.

Enmetena ensured there were fully shaded tents for the siesta. He invited Saba's party to return and spend a few nights in Mari with Abram and his wife, but Saba begged to be excused; she would accept his invitation at a future date. When all were rested, the sporting party set out once again with dogs and beaters. The King was insistent that Saba take one of the casts, preferably using his bird. After some argument it was agreed she would fly one bird for each party to allow her skill, or lack of it, to be shared equally, and to make the match more exciting, she would take the last flight for each. For the eleventh cast, each sent out a peregrine falcon and each bird brought back a hare. 'Beyond doubt the gods oversee this bout,' declared Enmetena. 'I will have the last cast of the day.' Saba flew Abram's peregrine on hearing the beater's cry and when the bird did not return, two dogs raced off to help carry back the catch. They returned sharing a great bustard in their mouths.

'You won't catch much heavier than that!' gloated Abram at Enmetena.

Enmetena sneered haughtily at Saba. 'Never fear, the god Shamash will not deny me.'

He turned around and selected his golden eagle. Bethel protested the bird was too heavy and dangerous for Saba but she shrugged and pointed out that a god was going to decide everything. Aengus grabbed an extra thick leather sleeve from Abram to protect Saba's arm before the eagle was given to her. It glanced at her with fiercely searching eyes, meeting a hypnotic stare equally unnerving. It seemed eager to spring, so she hoisted it upwards and it soared away with what seemed to the waiting group an amazing momentum.

'Congratulations! A superb cast. I knew you would not fail me.' Enmetena grasped her arms with emotion.

'I'll wager a knuckle of gold the eagle will win,' called Aengus, but no one took him on. Abram's party were angry at such an unsporting gesture, using an eagle when the opponent had none to match it.

Saba turned to Aengus. 'It's a pity your father was not here to accept your bet. He could never resist one.'

After what seemed an interminable wait, a dot appeared in the sky and rapidly grew larger. The eagle was carrying what seemed a heavy prey. To everyone's bewilderment he dropped his quarry in front of Enmetena then returned directly to Saba's arm. Abram and his party glared at it in silence and Enmetena said nothing. The quarry was certainly heavier than a great bustard. It was, in fact, a young goat.

'I thought the match was for game. Is that game?' asked Bethel mischievously.

Saba gave the eagle back to her handler with a stroke and a series of low whistles.

'Did you communicate with her?' queried Tara. 'It's not like talking,' Saba replied. 'I'll explain this kind of empathy when we have lots of time.'

'I'll wait as long as it takes, because I'm deeply curious,' murmured Tara quietly.

'Join me. I'm first in line,' whispered Bethel as Enmetena began talking with Abram.

'Shamash has put down my pride most prettily for choosing to win our match with this goat and therefore disqualifying my eagle.' The courteous apology mollified Abram, for he clasped Enmetena by the hand. 'I look forward to many contests in the future.'

'Indeed, and I hope you will bring this good queen with you when you visit. I would invite her and her consort to honour me by joining my court but I hear she has already refused to rejoin the Emperor's council, where her advice shone like a star across his dominions.'

'Your Majesty is better informed than I, but I will let her speak for herself,' replied Abram.

'Thank you,' said Saba. 'But I would prefer to remain with our good friend Enheduanna and strive with her to enhance the culture of that ancient city.'

'I will offer prayers for your endeavours. Mari has been a great city state several times before too. We all live in the favour of the gods.'

Abram offered his apologies for not returning to the palace this time, as he and Sarah intended to accompany Saba's party. They took their leave of Enmetena. It was close to evening and they decided to spend the night there and depart early in the morning. As they entered Abram's lands, Sarah showed Saba and Tara the couple's pine tree and told them how they reconciled their differences.

With his abilities restored, Aengus found his old forgotten enthusiasms flowing back like a dammed up stream that had been released. Next day he took one of the hunting bows and pointed his mule into the desert. Towards evening, Tara began looking anxiously towards the south. Then she brightened.

'I see him on the distant dune,' she called. 'Good,' growled Bethel. 'I've an appetite for a bit of fresh meat. Let's halt and light a fire.'

'How do you know he's killed anything?' Abram asked. 'I've long experienced his hunting skills and I'd wager anything on him.'

'In that case I won't take you up.' Abram smiled. They did light a fire and eventually Aengus plodded into camp with a young oryx buck draped over the mule's back, placed to permit the very long horns to point backwards and not to annoy the mule. 'I wasn't sure the mule could carry anything heavier in the sand, or if I could even lift it,' Aengus said bashfully under a shower of congratulations. Abram's servants hauled the buck down and set about flaying him and grilling choice cuts from loins and pluck on the hot embers of the fire. 'We will not lack fresh meat this trip. There are large numbers of these animals around but I saw no sign of any water – not even a dew pond,' Aengus remarked. 'They find sufficient to drink from the desert itself. As far as I know, oryx are the only ones who can,' Abram told him. 'They sip the morning dew from dried-up scrub tips and cobwebs, so they are very active before the sun rises. They also dig up succulent roots and bulbs.'

The evening was still warm and Aengus was hot and dusty after his hunt. He removed his vest and kilt and Tara brought a wet cloth to rub him down. Since his cure, Aengus was much more confident of his physique and fitness, and he became once again a splendid figure of young manhood. Tara was equally athletic in appearance thanks to her yoga practice. Her svelte, wiry figure contrasted with the rugged frame that Aengus had inherited from Fion, so that the eyes of all, even the servants, were drawn towards them and their obvious devotion to each other.

'To celebrate the return of your skills, I suggest we prepare to re-enact a devotion of love to the goddess tonight,' Tara whispered. Aengus grinned and nodded firmly. If anyone were listening after the group retired for the night, a series of sounds and mantras might have been detected issuing from a particular tent. This precipitated an electrical excitement akin to that generated in the air before a violent mountain or desert thunderstorm. It seemed to permeate the fabric of their tent.

'That must be an entrancing performance,' Bethel whispered to Saba. 'Yes, Tara was explaining many of the asanas and mudras to me. Part of the ritual requires the extra development of the thorax and sphincter muscles in man and woman. This enables her to lock him in at will and with his help, prolong his erection for extended periods and control ejaculations. They can also generate electrical and spiritual power from these organs through their spines to parts of their heads and achieve ecstatic trances.'

'If God allows them to do these things, as Abram would say, surely he would allow us also. Could you teach me?'

'With pleasure, my darling. We might require some instruction and training, but I'm sure Tara would be glad to help us.'

'Do you think she understands lucid dreaming? If not we could exchange that information with her.' Saba agreed. 'I'm sure we can teach one another a great deal. Do you think Tara's rituals would appeal to Abram's strict codes?' Bethel slapped his thigh. 'That could be very funny. I can just picture his reaction, and Sarah would be in fits. However, I'm not broaching the subject before this caravan trek ends – it's going too smoothly. Perhaps in Byblos if we are having fun some evening.'

'We will be there soon – the day after tomorrow. That oasis Tadmer was halfway. I am looking forward to seeing Amlodi again.'

'How do you know he's coming?'

'I can see him talking to Hermes on his ship. But they have not left yet. They are waiting for others – and I don't know who, before you ask me.' Bethel hugged her. 'Let's sleep, it will soon be morning.'

Byblos was a surprise. The outlying state lands did not extend as far as those of Mari, but the inner city was much larger, with more shops than they'd seen elsewhere. The streets were well tiled and very clean. The central drainage channels appeared to be cleared daily. Many of the buildings were three storeys high with the usual flat roofs and were constructed around central courtyards. They stabled their animals off a large square prepared for traders, with lots of accommodation like the one in Mari's palace. Saba wanted to surprise Aine and Kalliste. They entered the city anonymously, without fuss, and sent to enquire where the principal habitation of the Sabians lay. It turned out to be a small palace overlooking the sea and housing fifty or more people. The girls, as Saba still thought of them, rushed to greet them with cries of delight. Aine pretended to be annoyed that Saba had not telepathised with her in advance and dispatched servants to go and procure a range of extra provisions with which they could entertain their beloved friends.

'Have you rooms for us all?' Aengus asked. 'Of course, and for whoever is coming on this Kretan ship Saba is talking about,' Aine replied.

'We'll have time to compose ourselves and look around the city,' Sarah remarked. 'I suppose most people can speak Akkadian?'

'Yes, and Egyptian,' Kalliste volunteered. 'Although the buildings and decorations look Kretan, the customs and manners here are more Egyptian. I don't think you've met Bethel's friend Merer. His palace is close to ours. In fact, he found this building for us and sold it to the Sabians.'

Bethel laughed uproariously. 'The cunning dog, he probably owned it himself. Wait until I see him.'

'Do the ladies' shops have dressmakers?' Tara asked Kalliste who seemed the most style conscious. 'Indeed they do. I've found a clever seamstress who can run up any style. But I prefer the Kretan clothes and she has made me dresses from the most superb coloured silk. That's a fabulous material, thin and light as a cobweb, from somewhere in the far distant east. I'm told it takes about two years by caravan to bring it here.'

'I've journeyed part of that route with my guru. It's very difficult, so I imagine the cloth must be as expensive as rare spices,' said Tara. 'I suspect it is. I wasn't allowed to pay for it. Merer presented it to me as a gift. You see, because Aine is now their leader, she's not allowed to buy anything – the Sabians would be offended.'

'Is that not embarrassing for her?'

'Yes, but she's getting used to it. She returns the compliment by giving up a lot of her time to their ceremonies. I can get Merer to buy me things that make Aine feel less pampered, and if something is too expensive, I know my mother will reimburse him. They work in partnership with their trading ships.'

Within a few days the Kretan ship arrived in the harbour carrying, to everyone's surprise, Kalliste's mother, Queen Ariadne. To her chagrin, the current consul of the city was not there to greet her. Kalliste explained that the ceremonials of Byblos were as egalitarian as its code. Unlike the pomp of Egypt and its 'god king', the city was ruled by a republican council and three elected consuls who shared the tri-yul term of office between them.

'We couldn't notify him because we didn't know you were coming,' explained Kalliste.

'Surely Saba foresaw that? I thought she could foresee everything,' Ariadne retorted.

'Well, she obviously didn't see that.'

'I wonder! Perhaps because she is so powerful over here, little slights don't matter,' said Ariadne.

'Mother! She would never even think of slighting you.'

'That's just the trouble. Anyhow let's forget it.'

Amlodi was embracing his companions and getting to know Sarah and Abram. 'I've really missed you all, especially working with Aine and her musical illustrations. Have you painted any more since we parted, Aine?'

'Sadly no. I missed your encouragement, so Kalliste and I have been working with metals and gemstones. There are so many new techniques in Akkadia and Egypt for us to copy. Later we will show you all some of our efforts.'

'Yes, you should see Aine's scarabs from lapis lazuli set in silver and gold. They are stunning.'

'So is Kalliste's silver lyre,' Aine added.

'Amlodi, you are the man I need to help me tune the strings,' said Kalliste, grasping him by the arm and giving him her most appealing look.

'How could I refuse!' Amlodi said, grinning with delight.

'It looks like we have lots to get on with,' said Hermes cheerfully. 'I can't wait to hear these new plans Saba is proposing. When is Merer coming? I believe we need his presence to complete our council.'

'He's coming for supper this evening,' Aine replied.

'In the meantime, show us some of these precious toys,' Ariadne said, taking Kalliste's hand.

FORTY-FOUR

PEPY'S PYRAMID

Supper was coming to an end. The assembly sat grouped around low tables, sipping wine and munching pistachio nuts. Merer, seated beside Saba and Tara, was his usual merry and mysterious self.

Saba began by describing her experiences with the Gutians, from the occasion of Shar Kalli Shari's assassination to her capture and dispatch to Naram Sin of the Gutian chief. Her searches into the future confirmed the threats to the Akkadian Empire made by the Gutians, threats that Naram Sin refused to take seriously enough to strengthen the weak garrisons of the southern city states. Saba was determined to save them, Ur in particular, by doubling the numbers of fighting men in the garrisons.

'It's the next part of the plan that will interest you, my friends,' Saba stated. 'We will need a fleet of ships to transport the men. They need to be of the same calibre as the Kretan transport ships and able to cross the rough seas of the southern ocean – nothing like the Egyptian flat barges used on the Nile or along the coast to Punt to fetch slaves and trade goods.'

On a signal, Merer handed her a sheet of papyrus, pens and ink upon which she began drawing a map of the Nile Delta, the Gulf and the Red Sea.

'You will all notice that the top of the gulf is almost level with the nearest delta river on the Byblos side, where it joins the Nile, and the land between is flat and marshy. No hills or rough terrain. A wide three-runner sleigh could be dragged across by mule. Now, six ships could be partially dismantled, dragged across and reassembled at the head of the gulf. These ships could recruit fighting men from the famous Punt warrior tribes, that the Pharaoh uses in his army, and bring them to train in the lower city states.

'You may well ask, why go to all this trouble and expense to save the city states?' Saba continued. 'What then do we do with the fleet of ships? We use them to carry freight from Meluha and Punt to Byblos. By using large containers that are sealed in Kuntasi or Mohenjo-daro and loaded directly onto the deck with the same kind of hoist, or sheer legs, which the brilliant architect Imhotep designed to lift the giant blocks of stone when building the mighty pyramid of Khufu. A pair of legs could be constructed on the deck of each ship and on the deck of the Nile barge, meeting each crate and loading it from the sleigh in the delta to convey it to Byblos harbour. Only when landed will the seal be broken and the crate opened. This will prevent accidental loss and pilfering of the cargo, a lot will be of precious spices.'

'Each crate would have to be made of thick hardwood to be really secure,' Merer observed. He had been following Saba's account with great eagerness.

'It's a truly ingenious plan, and one which could yield vast profit,' Hermes declared.

'True, but there are lots of imponderables to overcome. I wonder, is it possible?' Ariadne queried.

'We would need to examine it in minute detail – especially the delta section – but I believe it just might be technically feasible,' Saba replied. Merer grinned. 'Whoever does it will not be popular with the Akkadians.'

'Perhaps. As Saba foresees, their empire won't be there anymore,' Aengus quipped.

'Ah! But there were caravans travelling the ancient silk road before the Akkadian Empire existed. The local toll towns will still be there also,' Bethel pointed out.

'Then they may have to go to Meluha to collect their tolls,' Aengus objected.

'This mighty scheme will take time to organise. How do we know it will be ready before the Gutians attack?' Ariadne asked.

'I don't know for sure, Ariadne. Within a yul or two at most. There may just be time. But your and Hermes's ships will continue to trade long after.'

'There is one major permission required – that of the Pharaoh Pepy and perhaps his Vizier, since the Pharaoh is old and unwell,'

Merer pointed out. 'This matter will require considerable negotiation with him and his advisors.'

'That will be our first priority. I'm sure you must have met Pharaoh Pepy. Is he amenable to argument? What are his interests?' Saba asked and drew Merer aside.

'I do know him,' said Merer. He is the most astute old fox I've ever met and will seek a large share in the enterprise. As to interests, he and his Queen Neitkrety are fond of theology and music.'

'I must start learning his language at once. Can you arrange it?'

'Of course. At the speed you mastered Akkadian, it won't take long.'

His eyes rested caressingly on her labreus pendant with the tiny butterfly trapped inside the left axe blade. 'It's my favourite amulet,' Saba said. 'I need all the protection available. These are dangerous days.'

'I offer you my life as protection, Bethel apart.'

'I appreciate your offer and I know you mean it.' Saba glanced up quickly to see Ariadne staring at her. 'I fear not everyone thinks so kindly of me.' Tara stepped across to them. 'My new mother has given us much to think about and sleep on. We should continue our deliberations tomorrow. Rest well, Merer. I would like to discuss how some Egyptian and Meluhan customs blend so well in Byblos society.'

'I am at your disposal, beautiful lady.' He took her hand and kissed it.

Next day, Merer dispatched a team of professionals to the delta to test some of Saba's ideas. Hermes and Ariadne declared themselves in favour of the scheme, so long as everything else proved feasible. They would provide the ships and open seafaring experience. Hermes and Merer held long talks with their technical staff about the feasibility of what they called the delta scheme and eventually decided all the challenges could be met. Saba, Aine and Amlodi began exchanging ideas with Tara and Aengus about preparing a version of his whale symphony to play in front of Pharaoh Pepy and Queen Neitkrety in Memphis, the royal capital.

Merer sent his emissaries to Memphis to request a private audience with Pharaoh Pepy. The whole matter must be kept utterly secret as anyone not involved might was a potential enemy: the proposed shipping route would overturn all existing trading customs and revenues derived from goods out of Meluha and the east. It was fortunate that Merer's rank in Egypt entitled him to a sufficiently high status to be granted a one-to-one meeting with Pepy himself; the plan need not be shared with the horde of avaricious grandees guarding the steps to the throne. He knew that the Vizier and Queen Neitkrety were party to all the Pharaoh's secrets and would have to be informed, but at least he might get first strike, and even introduce Saba for a private audience before other, possibly biased, opinions could interfere and cast a shadow on the venture.

Merer decided he would use the announcement of the musical concert with an innovative theme of orchestrated animal sounds as the principal reason for their visit. This might disarm any curiosity about his request for a private audience with the Pharaoh, whose intense interest in music was widely known. His need to question several of the exceptional performers would be understood.

The barges bound for Memphis eventually included the entire party from the first evening, for all of them wanted to experience the famous centre of luxury and power from such an elevated perspective as that afforded to an ambassadorial mission. Ariadne was determined that her status as a Queen of Krete should be held in higher regard than a queen of some mere northern island, of which no one in the civilized world had heard. As to magicians and Seers, they were common in the court of the Pharaoh and among the priests of the Temple of Amon.

While they proceeded in litters towards royal apartments appointed for them in Memphis, they were amazed at the immense size of the state buildings and temples. Erected as though to accommodate the gods themselves, the doorways, pillars, colonnades and ceilings were up to thirty paces high.

'Don't forget, Pharaoh is a god king and the entire royal family are all children of the gods and entitled to the same veneration wherever they go,' Merer advised them.

The day they arrived, Merer was summoned to the Pharaoh's presence. After a short period, Saba too was summoned. She was in a day room, resting and chatting with some of the others after their journey. Ariadne was among their number and when she realised that Saba was going to be presented before herself, she flew into a rage and demanded, through an interpreter, that she be presented first as she was of higher rank. She made a considerable commotion and was overheard by a lady-in-waiting to Queen Neitkrety who happened to be passing through one of the open corridors. The lady-in-waiting approached Ariadne and assured her that the complaint would be conveyed to her mistress, the Queen. She was joint ruler with the Pharaoh of the Two Lands, as Egypt was affectionately known at home. But by this time, Saba had already been led away for her audience, so Ariadne was left fuming with rage and plotting appropriate revenge.

Pharaoh was in the sixth of a series of long halls of white marble, each leading from the other. He was seated on a low dais conferring with Merer and another councillor who withdrew at his nod. He was wearing his lighter nemes crown of folded linen. Rising from his forehead to secure it was the gold band of the uraeus – the golden cobra Buto, goddess of the delta, with hood flared and jewelled eyes glittering, symbol of his powers of life and death. His crook and flail lay beside him where he sat, with a shining white linen robe wrapped around his torso and kilt. His feet were shod in fine gold filigree sandals. He wore golden rings on most fingers and toes, superb amulets adorned his upper arms and a delicately crafted gold crocodile bracelet encircled his left wrist. His skin was nut brown and so wrinkled that it was difficult to estimate his age. His eyes were friendly and he greeted Saba warmly as she and Merer knelt and touched their foreheads to the ground before him.

'I hardly know how to begin, for Merer says you can read minds.'

'That is true, Your Majesty, but I cannot connect with your gods unless they speak to me first. I will assist you in any other way possible, such as reading the minds of any of your subjects, as I did with Naram Sin.'

'Merer has told me a great deal about you, and your past adventures and encounters with other gods and supernatural beings. In that I am greatly interested, as well as in the musical spectacle you propose, and will interview you all together about that delectable prospect. Who are your guardian spirits and how did you come together?'

'My grandmother was a powerful shaman. She still helps me from the afterlife. My father was a Fin shaman from the far northern icelands. He introduced me to the spirit of Narwhal, who guides me and has generated in me a mutual empathy with marine creatures. One of these will come when I call, even if it is days away, and we communicate together.'

'What sort of creature is that?'

'An orca. They resemble us a lot in intelligence. They can teach us so much about everything under the sea. In age, my friend's grandmother is over ninety yuls and still strong.'

'By Osiris! How can you speak to it and what do you talk about?'

'I go for rides on his back and we discuss things by telepathy. He wants to know if orcas and people in general will ever be friends and co-operate in sea work. I have told him it will be a long time away, in the age of Aquarius. I've not met anyone who shares your shapes and images Lord Pepy.'

Pepy paused awhile. 'But that is thousands of years away. How do you know that?'

'Other voices talk to me as well,' Saba murmured.

'Now I know you are the one I have been seeking!' Pepy exclaimed. 'I will agree to your request about Merer's ships crossing our delta if you will help me in my funeral arrangements with the Lord Anubis. You must work with the seven parts of my spirit after I die and my body has been prepared for the eternal rest. I will teach you the thousand necessary spells in case my Ka and Ba mistake or forget any vital answers before the scales of Maat. Thus you will enable my Ba to traverse the Duat and ascend through the shining ones to live with Lord Osiris in Amenti. You must know that my doctors predict I have very little time left. You can visit me and my funerary scribe in my private apartments every evening. We shall begin teaching you the sacred spells. I shall arrange it.'

When Saba and Merer arrived back from their audience and told Bethel and Tara of their success in securing Pharaoh's consent, they thought it a joke, for they had expected many days or half-moons of negotiations. On being persuaded it was true, they could not understand how Saba had achieved it. She told them privately of Pharaoh's needs and swore them both to silence, mentioning how Ariadne and her jealousy could wreck the entire plan, even without her intending to.

Next day Ariadne was accorded a state audience, as a major Queen of Krete, with Pepy the Second and Queen Neitkrety. Afterwards, she confided to Kalliste that Neitkrety had been extremely disturbed when she learned about Saba's evening visits to Pepy without being told the reason for them.

Pepy was eager for Amlodi's concert to take place while he was still able to sit up and concentrate on the music so it was scheduled to take place at full moon in eight days time. Pepy controlled a large band of musicians and placed them all at Amlodi's disposal. Amlodi began practising at once, moving his old friends Kalliste and Aine from lyres on to flutes; Aengus and Tara were the leading voices. The forty Egyptian players counted many lyre, lute, harp and timpani players in their number, as well as extra flautists. Aine unrolled and set up her painted backdrops in the most appropriate areas of the great hall of music. The acoustics were as impressive as those at the Kretan rock caves when they performed their first concert. Amlodi composed special song and animal sound roles for Aengus and Tara after he heard their voices. The rag, or melodic chant, drew its audience in until listener and performer reached a state of sympathetic vibration.

The concert and whale symphony proved as wild a success as it had in Krete, especially as Pharaoh was seen by his senior courtiers to be ecstatic about it. Saba noted that the Queens Ariadne and Neitkrety sat together and chatted secretively during the most lively parts of the performance.

The following morning Saba, Merer and the principal performers were called to a private audience. Pepy was as excited as his condition allowed him to be and heaped congratulations on everyone, including Abram and Sarah who had acquitted themselves with distinction on the flute and lyre respectively. Amlodi told Pepy how he had become interested in water sounds, and later, in marine creatures and the world of undersea music with Saba's tutelage. Pepy exclaimed what a novelty marine music was to him and his court.

'The soul communicates to us through dreams and music as well as refined sensory perception in some people. The more refined and detailed the music, the more profound are the levels of consciousness explored and expanded. This is my central field of interest. I can play the instruments and compose music myself, but not such music as yours, Amlodi.' Pepy smiled at the blond giant, then at Tara and Saba.

'Music is also the spiritual language of the emotions. Since you two are so proficient in activating and interpreting dreams and sounds, I would love to be guided in imaginative dreaming with you both. And perhaps, Amlodi, we could create some novel compositions using the experiences you all possess in animal expression – especially with whales and birds.' Pepy stared at Amlodi. 'I always see images when I hear music. When music is playing, I see little circles or vertical bars of light, getting brighter for higher pitches or becoming a deep maroon for lower ones. Successive ascending notes produce increasingly brighter spots or bars moving upwards. High notes on strings make sharp bright lines. Several harps or lutes playing together evoke spirals of light of different shades, shimmering together. A whole chord will completely envelop me. Do you have such sensations?'

'No! Since I was born, I have seen sounds of all sorts in colour. Human and animal voices, thunder – all sound is continuously transformed into a flowing world of colours and shapes. I see symbols and numbers and days of the moon in different shades. Listening is enhanced, never distracted, by the stream of musical sensations that accompany it. It helps me when composing. I have songs, fragments of tunes and ideas for others always running through my head. My colour schemes are critical for their development. Colour is not added to music, it's part of it. When young I thought everyone shared this and only discovered they didn't as I grew up. My colours are completely inward and never confused with outward ones. I've not met anyone who shares your shapes of light.'

Saba became excited.

'Tara has taught Aengus and Amlodi the deep growling Bon chants of her people from beyond the roof of the world, when using these they can sing with one and even two overtones. They start with a single note and alter it's harmonies by opening and closing their mouths and tensing their vocal chords. Then a shrill melody rings out one or two scales higher, but using the same harmonics, almost as though it's coming through them from somewhere else. Also by visualising that first note as being coloured or scented, the singer is able to develop extra energy with greater healing effectiveness towards his target, be it a whole body, a particular organ or even the bone skeleton in order to restore it's normal healthy vibration.'

Tara nodded enthusiastically at Pepy's questioning look.

'Music creates a resonance which vibrates through the world and transcends the denseness of matter. It touches every atom of a living being through harmonic vibration and creates a fresh life energy that lends joy to existence and liberates us from the feeling of time.'

She looked to the others for affirmation and Saba added. 'You will probabally agree my Lord that a sympathetic piece of music enables the listener to travel deeply into their own consciousness in a mind altering experience, more effective than ingesting a god plant. If only we had met you a few yuls earlier, we could have at least have made the final term of you life more active and carefree.'

The Pharaoh softly inclined his head. 'More ancient than words, it's harmonies and melodies preceed language and let us commune with the divine ones.'

Saba and Tara asked Pepy if they could give him some healing as they could sense his pain. He assented and they placed their hands on his head and stomach. After a short while he smiled and announced his pain had eased. They suggested giving him additional healing each day and he was delighted to agree. They glanced at each other and Saba explained to him that while they could ease his pain, they could not cure him. The disease he had would surely kill him, for his lifetime was ordained to end. He must tell his family and his doctors so that she and Tara would not be accused of contributing to his death.

Within a moon, Pepy's life had ebbed so low that his family were summoned to bid him farewell. Saba was at his bedside, by command, to continue easing his pain. She had got used to the antagonistic glares from Queen Neitkrety, who obviously saw Saba's presence as intrusive.

Aine met Saba one evening on her return to the guest palace, as it was known, and sat her down for a quiet chat. Kalliste was in regular conversation with her mother and knew all about her jealousy of Saba and how she managed to direct Queen Neitkrety's attention towards her. This had apparently stirred up a greater hornet's nest than she anticipated. Neitkrety, initially resenting Pepy's close involvement with Saba, had become obsessed with the idea that Saba was interested in his treasure. Obscene amounts of gold, silver and objets d'art were being stacked within the pyramid treasure rooms now that his funeral was imminent.

'But, Aine, what could I possibly want to do with talents of gold or chests of jewels? Store them somewhere else to be stolen afresh? Even supposing I found a miraculous way of removing them from the pyramid. Why would I? You know I have the ability to generate any amount of wealth if it were needed. I would not have to carry it around like a shell on a tortoise or hide it like a squirrel. Surely Neitkrety has sufficient wit to realise that.'

'Even if she did not, she now fears something even worse – that you have designs on his Ka which might endanger the future prosperity of all Egypt.'

During Pepy's last days Saba found Tara's psychic healing powers as efficacious as her own. The bond between them as new daughter and close friend grew ever stronger. Given the outstanding similarities in their features – apart from hair colour, which made others believe that they both stemmed from a different race – Tara wondered if perhaps their fathers' tribes in the distant north were related. They shared a love for music made on stone gongs, flutes and strings. Could this be an ancient bond, like fire and cooked food? On reflection, Saba decided that Tara would benefit from an introduction to her numinous dreamtime friend the Root more than Aine or Bethel, if she could take her, because it could help her best with her healing procedures. This fabulous experience was too precious not to bequeath to someone in case of her death. She had recently experienced presages of danger and mortality and knew she had determined enemies. She was not sure if she could take Tara, but they both shared the dreaming qualities that might enable them to travel into time together and not get lost. Only Saba's inner self had originally heard the Root's dreamtime cry for help and traced the pathway there and back in her mind. It was not like dream flying to the moon or a visible star; its location lay beyond interstellar space and, bizarrely, outside their time zone. There was high risk involved in ever getting there or returning.

Saba explained the project to Tara, who was mystified and over-whelmed at the notion, but excited and resolved to go. One evening in the guest palace, they settled down on two pallets drawn together so they could clasp hands. Tara was advised to sleep lightly. Saba slept, dreamt lucidly, then linked up with Tara, steering her into the lucid mode when they could talk and tighten hands.

'Stay close with me. We travel into darkness at speed of thought, but try and tune your mind with mine, like twin yoked oxen, so you can sense the way back.' Their experience was like hurtling through a glass tube at enormous speeds, like flashing thoughts beyond their invisible interstellar space. Then they were there. The mangrove tree now towered above a small forest of offshoots. Saba led Tara across the tangled overground roots until they could lay their foreheads against its trunk and hug it with their arms while waiting. Water lapped gently over their feet in utter stillness.

'Have you thoughts of death that you bring a friend?' rumbled a deep-toned voice in their heads.

'It has crossed my mind,' Saba admitted. 'If that should happen, I've chosen this dear friend and daughter to remain in touch with you, if you allow it.' There was a pause. 'I did not expect another with a tuned psyche like yourself.'

'Tara is a yogin and sound healer, and would love to be able to consult you.'

'I have shared her mind and she pleases me, so I accept your request, providing neither of you ever abuse any knowledge or rapport I might bring you.'

'Tara, do you recall the heaven's breath instrument I gave your father?' Saba said.

'Of course. It helps him breathe and I think prolongs his life.'

'Well, that was a healing apport from our godlike friend here. Oh Root, can you inform Tara of anything helpful?'

'Only to say that one of her children will maintain our contact.'

'Are you satisfied with your regeneration?' Saba enquired.

'Yes, I have made many connections, some old and some new like yours. The sentient cosmos will slowly advance in expanded consciousness and wisdom, partly due to your joint contributions. For you, Saba, I foresee danger and possibly extinction, but the outcome has yet to be established. There are indications of death and sadness.'

'Why do you choose to live in a tree?' Tara wondered.

'I am this tree, leaves and roots, because I enjoy the seasons of the planets who possess them, including your little Earth, which I have visited with beings and machines you can't imagine. I have learned to outlast even such beings and choose as close to everlasting existence as possible. Trees are good. One can continue by way of their seeds or roots and fungal extensions to transfer to a different tree if the original one perishes. To exist as a boson or any other sub-atomic particle is not so satisfying. The tranquillity of a tree allows me to meditate for hundreds of years at a time and still enjoy the seasons – and my new pastime. I have enabled another planet in our galaxy to develop. It is like your Earth with its continents, oceans and mixtures of gases. The creatures have evolved close to your status but they still inhabit the sea coasts and lake shores as your own people did at an earlier stage. They can use the water almost as well as seals and otters but still remain permanent Earth creatures. This alters their evolution in small but important ways. For example, they have learned the true value of interdependence, not just co-operation but empathy with and reliance on each other; this inculcates a deep and permanent kindness. This begins in your own children but falters and often dies as they grow up, and adults, even if they understand it, seem unable to recover it for themselves. It would be a step in their expanded consciousness if a Mother Goddess could help these people maintain this state of kindness and avoid the isolation of selves, alienation, fear of outsiders and wars, and the conflicts to which these flaws lead. Artistic creativity is also required to make knowledge truly interesting to enjoying and suffering beings. Knowledge without love can be profoundly corrupting. Since you both possess these abilities and understand the meaning of acausal connections in this unfolding multiverse, perhaps I could prevail upon one of you to undertake such a compassionate role. I will always be there to assist you. You appear to forget, we are sharing minds.' Saba stared at him. 'You mean give up our life on our own Earth to become the guide of these people in another world? That needs a lot of thinking about! Also, I find it very difficult to share your mind.'

'I will teach you easier ways to access my thinking and wisdom. I leave the suggestion with you to ponder until the time comes for you to move on.'

'Pharaoh Pepy expects me to outwit Anubis and the other underworld gods to ensure his safe conduct across the Duat to join with Lord Osiris. Can you help me with that?'

'Any god in each civilization is only as powerful as the faith fostered in the pantheon of deities of that civilization. The Egyptian gods like Auser, or Osiris, and Auset, or Isis, have been developing for millennia, long before the dynasties, before the Sphinx and the Zodiac system of counting the aeons of time. When belief in them wanes, so does their power to affect the minds of anyone in conflict with them. Anubis has all the psychic energy of the Egyptian collective consciousness, and when you are in his spiritual domain you will need my intervention, combined with your own powers, to resist and persuade him. Your daughter could help as well, whether inside or outside the pyramid. I am so far removed in space and time that all your gods seem like pawns in that game you play in Meluha and Ur. My help will require huge exertion, like yours was for me when you walked up the dry riverbed and struck the rock to draw up the spring for this lake. When you need my assistance, you must both think of me at the same moment.'

It was time to leave. They bade farewell to the Root and found themselves back in that flashing time warp, only to stop almost before they started. In front of them lay a vista of snow and ice.

'The north lands,' Tara gasped. 'It would seem so,' Saba agreed. There in the sky, beyond the horizon of snow, appeared glowing curtains of green lights – then they were green, yellow and white, rippling and sliding across the sky as though the spectacle existed for their benefit only.

Finally the curtains began flickering and slowly turned into an axis whorl with three bent arms circling after each other.

'What does it mean?' Tara asked.

'I've no idea of the meaning, but we must fix the memory in our minds and paint the dream when we return to Egypt and Ur.'

'Great notion. We can fix it on skin or papyrus to carry around. It may be important and someone may understand and interpret the signs.'

Soon their dream was speeding them onwards again and they awoke on the pallets back in the bedroom in Memphis. 'That was an incredible experience, Saba. I shall remember it all my life,' said Tara.

'You must also remember how to travel there and back when you have something important to ask or obtain. The Root is a fountain of knowledge from older worlds outside our sphere. He can travel millennia of yuls into the future where new discoveries are made, like cures for diseases. He has brought me back healing objects from these other time dimensions that can help our peoples. Don't mention our adventure to anyone, including our partners, because they will want to share our visions, and how could we refuse them without destroying our mutual trust. The Root does not usually tolerate visits from people he does not know, and will find a way to get rid of us all.'

'I understand your reasoning. We have so many good friends who might get wind of it.'

'I have to sort out Pepy's problems in the Duat underworld when he is entombed in just twenty days time. I must know many more of these funerary texts and riddles before I enter the tomb at his side. Merer has told me he had many obstacles to sort out. However, he will shortly have six ships reassembled in the Red Sea. They will be fully manned by experienced crews and captains. Pepy, before he died, had his decrees authorized by Neitkrety and his Vizier. He allowed us to use his connections with the warrior leaders in Cush to choose some of their top fighting men for Ur and pass them over to the Kretan ships' captains for transportation as soon as they arrive at the coast. Sarah and Abram will travel back on the ships with Enheduanna and Namu, the young city leader.'

They found Bethel, Merer and Hermes down in the new port named Said in the gulf at the top of the Red Sea. It had been created for the reassembly of the ships and transfer to the sand-sleighs of the proposed cargoes of spices from Meluha, across to the delta at Giza near the three sky pyramids, and onwards to Byblos.

'Well done, Merer and Saba! You have fulfilled your roles superbly. Now it's up to the Kretans to play their part. I promise we won't let you down,' Hermes pledged.

Saba took the opportunity to draw Bethel aside. 'My love, we have promised ourselves a little holiday for ages. Now is our chance while we wait for the end of Pepy's embalming. Why don't we hire a felucca and sail it up the Nile? We can dine and sleep in some of those small luxury temples in the lagoons prepared for private guests.'

'Stupendous idea! The winds are favourable this moon. All we have to do is lie back and you can answer all the questions I've been pestering you with since we left Er-rin.'

'All right,' Saba said. 'This time I won't refuse any subjects and we can talk for a half-moon if you wish. Unless, of course, we might be otherwise engaged.'

'Well, we won't have to prepare food, and you won't have to fend off crocodiles and river horses all the time.'

'Let's do it as soon as possible. I'm going to order a boat and provision it as soon as we get back to Memphis.' A few days later, Saba and Bethel, like eager school children, slipped away from the palace at dawn with their bundles. Bethel had the felucca moored in the harbour under the care of an old boatman who untied the craft and pushed them off. They raised the lateen sail and began making good time as the boat eased out to the centre of the mighty river.

Soon the city of Memphis faded into the distance. There were few ships of any kind on the water because it was the mourning period for Pharaoh. Half a moon had passed since they last made love and both their bodies were aching with passion. They flung off their loose robes and clung together, tasting each other like two starving people at the beginning of a superb banquet. Each thought they knew the other so well, yet every taste revealed something unexpected and gratifying. After several consummations, they descended into a relaxed swoon.

His anima projected into his consciousness, which blended with hers. Poignant wisps of poesy entered his mind and he whispered them in her ear.

'When our bodies join, there is no touching here, nor touching there, nor straining joy. For whole is joined to whole in ecstasy.'

Saba began to hum an ancient air, soft as a lullaby yet producing magically exciting notes that would not permit the hearer to rest or sleep. She bestrode him again. The rhythm pulsed in their bodies and in the air around them. The wall of identity between them dissolved and their awareness was as one, a joint awareness of the entire cosmos and their embeddedness in it. Saba knew herself to be impregnated physically and psychically.

Yet at the same moment she received a fleeting insight, which ravaged and infuriated her. Surely it was mistaken! But an insight cannot be given back; one can never return to the moment before. She was infuriated because the warning of mortal danger did not supply sufficient information about how to avoid it, as her intuitions usually did. Saba put these thoughts behind her, determined they would enjoy the holiday to the best of their ability.

They fished for a while each day, or stalked and shot marsh fowl with a stealthy arrow and brought the catch, if a choice one, to whichever of the attractive little temples appealed to their taste towards evening. The temple servers were delighted to cook and add the fish or fowl to whatever other delicacies were on offer and accept the surplus as a gratuity.

One evening, in the lagoon shielding the famous temple to Hapi the river god, where they were planning to spend the night, Bethel's trailing bait was swallowed by a large Nile perch. He had pulled it close to the boat when the fish was seized by a huge crocodile hurtling forth from a papyrus bed. Saba was holding the bow and arrow on the chance of glimpsing a crane among the leaves. Shocked by the sudden attack, she strained and released the arrow which entered the animal's nostril. It reared up the side of the boat, opening its jaws with a roar of pain. Bethel hurled the heavy flint-tipped spear into its throat. It came out through the top of its head and the animal fell back, its sheer weight pulling Bethel into the water on top of it. Saba, fearing the beast might take a final bite or slash him with its claws, leapt onto its chest clutching her fishing knife. But no further action was needed, the crocodile was dead. They tied its body to the side of the boat and towed it up to the temple wharf where it was warmly welcomed by the applauding servitors and cooks who had watched the entire proceedings. The crocodile stew which resulted that night from everyone's joint exertions was deemed the most delicious dish of their cruise.

The embalming process was over and the entombment of Pharaoh was almost complete. Saba had taken her place beside the granite sarcophagus which contained his golden coffin. She was holding her bundle of papyrus scrolls inscribed with the prayers and riddles needed to support her intellectual and magical battles with the Lord Anubis and the other gods of the Duat. An army of craftsmen and artists had laboured for years to complete the magnificent murals that decorated the passages and subterranean chambers of the tomb. Five store rooms were crammed with all the treasures carried in during the recent moons. The entrances of these had all been sealed and painted over, as were the mouths of the vertical shafts so that they appeared to be smooth, floor and roof, to confuse potential tomb robbers. One moon's fresh food and water were provided for Saba as well as the traditional food and wine for Pharaoh's journey. The priests retreated backwards, holding their pungent oil lamps that polluted the dry air with black smoke, and joined Queen Neitkrety, the Vizier and Bethel outside the tomb where the guards would let down an exterior stone slab to protect the burial chamber itself while Saba communed with the gods for the final moon.

Tara was standing with the rest of the crowd of close mourners outside the pyramid. As the last of Pharaoh's private guards emerged, she saw a dark shadow appear over them and knew something had gone seriously wrong inside. Queen Neitkrety and the Vizier were already leaving in their respective litters. The guardsmen would permit no one to approach or answer any questions.

Where was Bethel? Had he decided to stay with Saba after all? He had wanted to.

Tara turned to Aengus and Aine. 'Did you see Bethel leave?' They shook their heads. 'Then he must have remained with Saba.' Tara tried to contact Saba, as did Aine, but all was dark. When Merer tried to enquire, he was informed by the guards' captain that everything had gone according to plan. Saba's party dispersed back to the guest palace where Tara, in the quiet of her room, managed to commune with Saba who transmitted the awful news that Bethel had been crushed by the three giant slabs of rock that were initially designed to slide down, one behind the other, blocking the entrance corridor and sealing it off permanently. They were all given to understand that the single slab to protect Saba and the tomb would be lowered gently to rest on raised bars until the other two were crashed down into their final slots after Saba, magical work ended, left the tomb.

As soon as she had seen all three slabs trembling, Saba realised the betrayal and how cleverly it had been staged. No one could ever prove there had not been an accident. Bethel, who also realised what was happening, tried in vain to hurl himself through the vanishing gap to be with Saba. The two remaining witnesses and the guards' captain had simply turned away, task completed, and Saba had been permanently immured.

Tara, her initial shock and horror subsiding a little, asked Saba what should be done. Knowing that only a miracle could save her and that Bethel could not be restored to life, Saba had decided to inform no one. She had a moon before anyone need realise she and Bethel were dead. Now that Neitkrety would feel her to be no longer a threat, their scheme could proceed smoothly under Hermes's supervision while Merer could maintain good relations with the Egyptians. She and Tara should not communicate with Aine to avoid burdening her with worries. Aine would merely think the pyramid was blocking her telepathic sensitivity.

Tara suggested that she and Saba should do as the Root had advised them when an emergency arose and contact him simultaneously. It might have some ideas about what could be done. After a half-moon they received an acknowledgement. It had found a reference in a digital library in the Aquarian age to the pyramid of Pepy the Second, which had been destroyed in the Piscean Age. A computerised reconstruction had since been made. This showed that a secret passage led from the burial chamber and joined to an angled star shaft opening near the top of the pyramid. Root was searching the plans.

FORTY-FIVE

ESCAPE TO UR

During her period of incarceration in Pepy's funeral chamber, Saba reacclimatized herself to the enchantment of silence as she recalled it in the Raven cave of her childhood. But the serenity of the darkness was interrupted by her inrush of memories of Bethel, and the shattering effect of his sudden death blasted the psychic harmony and balance of both their minds, for his had never gone away; indeed, it was clutching onto hers in fear and anger that she knew would take a long time to soothe.

She didn't blame Pepy for Neitkrety's machinations and was determined to keep her part of the bargain they had made before his death. She would assist his examinations and passage through the Duat by completing her prayers, incantations and prescribed rituals as and when required by Anubis and the other gods and goddesses who served Osiris. When in doubt, as in the 'Opening of the Mouth' ceremony to invigorate Pepy's Ka spirit, she contacted Tara to help her invoke the Root's advice.

Saba needed to show that, during the course of his life, Pepy had attuned himself to the system of Ma'at in all its different meanings of order, truth and justice. It was thought that Ra had ordained this perfect system of checks and balances throughout the universe. She pointed out that this man had indeed recognised his place in the great god's creation, which could not be improved as it was perfect at its inception. Pepy, as an individual and as a part of society, did not fall under his passions but lived in tranquillity; he was integrated with the life of nature and the experience of that harmony was the highest good he could achieve. He therefore deserved his place with Osiris.

Saba was confident that sooner or later, Root would uncover

the blueprints of the original pyramid that had been reconstructed by computers in the extraordinary Aquarian age, set far into the future. He would be able to supply her with the necessary coordinates to locate the secret star passage that led from inside the sarcophagus chamber to the pyramid's exterior, facing the constellation of Osiris during the appropriate season for Pepy's Ba to ascend and become one with him.

The news reached her in a lucid dream just after the end of the first moon. She carefully fixed the measurements in her mind and visioned them to Tara. She in turn explained them to Merer who had been waiting in an agony of suspense. He doubted that such things could be possible but was prepared to try anything to save Saba; besides one could never be quite sure what was possible with these people who were adepts in the mysteries.

During one of Saba's many dreams in the pyramid she found herself back in Garnac and communicating with Melusine who had returned there after a few moons with Sedana. When she heard of the earthquake, of the mischievous behaviour of the Kretan sailors, of Bethel's bruited blasphemy on the sacred island of Gavrinnis, of his and Saba's weird dealings with sea monsters and his misdeeds with Aelise and Sugaar, she felt impelled to return there by the first available boat. As considerable time had elapsed and the venturers were by then at the eastern end of the Tideless Sea, Melusine had found any telepathic contact with them beyond her geographical limit. Saba now managed to explain Bethel's predicament with Aelise and her subsequent behaviour. Finally, the announcement of his tragic death exonerated him, in Melusine's eyes, from being the cause of her daughter's attempted sacrifice at the volcano. Saba resolved that if she indeed escaped from her living tomb, she would go back to Ur and Enheduanna, have Bethel's baby there and make arrangements for the coming war. Then she would attempt to reach Er-rin and try to sort out the trouble that seemed to be brewing there. Melusine had maintained psychic contact with Sedana and with Pilar at the Mother Lake. She told of deep dissension about white clay supplies between the Eelfolk, who were being ordered to deliver five times the previously agreed annual amount as the stuff had become fashionable and as much in demand as gold dust. They demanded compensation.

Saba found a bronze strigil among the tools and ornaments laid out for Pepy's use in the afterlife and managed to pick out and loosen the mortar holding the block that concealed the hidden shaft. It was quite narrow and she was just able to insert her still slim body and wriggle down the little horizontal tunnel which eventually slanted steeply in a long diagonal towards the exit.

Taking with him a climbing expert, Merer was waiting three quarters of the way up the pyramid, in the darkness, as arranged. It was a long haul for Saba; she had to rest many times to ease her muscles and to allow air to seep upwards in sufficient quantities to satisfy her lungs and blood stream. Fortunately for Saba, tiny air vents were incorporated to keep the sarcophagus chamber fresh and Pepy's Ka alive and strong. Finally the exhausted woman tapped on the outer block with the strigil she had thoughtfully tied to her wrist. Her rescuers heard the note as from a tuning fork and hacked at the stone until they could ease it away, grasp Saba's arms and pull her gently out. The pyramid guards were spaced well beyond the perimeter and no one saw the three shadows making their way slowly down.

They withdrew to a secure resting place and while Saba recovered, they plied her with fresh fruit and water. Merer and she left quickly for Port Said, the dock from which Hermes's ships dispatched their cargo across the marshes to connect with the Nile tributary barges, and thence to Byblos. Tara and Aengus, Sarah and Abram eagerly awaited them on board and she was welcomed back like one from the dead, for both she and Bethel had been assumed as such by all save Tara. Sarah hugged her and swore she would never doubt her magical powers again, even though she could not save Bethel. He and Abram would always be the two loves of her life. Saba told her that she was still able to exchange feelings with him and soon Sarah would also. His spirit would always be available to them in time of need.

Aine and Kalliste remained in the Sabian palace at Byblos to allay any suspicion of trickery in the minds of the queens Neitkrety and Ariadne, and Saba decided to remain officially dead for as long as convenient. Amlodi, who was in Byblos with them, was joined by Orthonac from Krete with the two girls Medea and Stephanie, who remained loyal to their chosen men.

The ship's voyage led them first down the Red Sea to Cush to collect, because of the additional passengers, a smaller than usual contingent of warriors for Ur; then they went straight to that famous city. Enheduanna welcomed them also. She had heard of the tomb tragedy from one of the ship captains and broke the news to Lao Tzu, who was consoled by Tara and Aengus. They remained with him for the duration of their visit. Tara explained to him about her secret and incredible journey to meet the Root. She was amazed to hear that he had been shown many of the events she described during his dreamings. He was deeply impressed and urged her to seize and follow the wisdom of such an amazing entity as the Root after he himself was gone.

He again expressed thanks to Saba for her gift of the oxygen machine. It helped him to breathe better and this allowed him so much more energy. She told him that she was given it by the Root: because of his vast knowledge he was able to procure technical artefacts and discoveries from the distant future.

Saba arranged a conference with Enheduanna's protégé, Ur Namu, whom, as the ablest leader of the city's soldiers, she had chosen and trained in the ancient culture, not forgetting the arts of love. She and Enheduanna both foresaw an illustrious future for him and his family. Enheduanna prophesied that he would successfully fight off the Gutians, rebuild Ur to great heights with the largest ever known ziggurat to the city god, and begin a new dynasty to last for generations. Enheduanna, Merer, Abram and Sarah were all there with important functionaries of Ur and the other cities close by. Tara and Aengus also attended; because of Saba they too had the welfare of Ur and its people close to their hearts.

Arrangements were completed about restocking and training the garrisons in Ur and the adjacent city states. Saba advised them about as many of the events in the approaching Gutian war as she could foresee.

Saba and her friends stayed with Enheduanna until after the baby was born. It was a boy and she called him Bethel. She recalled her last birthing when the twins had arrived and she had to decide which to keep and which to share with her mother. So much had happened since then; her pilgrimage still seemed unending. She studied the baby and was glad that he looked as much like his father as Aengus had resembled Fion. She found it usually made life easier in the future. Everyone offered to protect and nurse him when she had explained her pledge to perform an important mission back in her own country; it would take one or two yuls to complete. She decided to leave the baby with Sarah and Abram, partly because she knew Sarah very much wanted a child and would love and care for her blood nephew as she had for his father. At their peaceful oasis Sarah and Abram could provide the stability that a baby needed, and Sarah possessed the seniority and experience of Abram's premier wife to protect him later, even if Abram ever formed other alliances and new progeny in the future, as his faith permitted.

Tara was startled by the arrival of several students who had just disembarked from a cargo ship from Meluha. Three of these boys had worked alongside her in the same ashram under the tutelage of Lao Tzu in Mohenjo-daro. They lost no time in presenting themselves to Tara and Lao Tzu who, they presumed, would have died by this time and they were most surprised and a bit disconcerted to find him alive; he even remembered them. There was little chance of being able to boast about imaginary exploits while he was around. They had been discharged for improper conduct and this was reported to Lao Tzu by Tara. They were even less pleased to discover Tara had a partner. She was the most popular and celebrated girl in the ashram, even in the city, because of her looks and personality. They had never been allowed an opportunity of partnering her in the Tantric workshops, particularly with the Maithuna exercises. Here in Ur, with her mentor dead and she perhaps more vulnerable, who knew what occasion might have presented itself. But they were all handsome and personable young men and were soon content to make a favourable impression in the high society of young people in Ur by putting it about that they were old pupils of Lao Tzu. Lao Tzu was not so well pleased, and reminded Tara and Aengus that the boys had been sent away because of their undisciplined minds and behaviour. He would never consider them trustworthy.

One of the summer festivals was soon to be held. The venue was outside the city on the banks of the mother river Euphrates, to allow a pleasant space for the games and amusements. There were rowing and canoeing races on the river itself, high and long jumps, short and distant foot races, javelin and discus throwing, gymnastics, horse and donkey races and a wide variety of amusements accompanied by feasting and dancing. The group of Indus river students were keen to enter the competitions to represent Melhua and came to Tara with the proposal that they could put up a good gymnastics team if they only had a really athletic girl to balance on top of their final event pyramid. They pleaded with her to help them out, for old time's sake. Gymnastics was not popular in Ur and athletic men, never mind girls, were thin on the ground. Although Tara listened to Lao Tzu's admonitions, she agreed to work with them if Aengus, Saba and Merer could come with her as well. When Ur-Nanshe, the famous artiste, heard that Aengus was attending the festival, she begged him to join with her in the main singing competition. He agreed willingly, having enjoyed singing with her previously at Enheduanna's gala performance. They decided to sing a famously difficult duet from one of Enheduanna's own compositions and rehearsed it several days beforehand. Tara and the young Melhuans did the same in the arena of Ur, as it proved difficult to find an area of hard, flat ground that lent itself to gymnastic leaping and springing.

The festival omens were promising and the procession set out southwards from the city, the contestants followed by large crowds of spectators. Amusements and vendors' stalls had been erected the day before and were in full swing when the consumers reached the venue.

Everyone seemed happy except Saba who, when asked, simply said she had woken up feeling out of sorts. She smiled and tried to be agreeable but half wished that Old Mother was still alive and she could go to her for advice as she had done in the past. She recalled how, as a girl, she had discussed her agonising choices after the epic misadventure with Cairla and Fion.

'You will have choices like these to make all your life and provided you choose wisely, you will become famous,' Old Mother had assured her. The only hard and level site the gymnasts could find lay on the other side of a small hill beside the main proceedings. It turned out that the gymnastics demonstration was scheduled near the end of the day. Aengus had gone off with Ur-Nanshe at mid-afternoon and still not returned. Saba, who would have loved to watch them sing, would not leave Tara on her own, and Merer would not leave Saba, so the three of them went to join the gymnasts who were already waiting. Tara was surprised to see the number increased to twelve in the troupe instead of eight as they had rehearsed. The others explained that the extra men could not leave their other jobs earlier for the rehearsals but that tiers of six, three, two, one, plus the girl on top making thirteen were safer. After the normal routines ended, they called Tara in for the climax. By arrangement, she was wearing the same golden coloured loincloth as the others, with no sandals or top and a thin rope circlet on her head. The gymnasts conducted a series of pyramid-building exercises, each culminating in a tier higher, eliciting gasps and whoops from the huge crowd that had collected for the performance. Finally Tara began climbing the four-tier-high group in complete silence, none of the spectators had ever seen a fifth level before. She climbed slowly and carefully, finding the single man on top the most difficult. When she reached his shoulders she raised her legs in the air to a handstand with her arms straight above his shoulders. The crowd were cheering their heads off believing this the climax, but Tara had managed to balance her head on top of his and now extended both her arms horizontally. The audience, including Saba and Merer, were ecstatic and declared this exhibition best of all in the festival.

The pyramid stood for a brief while, but as soon as Tara felt it start to waver, she reverted to her handstand and then began to climb down with equal care. The members of the pyramid broke up as quickly as they could and were elated to hear of Tara's balancing act and the crowd's acclaim. They broke open leather bags of palm wine to celebrate their victory. When the crowd saw there was no wine coming their way they dispersed quite quickly and returned over the hill to join in the remaining feasting. A few of the gymnasts suggested they do the same but others wanted to finish the opened wine bags. They had eaten nothing that day to keep their fitness at a peak and had forgotten the strength of the new wine, especially in empty stomachs. Some of the men began murmuring it was time for a little fun after all their hard efforts. Instead of remembering there were plenty of women back at the festival, they were overwhelmed at the beauty and attractiveness of the two women in their company. Saba perceived what was happening and suggested to Merer that they leave immediately. He agreed and went to fetch Tara, who was suddenly finding it hard to get away from hugs and pawings. Merer felt a blinding pain in his head and everything went dark. The entire atmosphere changed; all the spectators had left. Saba noticed that the gymnasts had divided into two groups, one around her and one around Tara, who was already on the ground, Saba's group began stripping her clothes off. One man behind her put his arm around her neck, squeezing her vagus nerve and windpipe, while the others grabbed her and pushed her down on top of him; another man was on top of her with his extended member pressing forcefully. She could hear Tara's cries and knew the same thing was happening to her. A vision entered her mind – that of Naram Sins's tiger at the open door of his cage, licking her hand.

Almost instantly she felt her neck thickening and similar sensations to those she had experienced on what she would never forget as the day of the bears, when Fion and Maeve were killed. Her body swelled and changed utterly; she could sense powerful teeth and claws and raging fury in her mind. She had become a lioness. The man under her was screaming as were the others above and holding her; she whirled on them like lightning, slashing and biting every biped within reach. Few escaped injury as she leapt to her feet and raced over to Tara. The man on top of her had the back of his head and neck bitten out and while the others tried to hurl themselves away, most of them received fearsome slashes to the bone on torso and legs and even more savage bites as the lioness circled them and chose her target areas at will. The gymnasts who had any wits left to employ could only think that the lioness must be an evil entity, perhaps called up by this witch queen Saba, as some named her, so even if they had weapons like spears, they would have been useless against such dark and terrifying powers.

Tara could only sit and watch in stupefaction as the carnage continued. She counted eleven men on the ground, dead or wounded, and a great deal of blood. She herself was covered with it by the man bleeding over her, and she did not much feel like offering sympathy or help to the moaning sufferers dragging themselves around. She found Merer lying where someone had bashed his head and managed to revive him by breathing into his mouth. By the time she told him all that had happened, the wine, the attempted multiple rapes, the huge lioness appearing from nowhere and the subsequent maulings and killings, the lioness could no longer be seen. Saba's clothes were lying where they had been ripped off her but she was as absent as the lioness.

Then they saw her, naked, her red hair gleaming in the orange rays of the setting sun as she climbed up the sloping bank from the river. Merer still bore the dried blood from his head wound and Tara had no opportunity to wipe the blood from herself. Saba clasped them to her and walked them back down to the river to cleanse themselves as she had done. All she would say was, 'They needed instant punishment and my guardians found and helped me. We were not a moment too soon, were we Tara?'

They looked meaningfully at each other. Merer apologised for not being able to help and for allowing himself to be tricked so easily. But Tara told him not to worry; what could he have done against twelve opponents? Besides, she felt the whole show was a deliberate setup to trap and overwhelmingly outnumber them. Even Aengus could not have staved those men off; they were determined to defile us both to the last man. Perhaps the remaining wretch will repeat the story as a timely warning.

The women remained on the river bank until Merer came back with Aengus, Ur-Nanshe and some fresh clothes. They were both horrified but no one dared ask further about the origins of the lioness. With a quizzical grimace, Saba said she thought she saw it swimming across the river, but it might have been a hippopotamus. She asked Ur-Nanshe how the competition went.

'Naturally, we won. With Aengus singing how could we not? And we had to sing endless encores. You must never leave us,' she ordered Aengus, throwing her arms about him. Saba told them about Tara's marvellous balancing feat on the twelfth man's head. Aengus swore he would get her to repeat it even on one man on the ground. The festival was still in full swing but none of them felt like staying and they returned to the city. As such a severe and widespread punishment had been inflicted, Tara and Saba did not seek further sanctions, and apart from telling Enheduanna and Lao Tzu, the subject was dropped. They had no doubt the wounded men, when recovered, would search out another refuge.

Saba began making plans with Aengus and Tara to sail back to Er-rin on one of Merer's vessels on the Tideless Sea. This way she would avoid any traffic with Ariadne. She had a long argument with Merer who wanted to accompany her. He acknowledged how important his experience would prove in preserving Ur in the probably imminent conflict. At last he reluctantly agreed that she might be able to undertake the journey without him, but insisted on making her the owner of the vessel and in charge of whatever captain was appointed. It was accepted that Aine and her inseparable companion, Kalliste, should stay in charge of the palace in Byblos. This gave her a position of considerable power should decisions be needed during the instability in Egypt and Akkad, and should Merer and his allies require wider support with their enterprise. Saba wanted to take Amlodi, Orthonac and their girls, as both men were extremely experienced and intensely loyal to her. She had presentiments that not only she, but Aengus and Tara would need their support. Saba decided to return by the route they came and transfer to her own ship in Byblos, where she could collect the others and say goodbye to Aine and Kalliste.

Their farewells were poignant and heartfelt. No one was certain if and when they would meet again, especially after what had happened to Bethel. Merer commandeered a ship, just arrived with a fresh party of warriors, to return them directly to Port Said rather than pursue its voyage to the Meluhan ports of Amri or Lothal, exchanging the delights of Ur for a return cargo of gems like etched carnelian, lapis lazuli, gold and breathtaking spices. Enheduanna resolved that she would copy Tara and Saba, who were performing Tantric yoga exercises before sunrise each morning. 'Do you believe I too can awaken the sleeping serpent at the base of my spine and have its power enter my mind?'

'We have no doubt that you can if you follow our directions. It will happen, and with such expanded powers you will be able to telepathise with us no matter how far away we are.' Tara began to explain the bodily sensations she should experience, then suggested that Saba could better describe them since her reactions were more recent.

'Since I am well used to deep meditation success came quickly,' Saba said. 'I concentrated on a white flower on top of my head. One morning I felt a strange sensation where the base of my spine touches my seat on the floor, the sensation was so unusual and so pleasing that it distracted my attention from focusing on the flower and as soon as that happened the feeling stopped. When I began to focus again the feeling recommenced. This happened several times until I determinedly persevered with my meditation on the flower. Then the sensation reappeared and extended up my spine, growing in intensity until reaching the top. I heard a sound like a waterfall and felt a stream of liquid light entering my brain through the spinal cord. The light grew brighter and the sound louder until I felt my consciousness and awareness spreading outwards in a widening halo. My perceptions no longer seemed tied to my body, which receded to a tiny point in the distance. My consciousness appeared to have become an ocean of light without barriers or obstructions and I was interrelating with other feelings, not my own but sharing themselves with me. After a while I felt the vast pool of light contracting, becoming smaller and smaller until I was aware of my own body and surroundings, with exterior noises and other objects intruding on my senses in a normal manner.

I looked around and saw the sun had risen but little time had elapsed. Tara across the room was still meditating. In future exercises I found the same result occur when I focused on the flower and repeated my chosen mantras. Somewhat alarming was the way my mind behaved after the first flowering of the current rose continuously from my loins up into my brain. I felt as if I were looking at the world from a higher elevation than that from which I saw it before. It seemed as though my thinking faculty had undergone a transformation and I was mentally expanding and contracting, regulated by the fluctuations of the current flowing from my spine.'

'That sounds extraordinary!' Enheduanna exclaimed.

'And so you will know the feelings are real, during the vision of consciousness, you will still be able to make a comparison between the extended state of consciousness and your normal one. You will feel the contractions while the halo is fading. Each experience will last longer until you eventually find you can control the duration to suit your convenience. The serpent power should travel up a nerve on the left side of the spine, not on the right. That would be dangerous. If the right side ever feels activated, stop at once,' Saba warned her.

'Remember, no matter whether it takes days or moons after we have gone, as soon as it happens try to make contact with one of us,' Tara added.

She thanked both women effusively as they exchanged last fond farewells with her and Lao Tzu.

They spent almost two moons in Byblos. Sarah and Abram were there in Aine's palace as her guests. Aine and Kalliste had wanted to meet and bond with Aine's new baby brother, Bethel, and create a larger family group with Sarah and Abram. They had all come to love Bethel, so his half-sister and playmate must possess equivalent worth. They already recognised Aine as part of Saba; in time, they would judge Kalliste her chosen one. Saba found it almost impossible to part herself from little Bethel; he had his father's features. She felt like a traitor when she finally left but a presentiment warned her it would be foolishly dangerous to bring him with her. As the danger apparently connected with the seas, the warning seemed appropriate; all voyages were hazardous whether they involved long skin boats or larger wooden ships.

Remembering the long and risky journey from Er-rin by sea and land to reach Krete, Saba held many protracted discussions with Aine and Sarah about the baby, as well as about other facets of their lives in the future. She advised Aine that it would be good for her to have a baby, that she must not allow her inherited talents to be lost; women would need all the assistance available in the course of the next few ages of the Zodiac. Kalliste should have one as well and they could be reared together. To be a mother was a highly fulfilling stage of physical achievement for a woman. Besides, then little Bethel would have playmates from his own family. She knew how fascinated Merer was by her family and proposed him to Aine to father her child. It would also cement their alliance and provide the baby with an influential father in this time when fathers were becoming increasingly important.

The ship destined for Er-rin was finally stocked with provisions and gifts, the crew organised and Amlodi appointed second-in-command in case Saba wished to remain in Er-rin for longer than she initially intended. He reminded her how they thought she had abandoned ship by disappearing on the back of her orca during the outward voyage. Merer reluctantly joined her family on the quay to wave them farewell.

FORTY-SIX

THE UNKNOWN PLANET

Saba's ship passed from the Tideless Sea, between the Pillars of the Giant into the Grey Ocean, and turned northwards, keeping the coast of Iberia within sight to starboard. But only a day later, a rising storm prevented them from calling at any of the known fishing ports. There was no shortage of fresh drinking water as their spare deck sails and containers were continuously filling and they carried plenty of dried food stocks. As the winds were south-westerly, short sails constantly hoisted kept the vessel racing before the gale. The pilot helmsman who had been on the previous voyage to Er-rin with Hermes and on several ventures to Garnac, claimed it would be one of the shortest journey legs he remembered.

They reached Orthonac's home port of Biskayne nine nights after leaving Byblos; the ocean had nursed a gale all the way. They were all grateful for the relieving shelter. Orthonac was eager to meet his people, as he had received no news from them since the Kretan traders' misdemeanour with the haughty, independent Euskerran women in Garnac. There had been only frosty communication between Euskerran and Kretan fishtraders on the few occasions they had been in contact since.

They made for a small sandy cove behind a sheltering cliff. The sleepy rowers, who had been required to steady the ship's direction during the storm, delightedly leapt into the wavelets and dragged the boat up a narrow channel carved out for larger Euskerran craft. A few children were digging razor clams in the wet sand. Some ran to fetch their parents to meet the strangers.

The crew was composed of Egyptians and Carians recruited by Merer and Medea. The pilot was a friend of Merer from Byblos. No Kretans were chosen in order to avoid any embarrassment, as the ship would be recognised as Kretan built. Orthonac remembered one of the fathers as a seasoned fisher trader with whom he had often worked. The man, in turn, was joyful to see Orthonac and the two were able to guarantee the ship's crew to the headman of the port as authentic sailors and not pirates. After they had been introduced and settled down, Orthonac told Saba, Tara and the others about the severe trouble happening over the entire northern side of the Euskerran nation. Each community of Euskerrans was led by a wise woman and usually a male shaman who shared joint guidance and leadership of the people. Over the rest of the Iberian mainland a patriarchal system was in process of taking over from the matriarchy and many of the Euskerran men were in sympathy. There was resentment on both sides of the leadership.

Etxeberi the shaman, leading Orthonac's community, told him that the Mother Protectress, who they knew and worshipped as Laminak, had turned against the people. He and the other shamans had been contesting power with her for some time. Like Orthonac, Etxeberi had spent a considerable period of time away in other countries and strongly favoured male dominance.

He was prepared to go to any lengths to ensure that El, a new male god he and some friends had introduced from the Tideless Sea, would become supreme in the homeland. Orthonac, who remembered him from when they were young, knew his nature possessed a mean and vicious side, so never entirely trusted him even while respecting his position as the shaman. Some of his comments about the way Laminak had mistreated her people made him wonder, especially the rumour that she was kidnapping children and demanding ransoms of the food and gifts that people used to present at her temple. The worshippers had stopped leaving gifts when she began sending poor crop years, letting their animals die and inflicting epidemics of sickness on the populace themselves.

Some of the high lands in the mountains were considered by the shamans to be too dangerous for shepherds and their flocks to live on any longer. They took them over and protected them from the Laminak themselves. They had begun holding rituals and ceremonial dances each quarter moon to protect the people from this evil water goddess. Offerings were now given to the new god, El, whom they hoped would do battle on their behalf and drive away the Laminak.

Saba's offer to help in every way she could was warmly appreciated by the wise women and their followers. The shamans shrugged and doubted if it would make a difference. Next day, she and Tara made their way to the ancient temple of the Laminak. It was hewn from a rocky cliff, and though abandoned only recently, was already being absorbed back into nature's care. Both women decided to lie down and dream on the altar slab, the quickest way to make contact. Since engaging in their joint Tantric exercises each morning, they were accustomed to synchronising their minds and bodies; within moments they were asleep and dreaming. A tall, well-built woman with long blond hair and wearing a white feathered robe stood before them. Her feet were like eagles' feet with white feathers reaching up to her human-shaped ankles. She was smiling a welcome to them both.

Saba began: 'You are the Laminak and we salute the spirit within you. Shall we introduce ourselves?'

'Not necessary. I already know a lot about you both and welcome you with all my heart. You are partly aware of the miserable situation which has developed here, and now that you two have arrived, I hope we can plan to resolve it together. You both have positions of power in your own country. I pray we can have many long discussions and enjoy each other's company.'

As all three of them were telepathic, they could exchange thoughts, feelings, ideas, narratives and pictures at electric speeds, unhampered by the slow time constraints imposed by language. The Laminak explained to them that all the troubles had been engineered by Etxeberi. He had made himself the chief shaman of the northern Euskerran tribes; since returning from his travels he was determined to supplant the notion of matriarchy in the nation's mind and replace it with the patriarchal system. He told his followers that males had really always been dominant over females – were they not stronger, more determined, less vulnerable to emotional persuasion? – so of course they were the natural leaders. In ancient times they had been hoodwinked by women who claimed superiority simply because they were the mothers who received the babies from the spirit ancestors, and grew and reared them, and because they knew about medical healing with plants and provided more constant food from roots, seeds and fruits than the men did from fish and meat, which could only be caught in season. Yet it was men who gave them babies by pouring their seed into them, just as their stock animals did. Women were not wiser or more enduring;

nor did they possess any other qualities over men. Etxeberi decreed that women must now do as they were told, like children and animals with limited sense and understanding. She also explained how Etxeberi had brought back a toxin and secretly placed it in the drinking water. It made people and animals sick; then when they worshipped the male god and brought gifts, he put an antidote in the water and everyone got better. The sickness is naturally blamed on the Laminak and the cure attributed to El. The Laminak had told all this to the wise women in dreams and these in turn told the other women in their community. They could not make their menfolk listen. Instead, they were punished like children for inventing lies. Meanwhile, the image of a benign male god was being developed in the minds of the people.

Saba remembered the poison Bethel had slipped in the drinking wells of the Mother Lake Folk disloyal to her family and the Old One, and told Tara about it.

'A clever but simple ruse, once we know about it. The simple plots are always the most effective,' Tara volunteered. 'We need to be wary of this Etxeberi. He's plainly no fool.'

'I can't tell you how greatly I appreciate your help and friendship,' said the Laminak. 'I have lots of ideas to counter his mischief but I can't put them into operation without help from able human accomplices. You must both return soon to my private refuge in case this temple is being watched. I will be able to materialise, sup with you and express my feelings properly. Can you bring a truly trustworthy Euskerran man friend who would help with my plan? That would be exceptional fortune.'

The two women returned to their friends in the port and told the wise woman they had met the Laminak in dream. She had said she would explain to all the people how a great mistake was being made. She would try to put things right with all the people, men and women. The wise woman must tell only her peer sisters, no one else. They explained the full situation to their close friends and how the Laminak had a plan which would soon restore Euskal Herria, as Orthonac called it, to a new and happier state. His own family held high status in the country. His parents were the biggest traders, and owned many of the fishing and trading curraghs that travelled along the entire western coast, exchanging goods from north of Garnac to south of the Giant's pillars and the sandy Berber lands with their great mountains, where the Giant held up the world on his back.

Some of the rescued children explained to Saba and Orthonac how they had been accosted by a laughing, fair-haired woman while they were gathering berries and roots. She had promised to show them a place where the bushes were laden with strange luscious berries which made marvellous wine that would delight their parents. They went with her, happily thinking their parents would be delighted. She exclaimed that as the spot was secret they must be blindfolded to reach the treasure; they would have it to themselves. But she led them to a series of underground caves and passages from which they could find no way out. They slept in a large cavern and were fed wild honey and nut cakes by the woman and a man who talked to her in a language they did not understand. There was a crystal clear waterfall to drink from. Finally, they were blindfolded on the way back and released near their village. Apparently, the berries were all stolen by a wicked witch. The fair-haired woman was short in stature and did not look like the description they were given of the Laminak, but then they had never seen her or any bird goddess with either claws or webbed feet.

Saba awoke in surprise to find the Laminak in bed beside her. The Laminak pressed her forehead to Saba's head and clasped her closely. 'Now we can communicate totally if you wish,' said the Laminak. 'You hold greater mysteries than Tara; I sensed them in your deep mind. I have talked with Lao Tzu. He visits the spirit world a lot now, and I understand Tara's yogic and healing abilities. But you have so many powerful helpers in spirit, and with your past experiences you could become one of us, spirits outside time, and serve the Great Mother by guiding a whole nation to expand their consciousness and transformative powers. In an older incarnation you were named Sekmet. She had a lion's head and the body of a beautiful woman. That's your connection with wild cats and lions, and from one of the ice ages come your experiences with bears and whales.'

Saba explained to the Laminak the new and exciting connection she had established with the Root and how he had asked her to do just that – protect and guide early peoples living in a new world. She hoped to help them avoid male-dominated barbarities, for the Root predicted that because of lust for selfish power and greed for lands, water and possessions, wars might rage until the planet faced a holocaust of destruction in which all mammals, including humans, became extinct.

'Yes,' replied the Laminak sadly. 'Just when humans come close to achieving a share in the organo-spirit world for themselves, and for all conscious entities in their universe, they will have the opportunity to populate enough to transform themselves over aeons of time. Tara's adopted father mentioned this entity of yours, the Root. He must be a kind of god if he can create a planet and its inhabitants. He has offered you an incredibly important position in the cosmos. How can you refuse?'

'I have not refused, but Aengus and I want to try and save our tribe from warfare and probable annihilation. Our people occupy only a small part of our island; however, it was prophesied that we would rescue them from such a fate.'

'I am certain you will find a way to do that as well. If later you accept the Root's appointment, your biggest problem will be finding ways to adjust the pendulum of gender control between men and women. It is vital that by some phase of temporal existence, say Aquarius for this planet, they can exercise an elastic balance of power. Under patriarchal jurisdiction, wielding power becomes the right and privilege of those appointed by collective authority – king, priest, army, father – to rule, conquer, repress and punish. The use of psychic power by the Mother – wise woman, guiding spirit, queen, priestess – is condemned as magic, sorcery and heresy against fatherhood and the male gods. So to each gender in turn the very idea of power becomes suspect: people worry that absolute power corrupts absolutely and become afraid of concepts like hubris, repression and destruction. When power as a positive force seems scary it is left to those who claim it for personal satisfaction, even those unconscious of their selfish motivations – dictators, do-gooders, fanatics or greedy entrepreneurs amassing goods, property and slaves, like the shaman Etxeberi here, who would organise a dictatorship.'

Saba agreed.

'Both genders must realise that power is a manifestation of natural energy, the creative force of world play, shaping and dissolving form,' the Laminak went on. 'It is the life process itself in which our human "I" experiences its own nature, its vitality and motivation.'

'Yes!' Saba replied. 'Life is power at play. Tara calls it "Shiva dancing". With his inseparable Shakti, Shiva is the supreme god in her pantheon of immortals.'

*

Saba and Tara brought Orthonac to their meeting with the Laminak in her secret cave. She had materialised and was standing in the entrance. As they saluted each other, Saba thought they made a well balanced pair. Orthonac's height and muscular frame, which at seven feet equalled that of Amlodi, enabled him to look down on her mere six feet. Her equivalent frame and shining charisma enhanced her presence and ensured one's gaze was attracted to her above anyone.

The Laminak explained the full details of the situation and the Mother's anger at children being dragged into it. Orthonac questioned her from his extensive knowledge of the background and was eventually satisfied that Etxeberi had launched on one of his old power trips to rule the nation, regardless of what damage was wreaked on the people. The Laminak, during the questions, had been judging him keenly. She asked him if he would be prepared to remain with his people in Euskerra as a secular leader and work alongside the wise women to help her maintain a balanced society. When he indicated that he would be proud to act with her, she suggested that because he seemed to be what Tara's tantrika friends called a Vira – someone capable of deeper psycho-spiritual experience and with the inner strength to play with fire – she was prepared to inaugurate him into the discipline of an asana. Tara and Saba explained that this was a psycho-yogic practice to test his faith and to know him intimately; the Laminak and he would even be able to telepathise together. The retention of seed transmits the sex force into a potency so strong that the serpent power up his spine was liberated to the top of his head and 'ananda', the spiritual joy of union, is experienced.

He stripped and stood to attention as requested by the Laminak. She laid him on his back and proceeded to mount him, moving with degrees of rhythmic excitement to which he responded nobly. After a while the Laminak nodded to her companions and said, 'He needs help.' Tara inserted her fingers with medical precision into the area of his groin around the scrotum while Saba pressed her thumb into the vagus nerve in his neck. His relaxation was instant and the onset of climax died away, enabling the couple to proceed in their motions until they murmured simultaneously, 'The serpent power', and froze in deep meditation.

Later, the Laminak pushed a wedge of wild honeycomb between his lips, congratulating him. 'We understand each other fully now and should work successfully together.'

During supper they agreed on a course of action. Orthonac would obtain supplies of the particular toxic rhizome and its antidote, which the Laminak told him Etxeberi stored in the shaman's lodge. He chose a time when the shamans were performing their quarterly ceremony at the sanctuary allocated to El. He found the rhizome in a covered basket, but took so long to discover the antidote, which was another plant soaking in water, that he was interrupted by a returning shaman who was highly suspicious when he saw him carrying materials in a bucket. Orthonac had to pretend he was bringing something unusual to show Etxeberi. When the other shaman became curious Orthonac put down the bucket to let him peep in, then seized him by the neck and snapped it. Then he had to hide the body. Fortunately the lodge was well secluded and he slipped away between the trees, bucket in hand, the body slung over his shoulder.

It was nightfall when he returned to Saba and Tara's lodgings. But they had left to meet the Laminak, who was going to show them the hidden passages where the fair-haired woman and foreign man lived with the children they had enticed away. The trek through the mountains was long and the first streaks of sunlight were paling the stars when they entered the entrance caves and quietly made their way to the central cavern. Listening, they detected faint sounds of breathing. Saba and Tara pounced on the sleepers before they could move. As soon as they opened their eyes, Saba hypnotised them both. Answering her questions, they said that they were Berbers, and that Etxeberi had told them he would give them a farm and make them rich if they did exactly what he ordered them. The woman said she had been unhappy about the children but made sure they were never harmed. Saba told her that if she repeated her story to an assembly of people exactly as she had just told it to her, she and her man would not be punished.

Orthonac and Saba summoned the inhabitants of the entire area for the following day to listen to an announcement of vital importance. The news had spread during the days since they landed that Saba was the paramount queen of an important trading country to the north visited by their curraghs for gold and precious axe heads. They were already impressed by her appearance, bearing and charisma. Her handsome son and his exotic partner stood beside her. When she began speaking, Orthonac translated for her. She began by recognising their ancient status and language and pointing out that her country, like theirs and others she had visited in the Tideless Sea, still followed the Mother Goddess. She was most distressed to witness the great mischief that was being perpetrated against their guardian spirit, the Laminak, who had always protected them, while the lower lands around them were awash with strangers who preferred male gods. There were shouts of protest by the shamans, claiming that the Laminak had deserted them and was a traitoress. Saba's voice rang out like a clarion: 'You don't understand how you have been duped by your own head shaman.'

'Prove it,' they yelled back.

'I can,' Saba called. She turned and led out the Berber couple who were standing behind her. 'This woman will tell you her story in your own language, which she speaks well enough to please your children. The woman told them the truth, exactly as she told Saba. The children in the audience, who recognised her, gave a cheer. They had all liked her and asked their parents if she could be their teacher. 'That deed turned back towards you, Etxeberi,' laughed Orthonac. Saba turned again and produced two sorry-looking goats. 'Now for the fake sickness supposedly sent to us by the Laminak.' She held up the rhizome. 'Etxeberi put this plant in all the drinking water wells, and when you brought your gifts to El, he put this antidote in the water to cure you and the animals. Look at these goats now they have drunk the antidote.' She had let them slake their thirst from the bucket handed to her by a wise woman and already the goats looked brighter and livelier.

Etxeberi exploded with a screech of fury and ran at Saba with a wickedly curved flint knife. Orthonac, standing close by had been anticipating his reaction and seizing his knife arm broke it neatly at the elbow. He offered the knife to Saba, gesturing that a coup de grace would be appropriate. Instead, she and Tara knelt towards a spirit image of the Laminak, which appeared on the hillside facing the people. 'Kneel and ask her forgiveness,' Saba called to them and even the shamans bowed their knees. The Laminak uttered a sequence of musical sounds that rolled over them like music from a pipe organ and filled them with awe. This time Saba interpreted. 'The Laminak grants you peace and her love. If you restore her shrine and her worship, she will permit those of you who wish to present token offerings to the new male god who seems blameless in this sad affair. Etxeberi is to be ankle fettered and left in the Laminak's grotto as she wants to heal his sickness. Orthonac is to be appointed as new secular chief of the northern lands and his companion, Stephanie, will be "first wife". The Berber couple may remain. They are productive and so positive.'

Saba ordered her ship to be provisioned and ready to set sail within two days, allowing time for a parting celebration.

The storm which followed the ship up to Biskayne had vanished, swallowed into the endless waves and swells of the Grey Ocean, and the sunlight played beams over them daily as they rowed slowly past Garnac and the Armorican peninsula, a small wind just fluffing the sails.

As the ship traversed the sleeve of deeper water separating the three lands, Saba, Amlodi and Medea stood watching the white wake trailing from either side of the keel, stridden by the usual group of gambolling dolphins. Amlodi was piping one of his mournful plaints when Saba nudged them. 'Look further back in the water,' she said.

He started and Medea chortled. 'I've been watching them each day since we left Biskayne,' Medea said. She turned to Saba. 'I suppose you have been talking to them.'

Saba nodded. 'I have. They've followed us since Byblos, I believe. They feel I belong to their pod as a land-based member and pods must stick together for survival. Amlodi, you recall – they lost a young brother at the volcano before the Isle of Bees, when the lava fell on him as he surfaced for air. I was adopted then to take his place and they vision me in their mind set as clearly as him. However, only Hroom communicates with me. You can know him by the scars near his big dorsal fin The other three just listen. They think of us as a bizarre pair.'

'So it's a male with whom you have the long discussions, or is it envisionings? What genders are the other three then?' Medea asked. 'All female, a mother and two younger ones,' replied Saba. 'Pods are usually led and guided by a mother. They can live as long as the oldest humans and seem to be able to retain and use their memories better about things such as where and when there were good feeding grounds during a bad cycle of seasons. Don't forget they use all the seas and estuary-fed lakes on the globe of the world. As to language, there are varied kinds – a simple telepathy of exchanging pictures, a very complicated series of clicks and whistles. I'm still learning these. Then musical notes and sounds for feelings, utterances and dreams. They dream a lot through all three modes. Then dreams get involved with intentions and aspirations. This is very difficult.'

'I would still love to communicate properly with them.' Amlodi sighed. 'If you persevere and make enough time, there's no reason why you shouldn't.'

'When did I ever get enough time. I haven't lived near a shore for yuls – not since I was a child in the northern Baltic seas and hunted for amber, and since you introduced me to these fascinating animals. I only see them when I'm on a ship with you.'

'Perhaps some day we'll manage it.' Saba viewed him speculatively. 'If you really want it enough! I'm sure Medea would love to live by the sea again. It was your life was it not?' Medea nodded. 'But hopefully a warmer sea than this one! I would give you both swimming experience. In fact you need to relearn more efficient movements.'

They avoided the Kaheen's court in Er-rin and ran the ship further up the coast to Boand's river leading to the Temples of Light. Saba wanted to meet her old friend Bride, leader of the Seior, and hear her balanced views before talking to Sedana and judging any discrepancies involving the Eelfolk's opinions. Bride was treated to, and thrilled by, a summary of Saba's adventures. She threw her arms around Amlodi and welcomed Tara with a long scrutiny and a kiss of offered friendship. Finally, she had a long chat with Aengus, establishing his complete restoration of health and recent mental development. 'The damaged goods are now resplendent,' she remarked to Saba with a smile. 'But I am not happy about this clay business. Up there they are on the edge of war about it, Pilar and Marcos are not the problem. A strong personal animosity has sprung up between the one they believe to be the Kaheen and the majority of the Folk, and every moon it has been allowed to fester brings us nearer to conflict.'

Sedana waited only two days before arriving at the Temples of Light. She had become more imperious in manner. She chided Saba for not visiting her first and showed her disappointment, failing to discuss how they might arrange their identities. Saba explained that she had no intention of upsetting the status quo and had only come to help her sort out what appeared to have become a perilous impasse. The Eelfolk, apart from Pilar, still believed the real Saba was Kaheen and had betrayed them. The penalty for this was death. Sedana was afraid to confront them under either guise, so would neither go north to meet them nor invite a delegation to come south. She was already very angry about everything that had occurred. She felt that Saba would want to take back the Kaheenship no matter what was said. She enjoyed being the most powerful person on the island, keeping a harem of lovers, and had no intention of giving up this position.

Saba knew that Pilar would like to assist her, but could do little because the Eelfolk barely tolerated her as co-leader, with Markos, of the whole tribe, knowing she was related to herself and Sedana. So Saba announced that she was prepared to travel alone to negotiate a new agreement between them and the rest of the island. She forwarded this proposal to the tribal elders via Pilar. Her courage impressed them and they agreed to hold a council to discuss the matter with her.

Sedana plotted a scheme to be rid of Saba permanently. One of her most trusted lovers belonged to a faction of the Folk who had always disliked Saba since long before the White Clay War, when she was linked to Fion the Outsider. He proved eager to help carry out her plan. He was sent north secretly, to rally and enlarge this faction of her old enemies so that when alerted they would attack and destroy Saba, her friends and any of the council who dared come to the meeting place. Remembering and fearing Saba's uncanny ability to escape from every deviant situation that threatened her, Sedana decided to go herself and ambush her on the coast, taking five of her trusted and deadliest bowmen along with the Eelfolk's renowned poisoned arrows. Aengus and Tara pointed out to Saba that she could not paddle a curragh alone, as she intended to meet the council at Redbay, a part of the coast where a great band of rock in the cliff is bright red sandstone instead of basalt or granite. Medea, who had become close friends with Saba on the long voyage from Byblos, asked as a special favour to be chosen, as she must have at least another paddler in the curragh. But Amlodi would not hear of them going without him and Aengus agreed. If Amlodi did not go then he would go himself.

Saba had great misgivings about the outcome of her meeting. She had imaged Lady Spider and all she glimpsed was a glistening web with a ball in the centre. She particularly did not want Aengus or Tara to be killed or injured as she felt they were about to accomplish a major part of their destiny. The future seemed vague for herself and for Medea; she knew Medea's prowess in diving and swimming and felt pleased and more secure with her company. She did not mention the private arrangement she had made with her friends, the orcas, anticipating that the final leg of the trip would be made by herself alone. There was still no track northwards through the dense forests to connect the Mother Lake with the Temples of Light. The traces in the landscape from the western lakes to the south-west corner of the Mother Lake made by Maeve's army had long disappeared. No trade existed other than that of the white clay. The Folk were only too happy to retain their total independence.

When Saba, Medea and Amlodi left one morning in their curragh, rowing down the Boand river and out to sea, Saba carried two extra lengths of a soft fibre rope. The others were too respectful to enquire its purpose; they reckoned that would become apparent – and their surmise was correct, although any guess would have been off the mark. Saba searched the water for four familiar orca heads. To Amlodi's joy and Medea's amusement, two orcas aligned their bodies on either side of the curragh. Saba slipped her lengths of rope around their bodies in front of the big dorsal fins. Amlodi and Saba held two ends each, giving them a whale-powered curragh. Partners were exchanged several times to relieve strain and monotony, and certainly a temporal leg record was established.

When they arrived at Redbay, Pilar and Markos were standing on the sandy beach, the first to greet them. Most of the council were there too and a refreshing meal awaited them. Saba deplored and apologised for the way the situation had been allowed to lapse. She fully agreed that adequate compensation should be paid. They established that sheep would be a desirable medium of exchange and accepted that forty per yul would be appropriate. These could be conveyed in twenty curraghs like the clay. This number would be increased if even greater quantities of white clay were required. Saba relayed this information to Aengus, Tara, Bride and Axular, now the chief Watcher, as the agreement was made.

At that moment an army of warriors erupted onto the beach, attacking the council members and heading for Saba's group. Everyone raced into the sea and swam for their lives. Saba, Medea and Amlodi easily outdistanced the Eelfolk who followed them and they were glad to see that Pilar, Markos and some others also escaped. Then three curraghs appeared, cutting them off and shooting arrows at them. Most arrows were aimed at Saba and two grazed her. One landed in Amlodi's burly back but Medea plucked it out and received a graze herself. The waters parted beside them to reveal Hroom, who took Saba and Medea on board, clinging to his fin. Three orca heads darted towards the pursuing curraghs and flipped them over with their flukes. One orca collected Amlodi on its back while Hroom swam to a red-haired woman, seized her long tresses, forcing her head under water, and swam out to sea. The other three followed close behind.

Back at the Temple of Light, Bride and Axular were seated with Saba's family. Tara received a telepathic vision from Saba and they impatiently awaited the news. Tara was white and grasping Aengus's hand as she described the unreal pictures entering her mind. 'Sedana is dead! Saba, Medea and Amlodi have gone out to sea with the orcas. They are all wounded by the poisoned arrows and are not returning.' Everyone groaned. Aengus threw himself on the ground. Bride and Axular left the temple and returned the following day.

'I have consulted with the Seior and the Watchers about replacing the Kaheen. They all remember Fion who acted as leader when Board was too old to function. As you, Aengus, are a living replica of him in character and looks, and the son of the real Kaheen, we will relinquish the Kaheenship for a period in order to have you as leader and guardian again. Saba's friends are welcome to stay or go as they wish and we are happy to accept Tara as your consort.'

Aengus thanked Bride and said they would be honoured to have her help, both as they learned their duties and later as a triumvirate to care for the island. They would, however, retain the right to travel when and where they wished on his mother's ship. Bride accepted their terms. She in turn would be pleased to work with them.

One of the Seiors handed Tara a white hare which licked her arm. She stroked it affectionately. 'Saba visioned pictures of these in my memory, she called them her sparring partners.'

'She left a pair with us to help us create our auguries, they are Mother Lake creatures, sacred to the moon and she loved them. I place them and their generations in your keeping.' Bride told her. 'Perhaps we will revive the ancient stronghold on our holy mount in the midlands and rename it in honour of the White Tara, the sacred protectress you have been telling us about. They sound so alike, she must be related to our goddess Board the White Cow.'

*

Saba's mind was spinning in light'ning spirals. Medea clasped her tight between her body and the fin. The Root's voice sounded in her head.

'I must take you now while you still live.'

'Where?' she breathed.

'To our new world,' he replied.

'Then take us all together and integrate us in your consciousness. We have only the idea that we make of ourselves to sustain us on this voyage of becoming.' Her thinking mind was drenched by scenes and images from the Root and from the deep well of her memory; old acquaintances and unknown ones, naked and long haired. The Spinner, with legs glued to her dew-glittering web. Aengus, Aine, Tara appeared in turn, and Bethel as she first saw him at Mother Lake, he was smiling and pointing at little Bethel cradled in Sarah's arms.

The voice deepened, 'Remember when guiding your new family, language can teach argument, poesy, logic, exploration, magical words and mantras, but people also need ineffable modes of communication like your telepathy, aleatory music, transcendent love, enchanting wit, healing resonances, you must tone harmonics with Amlodi as Tara and Aengus do. There is as much room in our minds as spaces between the stars for experiencing imagination and wonder. You will never be alone – exchanging visions with your present family and a vast company of beings who are interwoven with you. Everything in the multiverse is related, existence is unending.'

To a watcher on the cliff, the four dots swimming far out ceased to be visible, presumably submerged.

THE END

GLOSSARY OF TERMS & CHARACTERS

TERMS

Ambergris – a gelatinous, inflammable substance with dull grey variegations like marble, and possessing a sweet, earthy odour. It is secreted and disgorged from the stomach of the sperm whale and can be found floating in the sea or washed up on beaches in lumps from 40 grams to 40 kilos in size. Squid beaks are often found in it. It melts at 18°C to a fatty liquid and imparts a deep fragrance to perfumes. In the east it is also used as culinary flavouring and in pharmacy; see Christopher Kemp, Floating Gold (University of Chicago Press, 2012).

Bridskidney (Ganoderma lucidum) – Bracket fungus found from late spring to autumn, usually at the base of oak trees; it is soft and tasty when young. In the Orient it is named Ling Chi and used for the same reasons as ginseng.

Dree – accomplish; work out.

Epolar – also called orca/grampus/killer whale. About four times the length of a dolphin, it is related to them, and a highly efficient hunter and killer of creatures from seals to sharks and great whales, but never known to attack man. It can be trained like a dolphin and is kept in some seaworld parks.

Garefowl – Great Auks, the penguins of the north, were hunted to extinction in the nineteenth century.

Hermit boar – Wild boar, 15 – 30 years old.

Hupomone (Gk) – Patient endurance, for as long as it takes.

Liberty Cap (Psilocybe semilanceolata) – magic mushroom; has similar hallucinogenic properties to the fly agaric or ravensbread.

Narwhal – an Arctic whale, greyish-white with leopard-like spots, 15 to 20 feet long. In the male, the left tusk in upper jaw projects forward from the head with left-spiralling lines and tapers to a point almost as long as the body. Horns from harpooned or beached animals were represented as those of the magical unicorn.

Saithe – coalfish/coley/piltock; an important food since Mesolithic times. Adults grow to about three feet long; they shoal like cod and herring.

Torpedo fish (Torpedo nobiliana) – The Roman physician Scribonius recommended the electric shock from its head for gout and severe headaches. He successfully treated the Emperor Claudius in AD 47. Dioscorides, in AD 75, was treating paralysis and nervous disorders with it. By 4000 BC, Greek fishermen knew that a spear plunged in the fish could numb their hand for hours. It is found in shallow Mediterranean waters.

Tulpa/tulku – The incarnation of an entity. The ability to create a tulku, or the less lasting but more material tulpa, depends on the degree of power of the projector, and this in turn depends on the strength, amount of concentration and quality of the mind itself. Both concepts are used in Tibetan Bon animism.

Tupilak (Inuit) – spirit helper; can be part animal, part human.

Ulu – multi-purpose Inuit knife with half-moon-shaped blade, resembling an Inca tumi, with both ends honed to sharp points.

White clay – Large deposits of diatomaceous earth found in the flat banks of the lower Bann river leading out of Lough Neagh. Diatomite, as a natural colloidal silicate with over twenty-five mineral and trace elements, was prized by Amerindian medicine men. A variety of earth and rock dusts are eaten as a tonic by many peoples around the world.

Wyrd (Anglo-Saxon) – Destiny, magic. The flowing of life's complexities beyond the ability of words to comprehend. Not fate, but the inexorable evolution of the world, within which human affairs ebb and flow, sometimes in or out of harmony with the Tao or earth spirit.

Wyvre/wouivre – a fifth element (after earth, air, fire and water), in ancient lore. It has been translated as ether, telluric energy, mana, chi, prana, also water and serpent – a wavy animal spitting fire or lightning (hydre/hydra). One of the stones lining the north-eastern side of the entrance passage to the Gavrinis shrine in Brittany has three carved serpent-like lines appearing to rise from the ground onto the stone.

Zeroi – the Basque name for the sperm whale or cachalot. It can be up to sixty feet long, and has a huge blunt head one third of its body size. Its twenty-six lower teeth weigh an average of two kilos each and its favourite food is giant squid. In the stomach of one washed up in the Azores was found an intact squid measuring thirty-four feet from tip to tip of tentacles. Despite having been an age-long victim of man and now an endangered species, they tolerate the presence of divers who swim alongside and stroke them.

PLACES

Ailinn – Knockaulin, Boand's village.

Akkad – early empire from c. 2360 BC, covering approximately modern Syria and Iraq.

Albion – England; from the root Alb, Albina, White Goddess.

Amber coast – Baltic Sea coast.

Anu river – the River Liffey (e.g. Joyce's 'Anna Livia Plurabella'); also see 'Anu' in 'Otherworld entities'.

Axe Island – Rathlin.

Axe Mountain – Tievebulliagh in County Antrim.

Blood Mountain – Slievegallion in the Sperrin range, County Derry; a source of haematite/red ochre.

Boand river – the River Boyne; also White Cow river.

Boand's Plain – the great plain from the curragh of Kildare northwards.

Brid's Temples – Loughcrew hills and at Kildare where Brid's flame was tended by the Seior; see Brid/Bride/Bridgid.

Conal's country – Donegal.

Crom's Mountain – Croagh Patrick in County Mayo.

Cualan hills/mountains – Wicklow hills/mountains.

Cymru – Wales, land of the Cymry tribes.

Dancing floors – sacred areas enclosed by ring ditches or stone circles.

Dolmen – two or three upright stones topped by a large flat capping stone.

Eelway – lower Bann river.

Er-rin – island of Ireland

Euskualdun – the Basque peoples, or their area of influence.

Funeral mounds – barrows and tumuli aligned on specific stars like Deneb, Vega, Sirius, Altair, Rigel etc., which moved above and below the horizon, from where dead souls could be raised into otherworld habitations by the Star Lords on their journeys.

Gar – Garonne river in south-west France.

Garnac – old Breton name for Carnac, the site of the largest accumulation of megalithic monuments in the world.

Giant's face – natural formation in Cavehill rock overlooking north Belfast.

Giant's ring – Sunken rath c. 200 metres diameter with massive circular rampart, famous Neolithic site at south end of the marshes on which Belfast now stands.

Giant's Steps – the Giant's Causeway, in north Antrim.

Hecla – the Icelandic volcano whose eruptions had a drastic effect on Northern Europe. Hecla 4 c. 2354 BC was considered to be a major sky war.

Holyisland – Ram's Island in Lough Neagh; ramsons are a plant, also known as wild garlic; a spirit herb.

Holyisland river – Crumlin river; petrified wood is still found in its bay and waters.

Isle of Bees – Malta.

Kingdom of the Two Lands – Khemt/Qemt, ancient Egypt.

Larmorica – Armorica/Brittany; Larmor-land by the sea, called the Shaking Land because of the many earth tremors that occurred there during this period.

Longstone – menir; single standing stones used as tribal/parish/boundary markers or lodging for local ancestral spirits. Usually of quartz or granite in which the defect crystal lattices are transducers of energy; see Don Robins, Secret Language of Stone (1988), and Hans Jenny, Cymatics (1967) on the dynamics of vibrations.

Mananan's Island – Isle of Man.

Meluha – Akkadian name for India and Pakistan (Indus valley civilization).

Mother Lake – Lough Neagh.

Mountain of the Winds – Slemish Mountain, County Antrim.

Narbac – Mediterranean port at the end of an ancient trade route that passed down the river Garonne to where Toulouse now stands, then overland via Narbonne.

Oyster Lough and River – the Foyle river, County Derry.

Sanctuaries – the sacred villages that protected the Eelfolk ancestors.

Seal rocks – the Skerries off Portrush on the Antrim coast.

Seior temples – located at Loughcrew hills and Kildare; they were astronomically aligned to the seasonal movements of moon and sun.

Shinan – Shannon river and Maeve's capital village.

Sleeping Giant river – the River Lagan, so called from the natural formation of the Giant's face in the Cavehill rock overlooking north Belfast.

Star lodges – stellar constellations to which worthy souls of ancestors were led.

Suil's springs – the hot springs at Bath.

Sundust river – the Avoca river and its tributaries in the Wicklow hills; it enters the sea at Arklow.

Temples of Light – the complex of structures at Newgrange aligned to astronomical features, some of which admit the sun's beams at seasonal highpoints.

Tideless Sea – the Mediterranean Sea.

Valley of the Ancestors – area around the Garonne, Dordogne and Lot rivers down to Pyrenees and across Southern France. It has been populated continuously since at least 50000 BC as it lay beyond the reach of the ice sheets.

White Clay village – by little Lough Beg, north of Lough Neagh.

White Cow river – the River Boyne.

SOCIAL GROUPINGS

Allmother – the supreme wise one. She resided at the sanctuaries, where she selected and trained the young female candidates whose supernormal gifts were developed in the Raven's cave. She also supervised the head elders and the Hearthmothers of each village.

Clans – general title of the European peoples of the north-west Atlantic coast and islands who followed the older Neolithic pastoral and farming traditions and still used megalithic structures in their religious rituals. They called themselves children of Anu, the planet Venus, which was one of the manifestations of the Mother Goddess.

Eelfolk – An unknown Mesolithic fisher tribe hidden by dense forests in the north of Er-rin. With unfailing resources, and protective of their traditions and telepathic abilities (as found in rare Amazonian cultures), they utterly rejected the farming revolution that long before had attracted and overwhelmed neighbouring tribes.

Elders – every Eelfolk village had an elected council of veteran males which worked with the Hearthhouse to guide the people.

Finmen/Inuit – The sea distances linking Greenland – Iceland – Faroes – Orkneys are 180, 275, 185 and 200 miles respectively, all feasible distances for a kayak equipped with harpoon and fishing lines, and paddled on a suitable current or blown by storms. It is recorded in AD 1700 that, on average, one Finman/Inuit per year was seen around the Orkneys, and often killed or chased away because it was believed they brought ill luck with them.

Guardians – each Clan had an elite flying troop of warriors who supplied the Kaheen's bodyguard; they were the executive arm of the law for Seior and Seers, and protected the coast from pirates.

Hearthmothers – the spiritual leaders of each Eelfolk village and Hearthhouse; they had shamanic and telepathic powers.

Kaheens – the spiritual and temporal leaders of each Clan; earthly representatives of the White Cow goddess, they worked with Bride, the Seior mistress.

Ker – title of elders in Larmorican villages.

Nymphs – trainee hearthmothers and assistants.

Scouts – young Eelfolk bowmen who helped train boys at the testing fields and acted as a kind of home guard against intruding strangers who might venture up the rivers from the coast.

Seers – the Watchers and recorders of all sky and earth movements. With the Seior, they preserved Clan rituals and customs, and regulated the sacred landscape.

Seior – spiritual and temporal guides, healers and lunar priestesses, they worked with the Seers to protect the covenants with the Sky Lords and prevent further catastrophes like volcanoes, earthquakes, comets, meteorites etc. They interchanged with their temple peers in other Clans and countries, travelling the sea roads like traders and artists.

Skyfathers – shamans who lived in a lodge at the Eelfolk sanctuaries and supervised rituals and the testing fields for young men.

Smiths – Wandering metal workers and miners from the central mainland, welcomed for their unearthly skills in extracting and working with metals. They were allowed to settle in their own villages by the Clans, with whom they traded, and left free to follow their own customs and gods.

SKY AND UNDEREARTH WARS

Our ancestors felt at one with all things in a world where every element that existed, be it a rock or a horse, was recognised as possessing some degree of universal animating spirit. They assumed that their passionate and devoted rituals had an influence on even the most awe-inspiring events.

They helped the sun to survive its midwinter crisis, tried to alleviate the calculated eclipses of sun and moon and appeased supernovae and comets (invading sky gods with flaming hair). Departed spirits of venerated ancestors could be persuaded to mediate on the tribes' behalf with otherworld lords when they went to live with them in their starlodges.

They offered sacrifices to assuage the dread lords of sky, underworld and the fecund earth goddess herself. It was believed that battles between these gods created such devastating phenomena as floods, volcanic explosions, asteroid or meteor strikes, which resulted in drought, pestilence, lightning fires and homelands being submerged by the sea. Today our law still recognises 'Acts of God'.

The last glacial expansion (125,000 years ago) began decreasing from c. 15,000 BC to 5000 BC. During this period, the average sea level rose by 120 metres in three major inundations. These also affected the frequency and violence of volcanic eruptions, land subsidence, climate flips, earthquakes and fault tremors like those at Garnac where the earth shook regularly from the weight of huge tides rushing into the bay of Morbihan (Brittany).

As most ancient societies lived along coasts and estuaries, their cities, fertile fields and land bridges were catastrophically submerged. Instances of these wipeouts are noted, for example, on the Scilly Isles, Malta, in areas around the Black Sea and Persian Gulf, and the Indus valley cities lost in the Gulf of Cambay and along the Malabar coast in c. 7000 BC.

Memories of such events in earth and sky were preserved orally for thousands of years in the myths and legends of survivors, shaping their responses to the supernatural. Apart from the possibility of close passing comets and meteorite bombardments, which may have triggered major volcanic eruptions as described, the great eruption in the Aleutian Islands of 3119 BC precipitated a mini ice age across the world, followed by floods six to seven years later, particularly noted in Mesopotamia, where melting ice from the Zagros mountains was supplemented by rising sea waters in the Persian Gulf and elsewhere. The Mayan Calendar dated from 3113 BC, presumably as a result of the new environment there.

In 2354 BC, the Hecla 4 eruption in Iceland produced environmental crises for ten years, not only over Northern Europe but as far afield as

Syria; see Marie-Agnes Courty, 'Causes and effects of the 2350 BC Middle East Anomaly' in Proceedings of the Second SIS Cambridge Conference on Natural Catastrophes during Bronze Age Civilisations (July 1997).

MENSURATION

Many spatial units of measurement were derived from parts of the human body such as:1 finger width – ¾ inch or 2 cms
   1 hand – 4 fingers; still used to measure horses (12-18 hands to shoulder)
   1 ell – distance from elbow to fingertips; a tailor's ell wand checked clothwidths
   3 feet – 1 pace/megalithic yard

Geometrical shapes were copied from nature, shapes found in things like tide marks or butterfly wings, and in the constellations. For example, the summer triangle – drawn between Vega in the Lyre, Deneb in Cygnus and Altair in Aquila – is close to the right angle used in lining up 'ovoid' dancing floors; the great square of Pegasus, or the divided oblong depicted by Orion. The circumpolar stars suggested how to describe a circle around a fixed point with measuring line and stick. An oval dancing floor (egg shape) was determined by a triangle of 3 x 4 x 5 paces/megalithic yards. Spirals are portrayed in shells, whirlpools etc.

Settled populations could establish short temporal units from measures of sun and shadow, with poles or marking stones acting as gnomons, as with a sundial. Employing a rule of thumb, the units of daily sunlight could be divided crudely into ten fingers, sufficient for hunter – gatherers. As a 'finger' denoted both space and time, pairs of fingers often invoked a magical/holy symbol for blessings or curses, such as in a Papal benediction, Polynesian good luck or the gesture of the horns in Mediterranean lands.

The new moon began with the first visible sighting of the silver horns, as it does for the Chinese or Muslim New Year's moon and Longer temporal concepts were obtained from the sky:
   One quarter of a visible lunation – 7 days
   7 x 52 quarters – 1 yul/year
   1 yul/year – 13 visible moons = one solar year, plus one day (the old fairy tale injunction to return in a year and a day).
The planet Anu/Venus appears alternatively in the evening or in the

morning sky when she is often visible during the day. This is followed by short phases of invisibility; those between evening and morning last three weeks; those between morning and evening last three months. For five such periods she wanders around the Zodiac in loops, and in her few weeks of maximum brightness each period she outshines all other planets. Each period lasts one year and seven months, so her complete cycle takes eight years.

The mighty storm god Agni/Jupiter takes a whole year to move through a single constellation and then becomes invisible for seven to eight weeks, so his course through the Zodiac takes twelve years (a Jovian year).

The Red Lord of Mischief, Mars, moves at erratic rates. He increases by four classes of brilliance over a year, but never quite matches Anu; then he decreases during the following year. The solar-lunar conjunction, which occurs approximately every 18½ years is measured as one great yul; this was counted as one generation by the Clans.1 Star yul – approximately 2200 yuls (i.e. the time it takes one zodiacal constellation to succeed another at the spring/vernal equinox sunrise). For example:

Bull/Taurus – c. 4400 BC – 1800 BC

Ram/Aries – c. 1800 BC – 100 BC

Fish/Pisces – c. 100 BC – AD 2600

1 Sky age – c. 26,000 yuls to complete a cycle of the constellations
    of the Zodiac

The Sumerians have left records of the Anu/Venus cycle since 3760 BC and the Hebrews also reckon their calendar from that date. China, Tibet and the Indus valley civilization have been using the twelve-year Jovian cycle since c. 2953 BC to calculate their New Year and to name their astrological round of animals. Calibrated dating of material found at ancient rock drawings, for example at Lascaux and Chauvet caves, and bone engravings, have shown that some star and lunar cycles were noted and recorded by early man as long ago as 50,000 BC.

Temperature in Northern Europe c. 2300 BC was about two to three degrees centigrade warmer than it is today, and less windy (mild Atlantic). This meant that highlands were easier to farm, the sea was more navigable for small craft and the deciduous forests and wetlands were closer to present-day Mediterranean warmth.

Tids (OE) – time, season, festival, opportunity, tidal reaches.

Tides – high and low every 12 hours.

Ebb – goes out twice in 24 hours.

Flood – comes in twice in 24 hours.

A spring tide – occur at every new or full moon, and is higher than usual.

A neap tide – occur at half new or half full moon, when sun and moon are working against each other, so at minimum strength.

Rip tides and races – created by the convergence of two, or even three, tidal streams narrowing through gaps between islands or peninsulas, for example. These may produce undercurrents, whirlpools, or turbulent waves dangerous to small craft.

CHRONOLOGY

Northern Europe : Major rises in sea levels – c. 12,000 BC, 9 – 10,000 BC, 5500 BC.

Iceland: (800 miles north of Ireland), Hecla 4 volcanic eruption took place – c. 2354 BC, perhaps induced by, cometary bombardment; it brought about ten years of immediate disturbance and longer term climatic change in the Middle East.

Old One – c. 2366 – 2266 BC.

Fion arrives at Motherlake – c. 2276 BC.

Aengus and Aine born – c. 2276 BC.

Saba anointed Kaheen of Eastern Clans – c. 2257 BC.

Akkadian dynasty: Seven years' drought – 2353 BC.

Sargon, Emperor of Akkad – c. 2360-2304 BC.

Rimus – 2315 – 2306 BC.

Manistusu – 2306 – 2291 BC.

Naram Sin – 2291 – 2254 BC.

Enheduanna appointed high priestess and poet of Ur by Sargon – c. 2305 BC.

Saba's literary collaboration with Enheduanna – 2255 BC (Saba 38 yuls; Enheduanna 65 yuls).

Aengus and Tara meet – 2255 BC.

CHARACTERS IN SABA'S CHOICES

(Names in italics are main characters.)

Abram – a pastoralist from the Harran area. He became the founder of the religions of the Hebrews, the Moslems and the Christians (he is also known as Abraham/Ibrahim). He married Sarah and Hagar, possibly among others.

Aelise – Melusine's daughter in Garnac and Bethel's lover there.

Aengus – twin of Aine, and Saba's son by Fion.

Aine – twin of Aengus, and Saba's daughter by Cairla.

Alan – Saba's second companion, a Seafolk man who fosters the twins.

Alaric – Olwen's companion, Fion's father-line from Larmorica.

Allmother – Old One or Salah, the wise one and matriarch of all Eel and Seafolk.

Amlodi – Eastern Clan's leading minstrel, from Amber coast.

Anan – Seafolk captive of Fion's mariners.

Ariadne – Queen of Phaistos, mother of Kalliste, sister of Hermes, consort of Hephaistos.

Art – Grainne's brother.

Axular – a sage from the Basque country who tutors the twins at the Temples of Light.

Baldan – Aengus's sworn enemy and Maolin's nephew.

Bandu – elder and shaman at Seafolk village.

Bethel – healer and traveller from Akkad on the Kretan ship.

Betla – Nana's helper at the twins' birth.

Boand – Kaheen of the Eastern Clans.

Bran – Fion's brother.

Bride – Seior Mistress of Er-rin.

Brude – Axe islander, later captured and brainwashed by Eagrin.

Cairla – Saba's uncle and rapist.

Celan – mole for Maeve among Eagrin's Watchers.

Chrestena – an Amazon girl from the Danube and Black Sea lands, companion to Ariadne.

Croesni – head of the Smiths in the eastern Clans.

Daran – elder at Holyisland village.

Datemi – Bee keeper and priestess.

Dectra – head Nymph at Holyisland Hearthhouse.

Dugan – a native of Firestone village.

Eagrin – Master of the Seers at the Temple of Light, Newgrange. He and Bride, the Seior mistress, direct the activities of the Clanspeople.

Eino – head fisherman at Seafolk village.

Ena – Aine's wetnurse.

Endil – scout at the testing fields.

Enheduanna – granddaughter of Sargon. In 2305 BC, as a precocious child of only 15, she was appointed head of the ancient Sumerian city and culture of Ur by Sargon. He required one of his bloodline to be in control under the goddess Inanna. She was chief priestess of Ur and governor of the Naditu in the city. Much of her poetry has been found and translated.

Etain – Kaheen of south-eastern Clanspeople.

Europa – Queen of Knossos.

Eurydice – Consort of Hermes.

Eva – head shaman at the Valley of the Ancestors

Fergus – Maeve's favourite consort.

Fion – born of Olwen, the priestess at Suil's springs, and Alaric the Larmorican. Ambitious leader of the eastern Clan guardians, Boand's favourite consort, Saba's lover and predicted to become instrumental in saving the Eelfolk.

Fleur – joint Seior mistress, with Melusine, in Garnac.

Goll – Maeve's war leader.

Grainne – Fion's early and later companion at Sundust river.

Hephaistos – Consort of Ariadne, cleverest gemcutter in Krete.

Hermes – Kalliste's uncle, captain of Kretan ship.

Hroom – Saba's favourite orca

Ikhaluk – Saba's spirit father and Mara's Inuit companion on Axe Island.

Jaim-es – Leader of the hunters at Holyisland.

Jen-ifer – Mon-ika's daughter, Ulan's partner.

Jes-ika – Mastell's sister and Markos's companion.

Johan – senior elder at Twinrivers village.

Kalliste – Kretan girl from the Tideless Sea. Daughter of Ariadne, niece of Hermes, friend of Aine.

Ka-ren – chief shaman in Valley of the Ancestors; Amlodi's sister.

Kev-een – Markos's second son.

Lao Tzu – Ancient monk and mentor of Tara.

Lara – Hearthmother at Sanctuary; Mara's mother and Allmother's daughter.

Larmor – Eastern Clan Artist And Kinsman Of Alaric.

Maeve – the bloody Kaheen of the western Clans who aspires to rule the island; bitter enemy of Fion, she becomes Saba's main antagonist.

Malin – friend of Tudic.

Maolin – jealous enemy of Saba at Holyisland.

Mara – Saba's mother and Hearthmother of Holyisland village.

Markos – Fion's Eelfolk friend, companion of Jes-ika, Mastell's sister.

Mastell – Fion's shipwreck island saviour.

Mat-hieu – Sky father and head shaman at Sanctuary Skylodge.

Medea – of Caria in Anatolia, sponge diver, stays with Amlodi in Krete, Aengus's companion.

Meilikhios – Persephone's python.

Melissae – Bee priestesses on Isle of Bees.

Melitodes – the Bee Mother and chief priestess.

Melusine – Seior mistress at Garnac, she answers a telepathic appeal to help her nephew Fion and Saba.

Merer – of Edfu in Egypt, perfumier and major trader based in the free port of Byblos, his ships covered the Mediterranean and Red Seas. He was an influential advisor to Pepy the Second.

Mikel – Aengus's friend at the testing fields.

Minerva – Bee keeper and priestess.

Mishe – Seafolk captive.

Mon-ika – Alan's sister at Seafolk village.

Nana – Midwife at Twinrivers and Sanctuary.

Neitkrety – queen and wife of Pepy the Second of Egypt.

Nesto – Seafolk guide to Axe island.

Niall – Maeve's war leader.

Ogden – Ena's companion.

Olwen – the name of Fion's mother and of his sister, who were successive priestesses at Suil's springs.

Orthonac – leading Basque/Euskerran fisher; kinsman of Axular.

Paulus – the Minos of Knossos, consort of Queen Europa.

Pepy – Pepy the Second, the last Pharaoh of the Egyptian Old Kingdom.

Phoebe – Bee priestess and healer.

Pilar – Mara's sister, and Sedana's mother.

Ruben – wealthy property owner; married to Sarah, killed by Saba.

Saba – Great granddaughter of the Allmother, daughter of Mara and Ikhaluk the Finman. She is gifted with exceptional hybrid powers, which she develops in the darkness of Raven's cave. Allmother predicts that an incredible destiny will be woven for her by the Spinner.

Se-Bastien – rescued from burning sea at Etna, training with Hermes.

Sarah – A princess of one of the main families in Carchemish and

Harran. She was born into the Sabian culture, half-sister to Bethel.

S' bastian – Master of Ker and Seers in Garnac.

Scathach – meaning 'shadow', Maeve's evil genius.

Sedana – Saba's half-sister by Ikhaluk.

Sefra – Ena's daughter.

Shar Kalli Shari – murdered son of Naram Sin.

Stephanie – rescued by Saba and Bethel from the burning sea at Etna; she nurses Orthonac.

Sugaar – curator shaman of the healing and dreaming shrines.

Tara – a western Chinese girl rescued at the Sin Kiang and Tibetan border by a sage, brought to the Indus valley city of Harappa and taught yoga and Tantric healing. She cures and partners Aengus.

Tudic – Maolin's companion.

Ulan – Jen-ifer's companion.

Ur Namu – protégé of Enheduanna; third dynasty king of Ur.

Ur-Nanshe – famous singer and dancer in Akkad; friend of Enheduanna.

Urthur – Maeve's favourite bear.

Volgan – Maeve's head smith.

Will – elder at Holyisland village.

Will (Clans) – leader of Fion's warriors on Boand's Plain.

Xanthe – Larmorican priestess; Axular's companion.

Yurba – Gutian terrorist chief.

OTHERWORLD ENTITIES

Agni – the Fire God, who was worshipped by the smiths in return for his gifts of magical skills. Fire itself was a religious element which purified and renewed (as when celebrants jump across the festival bonfires). The smoke from a burning sacrifice was its ascending soul and the ashes contained its qualities in concentrated form. To smear the face with ash was a symbol of purification; smith wrestlers covered themselves with soot and ashes for extra vigour, hence blacksmiths. Haematite miners and artists had to fast and sacrifice with their shaman to propitiate the Earth Mother for the use of her blood, red ochre. But the smiths' sacrifices were even greater for the use of the immature ores mined from the Mother's body and matured/ripened in the furnace. The extraction of the metal from the ore was regarded as a birth before its due time in the earth. For this, and in fusing two metals together in a sacred union, the magical role of the smith superseded the normal processes of nature, so he was required to observe many taboos to fit him for his sacred task. A master smith ritually handled red-hot pieces of metal and preferred to use divine fire from a tree or forest blaze begun by lightning and preserved in his hearth. Agni was equated with the planet Jupiter, who hurled the thunderstones and lightning. A spark of divine fire was thought to be embedded in the heart of all living things, and at their death it returned to the sun. 'The dry soul that has most fire is the wisest and best' (Heraclitus).

Anu – also Anna, Inanna, Anne, Aine, Dana, Suil, Tara etc. a wide-ranging ancient name for the Mother Goddess. She was revered by the Akkadians and Babylonians as Inanna-Ishtar, to the Phoenicians she was Astarte, to Hebrews as Esther, and variously in Northern Europe as Oster, Eostre, Easter. The Paps of Anu describe twin peaks in Kerry. Buan-Ann, Mamm Goz ar Vretoned, good mother of the Bretons, Suzanne or, in Christian times, St. Anne is still venerated in Brittany. A famous early Irish race was known as the tribe of Dana, Tuatha de Danann. The Danube was the mother river on which was based the civilization of Old Europe c. 6500 – 3500 BC, so well documented in the works of Marija Gimbutas (see bibliography). In Sumerian, 'inanna' means Queen of Heaven and refers to the planet Venus and her cyclic voyages below the sky rim. She was goddess of love and war, and the subject of some of the earliest written poetic myths, third millennium BC. Anu may also represent the central mother figure in the triple goddess concept, Maid – Mother – Hag. As Venus, her planetary influence was believed to make the copper ore grow in the earth; bangles made from her metal possess strong healing virtues. She is companioned with the planet Mars, the red god of passion and war; see Diane Wolkstein and Samuel Kramer, Inanna (1984).

Baubo – an epithet of Hekate, the ancient Greek goddess of death also related to the Hag. In her aspect as Baubo the toad, she suggests that death must present the human condition with a comic side. She shocks her audience into laughter with lewd jokes and actions, a recognised therapy for grief, trauma and depression. The same concept was demonstrated in many churches and castles of Northern Europe by ridiculous or threatening gargoyles and Sheela na Gigs, statues of frog-like stooping Hags with hands on their pudenda, indicating that the gates of death, sexuality and birth are, through her, one and the same for everybody, high or low. Evidence of frog/toad images in Europe spans 8000 years; see Marija Gimbutas, The Language of the Goddess (1986).

Brid – also Bride, Breda, Brigit; from the root 'brig' which denotes power, essence, the sublime one. Brig Boillsge means 'brightness'; maid/bride of light was an old Irish name for a midwife; Brid is midwife to the old world New Year. If the milk fails in January, there is a traditional Kerry saying: 'Brid and her white cow will be coming soon!' She inspired equal devotion whether as the Christian St. Brigid or the Neolithic goddess Brid. Her feast day, 1st February (new calendar), heralds the opening buds and new shoots, the creatures emerging from hibernation, but above all, the strengthening sunlight. Hence her vital connection with the ritual of undying embers and the atavistic hearthfire, which exercises such a hypnotic fascination. It is one end of a flaming axis reaching through the imagination to subliminal mysteries.

Brid's three and four-arm crooked crosses are ancient symbols of the sunwheel and whorl of energy. The Brideog doll, formerly of straw, signified the regeneration of the corn spirit passed on from last year's harvest sheaf – a promise of new life for all. Her straw girdle was passed over the body to obtain a blessing; the Brat/Brait Brid were intimate scraps of her cloth that were used as talismans and worn by travellers or expectant mothers. The numerous wells of the Holy Woman offered cures, especially for barrenness or sterility.

Cailleach – also Caillighe, the Hag, Old Wise One, were synonyms for the third aspect of the goddess trinity. The Cailleach was infinitely old but still had many lovers; her antiquity was hidden by her veil, or caille. When evoked, she dispensed stern advice and judgements, as well as prophecies and predictions. Her other aspect was more terrible: goddess of death, destruction, disintegration and putrefaction; the natural catabolic process before the energy whorl regenerated and transformed anew. The principle is still openly manifest in some cultures, like Kali/Durga in India; see Pupal Jayakar, The Earthen Drum (1980). Her feast day, 31st October (new calendar), Samhain/Halloween, was also the principal feast for the dead, now All Souls. Its universality is evidenced from the divinatory nuts eaten in Europe to the candied skulls of Mexico. It is the most enduring feast after Easter/Pasch, Christmas/Yuletide and little Christmas of 6th January, when she is again seen as the witch La Befana (Italy), distributing gifts and sweets to children, unlike her unpleasant counterpart in the Slav and Russ nations, Baba Yaga, the original forest ogress of the Hansel and Gretel story.

Crom – Crom Dubh, the dark, bent one; a version of Donn the dark one. Originally a harvest deity, he was reputed to have brought back from the underworld a sheaf of wheat. This was linked to Eithne the corn maiden (meaning kernel or grain), whom he kept underground with him as mistress. He was also paired with Anu as Aine in a harvest festival called Domnach Aine agus Crom Dubh, and contrasted with Lugh the God of Light; see Máire MacNeill The Festival of Lughnasa (1962). There is an obvious resemblance to the Mediterranean myth of Demeter, Persephone, Hades/Dionysus. Crom was probably associated with Saturn. Crom was also connected to a bull cult through the Rannach Crom Dubh, a large henge and stone circle of 113 megaliths beside Lough Gurr in Galway. It was associated with bull sacrifice and feasting.

Crystal – Spirit of the healing chamber in Garnac.

Laminak – Lamia, Laima; ancient bird-like form of the goddess, still found in the myths of the Basque countries and Lithuania. Like the Eyed Goddess, she has similar associations with life and death as with the stork and raven etc. and exists in the folklore of most countries. She was the guardian spirit of Euskaldunak.

Mag/Trickster – recognised in one of his earthly forms as the magpie (pied maggot eater), a master of trickery and sagacity; he also appeared as the raven. Linked with the planet Mercury, he is also known as Hermes and Odin/Othin; he acted as spy and devious messenger of the High Ones and guide of recently dead souls. In his capacity as the wise god who hung on the tree for nine days and gave one of his eyes in exchange for wisdom, he was consulted by the other gods and revered by humans for his guidance and compassionate clown-like humour.

Oannes – reputed Fishgod. Sumerian legends of the world before the flood tell of their ancestors living in five great cities that were inundated with water, and recount how their ancient wisdom was preserved by seven sages who emerged from the sea as mermen; their leader was named Oannes. Effigies of him show a man wearing a fish skin. Like the Egyptian Thoth, he taught the people technical skills, writing, geometry, laws etc. Before c. 12,000 BC, the greater part of the Persian Gulf was a fertile valley. Scholars have proposed that the earliest Mesopotamian societies developed there and were gradually pushed back by successive marine invasions. The island of Bahrain, which lies to the south of the Gulf near the last areas of submerged land, had deities with Sumerian names like Enzak and his consort Mes-kil-ak. After the flooding of c. 8500 BC, the Vela supernova appeared low in the sky due south. It would have been extremely bright and at night the spectacular rays would have seemed to travel through the seawater up the gulf on to the shores of Sumer and been taken as a visitation from a great god. This phenomenon was recorded as a miraculous event and associated with Oannes restoring to them the lost knowledge from their once fertile valley.

Persephone – Daughter/maiden of the tripartite goddess Demeter and Hecate. The full story is well known. In an earlier era, when the Great Mother was still powerful but conflict between paternal and maternal societies was in process, Persephone was regarded by the maternal societies as the earth's saviour goddess. After her abduction and rape, she had shared the sacred pomegranate seeds with the dark lord (that is, she had integrated with the shadow) and she brought back fertility and fecundity from the underworld every spring in ceremonies from Imbolc/Candlemas to Easter.

Root – a dreaming godlike entity encountered by Saba; perhaps part of her collective consciousness linked to a mind from the distant future, which has developed the ability to travel and to transport apports (solid objects) and live creatures across space and time.

Spinner – the Eelfolk's Spider lady weaving the fates; viewed as the constellation Cassiopeia. The spider and snake are recognised symbols of wisdom, contrivance and perpetuity in the folklore and myth of most cultures. In several of the Upanishads there is the metaphor of a spider at the centre of its web, issuing and reabsorbing its threads in concentric circles. They expand to a visible circumference, and though there are divergent lines and varying distances to be spanned, they all trace back to the spider. It suggests that all existence is governed by a single principle and that the point of origin of the supreme consciousness is also an infinite reservoir of collective energy from which everything proceeds and returns. This web serves as a bridge between different planes and unites the physical diversity of the world, folding and unfolding in infinite expansion and contraction. The concentric figures of the yantra/mandala imitate the symbols of unfolding or gathering energy, relating what they unite or divide to the centre point of integration. Like the spider in its web, the bindu (point) is a core of creation, the radiating source of energy that generates all forms.

Suil, Sul – from the Irish meaning 'eye', 'look'. Eyed Goddess of the hot springs at Bath; known to the Romans as Aquae Sulis. Suil's eyes and face are famously depicted on the rock interior at Gavrinis in Brittany, and on stone and pottery at countless other sites. She is related to the all-seeing bird goddesses in evidence from the Paleolithic to the Bronze ages and is often portrayed as owls, eagles, cranes and other water birds. The concept was common to all mythologies, e.g. the Egyptian eye of Horus, the Eastern peacock's tail etc.; see O.G.S. Crawford, *The Eye Goddess* (1957). The symbol of the divine all-seeing eye is still painted on some Mediterranean fishing boats and is universally employed in motifs.

BIBLIOGRAPHY

Achterberg, Jeanne. *Imagery in Healing: Shamanism and Modern Medicine* (Shambhala, 1985).

Al Khalifa, Shaikha Haya Ali, and Michael Rice (eds). *Bahrain Through The Ages: The Archaeology* (KPI, 1986).

Attenborough, David. *The First Eden: The Mediterranean World and Man* (Collins, 1987).

Austin, James H. *Zen-Brain Reflections: Reviewing Recent Developments in Meditation and States of Consciousness* (MIT Press, 2006).

Baillie, Mike. *Exodus to Arthur: Catastrophic Encounters with Comets* (Batsford, 1999).

Bancroft, Anne. *Origins of the Sacred: The Way of the Sacred in Western Tradition* (Arkana, 1987).

Barandiarán, José Miguel de. *Mitología Vasca* (Ediciones Minotauro, 1960).

Barandiarán, José Miguel de. *Obras Completas* (Editorial La Gran Enciclopedia Vasca, 1972).

Barrett, John C. *Fragments from Antiquity: An Archaeology of Social Life in Britain, 2900 – 1200 BC* (Blackwell, 1993).

Bibby, Geoffrey. *Looking for Dilmun* (Penguin, 1972).

Bohm, David. *Wholeness and the Implicate Order* (R and KP, 1980).

Bosley, Keith. (trans.) *The Kalevala* (Oxford University Press, 1989).

Bradley, Richard. *The Social Foundations of Prehistoric Britain: Themes and Variations in the Archaeology of Power* (Longman, 1984).

Brennan, Martin. *The Boyne Valley Vision* (Dolmen Press, 1980).

Brennan, Martin. *The Stars and the Stones: Ancient Art and Astronomy in Ireland* (Thames & Hudson, 1983).

Brú na Bóinne. 'Newgrange, Knowth, Dowth and the River Boyne'. *A supplement to Archaeology* Ireland, Vol. 11, no. 3 (1997).

Burl, Aubrey. *Megalithic Brittany: A Guide to Over 3350 Ancient Sites and Monuments* (Thames & Hudson, 1985).

Burl, Aubrey. *The Stonehenge People* (Dent, 1987).

Burr, Harold. *Blueprint for Immortality: The Electric Patterns of Life* (Spearman, 1972).

Cameron, Dorothy O. *Symbols of Birth and of Death in the Neolithic Era* (Kenyon Deane 1985).

Capra, Fritjof and Luisi Pier. *The Systems View of Life* (Cambridge University Press, 2014).

Carey, Nessa. *The Epigenetics Revolution: How modern biology is rewriting our understanding of genetics, disease and inheritance* (Icon Books, 2011).

Carlson, Kathie. *Life's Daughter/Death's Bride: Inner Transformations through the Goddess Demeter/Persephone* (Shambhala, 1997).

Clark, David L. *Mesolithic Europe: The Economic Basis* (Duckworth, 1978).

Clark, Grahame. *The Identity of Man: as seen by an Archaeologist* (Methuen, 1986).

Courty, Marie-Agnes. 'Causes and effects of the 2350 BC Middle East Anomaly', in *Proceedings of the Second SIS Cambridge Conference on Natural Catastrophes during Bronze Age Civilisations* (July 1997).

Crane, Eva. *The Archaeology of Beekeeping* (Duckworth, 1983).

Crawford, O.G.S. *The Eye Goddess* (Phoenix House, 1957).

Dalfes, Hasan Nüzhet, George Kukla and Harvey Weiss (eds). *Third Millennium BC climate change and Old World collapse* (Springer-Verlag, 1997).

Dames, Michael. *Mythic Ireland* (Thames & Hudson, 1996).

Dames, Michael. *The Avebury Cycle* (Thames & Hudson, 1996).

Daniélou, Alain. *The Gods of India: Hindu Polytheism* (Inner Traditions International, 1985).

Davis, Ronald D and Eldon M Braun. *The Gift of Dyslexia: Why some of the brightest people can't read and how they can learn* (3rd ed. Souvenir Press, 2010).

Devereux, Paul. *Earth Memory: The Holistic Earth Mysteries Approach to Decoding Ancient Sacred Sites* (Quantum, 1991).

Devereux, Paul. *Symbolic Landscapes : The Dreamtime Earth and Avebury's Open Secret* (Gothic Image, 1992).

Dupuis, Jacques. *Au Nom du Père* (Le Rocher, 1989).

Edwards, I.E.S et al, (eds). 'A Early History of the Middle East,' Vol. 1, Pt 2 of *The Cambridge Ancient History* (Cambridge University Press, 1980).

Edwards, I.E.S et al, (eds). 'Prolegomena and Prehistory,' Vol. 1, Pt 1 of *The Cambridge Ancient History* (Cambridge University Press, 1970).

Eisler, Riane. *The Chalice and the Blade: Our History, Our Future* (Harper & Row, 1987).

Eliade, Mircea. *From Primitives to Zen: A Thematic Sourcebook of the History of Religions* (Collins, 1967).

Eliade, Mircea. *Shamanism: Archaic Techniques of Ecstasy etc.* (Princeton, 1972).

Eliade, Mircea. *The Forge and the Crucible: The Origins and Structures of Alchemy* (University of Chicago Press, 1978).

Eliot, T.S. *Four Quartets* (Faber, 1959).

Eogan, George. *Knowth and the Passage-tombs of Ireland* (Thames & Hudson, 1986).

Ereira, Alan. *The Heart of the World* (Cape, 1990).

Franz, Marie-Louise von. *Alchemical Active Imagination* (Spring Publications, 1979).

Franz, Marie-Louise von. *Archetypal Dimensions of the Psyche* (Shambhala, 1997).

Franz, Marie-Louise von. *Dreams* (Shambhala, 1991).

Franz, Marie-Louise von. *Number and Time: Reflections Leading Towards a Unification of Psychology and Physics* (Rider, 1974).

Franz, Marie-Louise von. *Psyche and Matter* (Shambhala, 1992)

Frazer, James. *The Golden Bough: A Study in Comparative Religion* (12 vols; Macmillan, 1935).

Garfield, Patricia. *Pathway to Ecstasy: The Way of the Dream Mandala* (Prentice Hall, 1989).

Gieser, Thorsten. 'Embodiment, Emotion and Empathy', in *Anthropological Theory* 8.3 (Sept. 2008): 299 – 318.

Gimbutas, Marija. *The Civilization of the Goddess* (HarperSanFrancisco, 1991).

Gimbutas, Marija. *The Language of the Goddess* (Thames & Hudson, 1989).

Godagama, Shantha. *The Handbook of Ayurveda* (Kyle Cathie, 2003).

Goldman, Jonathan. *Healing Sounds.* (Element Books, 1992).

Gooch, Stan. *The Paranormal* (Wildwood House, 1978).

Graves, Robert. *The White Goddess: A Historical Grammar of Poetic Myth* (Faber & Faber, 1952).

Graves, Tom. *Needles of Stone Revisited* (Gothic Image Publications, 1986).

Hamel, Peter. *Through Music to the Self: How to Appreciate and Experience Music Anew* (Element Books, 1978).

Hancock, Graham. *Underworld: Flooded Kingdoms of the Ice Age* (Michael Joseph, 2002).

Hannah, Barbara. *Encounters with the Soul: Active Imagination as Developed by C.G. Jung* (Sigo Press, 1981).

Harrison, Jane E. *Prolegomena to the Study of Greek Religion* (Merlin Press, 1980).

Harrison, Jane E. *Themis: A Study of the Social Origins of Greek Religion* (Merlin Press, 1977).

Harris, Rivkah. *Gender and Aging in Mesopotamia: The Gilgamesh Epic and Other Ancient Literature* (University of Oklahoma Press, 2003).

Herity, Michael and George Eogan. *Ireland in Prehistory* (Routledge, 1989).

Ingold, Tim. *Being Alive: Essays on movement, knowledge and description* (Routledge, 2011).

Iyengar, B.K.S. *Light on Pranayama: Pranayama Dipika* (Unwin Books, 1988).

Jablonka, Eva and Marion J. Lamb. *Epigenetic Inheritance and Evolution: The Lamarckian Dimension* (Oxford University Press, 1995).

Jacobsen, Thorkild. *The Treasures of Darkness: A History of Mesopotamian Religion* (Yale University Press, 1976).

Jayakar, Pupal. *The Earthen Drum: an introduction to the ritual arts of rural India* (National Museum of India, 1980).

Jenny, Hans. *Cymatics: A Study of Wave Phenomena* (Basilius Press, 1967).

Johnstone, Paul. *The Sea-craft of Prehistory* (Routledge, 1980).

Joseph, George. *The Crest of the Peacock: Non-European Roots of Mathematics* (Penguin, 1992).

Jung, Carl G. *Collected Works of C.G. Jung* (20 vols; Routledge, 1980).

Kalweit, Holger. *Dreamtime and Inner Space: The World of the Shaman* (Shambhala, 1988).

Kaplan-Williams, Strephon. *The Dream Work Manual: A step-by-step introduction to working with dreams* (Aquarian, 1984).

Kearns, Hugh. *Newgrange: The Mystery of the Chequered Lights* (Elo Publications, 1993).

Kemp, Christopher. *Floating Gold: A Natural (and Unnatural) History of Ambergris* (University of Chicago Press, 2012).

Kerenyi, Carl. *Eleusis: Archetypal Image of Mother and Daughter* (Routledge & Kegan Paul, 1967).

Kluger, Rivkah Schärf. *The Archetypal Significance of Gilgamesh: A Modern Ancient Hero* (Daimon Verlag, 1991).

Lambeck, Kurt. 'Shoreline reconstructions for the Persian Gulf since the last glacial maximum', in *Earth and Planetary Science Letters*, vol. 142, Issues 1 – 2 (July 1996): 43 – 57.

Layard, John. *A Celtic Quest. Sexuality and Soul in Individuation: A depth-psychology study of the Mabinogion legend of Culhwch and Olwen* (Spring Publications, 1975).

Layard, John. *Stone Men of Malekula* (Chatto & Windus, 1942).

Le Guin, Ursula. *The Dispossessed* (Gollancz, 1974).

Leick, Gwendolyn. *Mesopotamia: The Invention of a City* (Penguin, 2002).

Lethbridge, Thomas Charles. *The Power of the Pendulum* (Routledge & Kegan Paul, 1976).

Levy, G R. *The Gate of Horn: A Study of the Religious Conceptions of the Stone Age, and their influence upon European Thought* (Faber & Faber, 1948).

Lewis-Williams, J David. *The Mind in the Cave: Consciousness and the Origins of Art* (Thames & Hudson, 2002).

MacNeill, Máire. *The Festival of Lughnasa: A Study of the Survival of the Celtic Festival of the Beginning of Harvest* (Oxford University Press, 1962).

Maisels, Charles. *Early Civilizations of the Old World: Formative Histories of Egypt, the Levant, Mesopotamia, India and China* (Routledge, 2001).

Maisels, Charles. *The Emergence of Civilization: From Hunting and Gathering to*

Agriculture, Cities, and the State in the Near East (Routledge, 1990).

Mallory, J P and T E MacNeill. *The Archaeology of Ulster: From Colonization to Plantation* (Queen's University Belfast, 1991).

Marinatos, Nannó. *Art and Religion in Thera: Reconstructing a Bronze Age Society* (Mathioulakis, 1984).

Marliave, Olivier de. *Trésor de le Mythologie Pyrénéenne* (ESPER, 1987).

Marshack, Alexander. *The Roots of Civilization* (McGraw-Hill, 1972).

McClain, Ernest G. *The Myth of Invariance: The Origin of the Gods, Mathematics and Music from the Rg Veda to Plato* (Shambhala, 1978).

McClellan, Randall. *The Healing Forces of Music: History, Theory and Practice* (Amity House, 1988).

McCrickard, Janet E. *Eclipse of the Sun: Investigation into Sun and Moon Myths* (Gothic Image Publications, 1990).

McLeish, John. *Number: From Ancient Civilisations to the Computer* (Bloomsbury, 1991).

McNeill, F Marian. *The Silver Bough* (4 vols; Maclellan, 1957 – 68).

Mellaart, James. *Catal Huyuk: A Neolithic City in Anatolia* (Thames & Hudson, 1967).

Mellaart, James. *The Neolithic of the Near East* (Thames & Hudson, 1975).

Mereaux, Pierre. *Carnac: des Pierres pour les Vivants* (Nature et Bretagne, 1992).

Metzner, Ralph. *The Well of Remembrance: Rediscovering the earth wisdom myths of Northern Europe* (Shambhala, 1994).

Neumann, Erich. *The Great Mother: An Analysis of the Archetype* (Princeton University Press, 1972).

North, John. *Stonehenge: Neolithic Man and the Cosmos* (HarperCollins, 1996).

Nunn, John F. *Ancient Egyptian Medicine* (British Museum Press, 2006).

O'Kelly, Michael J. *Newgrange: Archaeology, Art and Legend* (Thames & Hudson, 1982).

Perera, Sylvia Brinton. *Descent to the Goddess: A Way of Initiation for Women* (Inner City Books, 1981).

Postgate, J N. *Early Mesopotamia: Society and Economy at the Dawn of History* (Routledge, 1992).

Ransome, Hilda M. *The Sacred Bee in Ancient Times and Folklore* (Allen & Unwin, 1937).

Redgrove, Peter. *The Black Goddess and the Sixth Sense* (Bloomsbury, 1987).

Robins, Don. *The Secret Language of Stone: A New Theory Linking Stones and Crystals with Psychic Phenomena* (Rider, 1988).

Rohl, David M. *The Lost Testament. From Eden to Exile: The Five-Thousand-Year History of the People of the Bible* (Century, 2002).

Rudgley, Richard. *The Lost Civilisations of the Stone Age* (Arrow Books, 1999)

Ruiz, Ana. *Daily Life in Ancient Egypt* (Souvenir Press, 2004).

Sandars, N K. *The Epic of Gilgamesh* (Penguin, 1960).

Santillana, Giorgio de and Hertha von Dechend. *Hamlet's Mill* (Gambit, 1969).

Schultz, Joachim. *Movement and Rhythm of the Stars: A guide to naked-eye observation of sun, moon and planets* (Floris Books, 1986).

Sen, Amartya. *The Argumentative Indian: Writings on India History, Culture and Identity* (Penguin, 2006).

Singer, June. *Androgyny: The Opposites Within* (Nicolas Hayes, 2000).

Singer, June. *Boundaries of the Soul* (Prism Press, 1995).

Singer, June. *Loves Energies* (Sigo Press, 1990).

Steiner, George. *Real Presences* (Faber, 1991)

Thom, A and A S Thom. *Megalithic Remains in Britain and Brittany* (Clarendon Press, 1978).

Thompson, William. *The Time Falling Bodies Take to Light: Mythology, sexuality, and the origin of culture* (St. Martin's Press, 1981).

Ullman, Montague and Nan Zimmerman. *Working with Dreams* (Hutchinson, 1983).

Wilhelm, Richard (trans). *The Secret of the Golden Flower: A Chinese Book of Life with a European Commentary by C.G. Jung* (Routledge, 1931).

Willetts, Ronald. *The Civilization of Ancient Crete* (Batsford, 1977).

Wolkstein, Diane and Samuel Kramer. *Inanna, Queen of Heaven and Earth: Her Stories and Hymns from Summer* (Rider, 1984).

Wosien, Maria-Grabiele. *Sacred Dance: An Encounter with the Gods* (Thames & Hudson, 1974).

Wunderlich, Hans-Georg. *The Secret of Crete* (Macmillan, 1974).

Yeats, W. B. *Collected Poems* (MacMillan, 1959).

www.ingramcontent.com/pod-product-compliance
Lightning Source LLC
Chambersburg PA
CBHW030113030726
47498CB00007B/2363